Praise for Robin Maxwell's *ATLANTOS*

I wasn't expecting much from an Atlantis-themed novel, but Robin Maxwell's *Atlantos* is a tremendous, exhilarating, unputdownable SURPRISE with deep, engaging characters, and a clever plot full of twists, turns and unexpected challenges. These qualities, and the sheer sustained craftsmanship of the author from first page to last, combine to make *Atlantos* a brilliant read. But beyond that, this unique novel offers a plausible, completely unexpected explanation of the Atlantis mystery and with it some real food for thought for anyone interested in the secrets of humanity's forgotten past.

— Graham Hancock, international bestselling author of
Fingerprints of the Gods and *Magicians of the Gods*

"If you fancy titanic struggles of godlike beings at the dawn of history, then strap yourself in for a vivid re-imagining of one of our oldest and most mysterious legends. Maxwell has created a fantastic world so thrillingly described that the reader will want to live there for a long, long time."

— Christopher Vogler, bestselling author of
The Writers Journey: Mythic Structure for Writers

"Robin Maxwell surprised and delighted me when she jumped genres with JANE: The Woman Who Loved Tarzan. She's done it again with ATLANTOS. This novel is Robin Maxwell at her best, full of wonderful characters and world-building — a *tour de force* of historical fantasy…"

— C.W. Gortner, international bestselling author of
The Last Queen and *Mademoiselle Chanel*

ATLANTOS

ATLANTOS

The Early Erthe Chronicles

BOOK I

My darling Cynthia -
So glad we're friends -
love the lunches and laughs
we have. And thanks for
your unflagging support,
Love,
Robin

ROBIN MAXWELL

PIPES CANYON PRESS

Published by Pipes Canyon Press

Cover painting: *Poseidon* Oil on canvas by Tom Ellis
Cover design: damonza.com
Formatting: damonza.com

ISBN: 978-0-9963759-0-0

With gratitude to Plato for his dialogues,
Timaeus and *Critias*

BOOKS BY ROBIN MAXWELL

JANE: The Woman Who Loved Tarzan
O, Juliet
Signora Da Vinci
Mademoiselle Boleyn
To the Tower Born: A Novel of the Lost Princes
The Wild Irish: A Novel of Elizabeth I and the Pirate O'Malley
The Virgin Elizabeth
The Queen's Bastard
The Secret Diary of Anne Boleyn
Augie Appleby's Wild Goose Chase (with Billie Morton)
Augie Appleby's Trouble in Toyland (with Billie Morton)

EPILOGUE

THE WORLD, AS Poseidon knew it, was coming undone.

As the Great Plateau of their home continent came into view out the shuttle window he willed himself to steady. He knew what lay ahead. His belly clenched in a painful knot and his limbs felt suddenly leaden. Like every man in his crew he was rendered mute by what he was seeing. Towers of smoke and debris belched continuously from each of the nine volcanic peaks in the Central Range, and the ash was being driven eastward toward the sea and the city by fierce, howling winds. Jagged bolts of lightning jettisoned from the mountains into the black clouds lit them from inside to a fearsome effect. The plateau – with its patchwork of lush irrigated fields and orchards, vast meadows and forestlands – had itself ruptured in dozens of places, oozing up from below into rivers of brilliant lava.

The shuttle disk breached the headlands of the plateau, and the magnificent seaside metropolis of concentric rings came into view below. As the craft flew lower it became apparent that death and chaos reigned in Atlantos. Homes, public baths and neighborhood temples, the racing stadium, the Academy, and warehouses along the docks of the Outer Ring Island had been leveled by terrible shaking. People lay dead and mangled in the rubble, and though some feeble attempts at rescue were still underway most were fleeing down the once-elegant thoroughfares and surging across canal bridges now choked with panicked citizens. Poseidon watched horrified as a stampede began on the Middle Canal Bridge, neighbor trampling neighbor, bodies piling one upon the other until men and women, even children, were flying over the railing into the seething waters.

The pilot maneuvered the shuttle over the Central Isle and set it down before the massive temple that had been consecrated in his name. As the crew exited the craft and huddled together on the trembling ground he embraced each man and they slipped away, leaving him alone on the circular island that had long been his home. With the sprawling residence at his back he walked slowly towards the temple, steadying himself against the now-constant shaking of the erthe under his feet.

A series of deep, onerous booms from the mountain range rumbled through the atmosphere. The sun shone down with heartbreaking clarity upon what had once been the perfection of nature that encompassed the entire continent, but would soon lay in ruins – victim of the arrogance and stupidity of his own species. Poseidon strode across the Temple Plaza contemplating the final, merciful task he was about to perform. Hurrying up the broad stone stairs he pushed open the tall golden doors and disappeared inside.

ORIGINS

Then listen, Socrates, to a tale which, though strange, is certainly true...not mere legend, but an actual fact...

– Plato, *Timaeus* 4th Century B.C.

Let me begin by observing first of all, that nine thousand was the sum of years which had elapsed since the war which was said to have taken place between those who dwelt outside the Pillars of Heracles and all who dwelt within them...Of the combatants on the one side, the city of Athens was reported to have been the leader and to have fought out the war; the combatants on the other side were commanded by the kings of Atlantis which was an island greater in extent than Libya and Asia...

– Plato, *Critias,* 4th Century B.C.

PseudoMort

HE COULD HEAR his brother weeping brokenheartedly and his mother's soft voice soothing the little boy's misery. The great sobs that had racked Athens's tiny frame echoed under the stadium's cavernous dome. His cries, thought Poseidon, annoyed their father, embarrassing Ammon Ra as he'd said his goodbyes to fellow Federation men who now, one by one, were drifting off to various pod-zones to join their families.

Athens had always been a child of untoward emotions. Rages, tantrums, paroxysms of delight, unrestrained laughter. And fears. His fears were the worst of the impulses so frowned upon in their society. From his earliest days Athens had lacked all reserve or restraints, all moderation. And yet, Poseidon mused as he ran his hand over PM-Pod 74.888 – the narrow tubular chamber in which he would endure the first PseudoMortic hibernation of his life – this was precisely and paradoxically the reason that people adored his younger brother. Athens would, of course, grow out of such unfortunate traits, such evolutionarily ancient behaviors. They were, in an adult, unacceptable in their culture. Dangerous. Certainly requiring modification.

But in a four-year-old boy, especially one as physically beautiful and innately charming as Athens, the traits were tolerated. In the privacy of their home the boisterous, jolly child was an entertainment, a ray of sunlight in the waning years of the ever-darkening solar cycle. Each of them – his mother, father, himself – hoped that when they awoke from their long sleep Athens would have shed those qualities and grown into a proper Terresian man.

Still, now he wept as though his heart was breaking.

"You will enjoy your sleep, I promise you," their mother said as she wiped her younger son's tears with the hem of her garment's loose sleeve. "You will dream wonderful dreams."

"I don't want to sleep!" Athens wailed. "What if the *bad* dreams come?"

"They cannot come, child. This is not ordinary sleep, not at all the same as when I put you into bed at home. You're safe in your pod. No one ever has bad dreams in PseudoMort. You must trust me, Athens." She tilted his face up to hers and held his eyes. "Do you trust me?"

His nod was small, a single tilt of the chin, and his lips were pursed tight. But Athens's eyes were dry.

She grinned then. "When you wake you'll be all grown up. Your brother and your father will have hair sprouting all over them. Above their lips, on their chins and their heads."

"No they won't!" Athens was giggling now.

"Oh yes they will. Their hair will be so long it will fill up their pods. We'll have to dig through it all to find their faces."

Athens gave a small shriek of delight.

She had not said that their finger and toenails would be long and curled, Poseidon thought, as this might incite memories of Athens's many nightmares. In the extended sleep Terresian bodily functions were drastically slowed, micronomically close to death. But as the length of their hibernation was so severely extended, some growth did take place. Athens, as their mother had told him, would awake as a young man. Poseidon, himself a young man today, would emerge fully matured. His parents would age perhaps a decade. And their protein bio-locations – hair and nails – to the sleep engineers' chagrin, continued to grow unchecked throughout the long dark solar cycle.

Terresian technos was marvelous. It was, however, imperfect.

Their mother smiled and pulled her cheered little son to her breast. Poseidon found himself squirming uncomfortably to see this display of affection in a public area. At home her embraces – while frowned upon by their father – were welcomed by both boys. Manya had always been different from other mothers in this way. It had been the family's small secret. Poseidon had overheard his father chastising his mate, inferring that her over-affectionate ministrations somehow contributed to their younger son's intemperance. And now in the Sleep Stadium with the entire populace of Atlas City gathered for the most solemn public event of their culture, his mother and brother were displaying for all to see the most unsuitable of emotions.

Poseidon was grateful that decorum had been restored by the time his father joined the family on the 7000-row of pods.

"It's time, Manya," he said. "Shall I help you in?"

"No, I can manage." She gazed steadily into his eyes. "We've already said our goodnights." And more quietly, "Be gentle with the boys." Then she climbed into her pod.

Ammon Ra went first to Athens and bent low. Poseidon could hear nothing of their exchange, but he did see his brother's small hand reaching up to touch their father's face. When finally he approached Poseidon's pod the man's expression showed not a single trace of sentimentality. "Your first PseudoMort," was all he said to his firstborn.

"Yes, Father. I'm looking forward to it."

"Use the time wisely. Have you some problems to solve?"

"I do. The generalized displacement ratios of glaxin hydroxalide. A new simulation protocol for bio-stem endrites. And equivalencies for the inverted macro-vibrus paradox."

"Good. I'll see you in the morning."

With a brief pat on his son's cheek his father turned and climbed into the pod next to his. Poseidon did the same, positioning his body into its warm enfolding fiber-cushion. He knew that as soon as the lid closed and locked – as would all 92,785 of the others in the dome at the same instant – a narcotizing frequency would activate and lull him to sleep. The temperature would begin to drop slowly, then precipitously, till crytonic stasis had been attained.

He allowed his eyes to close. *I'll see you in the morning.* Were these passionless words all that Poseidon would have to remember before his thousands-year sleep? *No,* he decided. *I will remember my mother, her fragrant embrace, a kiss on each of his cheeks and the smile that had warmed him to the core.*

Sweet dreams, my son, she'd crooned. *Sweet dreams.*

ONE

"S IR, MARS IS *gone.*"

Poseidon pulled his gaze from the diffracted image of the Deep Crust Survey and stared uncomprehendingly at Cyphus. He could see that the brawny security captain, his most trusted friend on the Aerosean mission, was similarly baffled by the report he'd just delivered. Together they gazed out the shuttle window up the pink sand beach on the east coast of the planet's Central Continent. To the east was a vast ocean, to the west lay an entire landmass covered in a single species of giant tree ferns, the only vegetation that had yet evolved on Aeros – the fourth planet from the sun.

"How can he be gone?" Poseidon asked.

"Commander Mars was last seen on Selvon Beach two hours ago. He separated from the rest of the patrol to explore an inlet. When they looked for him, he'd disappeared."

Poseidon blinked stupidly, lost for words, and found the other members of the team in various stages of alarm. They were looking to him for an answer.

Cyphus spoke quietly. "You're second in command, Sir."

Poseidon felt the world shifting around him, some aspects blurred out of focus, others coalescing into razor-edged relief.

One pair of ideas in particular blazed clear and indisputable in his head. The small escape window for return to their home world was quickly closing. And Elgin Mars, before taking off for Selvon Beach, had once again dismissed the drilling site for titanum that Poseidon believed held the most promise. Now as Poseidon turned to Zalen, the vessel's captain, he hoped some semblance of authority was present in his voice.

"Send Gracos and three men to join the patrol – a search party." Then to Cyphus he said, "I want you to come with me."

"Come with you where?"

Now Poseidon addressed the entire team. "We're nearly out of time. I'm going back to Site 62 to take one more look."

There was a brief, surprised silence.

"There's nothing there," said Ables. He was, aside from Poseidon and Mars, the most knowledgeable geologist on the off-world team. "The best use of our remaining time is to explore 72 or 73."

"There's something in 62 that we're missing," Poseidon told him. "Come here and look at this."

Ables and the others gathered around the diffractor map of Aeros's crust, displayed before them at eye-level.

"Look between this layer of vitreous rock and granite," Poseidon instructed them.

"I see something," said Ables. "But it isn't titanum."

"I believe it is." Poseidon hesitated uncomfortably. "For the moment, I'm in command. It's my decision."

Zalen spoke up. "Shouldn't we wait for the report on Commander Mars?"

"We don't have the luxury of waiting," Poseidon argued. "Our launch window expires in seventeen hours. The search party will see to Mars. Of course they'll locate him, but meanwhile I'm going to find the deposit we came here for. Who's coming with me?"

Within the hour the shuttle disk had risen silently into the sky, but the gravity of the circumstances, the lovely beaches and endless, always-moving blue ocean below aroused so many warring thoughts in Poseidon that he found himself fighting to keep steady. Everyone believed he was sunk deep into his calculations but he was, in fact, considering the possibility that Elgin Mars – the greatest geologist of their time – would not be located before their launch window closed, and that Poseidon would face a dire decision.

He might be forced to leave the commander behind to die on a distant planet.

An irony seized Poseidon: this present, disastrous scenario had been forged more than four billion years ago. A shattering planetary event had rocked their solar system – the collision between a massive rogue comet and the giant third planet from "Helios," its sun – so violent that it sundered the unlucky world into three parts: a vast asteroid belt fostering billions of rock shards, the life-rich planet Gaia, and its twin sister, Terres – his home.

Both planets recovered, spawning fabulous plant and animal life-forms. But the frequent cosmic extinction events that Gaia suffered set its evolution back time and time again. Terres therefore evolved more quickly, more radically than its sister. The human animal was primitive and savagely warlike, but over millions of years emerged as a civilized society. Terresian sciences evolved as well, and a central unifying principle was discovered: *All matter and energy, at their most basic levels, were nothing more than vibrational frequencies.* The phaetron – a device that could harness and modulate the "vibrus" was invented. And that which powered the phaetron was an ore found on Terres – titanum.

Phaetron technos proved nothing less than miraculous. With its many uses, quality of life had been elevated. Back-breaking physical labor became a distant memory. Fabulous cities and grand monuments were built to celebrate this newly ordered world. The result – a conscious, peaceful society in which all were fed, educated, comfortably housed and entertained. Unfortunate conditions of both flesh and spirit became a thing of the past, and maladies that could not immediately be reversed found their solution in genomic re-programming and recalibration. The broader problems inherent in the race – greed, violence, mental deficiency and deviancy – were largely bred out of the population within ten generations. Eventually, off-world travel began. The most frequent destination was the diverse and fascinatingly wild sister planet, Gaia. Studying the evolution of its sub-human root species and genomic tampering with the creatures became a scien-technic obsession.

"Technos" was firmly established as the one and only religion of Terres.

Then Terresian luck ran out when a monstrous asteroid came crashing into their world. While Terres survived the collision, the result was a slow but inexorable destabilization of the planet's orbit. With each millennia it went flying farther and farther from Helios, trapped within an unnaturally long elliptical path, past the planets Aeros, Zeus, Chronos, Ouranos, and Radon, until – at its distal arc – it was five billion light-years past the solar system's outermost planetoid, Pluton. When Terres returned to its brief "inner circuit" it basked in the sun's life-giving light and heat. But during its protracted "outer circuit" it suffered in the dark, freezing reaches of deep space. It stabilized, finally, into the unfortunate, ultra-elongated orbit.

Terresians had been forced to adapt, squeeze all of their living, learning, arts, exploration and progress into the roughly one hundred years before leaving the sun's inner circuit. During the three thousand year outer circuit the planet grew more and more inhospitable. The atmosphere thinned and solar input grew so weak that sub-zero temperatures froze their oceans, turning the world into a permanent wasteland. The population had no choice but to condense itself into "hubs" – finite geographical areas that could sustain all life forms, both plant and animal. But these required a foolproof protective shield. Phaetron technos provided them. "Contour domes" over their cities, and artificial suns, kept the climate regulated. PseudoMort vastly extended lives through the wasted years of darkness. Dependence on technos became absolute, a simple fact of life for every man, woman and child alive.

When the veins of titanum – once believed unlimited on Terres – were found to be finite, none were prepared for it. Not long before Poseidon's birth the people confronted the unfathomable crisis ahead. Without the titanum-powered phaetron, without the domes, without PseudoMort, the extinction of all life on Terres was certain. With every new "tear" in the aging contour domes, the hand of fear tightened its grip.

Hundreds of expeditions were launched all over the planet to find new sources of ore. As each came up empty-handed, and every "revolutionary" alternative energy source proved insubstantial, cracks appeared within the ranks of the once compliant and prosperous, the self-possessed and progressive. Off-world missions requiring vast stores of titanum provoked virulent public debate.

It was then that Elgin Mars convinced Federation that interplanetary exploration was Terres's only hope. But as one after another planet in the Helios System was found devoid of titanum deposits, hope began to wither. Mars had been most persistent in his exploration of Aeros, despite it having been found barren of the ore. He insisted there was a vein of titanum there – one so long and deep that Terres could be powered indefinitely. Naysayers howled their disapproval of yet another futile and costly Aerosean mission. But Mars prevailed.

The man had been Poseidon's geology instructor at the Academy. When the new team was assembled, Mars chose his outstanding student – now a colleague – as his Second in Command. It was Poseidon's first off-world mission, and most believed it Terres's only chance of survival. The weight of their world rested on the shoulders of that crew. It was with unspeakable anxiety and blind faith that Mars would be proven correct that their craft was sent hurtling from the Terresian orbit towards Aeros.

Now, thought Poseidon, he might be forced to sacrifice a friend…in order to save a planet. But even that sacrifice would be in vain if titanum could not be found.

It *would* be found, Poseidon insisted to himself. At site 62. His readings had been at odds with Mars's findings. But titanum was there. Poseidon was certain of it. As certain as he'd been about anything in his life.

*

Elgin Mars was never found. But titanum was. The vein uncovered at Site 62, a mere forty feet below the deepest crustal layer they'd previously drilled, proved enormous — an underground river running a tenth of the way around the planet's equator. It was the one that Mars had believed was there, but had not himself located. They escaped Aeros with no time to spare.

That night Poseidon numbed himself with too much jog at dinner. He could feel the crews' eyes on him. It was natural for them to feel as though the world had been lifted off their shoulders. Of course it was. Terres's future existence had been suddenly resurrected and guaranteed.

"The truth is, Mars was wrong about 62," Zalen said.

"If you hadn't been so stubborn we'd be going home empty-handed," Cyphus added, knocking back a cup of jog.

The others nodded their agreement.

"He's a hero," Poseidon insisted. "He led us to Aeros. We have to make sure he's remembered."

"There'll be questions about his disappearance," Ables said. "Ones we don't have answers for."

"We should tell Federation the truth," Poseidon offered. "But they can tell the people he died during the mission."

"His body mutilated," Zalen added. "His remains...too unpleasant to view."

"They should rename the planet after him," Cyphus said, and everyone agreed.

What they at the table knew, but did not say, was that Poseidon – the recognized discoverer of titanum – could not help but be elevated to a status rivaling the long-abandoned gods of old.

It was a prestige for which he had no preparation.

Something else was weighing on Poseidon's mind. Their return to Terres itself – speeding away from the light and heat into the depthless dark – dampened his spirits more than he would ever admit. So few had enjoyed off-world expeditions and sun-filled environments. All that Terresians knew was the daily life manufactured by phaetron technos. They were content with excellent technological representations of nature. Comfort. Safety. Beauty. Refinement of culture.

All under the contour domes.

It occurred to Poseidon then that even in the years of Terres's near-orbit to Helios, when natural light and warmth were but steps away through the curved phaetronic walls, people more often chose to ignore them. True, the surface was largely desolate, a far cry from the lush gardens and lakes, blue skies and ever-changing clouds projected by the masters of phaetronic illusion inside the domes. But now Poseidon had seen the wonders of the *natural* world, and they had moved him to an extreme degree. The other members of the Aerosean crew seemed only eager to be home, content with the planet they knew so well.

Poseidon would keep his longings to himself.

*

As the shuttle disk set down amidst a massive crowd at Atlas City's Federation Headquarters, Poseidon could see his brother Athens among the primary greeters. He was wearing that famous smile of his, the one that caused everyone around him to feel unaccountably happy. He was so handsome. So full of natural masculine grace. How strange it was to know that for Athens, the adulation showered upon Poseidon that day and in the days to come would be next to unbearable. Athens had always been gracious in public, hiding both his great and petty jealousies, but as the off-world team filed down the ramp to the waiting well-wishers, Poseidon caught sight of Athens's eyes above the smiling mouth.

They were seething with envy.

When had it not been so? Poseidon wondered as the applause thundered about the crew. *When had his brother last wished him well?*

"Welcome home." Athens clapped an arm around Poseidon's shoulder. To anyone watching it would have been thought a warm gesture. But the mouth was tight, unsmiling, and the words whispered in Poseidon's ear – "You're quite the hero, aren't you?" – brimmed with antipathy.

Some things never changed.

As he pulled from the embrace he spotted Talya Horus. She was a woman of great, if chilly, loveliness, with a straight-backed figure and sleekly knotted blonde hair. They'd taken up with each other just before he'd left on the Aerosean mission. As preoccupied as he'd been on the mission, he'd found himself thinking about her. Now he was delighted to see her.

She graced him with a closed-lipped smile before he was mobbed by the Federation men. He would see her later. They would celebrate in bed.

TWO

STANDING WITH THE welcoming crowd at Federation Square Talya heard the phaetronic hiss high overhead. *Another breach in the dome's field*, she thought. Sunlight – if one could call it that – illuminated the day. She could see the actual tear in the synthetic blue sky and illusory cloud formations right through to the black of sunless space that altogether enveloped Terres. It would be months before the first of Helios's faint rays fell on their planet.

In other times such a breach would have been an emergency, an ugly reminder of the trouble they'd all been in. The conservative men at Fed Energy would have flown into crisis mode, calling for the start of titanum rationing. The loudmouths and hotheads at Energy would shout them down, insist that their new technos – in various stages of development – would, with sufficient investment, render titanum dependence obsolete. But the success of the Aerosean explorations had changed everything.

And Poseidon had come home a hero.

As she watched him turn to greet Elo Denys, High Commissioner of Energy, she found herself thinking that Poseidon Ra was the ideal man. Physically striking with a stunning intellect.

Disciplined yet adventuresome. She wondered how long she should wait to broach the subject of their breeding together.

She spotted Athens in the crowd. He was scanning it, lingering momentarily on the face and figure of every pretty girl in sight. It was said of Poseidon's brother that he had been blessed – or cursed – with the personality of five men. Now he was coming her way. She found herself mildly annoyed, for while Athens exuded tremendous charm, Talya mainly found his chatter inane. And the way he was leering at her he was probably picturing her in his bed writhing under him, groaning with pleasure. Right now what she wished for was a quiet moment with Poseidon.

Athens came and stood before her, blocking the view of Poseidon being mobbed by his well-wishers.

"Quite an accomplishment," she said of him.

"Not unexpected. He always attracts the greatest good fortune. Though being the savior of a world is a stunning accomplishment, even for him."

Talya could see that Athens was making sure to hold her eyes with a steady stare. Probably no one but she and Poseidon knew it irritated Athens to be forced to say a kind word about his brother.

"You have a new fissure," she said without looking up.

"Energy is already aware. Crews are on their way."

"Nice to know such things are no longer catastrophes."

Talya saw his eyes wander from her face to her throat. Perhaps, she thought with irritation, even lower. She was certain he knew this would annoy her, and did it all the same. Athens was the kind of man who believed those close to him would always disappoint him, so – without fail – he disappointed them first.

Talya startled when Poseidon slipped his arm around her waist, and she stiffened slightly. He was overly demonstrative, she observed, not for the first time.

"Welcome back," she said.

"You're the most beautiful thing I've seen in three years," he said, placing an affectionate kiss on her cheek.

"In historical times wars would have been fought over our Talya," Athens offered.

"How fortunate we are that such stupidity has been bred out of us," she said, perhaps a bit too pointedly.

But Athens was, if anything, thick-skinned, and his eyes had already begun wandering to a female student who gazed at him adoringly. He excused himself and went directly towards her, flashing one of his dazzling smiles.

Alone with Poseidon in public Talya felt a moment of discomfort. Their pairing was still relatively new. She wondered if everyone was watching them.

"When we were gone I found myself thinking about you – the last time we…" He didn't finish, but fixed her with his clear grey eyes.

"What a waste of valuable time."

Poseidon chuckled.

"Are you laughing at me?" she demanded.

"No. I imagine you're laughing at me. "

"You *are* overly sentimental," she chided him.

"Guilty," he said, then leaned over and whispered, "Come home with me."

"I thought you'd never ask," she said.

THREE

HOW I LOATHE *the sound of that voice,* Athens thought, consciously unclenching his jaw. He'd rather pluck out his eyes than endure the warm, commanding tones of Poseidon's debriefing at Fed Energy. It was the first strategy meeting after the Aeros expedition had returned, with leadership of future off-world operations high on the agenda. His brother headed the long conference table, the commissioners lined up on his right and left. Athens sat with the other junior engineers at the table's far end. A loud rapping of knuckles on the table – the most heartfelt ovation acceptable to their deeply reserved culture – was winding down, but Athens knew the commissioners revered, even worshipped his brother.

Plans had already been mounted to begin mining the newly renamed planet "Mars" for titanum, with a sizable permanent colony to be set in place there. With that success assured, the Scientechnos Academy had petitioned and won their bid to re-establish the programs of previous evolutionary scientists on Gaia. Talya Horus had been granted the head posting.

"So of course, Poseidon," said Commissioner Denys, "we are offering the Colonial Governorship of Mars to you."

Poseidon smiled and nodded with utter humility at all the

senior men at the table. "I'm going to respectfully decline," he finally said.

The dead silence exploded moments later into a barrage of shocked cries and objections.

"I'm honestly unsuited for this job," he insisted over the furor.

"How can you say that?" Denys pleaded. "No one knows Marsean geology better than you do."

"There's more to it than that. Please…let me explain."

Athens sat back in his chair, genuinely stunned. Brantus, sitting next to him, leaned over to whisper, "Has he gone mad?"

"I've been thinking about it all," Poseidon continued. "The colony is a permanent one. A large number of people are going to have to work productively in dirty, dangerous conditions for an extended period. They've got to be kept happy. They'll need congenial leadership, someone that will keep their spirits high. Of course the governor will need administrative skills and technological know-how as well." Poseidon paused before he said, "That's why I'm recommending my brother for the post."

Athens's limbs froze, yet he felt heat rising up to his cheeks. A hard thumping began in his chest. He chanced a look at the far end of the table where Poseidon was beaming at him, seemingly unconcerned at the long, uncomfortable silence, one that ended abruptly with a chorus of raised voices, all of them offering compelling objections to Athens's nomination. The argument grew more heated and less coherent. "Too young!" Denys cried. "Too volatile," offered Gracus, head of engineering, being careful not to meet Athens's eye. His humiliation was growing with every passing moment, every insult. Every comparison with his brother dissected in excruciating detail.

"My reasons for declining the post are not strictly unselfish," Poseidon interjected. "The sister mission to Gaia holds far more interest for me."

"Gaia?" Garam Praxis growled.

"So much of that planet is yet unexplored," Poseidon continued, "and I feel myself more an explorer than a geologist. I relish the Gaian mission above anything else in the world."

Athens could see the commissioners beginning to waver.

Poseidon pressed on. "If Energy wishes to reward me for finding titanum, you'll grant me Gaia. And if you're looking for an inspired nomination for Mars, you will seriously consider my brother."

*

All objections to his appointment had eventually, if reluctantly, been resolved – *if only to please their newly anointed godhead*, he thought bitterly. Before the commission adjourned for the day the Marsean governorship had been offered to Athens. He'd managed to accept it with good grace and a pleasant smile. But as the commissioners filed out the door he could hear as many voices grumbling as offering congratulations. The only one left at the table was Poseidon. Neither of them spoke for a long while.

Finally Athens found his voice. "Finding titanum was your glory, not mine. Everyone knows it. They're thinking, 'Oh how very kind of our savior to throw his brother the crumbs.'"

Poseidon's face contorted. "Can you not, for once, be gracious? Trust that I bear you only good will?"

Athens refused to answer.

"There's something you need to know about Mars," Poseidon said.

"The man or the planet?" Athens shot back.

"Both." Poseidon hesitated before going on. "Elgin Mars went missing shortly before we returned to Terres."

"We were told he'd died."

"A search party was sent out while the rest of us made one last attempt at 62."

"The attempt that was successful. The much-celebrated deci-sion." Athens narrowed his eyes. "You'd just taken command."

"Yes."

"But his body was brought back."

"There was no body. We left without him. The High Commissioners at Federation were told, but no one else."

Athens spoke carefully. "What happened to him?"

"The planet swallowed him up."

"That's rather dramatic, coming from you."

"It was a terrible thing," Poseidon said.

"Leaving him there, you mean."

"We had no choice. We'd run out of time."

"Well, that's quite a story," Athens said.

"It wasn't meant to entertain you."

"Why *did* you tell me?"

"Mars is your planet now. It has…secrets. Perhaps some unpleasant ones."

Athens stood there silent and still. As he gazed out beyond the sprawl of Atlas City to the mountains beyond, he could feel his newly forged destiny gaining form and substance in his mind.

"I'm sorry I gave you no warning. About the governorship," Poseidon said.

"It would have been nice."

"Surely you're pleased. It's an unparalleled opportunity."

"Yes. For failure of unparalleled magnitude."

"I believe in you, Athens. You're the right man for Mars."

He'd laughed mirthlessly and shook his head. "For Terres sake, let's hope you're right."

FOUR

"I'LL NEVER UNDERSTAND why you moved out of the city," she said, fingering the antique tapestry hanging above his bed. "It's a lovely place. A good view of the mountains…but it's awfully remote."

Talya could feel Poseidon's eyes on her as she explored his new home. He was probably hoping she would unloose her hair. She loathed it when he displayed that kind of ardor.

As if suddenly realizing his slavishness, he moved to the bedroom controls. "The noise was beginning to bother me," he said.

"What noise?"

"That's just it. When you've lived in the city all your life you begin not to hear the din that's all around you."

She shrugged and pulled off her earbobs, placing them on the bed table. "Then it shouldn't be a problem. Are you thinking of becoming a farmer?"

Poseidon smiled at her teasing. She knew that even her smallest attempts at humor pleased him. He programmed an image on the large bedroom window, and suddenly a low roaring sound was all around them.

"Good grief, what is that?"

"Out the window you are seeing waves crashing on a 'beach' on Mars. One of the great Marsean seas. Isn't it beautiful?"

She stared at the diffracted image for a moment. "I'm afraid it makes me queasy. Can you change it? Something soothing."

"The Plaza in Atlas City?"

"Now you're mocking *me*."

"I'm not," he said, coming behind her and pulling at the pins that held her pale hair in a tight coil. As it fell around her shoulders he kissed the back of her neck. "Really, I'm not."

Talya unbuttoned her sheath, allowing it to drop to the floor, then began tapping the inside of her right wrist with two fingers of her left hand.

"Could we...?" Poseidon began, placing his own hand over hers. "Let's do without it."

She turned to him. "Why would we want to do that?"

"We don't need it," he said.

"I prefer a richer experience," she countered, completing the sexual programming at her wrist. She looked into his eyes. "Are you having doubts about us?"

"No! No, I want it all to be perfect for you. I just thought..."

She kissed him lightly on the lips, then unfastened his shirt at the shoulder. "It will be. It always is. Here..." she said, "Let me."

Talya turned Poseidon's right hand palm-up and began lightly tapping the enhancer controls at his wrist. She imagined that he'd be feeling his heart rate quicken and warmth radiating through his genitals. She was right. In moments he was rock-hard, and as Talya pulled him down between her naked thighs she could see all sentimentality falling away. Enhanced coupling. Always rich. Always stunningly climactic.

Perfect.

*

Talya gazed at the face of the adult female subject suspended upright in the Scientechnos Academy's genomic preservation chamber. The adult male and the juvenile male never held her interest as intently as the "woman." Could this *Gaiae pithekos intermedius* rightly be considered a woman? Talya mused for the hundredth time. Or was she yet an animal? The debate raged among her colleagues: *How many Terresian genomes must a creature share to be deemed human?* The skeleton and musculature were all in place, even if the limb bones were thick and the legs bowed, the muscles anything but refined and sculpted, as they were in the Terresian anatomy.

The *pithekos* brain – ironically – was larger than her own, and there was rudimentary speech and the beginnings of consciousness. But the facial features were so coarse as to make Talya wince at the sight of the specimen. The protruding brow ridges made the female look monstrous, and the hair – so much of it – was wild and matted. The hairline around the face crept down low on the forehead and into the hollow of her cheeks. The irises of her eyes, open and staring through the phaetronic gas, were muddy brown, a color rarely seen on Terres anymore. Blue, green, grey were the norm.

And the specimen's hands – perhaps these fascinated Talya more than any other feature – had thick digits with palms like leather. They were much too reminiscent of the great apes that had come before, lower on the evolutionary ladder. The hands looked as though they could rip raw meat from the bones of a fresh kill.

This was *not* a woman, Talya decided. It was an animal.

She shuddered, turning away and entered her adjoining laboratory. At one of the trans-screens she called up before her a three-dimensional diffractor map of Gaia. It annoyed Talya that the previous expedition had failed to collect specimens from every continent. There might be species higher up or lower down on the evolvement scale, somewhere that they hadn't looked. Sixteen thousand Gaian years and countless generations – undocumented.

Who knew what would be found? *Pithekos* might have *devolved*, perhaps died out altogether, leaving her work in tatters.

She very much disliked surprises.

Talya consoled herself with the modest, no *minute* risk factor for extinction. The line – going back millions of years to the fur-covered, knuckle-dragging apes that evolved into the small upright, tiny-brained *Pithekos Afroencis,* to the bi-pedal, long-fingered, prehensile-toed *Erectus sapiensis* – was incredibly hardy. It seemed destined to survive.

Strange, Talya thought, glancing back at the female, the only thing that had killed *Pithekos intermedius* was removing specimens from the planet. Several dozen of the creatures had survived cryo-hybernation during the last voyage home to Terres, and most of them had accepted their pseudo-habitat provided them. The diffracted image of their sun rose and fell, the wind blew, the "seasons" changed. The creatures had gone on with their daily lives, subsisting on the vegetal foods provided them, and they'd even bred for several generations. Then they had begun to die, one after another. They'd buried their dead with a reverence that baffled the researchers, placing flowers and little stone trinkets in the graves. The *Pithekos* had been unaware that in the "night" the genomic team had exhumed the burial places and removed the bodies for autopsy.

It was found that no particular disease had felled their subjects. No viruses or bacterium. No obvious deterioration of vital organs. It was postulated that perhaps the pseudo sun had been insufficient for their needs. Lacrum Daes, in his infamous theorem, suggested an "emotional" cause for death linked to a purposeless life without the hunt. The simulation of their environment, while geologically and climatically perfect, and planted with familiar species of vegetation, was enforced by boundaries beyond which *Pithekos intermedius* could not travel. "We imprisoned them in a false environment," Daes insisted. "Consciously they were unaware of the difference to the authentic environment – save the lack of game to hunt – but their bodies and brains suffered nevertheless."

The idea had been roundly scorned by the scientific community for its sentimental bias. But one way or another every last *Pithekos* had succumbed, their bodies preserved and stored in hydrone gas for later experimentation. Only this small "family" remained displayed in the laboratory, a constant reminder to Talya of the challenges that lay ahead.

Her curiosity was intense. How far forward had previous modifications taken the creatures in their evolutionary process in the intervening years? During the coming mission they would finally implant the genomes that would "take the savage out of the beast." Allow the Gaian species the tools to begin building a modest culture. Of course she couldn't expect Terresian levels of intelligence and consciousness, but she hoped to be getting close.

There was, she was forced to admit, another challenge that rivaled the scientific ones. Her own mating with Poseidon needed to be carefully managed. He'd come from solid stock and proven more than fit. Outstanding really. His mind and character fascinated her. She thought him quite the perfect man, and had decided that upon their return to Terres he should father her child. Only his trait of over-demonstrativeness concerned her... though he could be modified.

What if he shared the same disturbing geno-sequencing as Athens? she wondered. *A latent strain?* Athens *was* a bit of a mutant. But his problematic qualities – just outside normal boundaries – were also the ones that caused a certain breed of Terresians to cleave loyally to the man. She wondered if a significant proportion of those who'd volunteered for the Marsean Colony carried the same genomes for jealousy, aggression, passion. Perhaps she should look more closely into Athens's profile. Learn whether his parents had ever had him re-calibrated when he was a boy. It might be that the mother, Manya, was the culprit. Poseidon often spoke with inordinate warmth about the woman and the plethora of physical affection she had lavished on both boys. This was less easy to correct, she knew, and Poseidon would have to agree to re-calibration.

Overall, Talya relished the future. She looked forward to Poseidon and herself as colleagues on the coming mission. She believed his choice of Gaia rather than Mars had been at least partially predicated on her own place on the Gaian team. Like herself, he must be aware that the time together would shape and solidify their pairing. There would be adequate opportunity once they'd reached their off-world destination to discuss such things. The timing might appeal to Poseidon's sense of the exotic. With her scientechnic studies laid out for a good many years, with Poseidon as her mate and child's sire, a mutant sequence or two would prove inconsequential. Her life would be complete…

Talya checked herself. She was being foolish. She must silence these endless ruminations about the man. What kind of scientist would she be if she spent the entire Gaian mission in a state of single-minded focus on a colleague…and her commander at that? There was so much to accomplish. She needed to get hold of herself. Re-focus her intent.

On the trans-screen Talya magnified the equatorial land mass lying south-southeast of the huge, vaguely triangular Indus continent, and began mapping the most likely locations for her studies. This posting would be the triumph of her scientific career, with or without Poseidon.

Focus… now, she admonished herself. There would be sufficient time for pairing on Gaia.

FIVE

JOURNEYS OUTSIDE THE dome always unsettled him. This day riding solo to the launch hub in the trans-car train, Poseidon found himself more disquieted and more stimulated than usual. Since childhood he'd always sensed that the farther he sped from the population hub into the planet's desolate reaches, the further back into Terres's deep history he was traveling. The initial shock of piercing the phaetronic force field that blanketed the contours of Atlas City, the farmland surrounding it, and the hill country to the west was one not simply of passing from light to pitch blackness and warmth to shattering cold, but from safety to danger, the known to the mysterious, tranquility to chaos.

Certainly the industrial and mining hubs along the track glittered hospitably under their domes, but these became fewer and much farther between. Out beyond in the dark regions, Poseidon knew there lay massive continents with their jagged mountain ranges, long-dead volcanoes, great plains, deserts surrounded by vast frozen oceans. But they were invisible in the dark.

All dead now.

Even the years of Terres's "close orbit" to their sun and its warming rays did nothing to revive the land or seascapes. They were permanently and irrevocably bleak. Poseidon believed that Terresians, perhaps to spare themselves the pain of their lost world, had all but forgotten what lay outside the domes. In those places the race's raw animal evolution and desperate bloody history had unfolded.

Best forgotten.

Better to contemplate and celebrate the splendid civilization they had created. It was a relief to regard their myriad blunders of long ago as resolved, the stupidity of passions, idolatry and wars behind them.

Poseidon squirmed in his seat recalling his recent questioning of the phaetron's sexual enhancement function, and Talya's dismissive response to it. He remembered the explosive orgasms they regularly shared and decided that he really should keep his subversive thoughts to himself.

Now up ahead were the glittering lights of the Launch Dome. Beside it in the blackness he could see in reflection and shadow the shape of the discoid mothership that would take him far across the solar system, and beyond this the massive trapezoidal transport vehicle, by now most certainly boarding its five thousand colonists.

The car slowed and came to a stop at the Launch Dome. Poseidon alighted to find that the crowds had already thinned, most of the passengers aboard their ships. There among the remaining few was his mother, Manya. It didn't surprise him that she'd come to see Athens and him off. He closed the distance between them and embraced her. The scent that wafted from the silky silver hair she defiantly wore loose about her shoulders recalled the kisses and goodnights of his first PseudoMort those many years before. Athens appeared from the boarding chamber door and joined them.

"Look at the two of you," she said, her mouth trembling with pride.

"Do you wish Father was here?" Athens asked her.

"Absolutely not," she said of her recently self-deceased mate. "Imagine calling his long, wonderful life 'tiresome.' He was the one who'd become tiresome."

Before his death Ammon Ra had committed himself to the "Graviteur" stage of life, binding himself relentlessly to its strictures: he must be reclusive, care for no one, feel nothing.

"Your father was an old fool," Manya said, placing an arm around each of her sons. "Permanent tranquility? Retreat from living when one is fully functional? Choosing death over life when there is so much left to study, to explore? He could barely rally a 'Well done,' when I brought up your achievements. His choice, not mine, boys." She pulled them close with her strong slender fingers. "I'm so proud of you both. What a glorious adventure lies ahead!"

Athens was called back to the loading platform. Poseidon hung back to give them a moment alone. For the son who would not be returning from Mars, Manya reserved a poignant farewell, allowing tears to fall freely. Poseidon could not look away as Athens clutched her tightly, his eyes over-brimming. Then his brother hurried away.

"And you," she said to Poseidon, wiping her cheeks with the back of her hand, her lips twisting into a smile, "You, I will live to see again. That makes me very happy."

"As it does me." He thought for a moment before he asked, "What do you think of Talya Horus?"

"You're a grown man. Why ask me?"

He didn't know the answer. It wasn't approval he was seeking, merely guidance.

"She's very beautiful," Manya offered. "Brilliant in her field. She could not be a more perfect Terresian woman."

"But...?"

"Does she move you?"

"Move me? I don't know what you're asking."

"Do you dream of her?"

He considered this, then said, "I can't remember dreaming of Talya. Does that matter?"

"Perhaps not." Manya laughed softly and touched his cheek. "I hope you find what you're looking for on Gaia."

"What *am* I looking for?"

"Don't you know?"

He shook his head.

"You'll tell me if you found it when you return. I hope it's wonderful. I hope it surprises you."

"If it surprises me half as much as you do, Mother, I will hold myself a very lucky man."

SIX

SUPINE IN THE MicroMort pod aboard the mothership Poseidon drifted in the last moments of Free-Dreaming. The Work Protocol – by far the longest phase of his hibernation – had finished several days before and had been quite productive. Now he rested in a period of blissful sleep in which his mind had wandered to the far boundaries of unconscious cognition – random phantasms of light, color and sound, preposterous dramas and domestic chatter. Even asleep he was aware of the mild phaetronic vibrus in the bones of his skull as the first sequence of pre-programmed stimullae fired, and his slumber began its shift into its final phase: Approach Protocol.

This allowed the last days on Terres before launch to be replayed to assist in pre-landing re-orientation to the mission. Poseidon noted that there had been unusual spikes in emotional responses, disquieting fluctuations in his thoughts and impulsive – even impetuous – behavior. He knew that as commander of the Gaian expedition nothing was more important than a carefully controlled state of mind – the hallmark of Terresian intellect.

Thankfully, no extreme oscillations or instability had marred his pre-arrival dream-state, and as he re-entered Waking Mode he was more than confident that he was prepared for the mission ahead.

SEVEN

P LEASE, *LET HIM be of good cheer,* Poseidon thought as he watched, from his ship's bay window, a shuttle pod crossing the distance between Athens's ship and his own. Before launch there had been a fair amount of grumbling – comparisons made between their vessels and expeditions. It was true, the two crafts that had been speeding on parallel courses toward the center of the solar system could not have been more different. Athens's transport – the one across the way – was a huge lumbering thing. Never even given a name, it was nothing more than a shapeless freighter, an unlovely mover of goods, plant life, all manner of Terresians – five thousand of them – and every conceivable necessity to begin the colonization of Mars.

Poseidon's ship, the *Atlantos,* was a gleaming disk, an elegant slice of silver amidst the stars, housing an elite, all-scientechnic team set to explore Gaia. This vessel's form was enhanced by function – stark, refined and exquisitely advanced. It was a circular craft of five levels, comprised of five master corridors that symmetrically extended to its distal edges like the spokes of a perfect wheel. Its lavishly appointed laboratories and extensive library were fully equipped for each of the major branches of Terresian science.

This was precisely the kind of contrast in his and Athens's

circumstances that had deeply grieved his brother from the time they'd been small. But the transmission Poseidon had received from Athens the day before had sounded uncharacteristically cheerful. Perhaps the work his brother had done aboard the transport in MicroMort had produced a healing between the two of them. Hopefully this meeting would be a pleasant one. Poseidon dearly wished it so, as it would be their last encounter for a good long while. After the long voyage from Terres the two vessels were approaching the point at which their paths would diverge – the *Atlantos* to Gaia, the transport to Mars.

Poseidon watched the transport's boxy but functional pod glide noiselessly into the landing port between several of the *Atlantos's* discoid shuttles and set itself down. The great door closed and the bay's pressure and gas levels were stabilized by the engineers behind the glass of its control center. Athens emerged from the pod's door and greeted the crew that had spread out onto the bay floor. They were all smiles as he moved among them, and Poseidon marveled at the effortless charm, the intense magnetism that caused both men and women to devote themselves ardently to his brother.

Athens caught sight of Poseidon and smiled his winning smile. His gaze was calm and steady as he approached, and for a moment Poseidon felt confident the tension between them had eased. They clasped arms.

"Was your waking comfortable?" Poseidon asked.

"Comfortable enough. And yours?"

"More so than the sleep. The anticipation in my dreams was close to unbearable. I can hardly wait to arrive. You must feel the same."

"I do," said Athens with a wry smile. "Every young unmated woman on the transport has already thrown herself at me." He hardly took a breath before adding, "And have you taken up again with Talya?"

"Bloody stars, Athens! We've only been awake forty-eight hours. You'll be seeing her shortly. We're dining together."

"Is that all?" Athens said with a playfully salacious leer.

"Behave yourself." Poseidon shook his head, amazed at his brother's tastelessness, but in truth his relief was greater than his disapproval. Athens was truly at ease.

*

The meal had been superb. If Terresians held one sense above all others it was taste. Athens, Talya and the mission's anthropologist, Symos Korber, sat with Poseidon in his private quarters beside its window overlooking the colonial transport – now framed by a great expanse of stars – commenting on the subtle flavors the staff cook had masterfully blended, and drinking a considerable quantity of the fermented brew called jog. Their conversation had, so far, waxed pleasantly mundane.

"You already know I think you're something of a deviant," Talya said, fixing Athens with a semi-serious gaze. "What I'm coming to believe is that every one of the colonists who volunteered for the Marsean mission shares that same genetic mutation to one degree or another."

Athens poured himself another cup of jog, trying but failing to assume a straight face. "Because they wish for adventure?" he asked. "Because they'd like to live in natural sunlight for the rest of their days?"

"Because every female onboard the transport would like the opportunity to bed the governor?" Korber suggested with a grin.

"I believe you're jealous, Korber," Poseidon teased the pudgy anthropologist. "You'd like a few of those healthy young Marsean emigrants falling all over *you*."

"Yes, I would," he agreed with a straight face.

Talya waited till the male laughter died down, then persisted with her over-serious theorizing. "For so many thousands of years we've been moving in the direction of peace, reason and dispassion. Now a significant portion of the population appears to be regressing."

"Some feel we've gone too far in that direction," Korber offered more soberly. There's barely enough passion to keep procreating the race. Look at how few women choose to carry their fetuses to term these days. Incubation centers are always full."

Talya shrugged. "For good reason. The female body is evolving in consequential ways. Fewer women possess the ability to lactate."

"Our mother breast-fed both Athens and me," Poseidon interjected.

"Perhaps that's the problem with the pair of you," Talya countered, with a barely perceptible hint of humor.

"Did you know, brother," said Athens, "that Talya believes us equally afflicted?"

Though Poseidon smiled at the jab, it did make him wonder. He knew that the warmth and affection he showed Talya annoyed her. Now he wondered if she believed he was indeed a deviant. He watched as Athens moved to pour more jog into Talya's cup, but she placed a hand over it.

"Four or five generations down the line," she said, "I'd like very much to test my hypothesis on your 'New Marseans' and see just how much recalibration they need."

"Perhaps they'll reject recalibration," Poseidon suggested.

"Quite right," Athens agreed.

"You would let society devolve into chaos?" Talya asked him.

"Your definition of chaos...?" he challenged her.

"Unbridled emotion. A throwback to ancient Terresian madness."

"My brother tells me he's thinking of feeding his colonists creatures from the sea," Poseidon added, well aware he was adding fuel to the fire.

"Then you've already gone mad," Talya snapped. "That is

utterly irresponsible. Our bodies will not tolerate eating flesh. You'll poison the entire colony, and where will that leave your mining efforts? Terres will die."

"Introduce the 'sea food' gradually," Korber suggested evenly, "and the Terresian body will adapt. If females can cease lactating…"

Poseidon observed Talya's beautiful features grow rigid with irritation, but it was Athens that cheerily eased the strained moment.

"I propose a toast!" he cried and lifted his cup high. "To the Gaian and Marsean missions. May we double the accomplishments set forth and bring a long, secure future to our beloved home planet." Then he turned and gazed at Poseidon. "And to my brother, who made this mission possible for me."

The others raised their cups and even Talya, relenting from her harsh opinions, smiled.

Indeed, thought Poseidon sipping his jog, something wonderful had come over Athens. He had emerged from his long sleep a new man, hopeful and optimistic. All bitterness and jealousy had vanished as though it had never before infected their lives.

His heart full, Poseidon raised his cup again. "*My* toast – to Athens! May he…" The words caught in his throat as he became aware of a flash of unexpected movement outside his window.

A cluster of glowing amber plasma spheres was speeding toward the two ships! They moved at so great a speed Poseidon had barely time to cry out a warning when the spheres flashed within a hairsbreadth of Athens's transport, covered the distance between the two vessels and collided with the *Atlantos*. Reflexively bracing for massive impact, all at the table were astonished when none came. But in the next instant one of the spheres – not solid but *pure energy* – pierced the ship's hull without breaching it, sped across Poseidon's quarters and missed the diners by less than an arm's length. Instantly it disappeared through the opposite wall into the body of the ship with no material damage to anything surrounding it.

Then the craft shuddered violently and all magno-electric systems ground to a halt. Lights died momentarily before emergency systems switched on, but when even these faltered momentarily, the true damage became apparent. The orbs had, during their trajectory through the *Atlantos*, crippled the energy matrix of the vessel, and even the crew's wrist phaetrons.

Life support was going down.

"Everyone – to the shuttle port," Poseidon said. "Pray the shuttles are still functional."

The elevator beam at the ship's hub was nonoperational. All aboard were forced to scramble down the ladders to the shuttle bay. When they arrived it was clear Poseidon's prayers had been unanswered. The technos crew was helpless. The shuttle disks were dead. Air in the ship was growing noticeably thinner, and even among these highly experienced scientists panic was rising. Then the lights flickered once more and finally died. There was silence in the pitch dark bay.

"We'll get everyone to the transport," said Athens, excitement thrumming in his voice. Even as children he'd made a challenge of danger.

"Captain Zalen," Poseidon called. "Help everyone into their life support suits."

Talya was at Poseidon's side. "We're not going out there..." she whispered.

"I've raised the transport," Athens said. Poseidon saw the faintest glow flickering in his brother's wrist, and heard a static-plagued voice emanating from the thing. Into the device Athens barked, "Prepare to receive entire crew of the *Atlantos*...What?" Athens put the device to his ear. "No, we have no shuttles, and I can't be sure that any of ours won't decommission if you bring them too close to this ship!" He seemed to devise the plan as he spoke. "String a tether between the vessels… a tether!"

There were sounds of rustling in the dark as one hundred and seventy-five terrified men and women donned the emergency suits they'd been assured they would never have to wear.

"The bay doors…" Poseidon said to Athens. "We'll open them manually." By the time they reached the doors, Cyphus – named head of security on this mission – was there already, feeling around in the darkness for the mechanism that allowed for emergency opening.

"I know you're all frightened," Poseidon announced, his voice echoing in the cavernous shuttle port. "But there's no need to be. We're going out there *together*. We'll be firmly attached to a blenium cable stretched between our two vessels. We'll keep our heads, and we'll all be across in no time."

He hoped his message to the crew sounded confident and commanding, but when the bay doors finally rolled open to reveal the vast expanse of lifeless space, all he could think – but did not dare say aloud – was, *Luck to us all. We are out into the void.*

Before terror could fully seize them the crew found themselves strung along a cable between the two ships, like jewels on some fantastical necklace. The dark of the bay's interior had been replaced by the welcome glare of lights from the transport. Dozens of Athens's colonists had donned their life support suits and were now floating out into space to assist in the rescue. One by one the *Atlantos* crew was pulled aboard the ship.

Talya had insisted on staying close to Poseidon, though he'd been last to leave the stricken vessel. Now hanging in the vacuum side-by-side he calmly assured her that the heavy clip holding them to the tether was foolproof, that there was no way she could break free and float off to her death in deep space. A moment later he heard her speaking to the man hooked to the cable in front of her – it was Korber – telling him not to worry, that everything was under control. When she turned back to him, Poseidon detected a hint of a smile through the faceplate. *She's an amazing woman,* he thought. *I'm fortunate to be sharing her bed.*

The second cluster of amber plasma spheres screamed out of the darkness and bore down on the remaining scientists with such velocity that no one saw them till they had severed the center of the human necklace in two places. Talya, Korber and Poseidon, still tethered together, were sliced away from the others and whipped along in the spheres' wake for a terrifying eternity before the glowing balls released them from their pull and disappeared into the blackness.

The three were floating in space, tumbling out of control. The sight of their receding ships was awful, but Poseidon forcibly stifled his fear. He located the stabilizing mechanism in his garment, righted himself, then began pulling his crewmates in towards him. Talya was first into his grasp. He had never before seen such naked terror in a person's eyes. Few circumstance in modern daily life on Terres jeopardized its population. It was a peaceful, modulated existence, and the people had become soft. But there was no time to comfort Talya now.

Korber was still adrift.

"We're going to reel Korber in," Poseidon told her. Together they tugged on the length of tether. He was within a dozen feet of them when a single rogue energy sphere sped out of nowhere. It smashed through Korber's body and was gone before Poseidon and Talya could react.

The anthropologist's violent spasming was, moments later, replaced by limpness inside the suit. Poseidon's stomach turned at the sight. Together Talya and he began pulling him toward them, an awkward feat, the tether wrapping itself around Korber's legs. Their bulky, inflexible suits made movement difficult, and the physical effort they expended destabilized them further. Arms, legs and cable became dangerously tangled. All thoughts had been for Korber's rescue, so that when one of the transport's pods appeared suddenly beside them and deftly maneuvered itself close to the trio, Poseidon gave up his struggle and allowed himself and his battered colleagues to be hauled aboard by the pilot.

It was Athens.

Inside they unsuited Talya and found her unharmed. It was with terrible trepidation that they removed Korber's helmet, the faceplate glazed into opaqueness. All that remained of the man was a pile of crumbled bones encased in a bag of seared skin.

Silenced by shock and the knowledge that nothing more could be done for him, Athens regained the controls and flew them back to his vessel.

EIGHT

MY OWN LITTLE *kingdom*, thought Athens as he walked with Talya and his brother through one of the transport's large common rooms teeming with cheerful colonists. Many greeted Poseidon with respectful nods, but it was gratifying to see it was for their governor that they reserved their warmest, friendliest smiles. Nearly every young woman gazed at Athens with what could only be described as blatant invitation. He could feel Poseidon's disapproval – no one aboard seemed particularly moved by the loss of one of their own.

Poseidon and Talya would never, Athens knew, understand that the colonists' spirit of celebration for their coming adventure was immutable, unshakable, even in the face of death and that he, Athens, symbolized their glorious future. Of course he was sickened by Korber's violent end. Nevertheless, this mission was proving a particular balm to the wound that had perpetually afflicted him since childhood. Despite how the posting had come about it was now something of Athens's own. Since his waking he had enjoyed a new buoyancy, a certainly that he and his colonists would live in great contentment on Mars. Even the notion of manual labor in the titanum mines did not appear to blunt their enthusiasm.

They were to be bold pioneers on a sunlit planet.

Persus Elrah – the short, stocky and mildly unattractive young assistant assigned to Athens by Federation – hurried up behind them. She nodded respectfully to Athens, silently asked for and was granted permission to speak to Poseidon.

"Repairs on your ship are going to be extensive, Sir, " she reported. "I don't think we can afford to delay our landing much past the estimated arrival schedules. The transport can tow you, and repairs can continue on route. But if the fixes aren't made before landing we'll have to maneuver the *Atlantos* to Gaia's surface somehow. And this vessel is anything but maneuverable. Perhaps a number of our shuttle pods would do the trick."

"Thank you, Persus," Poseidon replied. "That sounds like a workable plan."

"Shall I gather the pilots, navigators and engineers in an hour – shuttle bay?"

"Yes, but walk with us for a moment," Athens said to his assistant, gracing her with the warmest of smiles.

She blushed with pleasure and stood just a little straighter in her Federation uniform.

Now as the four of them entered the transport's sparse, functional living quarters they were arrested by the sight, out a window, of the crippled *Atlantos*, and shuttles ferrying repair crews between the two vessels. If the colonists had been unperturbed by Korber's death, it seemed that Talya and Poseidon had been particularly shaken, perhaps by the knowledge that they might easily have shared his fate. The scene outside reminded them all that the cause of the calamity was still a mystery.

"How can you believe that anything but an intelligent force was driving those spheres?" Athens insisted, revisiting a conversation begun moments after he'd brought Talya and Poseidon aboard the transport vessel.

"Our sensors found them to be composed entirely of energy,

their trajectories random," Poseidon countered. "If they'd meant to harm us, why did they miss the transport, filled with people?"

"We've never seen anything remotely like them occurring naturally on Terres," Athens persisted. "Or reported on Mars, or Gaia on previous expeditions."

"That's not altogether true," said Talya. "We know that on the surface of Gaia there are electrical storms that produce ball lighting that moves in similar ways."

"In an *atmosphere*, Talya," was Athens retort. "What could hold a charge like that together in a vacuum, and propel it with such precise direction?"

"But they moved uni-directionally," Poseidon said. "If the spheres had changed trajectory, made even one angular course correction, then I'd have to agree with your notion of an intelligent source."

Athens grew frustrated. This was another old, sometimes bitter argument between the brothers. "Did you see the energy spheres, Persus?" Athens asked his assistant.

"Yes, a diffractal of the events. Both of them."

"And?"

"I don't know what you're asking, Sir," she said.

"My brother believes there was an intelligent force driving them," Poseidon told her. "Most in the sciences are certain that there is intelligent, perhaps technos-advanced life somewhere in the universe, though we cannot conceive of how they could have solved the problem of interstellar space travel – which would assume exceeding the speed of light – something that we ourselves have never managed. Athens is among a small but vocal minority who suppose intelligent life exists within our own solar system, or has visited our solar system."

"And that might account for certain unexplained leaps in Gaian evolution that occurred even before Terresians began tampering with the genomic structure of *Pithekos*," Talya added.

"Certainly it's tempting to fill the gaps in Gaian evolution with the intervention of other intelligent alien visitors besides ourselves."

"Correct me if I'm wrong," Persus interjected, having found her voice, "but when the first Terresian explorers set foot on our sister planet fourteen sun cycles ago, two species were discovered. The first was genomically and structurally similar to ones that had developed on Terres, and from which modern Terresians long ago evolved. But the other creatures they found on Gaia were strange intermediate beings – dull-witted cave dwellers with thick bodies and monstrous heads – more than an ape and less than a human. By Terresian calculations – considering the many shattering cataclysms and massive extinctions that hurled Gaia's development back by eons – these creatures were *too far advanced* in their development…by several million years. That was when the first expedition scientists, believing they were fulfilling a moral obligation to their sister planet, immediately began a genomic program, escalating the evolutionary process even further. This species was, indeed, a mystery, one that could be explained by 'intervention' by someone – some *thing* – other than ourselves."

"Well said, Persus," Talya said. "But I think the governor will have to provide some hard evidence of alien life forms tampering in our solar system to change my mind…or anyone's, especially his brother's."

"Surely you're not saying you think it even remotely possible," Poseidon said to Talya.

Was this a simple rhetorical question, Athens wondered, *or Poseidon's condescending tone that always made his blood boil?*

"Let's just say I feel the theories – and they are both merely theories – are equally valid," Talya replied.

"Or it could be that a third theory, one that hasn't yet been explored, will solve the mystery," Persus added.

This line of reasoning relieved Athens, quelled the sudden bolt of anger his brother had kindled. He'd been feeling uncharacteristically warm and gracious towards Poseidon since his waking. And today, as the entire colony watched, their governor had shown skill and heroism rescuing the beloved Terresian savior. Athens could afford another generous gesture. He placed an arm around Talya's and Persus's shoulders.

"I think Federation has mistakenly given our jobs to the wrong people," he said. "These are two extraordinary women. We're lucky to have them." To Persus he said, "Go along and find the others, and we'll figure out a way to get my brother's ship safely to its destination."

Then he smiled at Poseidon and he found, to his deep satisfaction, that the smile was genuine.

NINE

HOW MANY TIMES had Poseidon watched the diffractal called "Gaia Approach"? Studied the multi-dimensional image of the blue and green orb with its anarchic pattern of clouds swirling above it, suspended in the pitch blackness of space? It must be hundreds. But now, viewing Terres's sister planet from the sub-bridge of Athens's transport, he was stunned, speechless at the heart-stopping immensity, and its beauty – both seen and unseen. Beneath the crust its molten core roiled with oozing red magma, the warm seas teemed with unfathomable species. The continents thundered with hooved herds. Endless forests blanketed vast plains and mountains alike. Skies were blackened by great dancing clouds of winged creatures. With the actual planet before his eyes spinning in slow majesty on its invisible axis, Helios bathing one half in light, the other half shadow-bound and awaiting its moment in the sun, Poseidon knew that nothing – neither his studies, his previous explorations, nor his discovery of titanum – could have prepared him for this moment.

The realization that this was the moment of his destiny's turning – was shattered by the sudden noisy arrival of his team leaders. Talya: population and genomics; Ables: climate; Chronell:

geology; Leones: biology; Zalen: Captain of the *Atlantos;* Cyphus: security.

First sight of Gaia was something best shared. Posidon had called them together, eager for their initial observations. A final decision about the location of their headquartering needed to be made as well.

Ables was the first in, and the first to catch sight of Gaia. He was virtually stopped in his tracks. "There she is," he intoned with reverence.

All conversation ceased and everyone fell silent as their individual calculations began. After a few moments Chronell began whispering excitedly into his wrist device.

"Tell us what you're observing, will you?" Poseidon said.

"Certainly. Captain, will you magnify for us – 12 pvs?"

Zalen moved to the console, and loading the image into the diffractor presented a three-dimensional Gaia that now floated between them, spinning on its axis. Details invisible from a distance were now revealed.

"Chronell continued. "Observe North Platos."

The geologist referred to the huge northern continent of the two that were stacked one atop the other, linked by a narrow volcano-heavy isthmus.

"Look at that!" Ables cried.

"What are you seeing?" Talya demanded impatiently.

Chronell pointed to the northernmost portions of North Platos. "During the last Terresian expedition – and for 100,000 Gaian years before – this continent was covered by an extensive, miles-thick ice sheet. It's all but gone now. Only polar ice, north and south, is left. Extraordinary."

"What conditions might have caused it to melt?" Poseidon asked. He looked to both men.

"Internal warming?" Chronell surmised. "Increased volcanism on a grand scale?"

"Collision with a space rock," Ables suggested. "Asteroid. Comet. In either case, the initial fires and a full atmospheric dust event would have caused another severe planet-wide freeze. But it appears largely temperate now. It'll take us some time to calculate when it happened and its cause."

He and Chronell exchanged a look of happy anticipation. Their mission had just become an official adventure, a mystery to be solved.

"Correct me if I'm wrong," Talya said, addressing Chronell as she halted the planet's rotation with a finger to the image, "but was *this* not once a single piece of land? Magnify, Zalen."

The area in question – what had been the long South Asyan Peninsula, just east of the Indus Sub-continent – was now significantly shorter. Its southern half was separated entirely from the continent by hundreds of miles of water.

"Chronell leaned in and took a closer look. "There must have been monstrous flooding and permanent sea level rise even that far from North Platos. Fascinating!"

Ables tapped the image to start its rotation again. "Look here," he pointed, "and here. Those were land bridges. Gone now."

"Nominations for our headquartering," Poseidon requested.

"Central North Platos," Chronell suggested.

"Afros," Leones said. "Unparalleled for bio-diverse flora and fauna."

"And where the preponderance of early human evolutionary activity occurred," Poseidon added. "Where most of the previous Terresian expeditions quartered."

"Something equatorial," Ables suggested. "Stable climate."

"The new South Asyan island." Talya said this with such startling command it seemed as though the decision had already been made.

Everyone turned in surprise and stared at her.

Unruffled, she added, "Or are we calling it a continent?"

GAIA

In this mountain there dwelt one of the earth born primeval men of that country, whose name was Evenor, and he had a wife named Leucippe, and they had an only daughter who was called Cleito. The maiden had already reached womanhood, when her father and mother died; Poseidon fell in love with her...

– Plato's *Critias,* 4th Century B.C.

TEN

NIGHT WAS FALLING and the *Atlantos*, perched on its five retractable legs, gleamed in the sunset's light. A dozen pods – those that had towed the damaged ship to the ground – prepared for departure to the transport, now hovering several miles overhead. The brothers stood looking out across Gaia's landscape –the broad central plain, an immense range of jagged mountains serrating the eastern horizon.

"You know I envy you, Athens."

"Nonsense. Look at this place," he said, sweeping his arm before him. "It's breathtaking. Mars has precisely one species of land vegetation and a featureless ocean."

"True. But my stay on Gaia is short. We'll have only begun to enjoy it before we have to leave for home."

"Trade with me then," Athens teased. "You take my post on Mars with twenty-five hundred nubile girls panting after their hero, and I'll stay here in paradise with the lovely Talya. That's fair."

Poseidon laughed aloud.

Athens fixed his eyes on his brother. His features seemed somehow more defined, and a kind of energy radiated – no *pulsed*

– around his body. Was it merely the quality of light on the planet, he wondered. Or was Gaia playing tricks on his own mind?

"Something's changed," Athens said impulsively. "Something in you."

Poseidon straightened, looking suddenly uncomfortable. "Nothing has changed. I'm who I've always been. Your aggravating brother."

Athens looked away, scanning the landscape for a hint of the curious affinity he sensed between Poseidon and this world. As though they shared a frequency. A vibrus. But how could that be?

"Brother…" Athens continued in a tone that sounded, even to his own ears, remarkably affectionate, "…thank you again for making the post on Mars possible for me."

"There was no one more qualified than you."

"We both know that's a lie. It was a brotherly gesture, a peace-offering."

"One that I would never have made had you been in any way lacking. I may have wanted peace between us, but not at the expense of Terres."

Athens embraced Poseidon impetuously, then abruptly turned away and strode off to his waiting shuttle without another word. He sped through the pale blue atmosphere towards the darkening sky joining the others pods, and beyond to the glittering lights of the transport. As one by one they were swallowed up by the great craft Athens allowed himself a final thought of his strangely transformed brother and the third planet from the sun…before snapping his attention inward.

The colonists awaited, and Mars. His own adventure was about to begin.

ELEVEN

FIRST DAWN ON a new world.

Poseidon rose earlier than the rest, dressing in the dark to hasten from the confines of the *Atlantos*, now humming subsonically with the vibrus of a thousand life support machines, those that the technos crew had managed to make operational. At the craft's hub he stepped into the center of the beam elevator, a vertical blue shaft of light whose inner core transported one downward, its outer cylinder sweeping the passenger upward. At the lowest level of the craft a round door slid open under his feet and the blue beam shot through thin air to Gaia's surface.

He stepped out into what was left of the night, a wide band of stars still winking in the west, a diffuse, promising glow to the east. The moment he exited the elevator beam he felt himself overcome by an avalanche of sensations. The moist breeze that ruffled his hair had brought with it smells of rich, dew-dampened topsoil, a strong vegetal fragrance gathered, he guessed, from the profuse forest canopy nearby, the pungent scent of a distant herd – odors foreign to his senses, but all vaguely and mysteriously familiar. By habit he moved to switch on the enhancer function of his wrist device, but thought suddenly with a jolt of surprise that it was unnecessary.

I hope it surprises you, his mother had said. *Here it is,* he thought, *the first surprise...*

Even before the tiny startling point of sun made its appearance on the horizon the eastern sky filled with streaky, haphazard clouds of brilliant orange. As each second passed everything around him began turning a sharp, deep unimaginable blue. Poseidon had seen sunrises before. First dawn after the endless Terresian hibernation was cause for celebration. But nothing, he thought, walking quickly to be gone from the vessel's suddenly unnatural shapes and surfaces and burnished metal, *nothing* had prepared him for this. He knew in his scientist's mind that what he was seeing was merely a coalescence of the surface weather conditions and upper atmosphere causing cloud formations, enriched by splendid life forms. Still he was dazzled. Over-awed. Even bewildered.

Then the sun burst over the horizon in an explosion of phosphorescent yellow in the full spectacle of Gaian dawn. To the east was a vast grassy plain. Underfoot was loamy soil sprouting a cover of large pale flowers with insects buzzing round them like planets orbiting a miniature sun. Standing in place he turned in a full circle, feeding on these visions, growing fat on the feast of beauty. In the silence, without the enhancer, he could hear the blood pounding in his ears, feel a sweet tingling the whole length of his limbs, and a warmth spreading outward from his chest that rivaled the heat bathing his body from Helios. Breath escaped him in a long deep sigh, and suddenly he realized with as much certainty as incredulity that he had traveled nine-hundred-and-forty-million miles through the vast reaches of space to find himself, inexplicably, home.

TWELVE

POSEIDON MADE A habit of solitary early morning explorations in proximity to the ship. This morning he roamed through the forest floor, speaking a report into his wrist device, quietly, reverentially, meant to disturb nothing. *Ninety-two days post Gaian landfall,* he began. *Phaetronic depictions of the planet, no matter how detailed or vivid, provide only a pale imitation of living reality. Standing in an ancient grove of trees makes me dizzy with its fragrances. Animals and insects in number and variety stagger my imagination. How can I describe the exquisite pleasure I receive from a tiny furred creature simply returning my gaze? This morning I attempted to catalog each and every shade of green around me, but after the second dozen I abandoned the project, feeling silly, and afterwards simply enjoyed the plethora of greens for their own sake. I believe I've come to an understanding of reveling in an experience. I'm afraid it could easily become a habit.*

As he emerged from the tree line, the *Atlantos* – now in its final stages of repair – came into view. Rooted to the spot, Poseidon felt the breath go out of him. As though his eyes had opened for the first time he could see that the ship, with its neatly functional form and smooth metallic symmetry, was no more than a blight upon the Gaian landscape. *The ship,* he continued in a trembling voice, *is completely antithetical to its surroundings, an affront to this rolling meadow. It is… a weapon's cold blade lying on the belly of a beautiful woman. Perhaps I should speak to the crew about burying it underground.*

Then a rueful laugh escaped him. *The crew will think me insane. Maybe I* am *losing my mind. Lately I've been entertaining a madly subversive idea: how wonderful it would be to ignore the Planetary Escape Timetable and miss the precisely scheduled escape from Gaia's orbit back to Terres. I don't want to go back. I wish I could live here forever.* These words spoken aloud for the first time rocked Poseidon on his feet. Frightened him. He straightened up and pulled the phaetron from his lips. There was no time for such erratic self-indulgences. He had to get his head straight. And under no circumstances could anyone know these strange turns his mind was taking.

Anyone.

THIRTEEN

POSEIDON STEPPED INTO the blue central beam, allowing himself to be whisked upwards into the heart of the craft. He consciously banished the thought that the air felt dead, the artificial lighting harsh and unpleasant, and hurried down the long corridor. He mustn't be late for another meeting.

Ables and Chronell, just returned from their initial field studies, were waiting for him in the ship's circular library.

"We can confirm it was a comet strike that melted the Northern Platos ice sheet twelve hundred years ago," Ables began, "and caused widespread flooding and significant changes in coastal geography all over the globe. We believe it submerged the lowlands across the center of the South Asyan Peninsula, causing this island's 'separation' from the mainland. The resulting smaller ice age has prevailed for the last thousand years. We expect reports from Leones and Horus describing major migrations and extinctions of plant and animal species as a result."

Chronell continued. "However, the northern and southern polar caps have not only held firm since the last Terresian mission, they've thickened. But we believe some changes are in the making." He slipped a small cylinder into the stationary phaetron pedestal at the far end of the library. An instant after the cylinder disappeared into the receiving slot, the three of them found themselves standing amidst a blizzard so fierce the barrage was horizontal.

"This is the northern pole," Ables announced. "I won't activate sensory parameters. We'd freeze, and the noise would deafen us."

The diffracted image of the snow appeared to penetrate and move right through their corporal bodies. Ables was right. Had he activated the sense memorizer, the howling and cold would have been unbearable. But a moment later the scene changed, the blizzard superseded by a serene landscape – endless pale blue ice and a sky of the same hue, but a dozen shades deeper. In the distance were rugged peaks shrouded white.

"The pole's grown so deep that pressure is building between the lower layers," said Ables. "The resulting friction produces heat."

The diffracted image changed again, and the three men were suddenly floating amidst a sea of icebergs, huge and grotesque.

"Ables believes the end of this ice epoch will occur because of the friction-produced heat melting the ice caps," interjected Chronell. "I don't agree. Gaia's excessive volcanism of is not yet a thing of the past. While we haven't seen the kind of activity that created the great mountain ranges, for example the Indus Himalayan Range, we envision much more to come. I'm predicting a moderate but widespread increase in volcanic activity in the next century or two. And of course activity at the rifts."

"A faster melt at the poles than with friction?" Poseidon said.

"In my opinion," said Chronell.

Quite suddenly the trio was again standing in the middle of the vessel's library. Chronell had removed his data cylinder from the phaetron and was packing up his materials.

It startled Poseidon to find himself back on the mid-level of the *Atlantos's* metallic hull. It was as if a lovely dream had ended. He was suddenly aware of how deeply he wished to begin his own travels. They'd been delayed far too long already. He noticed then that the two scientists were regarding him strangely. Were his emotions so apparent in his expression?

Quickly Poseidon twisted his face into the semblance of a smile. "Good work, both of you." He turned on his heels and left the library so abruptly it occurred to him that Ables and Chronell must have thought him strange, or even ill.

I must pull myself together, Poseidon thought as he moved down the long corridor trying to quiet his rapid breathing. He nodded to the crewmembers he encountered, then disappeared into a small alcove where he set his wrist device to the 'chemistry-balancing' function and held it up to his neck. The jolt of moderating vibrus surged into him, and he sensed his heartbeat and breath slow to their regular levels. By the time the phaetron signaled an incoming message less than a minute later, he felt almost normal.

"Yes?" He spoke into the device in his most commanding tone.

"Don't you sound serious?" It was Talya's voice, smooth and cool as one of the northern icebergs.

"You're back." Poseidon was aware that his reply was warm enough to melt one of them. He had missed her, he realized suddenly.

"I'm ready to make my preliminary report."

"In my quarters. Immediately."

"Immediately?"

He found the blood rushing to his face. *What is happening to me?* Poseidon's normal equilibrium was no longer at his command.

"I've missed you, too," she said.

But despite the sentiment he could hear the chill that was ever-present in Talya's voice. *It's her way*, he told himself. *It's everyone's way. Everyone's but mine.* He stepped out into the corridor and straightening his posture, made for his quarters.

FOURTEEN

TALYA WAS VAGUELY annoyed. Something was wrong with Poseidon. Her field report seemed to be falling on deaf ears. They'd had a brief private moment when she entered his quarters, but there was more urgency in his embrace than made her comfortable. She'd quickly launched into an account of her visits to several of the continent's aboriginal villages, but he seemed distracted.

"So you remained cloaked for the entire period of your study?"

Finally, she thought, *a meaningful question.* "In light of my predecessor's disastrous experience," she said, "I decided I should not reveal myself to the tribe."

"The Goddess Talya," Poseidon teased gently.

But she was in no mood for levity. "Our incorporation into tribal myths is an unacceptable contamination of the test sample. Don't you agree?"

"We've been tampering with the species at the most profound levels possible for millennia. A few small additions to the local cosmology seems a rather minor contamination to me."

"I wouldn't let your colleagues hear you say such things."

What's come over him? Talya thought. Her concern for Poseidon was growing with every conversation. Whatever emotional fluctuations had taken hold of him on Terres had been exacerbated by their presence on Gaia. Now she could see him suppressing a smile. The last time they'd spoken he'd accused her of being overbearing in her seriousness.

"In general the *sapient* species is substantially more advanced than we expected. We anticipated any number of evolutionary strides since the interventions of our last expedition. I was particularly pleased to see the short, once-yearly female estrus cycle replaced by a monthly period of fertility. It's the reason we've seen such an explosion in the population."

"Brain capacity has increased?" Poseidon asked.

"Not size so much as neural complexity. There have been some unprecedented advances. Many of the small wandering tribes our scientists saw on the last mission have settled into stationary villages. Primitive art, music, medicine are developing. I observed some rudimentary mining – flint for weapons, ochre for ceremonial uses. I spent a good deal of time with a tribe on the mid-eastern coast. They call themselves the Shore People. They've begun exploiting their proximity to the sea, harvesting edibles from the shore, as well as constructing simple vessels that take them to locations where larger sea animals can be caught. No navigation as yet. Females in this village seem to be on equal footing with the men. There was one individual of particular interest there – a woman. The subject – 4251 – is strong and healthy. More importantly, she's intellectually advanced beyond the others to a remarkable degree."

Talya punched up a sequence on her wrist device that began conjuring a three-dimensional image into the space near Poseidon's chair. "Factoring in the obvious cultural liabilities and rudimentary language, 4251's reasoning, logic and learning capabilities may be equal to our own."

The image was quite clear now. A tawny-haired young woman attired in animal skins knelt between the thighs of a pregnant woman who was obviously in the throes of labor. Her head bowed to her task, there were only glimpses of the brown eyes, high, rounded cheekbones, perfectly oval chin.

"At the age of fourteen, subject became the tribal doctor using medicinal combinations of plant and animal substances she concocted herself," Talya continued. "She's present at every birth. She devises simple tools and relatively sophisticated weapons, and her problem-solving abilities are superb."

Talya could see that her report had captured Poseidon's imagination. She went on. "While the general population is more advanced than we'd expected, this particular female's cognitive skills are superior."

"Are we to assume, then, that she's a natural – if statistically rare – mutation of the species?"

"Yes, I think we can assume that."

"How does the tribe view her?" Poseidon asked. He stood and moved alongside the image to get a better look at the young woman. "I'd imagine her differences would prove disconcerting to them."

"When she was still a girl she was single-handedly responsible for domesticating wolves and bringing them into the village. This initially caused a great deal of strife. Now the animals are not only accepted, but an integral aspect of the hunt. From what I can gather 4251 was an oddity from earliest childhood. But her parents were themselves tribal leaders who wielded a good deal of power. While they didn't understand this child any better than the others, they smoothed the way for her as best they could."

Poseidon seemed captivated by the diffracted image, moving slowly around it to view every angle.

"You must understand something about these people as a whole, Poseidon. They have a certain quality...I find it difficult to describe. Of course this is not my discipline. Korber could have done it far more justice." Talya relaxed back in her chair, momentarily allowing her finely-honed intellect to linger on the idea, turn it round to view from several perspectives before delivering her interpretation.

"They feel things intensely. No half measures. Parenting is a passionate endeavor, especially for the females, though even the fathers are fiercely protective of their offspring. Beyond that, every adult member of the tribe is affectionate to all the young. They've adopted a religion that revolves around a belief that Gaia – which they call 'Erthe' – is *itself* alive, a goddess who can bless or exact punishment on them."

Poseidon appeared entranced.

"Are you all right?" she asked.

"Of course. Go on."

"Every object, plant and animal in nature is imbued with a particular spirit. Like so many of the planet's mammalian species, these people are highly territorial — and they'll fight to the death to protect their food supplies and families."

Now before them, subject 4251 successfully delivered the infant and placed it on her mother's breast to suckle. She pulled a stone blade from her waist and skillfully cut the umbilical.

"Of course this means the natural aggression of their primate ancestors has begun escalating," Talya continued. "And with the growing population, the tribes will be coming into contact with each other more frequently, so I'm going to recommend in my final report that during the next mission we initiate GRP."

At this, Poseidon went decidedly pale.

What could be wrong with the man? Talya wondered. The Genomic Restructuring Program, to which all humans on the home planet were subject, was a protocol whereby the particular brain chemistry which produced aggressive and murderous behavior in their species had been bred nearly into extinction. During their long evolution the Terresians – not unlike the Gaian primitives – had made bloodshed a way of life. Greed, sexual jealousy, even differences in religious beliefs led to slaughter on a frightening scale. But natural evolution of consciousness and advances in phaetron technos – particularly the science of genomics – brought with it the discovery of a specific genome which, when excised from the basic helial structure, eradicated the impulse to fight.

It had been a revolution unparalleled in Terresian history. With each succeeding generation children grew up to be non-aggressive adults. War and crime ceased to exist except in the occasional mutation. Religious conflicts, once a common catalyst for great wars, no longer precipitated hostilities.

That was when the debate on the loss of "natural passion" in the species had begun. Talya knew her recommendation for instituting the Gaian GRP would spark controversy back on Terres. Some of her colleagues believed the previous expeditions' interventions with the primitives were already excessive. That Terresians ought simply to be *observers* of their twin planet's development, and careful about tampering with an extraordinarily pure lesson in the evolutionary process of a closely related species.

But Poseidon was not one of them. He'd always been among the majority of Terresians who were satisfied with their existence no longer plagued by violence. They believed it their duty to guide the Gaian primitives to a more peaceful planet.

Talya noticed that Poseidon was almost trance-like, unable to take his eyes off the young woman in the diffractor image. She decided she would not indulge his strange behavior, and continued.

"The males and females seem to have adopted monogamy, though there is a period of youthful sexual activity with random partners before the final mate is selected.

"And our special female," queried Poseidon, "has she a mate, or random sexual partners?"

"Happily for our purposes, neither. While she's considered a person of stature within the tribe, no man has dared to approach her sexually. Her strength frightens them. There is one young male of approximately her age, subject 2287, who appears to be interested. They must have grown up together."

"She must feel very alone," Poseidon said, more to himself than aloud. Then all at once he seemed to grow flustered, as though aware of his inappropriate sentiment and behavior, and added quickly with some semblance of professionalism, "Her name is...?"

"She's known as Cleatah, child of Evenor and Luna," Talya answered, perhaps a touch too sharply. She found herself troubled by Poseidon's personal interest, even compassion for an experimental subject. With a few touches of her fingers to her wrist, the image abruptly dematerialized.

Poseidon appeared shocked by the sudden disappearance of the image and Talya, growing impatient and unable to soften the sharpness in her voice, pressed on.

"Do I have your permission to visit the tribes to the north and west? I'm hoping to find suitable male sperm donors for the control study before we harvest the female's..." She corrected herself with the mildest touch of sarcasm, "*Cleatah's* ovum."

"Of course you have," Poseidon said. Then visibly pulling himself together he moved to Talya's side, his hand caressing her shoulder. "But you won't leave immediately, will you?" He smiled. "I've missed your company."

Despite herself, she softened under his touch.

"I've missed you in my bed," he said.

"Come to my quarters tonight," she told him. She would ignore his aberrant behavior. "We'll share a meal."

Of course they both knew she was promising more. Talya left Poseidon's quarters, the door closing behind her with a soft whoosh.

FIFTEEN

"I'LL BE TAKING Cyphus as my second, Fracsus and Lacorre from biology. Two techs are all I'll need. Volunteers?" Poseidon looked around the circular table. Helgen and Bial nodded their desire to join him. A moment before he had announced his first Gaian exploratory mission. For months he'd patiently stayed aboard the *Atlantos* overseeing the most difficult propulsion repairs, waiting until all the shuttles had become operational. Every member of the scientechnic team had already begun their field studies in earnest. All except himself.

From the moment of Talya's report on the Shore People and sight of the extraordinary female, Cleatah, his urge to begin his fieldwork had become consuming. He had not traveled millions of miles through space to languish indefinitely in the hull of a metal monster. It was high time to explore this glorious planet.

"Where will we head first?" Cyphus asked, looking pleased at his assignment.

"The mountain range to the east of us."

"Extreme volcanism there, and a rather complex rift zone," Chronell offered. "A good choice."

"Then we'll proceed across the eastern plateau to the central coast."

Talya sat up a bit straighter in her chair. "Your purpose?" she asked.

"I'd like to take a look at the village of the Shore People."

"That data – genomic and sociologic – has already been collected and recorded." Her words were sharp.

"There's more I'd like to know." Poseidon's tone was even, dispassionate, which seemed only to unnerve Talya further.

"Then I'll join you," she said.

"No, you'll adhere to the sperm collection program you outlined in your breeding protocol. We need the broadest possible sampling of the aboriginal population."

Poseidon wondered if anyone beside himself could see the pink flush rising on Talya's throat. *She's fuming*, he realized, an altogether anomalous condition of her being. He knew her mortification would be terrible if she believed anyone had noticed her weakness, most especially her colleagues. In the next moment, leaning back in her chair, with a long slow inhalation, Talya recaptured the chilly demeanor that so perfectly defined her.

She smiled at Poseidon. "Then will you collect some additional samples for me if I specify the subjects?"

"Certainly."

Poseidon smiled back at Talya, the deadlock unprecedented in the history of their pairing. This woman who displayed the most minimal of emotions was livid. Furious with him. He visualized – his imagination running away with him – that at this moment she would gladly have ripped out both of his eyes.

The thing was, he didn't care. Not in the slightest.

SIXTEEN

S UN GLINTING OFF the curves of the *Atlantos* and its shuttle disk – a thirty foot replica of its mothership – lent an air of celebration to all who were now gathered for the send-off of Poseidon and his team. Talya was self-possessed, but offered Poseidon an embrace that bordered on warmth. Strangely, as he boarded the shuttle with his crew, turning for a final wave, a phrase that had repeated itself a hundred times inside his head in the past week reasserted itself once more.

I should be making this journey on my own.

Of course it was a ridiculous thought. Solo missions on any alien planet were unheard of. Not only could the expected physical dangers be handled most expediently by the security crew, but the vast amount of detail work on so large and varied an exploration as this should be left to the technical assistants, leaving Poseidon free to set the itinerary and expeditionary goals, collect and process data. Why, then, did he envision himself entirely alone in the Gaian landscape? It was an odd fantasy, this, for these off-world expeditions were nothing if not team efforts.

Of course, he shared these strange emotions with no one.

Once underway he behaved as he was expected to. Each day the shuttle would fly from mid-continent, landing at a new location. Cyphus's security team carefully scouted the area before the science team piled out, eager as children to begin another day of what they believed the most enviable and exciting occupation to which a Terresian could aspire.

They drank in one thrilling sight after another: the tawny, long-fanged lion; huge herds of wooly, ivory-tusked creatures twelve feet high roaming the endless inland plain, tenderly minding their young, feasting on the plentiful grasses and wallowing in muddy watering holes; a great thundering waterfall that produced a constant rainbow in its midst; long-necked scarlet birds in so enormous a flock that when they took flight the sky became a flaming, sunless sunset. There were brilliantly hued trees which would, in a surprising explosion, be shorn of its "foliage" as fifty thousand delicate, large-winged insects blossomed into a fantastical cloud.

Following a dry riverbed between the sheer walls of red granite, Fracsus uncovered the perfectly preserved fossil remains of a monstrous reptilian creature that had lived two hundred million Gaian years before. Volcanism had produced many wonders as well – chasms, crystal caves and vast expanses of soil so fertile the variety of plant species were literally uncountable. Cloud formations – non-existent on water-starved Terres – were particularly dazzling. Sometimes Poseidon would find a private place, lie on his back and simply watch as the majestic flotillas passed him by.

But it was the massive, mid-continental mountain range that had beckoned Poseidon most seductively and mysteriously from the start of the journey, looming larger and more imposing the closer they came. Gathered storm clouds crowned the conical peaks on most afternoons, though the nine volcanoes themselves had been serene during their slow approach, not a single lazy tendril of smoke rising from any of their snowcapped tops.

Before they'd set out Poseidon had studied the range in great detail – aerial maps and geologic surveys that showed the peaks and jagged pinnacles, each neatly numbered. This morning the shuttle had landed at their base, a lush, semi-tropical forest teeming with life. As the scouts began their initial survey Poseidon stared up at the mountains, Cyphus at his side.

"They should have names, not numbers," Poseidon told him.

"What should have names, Sir?"

"The mountains." Poseidon had never before been prone to flights of fancy. "Don't you see faces and figures in the rock? There!" He pointed toward the saw-toothed foothills. "I see the distinct profile of a man lying on his back. There...a snake swallowing the world whole. And there – the throne of a gargantuan king."

Cyphus, amused by his commander's game, joined in. "Those two symmetrical mounds there? The ones standing apart from the others?" he said. "A woman's breasts."

"You sound like my brother."

The two men laughed.

Poseidon stared in silence at the tallest of the mountains whose graceful, snow-draped shoulders reminded him of his mother. "She is called Manya," he said quietly.

A moment later the moving cloud formations seemed to place a white giant on the rock throne.

"Do you see that, Sir!?" Cyphus cried. "It's a king with a crown on his head."

"I see it, too."

"Never in my life..." Cyphus said, trailing off.

"Nor mine," Poseidon whispered. 'I think right now we're the luckiest men alive." He waited until the king had dissolved into indeterminate puffs of white before he spoke again. "Cyphus..."

"Yes, Sir?"

"I've been meaning to talk to you. I'm considering making the ascent myself."

"Of course. I noticed that you've been eyeing the range for the last two weeks. Lacorre and Fracsus have their work cut out for them right here. We can get started within the hour. Helgen and Bial seem most eager for the climb."

"You don't understand." Poseidon attempted to make the words sound sensible. "I'd like to go solo."

"Solo?"

"Correct."

"I'm afraid I can't allow that, Sir." Cyphus spoke calmly, never taking his eye from the mountains, without a hint of control-mongering. It was a simple, incontrovertible truth. He was, by virtue of his assigned post, honor-bound to protect the crew of the *Atlantos*. More importantly, he held a strong personal affection for Poseidon. Nothing could be allowed to happen to the commander under his watch.

Cyphus's gaze was still fastened on the mountains. He could not grasp Poseidon's unusual state of mind but was content to wait for more clarity. In the meantime he would hold his own position.

"It's just..." Poseidon hesitated, uncharacteristically lost for words. "I don't want a great gang of enthusiastic...noisy..." He stopped, aware he was sinking deeper into incomprehensibility.

The pair of them stood in silence for a long moment before Cyphus spoke again. "I'd consider taking you up there myself."

There was another moment of silence, this one rich with Poseidon's appreciation and thanks. "How soon can we leave?"

*

They climbed the foothills, their phaetrons set for a detailed scanning of the area. Despite his brawn, Cyphus was a man of great masculine grace and tremendous strength. The two of them moved cautiously – though not nearly so much as Cyphus would have liked – through thick groves of gnarled, ancient trees inter-spersed with massive boulders which, in times past, must have been tossed like pebbles from the mouths of the volcanoes above. The air became crisp, and soon there were more rocks than trees

– fabulous angled outcroppings, many of them covered with vast colonies of varicolored lichen.

Poseidon stooped to record a rock-face covered in brilliant patterns of orange, yellow, green, black and rust. "They're the oldest living things on Gaia," he said. "Some believe lichen spores may have seeded the planet from other worlds and asteroids."

At every site of interest they stopped and recorded their observations, both verbal and visual. Sometimes Poseidon would have Cyphus stand near a boulder the size of the *Atlantos*, or a thousand year old conifer less than a foot tall, to illustrate their proportions. Cyphus complied good-naturedly, enjoying his commander's private company. For his part, Poseidon found Cyphus an excellent companion and was glad he had insisted on coming.

Following the natural paths between these piles of boulders they discovered numerous sinewy caves snaking far back into the mountains. Poseidon found himself drawn into each and every cavern he passed, overwhelmed with the desire to explore their dark mysteries. Only on Cyphus's urgings did they finally forge ahead, reminded that if he did not control this particular impulse they would lose the daylight. And Poseidon wished to reach the summit this day.

Above them the skies were no longer visible, blocked by turbulent grey cloud cover. The landscape – fields of black lavic rock – were stark and grim. The crust was jagged and brittle, still warm beneath their feet. Upon closer inspection, pulling away the topmost skin, was revealed red hot lava not two feet below where they stood. Cyphus held up a fragment of the black rock while Poseidon shone the phaetron's piercing light at it, revealing its interior – a surprise of glittering iridescence.

Wonder built upon wonder as they found themselves walking through a perfectly circular rock tube twice their height. Their shouts and laughter echoed in the tunnel that had been fashioned by a raging river of lava. But as they emerged from the tube cave a sulfurous stench brought Cyphus to attention. Poseidon had already moved out onto a flat expanse of shiny black obsydion rock seared smooth and sundered by hundreds of small cracks, now venting white steam.

"Stop where you are, Sir," called Cyphus, calmly but commandingly.

Poseidon obeyed, suddenly aware of how blithely he had moved into a potentially hazardous situation. He turned to retrace his footsteps but was stopped dead by Cyphus's upraised hand signaling him to halt. His face was dark with self-loathing at having allowed Poseidon to put himself in danger.

"What have I done, Cyphus?"

Never taking his eyes off his phaetron's readings he replied, "The crust you're standing on is extremely thin. Beneath it is a lake of molten lava."

"Shall I...?"

"Don't move a muscle, *please* Sir. I'm going to activate a tractor beam and get you back to me."

"I want to continue the ascent. Once I'm over the field I'll bring you to this side. Why don't I use the levitation platform?"

"Negative. Even the smallest motion to use your phaetron could break the crust. Besides, the levitation platform requires solid ground beneath your feet."

A moment later a vertical yellow beam of light the size of a tree trunk blinked on next to Cyphus and began its swift course across the lava field to where Poseidon stood. But simply bracing himself for capture was enough to crack the crust under his feet. As the tractor beam seized him and propelled him away to the far side of the broad black obsydion field, a geyser of scalding steam and globs of lava shot up through the rupture. His set-down was less than graceful, but from across the distance he could see Cyphus, still at the mouth of the lava tube, much relieved.

"Are you all right, Sir?" came Cyphus's voice from Poseidon's wrist device.

"Not a scratch. Let me bring you over now. I'll move several feet so I don't take you over the new vent I created. Move to the left of the tunnel. I'll aim right."

"Very good, Sir."

The yellow cylinder of energy arose from Poseidon's phaetron. He directed it back across the lava field towards Cyphus who entered it and began tractoring back towards Poseidon. Suddenly, with terrible splintering shrieks the crust below Cyphus began fracturing outward from the jagged hole Poseidon's foot had made. Slabs of the brittle black glass fell away under Cyphus, clouds of searing steam billowing up around him. The walls of the energy cylinder wavered and grew fainter in the intense heat. Then Cyphus disappeared in the sulfurous cloud.

Poseidon cried out to him but there was no answer. Should he accelerate the tractor beam, he agonized, or would that further weaken it, plunging Cyphus down to a gruesome death?

For a moment the entire red-orange lava lake churned and bubbled and steamed. Then a mountain of magma erupted violently from its center. Holding the phaetron steady Poseidon prayed helplessly for his friend, and a too-long moment passed before the steam cloud cleared. Cyphus emerged, still upright in the nearly transparent energy column and fell heavily into Poseidon's arms. There was an explosion of breath from his lungs, gulping his first inhalation since the ordeal had begun.

Thank the stars, Poseidon thought, *at least his lungs would not be seared*. The automatic climate control suit had protected all but Cyphus's face and hands. They were badly scalded – bright red with sections of outer derma beginning to peel and fall away. His eyelids were swollen painfully shut.

"I'm sorry, my friend," Poseidon said. "I don't know how I could have been so foolish."

"My fault..." croaked Cyphus. "...my job to keep you from acting foolishly."

Despite Cyphus's miserable condition they managed a small laugh.

Poseidon helped him lie down. "Let me take care of these burns."

First anaesthetizing Cyphus, Poseidon used the phaetron's tissue regeneration function, re-building the skin from the innermost layer to the outermost. Hardly a quarter of an hour had passed after the healing before Cyphus insisted on resuming the ascent, though he hesitated when discovering that his wrist device had been damaged – the only real casualty of the magma lake. Poseidon's phaetron would have to suffice for the two of them.

Three hours later they emerged into blazing sunshine on a gently sloped field of blinding white snow. Poseidon and Cyphus had reached Manya's summit. From her peak they stared eastward across the endless plateau all the way to the horizon. At this altitude the continent's edge was visible, as well as a slice of the glittering sea beyond. Directly below was Manya's eastern slope, the top third covered by a thick blanket of snow, and a massive glacier flowing down between two smaller, tree and boulder-strewn mountains at her base.

Despite the snow and ice all around them the noonday sun was warm on their faces, and they sat down on a rock to eat. They were quiet as they chewed their rations, both giving silent thanks to the other for their survival.

Bial hailing them broke the peaceful silence. The urgency in his voice brought Poseidon and Cyphus instantly to attention. "Sir," barked the tech, "we're getting powerful pre-seismic readings over here. "It happened very suddenly, but something's about to erupt."

"Coordinates?" Poseidon stared at his phaetron. It took a moment to comprehend what he was seeing. The readings flashed so rapidly they were a blur.

"That's the problem, Sir. We can't tell," came Bial's static-plagued voice. "It could be hundreds of miles from here. It could be right under our feet. The activity is so widespread...it doesn't seem possible, but the event may be continent-wide. We've called everyone back to the shuttle. As soon as we're all in we're coming to get you."

"We'll be waiting."

Poseidon switched on his positioning device, then he and Cyphus moved out into the open.

Gaia, he suddenly realized, *has cast a spell on me.* The mild weather, the extraordinary beauty and grandeur of the surroundings had wrongly caused him to perceive the planet as benign. Even their close brushes with death Poseidon had put down to his own stupidity, lapses in conscious observation. *This is a dangerous planet,* he sternly reminded himself. *I must always remember that.*

The first rumblings were little more than vibrations under their feet.

"I think we should move, Sir," Cyphus said. "We're too exposed here."

"Which way?"

"Down there."

The eastern slope was steeper than the one they'd traversed on the ascent, so to prevent an out-of-control tumble they were forced to tread with maddening care in the sometimes ankle-deep, sometimes hip-deep snow. Several times sharp tremors caused them to lose their footing, and they would slide tens of feet out of control, sometimes finding themselves buried over their heads in the fine, cold powder.

"Stay calm. Keep moving!" Cyphus barked. Poseidon struggled against exhaustion, the gripping pain in his legs, and the realization that they had nowhere on the mountain to shelter.

A great double boom sounded, but by now Poseidon and Cyphus had reached the end of the snowline. The slopes below it were a huge patchwork of boulders and trees, with the glacier nestled between them. Footing was slippery on so steep an incline, peppered as it was with small rocks and gnarled roots. As they bounded down the slope Poseidon wondered if he had ever been so perceptibly connected with his body, his feet somehow finding the perfect spot to land, the precise angle at which to strike it, correct weight allotted to toe, ball and heel. *If I were not fleeing in terror for my life*, he thought, *I might be enjoying this exercise.*

A suddenly violent tremor flung Poseidon off his feet and into the air. When his body began falling, the slope's angle rolled and tumbled him like a stone, down and down in the company of all that was, like himself, unrooted to the earth. He came to rest at the base of a huge boulder, bruised and bloodied but alive. He scanned the slope for Cyphus. He was staggering towards Poseidon from fifty feet away.

The phaetron signaled the shuttle's approach. They would be safe in a matter of moments. Poseidon watched as the craft cleared the summit, hovering momentarily above it to relocate its ground crew and lock their positions for rescue.

It was the last moment of the shuttle crew's lives.

Manya erupted in a monstrously tall fountain of molten fire. As Poseidon watched, its lava spout engulfed the vessel. The ship exploded with a violence that matched the mountain's fury, hurling burning metal projectiles in every direction, starting fires in the trees where they fell.

Poseidon stood stunned and paralyzed. All in the shuttle had, in that instant, been incinerated. But there was no time to mourn. Cyphus had just reached Poseidon when the eruption's true legacy revealed itself. The infernal heat had melted the mountain's enormous cape of snow. It was now a seething wall of water heading straight at them. Gathering what strength they still possessed, the two men bolted for the closest standing tree. They grasped and clung, climbing as fast as their battered limbs would take them, calling encouragement to each other as they went.

Halfway to the top the wave struck, the force of it uprooting the tree as if it was a sapling. It, and dozens of small boulders nearby, joined the flood that scoured the steep slope in a raging tide.

Choking water from mouth and lungs Poseidon clung more dead than alive to the tree, riding the torrent on the branched raft, submerged and grappling desperately among the limbs to find one above the waterline. The harrowing ride ended suddenly as the pile of debris washed up against a tall outcropping of rocks. The tree crashed to a halt, rocks and other trees battering it, crushing its thick branches like twigs. He cowered in a sturdy crotch while the last of the flood washed over him, spent itself and finally slowed to a few muddy rivulets. Then his eyes fell on Cyphus hanging motionless from a limb above. Poseidon tried to call out to him, but his lungs were still choked with water, and all that came out was violent coughing. Finally there was movement. Cyphus's head turned and his weary eyes met Poseidon's. *Thank the stars*, he thought. *We are both alive.* Then from above began the sounds of crashing and shrieking so loud that Poseidon feared looking up to see what new terror now descended upon them.

The glacier, pulverized into great, razor-edged shards and massive chunks of ice, tumbled and crashed down the mountainside toward the dam of rocks and trees where Cyphus and Poseidon still clung. There was hardly time to think.

Poseidon looked down at his wrist phaetron blinking in healthy sequence. He extended his arm and pointed it at the first ice boulder heading straight for their perch. The 'neutralize' function vaporized the projectile moments before it would have slammed into them. Cyphus, even had he been armed, was too badly injured to protect himself. Now, as the barrage came fast and furious, it was all a matter of aim. Poseidon swiveled left, right, center, one flying iceberg close behind another. A trio of them side-by-side. Once, he missed and was forced to duck as the ice rock came racing overhead, cleanly slicing away the limbs a mere foot above him.

Then came a terrible sound – a low, earthshaking rumble as the great grandmother – the very heart of the glacier, seventy feet thick – came sliding slowly, inexorably toward them. The phaetron, aimed at the monster, worked... but too slowly. *Too slowly!* Pieces were disappearing under the device's beam but there was more mass than could be dealt with. It was coming – what was left of the glacier's heart – and as it came crashing blue-white through the broken limbs, Poseidon wondered briefly what it would feel like to die.

*

How long it was before he regained consciousness was unclear, but the phaetron – still set to vaporize – had melted a substantial hole in Poseidon's icy tomb. He opened his eyes but they were awash with blood. His legs were completely trapped in heavy packed ice. He tried to move his arms but found himself instead screaming with pain. A bone was fractured. Several bones. *Is my back broken?* he wondered *My spine crushed?* He tried moving his feet and shouted with relief when they responded one at a time. He concentrated his effort and focused his will. He knew he must have the use of one arm, one hand if he was to survive. He tried the right one but found it fully outstretched at shoulder height crushed between a branch and a boulder – the source of the most excruciating pain. His left arm, which until this moment he'd not felt at all, was suddenly discovered pinned behind his back as the prickle of returning sensation replaced complete numbness. Slowly and carefully, arching his body to make room for movement, he slid the arm out to his side. Once freed the strained shoulder objected mightily at being returned to its natural position with a searing bolt of pain that brought tears to Poseidon's eyes. But the hand was free now, function returning.

By the time he was confident enough to try to activate the phaetron he felt cold fingers of confusion muddling his brain. He could not tell if it was the head injury or the onset of shock. *I will close my eyes for just a moment, a moment...*

*

The sun was beginning to set when Poseidon opened them again. His body was very, very cold. Throbbing pain in his right arm had woken him – perhaps, he thought, saved his life. He knew he must act decisively if he was to survive. With what strength was left he brought his right hand before his eyes and saw it had already turned a bluish-grey. He examined his head with his left hand and found a small but severe crushing injury to the temple which, he assumed, had caused his unconsciousness. He knew he must treat the head wound first, before attending to the shattered arm, before beginning his escape from this icy tomb, before losing consciousness again.

In Poseidon's present condition it was difficult to remember the phaetron function and procedure for healing. *But I must,* he blearily thought. *I cannot let myself die out here.* In the fading light he programmed the phaetron as best as memory served and held it, tremblingly, over the head wound. For a long moment he felt nothing but the cold skin of his wrist against his forehead. Then slowly heat and a mild tingling signaled that the healing had begun.

Poseidon's Report – Trans-Continent, Day 24

Muscle, bone and brain matter have mended at the touch of the phaetron, but I am exhausted, my spirit weakened considerably. I have allowed myself to be lulled into a sense of trust and safety on this planet – a false state to be sure – and I'm angry at myself at the deceit. While Gaia appears benign in its beauty, there is danger everywhere. Not simply the wild beasts and the fickle, sometimes violent weather, but the very ground under my feet is not to be trusted. Though I know the emotion to be ridiculous, I feel as though I have been betrayed, nearly murdered by a beloved friend.

I searched for the wreckage of the shuttle but found nothing of it at all — just the spouting column of magma that had claimed it — smaller now — and an endless river of lava flowing down the eastern slope of Manya, disappearing back into a great crack in the earth at the base of the mountain. The planet's blood seemed to be returning from whence it came.

I looked for Cyphus but when I found him wished I had not. His body had been crushed and pulverized by the ice, his head and neck sheered off his shoulders as if by a giant razor.

When I made contact with the Atlantos, *I reported to Captain Zalen with as much disbelief as sadness the loss of Cyphus and my team, as well as the shuttle. He said that the earthquake had shaken the continent from end-to-end, and the mothership had itself suffered extensive external damage when a massive crevace opened up beneath it. Zalen wished to send a shuttle disk to rescue me, but I refused. Despite our losses I can see no reason to abort my current mission. I will simply go on alone. I ordered Zalen to oversee all repairs to the* Atlantos *and signed off.*

Then I returned to one of the deep caves Cyphus and I had explored and set up a solo camp for myself. With the phaetron I synthesize enough food to survive, but nothing has any taste whatsoever.

Poseidon's Report – Trans-Continent, Day 25

For the past days I have experienced a rare bout of self-pity, mourning and brooding, cursing myself aloud, even weeping at my own stupidity and arrogance. How could I have made so grave a mistake in judgment? Then realized I had been so busy reveling that I had forgotten how to reason. I am determined to pull myself together and return to Terresian good sense. I'll assess the remainder of my journey and resume with a more realistic and responsible outlook.

Poseidon's Report – Trans-Continent, Day 28

My dreams, when I can sleep, are vivid – nonsensical colliding images one night, the replaying of painfully real events the next. Talya moves through these dreams, cool and silent, and I've glimpsed the woman Cleatah, more an ethereal presence than a creature of flesh and blood. I see geometric slashes of colors – brilliant red on a field of pure white – visions that wake me, bathed in sweat. There are soft rolling expanses of variable green – grasslands becoming thick Marsean forests becoming a strange green sky which then transmogrify to blue. After these dreams I awake feeling calm and discernibly stronger in body and spirit. But I find myself incapable of controlling this night-sport, a gift at which I've always been adept, the loss of which frightens me. Will I never regain it?

Poseidon's Report – Trans-Continent, Day 30

Even though my explorations of the cave's deepest reaches fascinate me – weird crystalline columns of dripping minerals and pale, eyeless creatures that hide among the crevices – the days are difficult. I frequently consider bolting, going on with the journey to ease my dis-ease. Inaction and this steady diet of contemplation is not my way. There are many times I think I'm going mad. But I steady myself, sure that this is a much-needed rest.

I believe I'm beginning to heal.

Poseidon's Report – Trans-Continent, Day 33

Restored in mind and body, I have set my sites to the east. Smooth and uneventful as my descent from the range was, I find myself frequently looking behind at the looming volcanic peaks, remembering their treachery. It pains me that I must be ever-wary of the natural environment, and restrained in my enjoyment of it. Never again will I be seduced by beauty, or surrender to rapture. Much as I hate the admission, Terresians have been proven right that these emotions are unnecessary, even dangerous. There is far too much that needs accomplishing. So many depend on me. I have been using the phaetron frequently, trusting its various functions to collect and analyze findings, or to carefully survey a new landscape before setting foot upon it for the first time.

The solo journey – ironic that I've gotten my wish after all – began serenely enough. But the nights are long and lonely. In the daylight it's easy to be rational and purely scientific. But lying awake under the extravagant canopy of stars, watching the planet's only moon move through its graceful and deliberate phases, I find my mind wandering freely – too freely, I sometimes worry. I think thoughts and dream dreams that are fanciful, even dangerous. Each dawn as the sun rises and floods the world with light I regain my senses, force myself to recall the horrors that my descent into passion precipitated. But each night as the shadows envelop me I again fall victim to my wandering imagination.

Poseidon's Report – Trans-Continent, Day 40

Last night I made the decision to meet the Shore People disguised as a primitive of Gaia…or "Erthe," as they call it. The idea burst upon me suddenly while waiting for sleep to overtake me, and it catapulted me into wide-eyed wakefulness. The thought, outrageous as it was, seemed perfectly sensible when analyzed. If I presented myself as I was now, I decided, the primitives would be so confused and awestruck that I'd surely be deified, and much data on the everyday workings of the peoples' minds would be virtually unobtainable. I could – as Talya had done, and what I originally planned on doing – cloak myself with invisibility. But then, I reasoned, I would learn no more from my observations than Talya had. Surely I was resourceful enough to carry off the pretense. I never slept the rest of the night, as I was deciding upon the details of my disguising.

But when dawn broke this morning the madness of the scheme was so obvious that even in my solitary condition I suffered terrible pangs of embarrassment. Best to forget the scheme.

Poseidon's Report – Trans-Continent, Day 45

Each evening for the past several days, as the sky began to darken, my idea reasserted itself as an original and vibrant approach to data gathering. It has not previously been imagined by Terresian scientechnoists because the aboriginals have never before been in a stage of development compatible with such a scheme.

So despite my misgivings I have decided to execute this plan. I've begun the process tentatively, recording into the phaetron detailed lists – all the elements of my transformation from a modern, technologically sophisticated Terresian into a primitive Erthan while on the final leg of my crossing of the Great Eastern Plateau. Firstly, I must force myself to think of the planet as "Erthe," not Gaia. And I will be making these reports more infrequently, as I believe the transformation is as much a state of mind as it is of body, and a constant reliance on technos will be confusing. I will be using the phaetron thoughtfully and sparingly.

Poseidon's Report – Trans-Continent, Day 62

I have begun to alter the appearance of my body. I've allowed my hair and beard to grow long and wild, even accelerating its growth using my device's "bio-stim" function. Discarding my clothing I've been working naked, and the sun has burnished my skin to a pale brown. While I'm in good physical condition by Terresian standards, I'm relatively soft. The primitives require great stamina and strength simply to survive. I have therefore given up the comforts that my phaetron-produced bed and protective shield provided me and now sleep on the ground, using only what cushioning I can find in my surroundings. Many nights I am eaten alive by insects, and more than once have been shocked into wakefulness as some slithering creature moves across my body.

I run great distances each day, locating every hillock and rock pile on the plain. I make endless trips up and down them carrying heavier and heavier loads. Where I find forests I climb trees. I create obstacle courses from fallen limbs and boulders, and practice in them to increase agility, speed and grace.

Using images of Erthan tools and primitive techniques I have fashioned replicas of stone spearheads, arrows and blades. The required skill and precision are much greater than I imagined. I practice throwing a spear at farther and farther stationery targets until I am able to hit the mark every time. At night my muscles complain, but I've determined not to use the phaetron's soothing effects, as I know the unpleasant experience will harden my mind as well as my body.

Poseidon's Report – Trans-Continent, Day 83

Yesterday was the day I had been dreading for so long. I knew I must learn to hunt, and hunt well if I was to earn the respect of the tribe, and that if I failed at this I could never hope to be accepted as one of their number. I'd have no chance of gaining close access to the woman I seek to examine.

The killing of the small, long-eared creature called "hare" was perhaps the most distasteful act I have ever committed. I've never taken a life, and besides saddening me it caused me to ponder the profound difference between the Terresian and Erthan cultures. Certainly our early ancestors on the home planet killed for survival, but the biological memory was so very ancient by now that it felt an entirely unnatural act to me. Skinning the animal with the sharp stone blade I'd fashioned was revolting. I persevered only by repeating over and over to myself that the end result was the acquisition of knowledge, and no aim was higher nor more honorable than that.

Building a fire with thin branches, grasses and a spark from a struck flint, I cooked the creature whole on a stick. It was only then, smelling the aroma of the sizzling meat that my primitive olfasenses registered the smallest hint of pleasure. When I steeled myself, chewed and swallowed the leg muscle of the beast, however, my innards rebelled. I vomited copiously, and even when the offending stuff was long gone from my stomach I continued retching.

That night I grew fevered and ill. My plan to pass myself off as a primitive suddenly seemed a ridiculous notion. My suffering was so great that I very nearly succumbed to using the phaetron to heal my physical body. In the morning, though ragged and sore, I felt triumphant at having survived. I hope that hereafter the kills will grow larger and the meals of flesh more bearable.

Poseidon's Report – Trans-Continent, Day 114

With the animal pelts I've collected I outfitted myself. I have now taken down and skinned an antelere, fashioning from it a sleeveless tunic using the front legholes for armholes. I stitched short trousers and boots with tough sinews on a bone needle. But try as I might I cannot find a way to soften the pelts sufficiently to be worn comfortably against my skin. After repeated failures I have finally relented and using the phaetron, made the fur and leather garments softly pliable. I've also made slings and carriers for my tools and weapons, and hang them from my shoulder and waist.

I've stopped bathing and find that not only does my body odor no longer interest biting insects, but my natural "fragrance" allows me to move closer in among the animal population, which makes hunting easier.

The pull of the wild might have been complete but for my infrequent communications with the crew of the Atlantos. I'd decided not to tell them of my decision to transform myself, reluctant to explain my motives, or engage in arguments with them. I therefore – once every seven to ten days – find myself in the strangest of circumstances. It makes me smile to think of anyone viewing me – a wildman dressed in the skins of animals, conversing in the most scientific and sophisticated terms into my phaetron, pretending to the crew that everything is as it always has been. Less and less do I enjoy these conversations, for deceit does not come naturally to me. As I draw closer to the eastern coast of the continent I have been preparing Zalen and the others for a drastically reduced level of communication. They are never to signal me, for fear that my disguise will be detected by the tribe. I will contact the crew only as necessary.

I admit that my resistance to the vast and mysterious pull of the natural world has been weakened by my transformation process, and so I frequently and strictly remind myself of the scientific purposes of the journey.

Poseidon's Report – Trans-Continent, Day 136

Several days ago I arrived on the coast of the Eastern Sea, and I found myself as spellbound as I had been on my first sight of the Marsean *ocean. Behind me was a range of low, rocky outcroppings, and on the plain between the sea and the rocks I spotted a grazing herd of magnificent, four-legged, proud headed creatures my predecessors had name "horse." I have lingered here for several days to watch the beasts which number more than forty, with most of the females tending skinny-legged but otherwise perfectly formed young. I hid myself in the tall grass to witness a birth, and was dumbfounded by the speed with which the newborn climbed to its feet and took its place among the herd. I've filled my phaetron's memory bank with copious data regarding the horses. I sense this is valuable information, and that this creature might be of some use to the primitives at a later date. If I am perfectly honest I must admit to a deep attraction to the horses, a tug in my chest as I watch them thunder in their numbers across the grasslands.*

Poseidon's Report – Trans-Continent, Day 138

I did move on, reluctant to leave the horses, but eager as well, because as I walked south toward the edge of the great plateau and the steep cliffs of the land mass's eastern coast, I had finally reached my destination. Here, Talya reported, live the tribe that calls itself the Shore People. I've spent considerable time on my journey contemplating this group who, like most of the other tribes on the continent, have given up their nomadic existence to take up permanent residence in a village. They gather and use in their diet a few root vegetables – though they have not yet conceived of cultivating grains. They hunt small animals as their ancestors had done, and more recently larger game. As Talya reported they have engineered rudimentary "sea vessels" and paddle through the shallow waters off their coast. Their diet is compromised in great part from what they catch from the ocean or capture in nets from the beach.

From my vantage point on the headlands I can see the Shore

Village. It is located on a "ledge" of land – a narrow plateau perhaps a hundred feet above the beach. There are some trees and terraced slopes where they grow their few crops. The village's several paths down appear to make access to the beach an arduous process, though it cleverly protects the settlement from even the highest of tides and wave action. Though the huts appear to be simple buildings of mud and straw the village has a sense of permanence to it. Perhaps two dozen of their sea crafts – what appear to be the hollowed out trunks of the trees surrounding the settlement – lay unattended on the beach. My interest and excitement about these people is increasing exponentially with every observation.

I can see from the headlands a number of villagers at work in their terraced gardens, and children playing. They are, as Talya's reports have shown, a people of strong, well-formed bodies, skin burnt to a tawny color and hair – worn long by men and women alike – thick and with few exceptions, dark and wavy. They're a handsome people with strong jaws and high foreheads. Talya had commented that had a typical member of the Shore Tribe been clothed and groomed as a Terresian, no one could guess them otherwise. This is no surprise, of course, as Erthan genomes have for so many generations been mixed with the life essences of Terresians.

As I descend the plateau to a beach just north of the village in preparation for making myself known to the Shore People, despite feeling confident I admit I'm apprehensive. It has always been my intention to pretend myself a solitary traveler from a neighboring tribe. To that end my newly toughened body, long matted hair, and animal skin garment support such a deceit. Since the earliest days of the journey, using the phaetron and lingual data Talya had compiled, I've been learning a rudimentary language common to several tribes, among them the Shore People. Any blunders I make I will ascribe to differences in local dialect.

It is time to move.

SEVENTEEN

POSEIDON TRAMPED ALONG the headlands searching for the least precarious route down to the beach north of the village. He assumed his most robust posture, making sure his tools and weapons were slung around his body in keeping with Talya's images of a primitive tribesman. He hoped his appearance and odor were appropriately unkempt.

Thus he made his way south along the coast.

Up ahead he could see several women with small children, all engaged in gathering sea animals from the shore in nets. Once he was close enough for the women to recognize that he was not one of their own he stopped, stood in place and opened his palms toward them to show he held no weapons. One of the children made a dash at him but was caught up by one of the women. They were now standing and staring openly at him with moderate alarm. One woman broke from the group and herding the children before her, climbed the diagonal steps up to the village.

Poseidon stayed where he was, trying to remain dignified and non-threatening with smiles and waves. It was not long before a grim looking delegation – four men and one woman behind them, armed with stone tipped spears and clubs – appeared and approached him directly. He could see several other groups fanning out along the village's perimeters and either end of the beach, clearly meant to determine if he was alone or had come with others for an ambush.

Heart pounding, Poseidon stood his ground, open-handed but attempting to exude manly strength and fearlessness. He remained silent while they talked among themselves and waited – as custom demanded in such a situation – for them to initiate communication.

Finally the leader, a tall, well-muscled man of middling years, stepped forward and stood chest to chest, eye to eye with Poseidon, facing down the "stranger." He held the tribesman's gaze and consciously slowed his breathing so that he might appear far calmer than he actually felt. The stand-off seemed to last an eternity, the Shoreman's muscles tensing, Poseidon's fingers poised to throw up a phaetronic shield around himself if attacked. Finally the leader drew several sharp sniffs and screwed up his face in a grimace. A word or two was spoken to the group and suddenly they were all laughing. Indeed, laughing at Poseidon. He realized the reason.

He smelled unpleasant to them, and a joke about his hygiene had been made at his expense. He was unsure if it was appropriate to laugh along with the delegation, but the situation *was* amusing, so he joined in. Poseidon's laughter did not stimulate any aggression. In fact it made everyone laugh harder. Feeling more confident he sniffed the pit of his arm, then made a terrible face. They all roared.

By this time many more of the tribespeople had gathered, wondering at the commotion on the beach. Poseidon drew a breath and tapping his chest, announced his identity.

"Poseidon," he said loudly. The laughter ceased and he repeated, "Poseidon." With a questioning gesture he requested the leader identify himself.

"I am Brannan," said the Shoreman. The three men in the delegation spoke their names in turn. Heydra. Elkon. Boah.

Suddenly the woman stepped out from behind them. He could see now, to his astonishment, that an adult brown wolf stood at her side, protective, its expression alert, the hackles spiked high along the back of its neck.

"I am Cleatah," she said, clear and bold.

For the first time since his encounter with the Shore People, Poseidon faltered. Suddenly confronting the very individual he had traveled the continent to see was itself startling, but the look and presence of the woman – despite his earlier viewing of her – was astonishing. She was tall, nearly as tall as Poseidon, and she was as lovely as a Terresian year was long. The tawny hair fell in soft curls on her sculpted shoulders flanking high, rounded breasts under the skins she wore. Her lightly freckled complexion gleamed with a sunny glow, and the gaze of her rich brown eyes was sharp and confident. The woman's limbs were long, muscles full but shapely. He forced himself to tear his eyes away from her, as such interest in a female would be thought highly suspect, even aggressive. And the wolf had never taken his eyes from the stranger.

As the people crowded round to accompany Poseidon up to the village he noticed about them an almost complete absence of rank body odor. Many appeared freshly washed. Talya had failed to mention this inclination of the Shore People towards cleanliness, but her omission had happily provided him with a natural and humorous introduction to the tribe.

He'd carefully studied Talya's images of the village environs and artifacts, but in the same way a phaetronic image of a forest or a mountain range never imparted the true impact of the place itself, the mud and thatch enclave on this broad ledge of the plateau was far more fascinating than its three-dimensional portrayal. As Poseidon came into the village surrounded by his welcoming party the sun was bright, bleaching the varied earth tones to a homogenous pale tan. Yet there was a mysterious quality here, and beauty to be found in the simplest and most unexpected places. A basket that sat outside the door of a hut was woven with intricate artfulness out of four subtly different colors of reed. An obsidian spear tip flashing momentarily in the sunlight hinted at artistry. The murmur of the villagers' voices as they had their first sight of the stranger sounded strangely melodic. Wolf mothers lay sunning themselves lazily, watching their pups rough-and-tumble in play. And the people themselves – this was the most astonishing of all – the people were beautiful to his eyes. Primitively dressed as they were, rugged and tan and rough, they all – every man, woman and child – exuded vitality. A healthy fire shone in their eyes.

When everyone had gathered a man from the welcoming party who had called himself Boah, began to speak. He was the youngest of the four males, and powerfully built. Poseidon now recognized him from Talya's data as the ranking young hunter of the tribe, his status recently elevated by a success during a daring and dangerous kill. He was the man who'd begun showing sexual interest in Cleatah.

Boah had been chosen by the elders to introduce the stranger to his people. It had been an interesting choice, Poseidon reasoned, as he himself would in the coming months be tested as a hunter, would seek status in the male hierarchy of the tribe, and most certainly come into conflict and competition with the man who was even now presenting him to this society. Poseidon's grasp of the language was still imperfect, but when the people broke into gales of laughter, he understood that Boah had poked fun at this stranger. Poseidon grinned, feeling foolish but unaccountably happy.

Eighteen

I T WAS A long, steep climb up the path to reach the Great Plateau above the village, but this day Cleatah hardly felt it at all in her legs or chest…for she was lost in thoughts of the stranger. As always, Sheeva bounded ahead, her scout and guardian. The name Cleatah had given the wolf was, in fact, the word for guardian, and in their years together they had become the closest and most trusted of companions. That morning on their way to the plateau Cleatah had stopped to stand in the shade of Jandor's hut and watch the seated circle of men carving arrow shafts, her eyes falling upon Poseidon among them. His head was down, and he worked with his flint knife on a hard wood branch.

This stranger carries within him a secret, as I do, she'd thought. Poseidon looked as the other men did, but something was different. She liked the way he looked, though could not say why. He was no taller than the other men, and not as brawny. He was more clumsy with his body than the males of the tribe, and could not dance. But he worked very well with his hands, was able to weave the slenderest threads of the lota plant into fine netting used to harvest brill from the sea. She had secretly watched him one day as he had examined the muscle inside a small, double-shelled sea creature. No one beside herself looked that closely or for that long at so common an object. In many small ways Poseidon was very ignorant. Maybe the customs of his people and his language being different from her own could explain this.

His story was a sad one. His inland people had been slaughtered by a hostile neighboring tribe while he and a small party were hunting. Not a man, woman or child had been left alive in the village. It had been decided by the survivors that they must go in search of new families and friends, but that they would be more acceptable to a tribe if they were one man alone.

Poseidon would smile and joke when the others did. He was kind to children and never stared too long at a woman, unless she was very old. But he seemed to take no real pleasure in his food, nor celebration in the blessings of the bounty. He had refused to eat of the sweetest white flesh of Cleatah's favorite long-tailed shellfish, claiming his tribe did not eat animals from the sea. She would watch him at a feast after a large kill, and though he had eaten his share, and even chewed on a second piece that was offered by one of his hunting companions, she could see strangeness in his eyes. A feeling with no name. Was it disgust? Of course that made no sense. He was a man like any other.

Still, she was sure he carried a secret.

Poseidon had looked up from his carving and saw Cleatah looking at him. His eyes stayed fixed on her and paid no attention to Sheeva pacing impatiently at her feet. She saw that he was studying her face the way she herself would examine the inside of a flower. Lamarak, sitting next to Poseidon, had poked him with his elbow and gestured to the bowl of pitch. Poseidon looked quickly away from her, grabbed the pitch bowl and handed it to Lamarak. *Too quickly, as if he did not wish to be caught,* she thought. The stranger with his secret was interested in her.

She spent much time thinking of Poseidon as well.

With Sheeva trailing at her heels, Cleatah had moved out of the shadows to pass directly by the circle of men before going on her way. They each called out their usual pleasant but reserved greetings. Now that her mother and father were dead no one strayed too close to her, for her differentness made them uneasy. She had grown content being left to herself as long as she had the company of her wolf, but now she found the stranger's curiosity warming. *Poseidon.* Different, like she was. She was glad he had come to the village.

She and the wolf climbed until they reached the plateau, cut by rivers and smaller streams, each one bordered by the thick patches of forest. From this height Cleatah was also blessed with sight of the far mountains they called Krakatoh, and the Great Sea, its horizon unimaginably distant. Since earliest childhood she had roamed these fertile flatlands with her mother Luna – the Shore People's healer – in search of the plants the woman had used in her treatments. Everything grew abundantly in the grassy meadows and along the rich wooded riverbanks, and the waterways teemed with life. Luna had instructed her daughter where to discover brushweed – used for stomach cramps – and golum, which together with the hard berries of the junip, relieved the swelling of joints. She had learned which willow branches were best to make splints for a broken bone, and how to find the orange mushroom that, ground into a mash, made the best poultice to draw poison from a festering wound. Her mother had shown Cleatah how to test each plant by taste – the tiniest nibble would tell the girl if it was fresh, ripe or fermented, and which was most potent. And of course she learned the signs that told if a plant would sicken or kill.

The recent coming of the great herds onto the plateau had changed the tribe's lives forever. Cleatah could remember how, in the short time since her childhood, the weather had also shifted. Longer droughts had driven many different animals that had once roamed the inland plains to the rivers near the Great Sea...and her home.

The mighty herds of hooved creatures had trampled much of the vegetation, destroying many of the plants her mother had depended upon. While the men celebrated the bountiful hunting grounds, never coming home empty handed, Luna had despaired. When a child died for want of a medicine that no longer grew her mother had cursed the buron, refusing any longer to honor their animal spirits – they who had taken from her so many tools of her calling.

Though not yet a woman Cleatah had been old enough to venture out on her own. She'd become the sole gatherer of whatever healing plants were still to be found. She enjoyed ranging far over the Great Plateau but she was always careful of her safety. She knew that a mistake in the presence of such large and numerous animals could mean terrible injury or even death. She learned to search out the medicines where the herds had not found them. Then she fashioned sturdy barriers from large fallen branches and built little untouchable gardens of the valuable plants on rocky ledges where the cattle could not graze on or trample.

Leaving the village this day with thoughts of Poseidon filling her head Cleatah followed the worn path leading to the closest stream she called White Waters. She tried to shake the thoughts away as she took notice of those plants that were in perfect readiness for picking – one, like the yellow fern that she would pluck on the way home for freshness – and others, like the sunwort which had already dropped its seeds and could be gathered now.

The path took her through a recently grazed field, Sheeva ranging ahead, her nose down in the grasses, scouting for poisonous vipirs. Cleatah knew by the shape and content of the large droppings that it had been a herd of antelers, and whispered a low curse, knowing that she would find no spirit mushrooms in this particular dung.

It never failed that gazing out over this lush meadow reminded her of a special day, soon after her first blood, when she had discovered the mushrooms. It had rained all of the previous night. The days following such showers were always the most pleasant and favorable for finding and collecting medicines. Cleatah roamed in many places, but on that day she chose to visit the most distant meadow. She had observed that the buron herds had left it three days before. The grasses always revived after a downpour and now new, tender shoots were springing up everywhere. She had stopped to switch her gathering sack from one shoulder to the other when her eyes fell on a large pile of dung, steaming as the moisture was drawn out of it by the morning sun.

Poking out of the dropping was a delicate, long-stemmed mushroom. Her eye was trained for spotting such things, but she had never before encountered such a plant. She knelt to look at it more closely and suddenly saw that all the piles of droppings nearby sprouted the same mushrooms. She had picked one carefully, and turning it in her fingers looked at it closely. It was brown with a long slender stem and small delicate cap. She saw none of the signs that it was poisonous. *Surely a small nibble – the way I had been taught to test plants – could not hurt me,* she thought. Cleatah could compare the taste and effect on her tongue and lips with the other mushrooms she *did* know.

She had bitten off the edge of the cap. The taste was earthy and slightly bitter, reminding her of the greatcap fungi that grew in the softened bark of fallen trees. There were no signals of danger so she had taken bite after bite of the cap and ate downward into the stem. She thought of how proud she would be to bring home a plant that her mother had never before seen. Together they would see if the mushroom had uses as medicine.

Then all at once Cleatah had felt a tightness in her throat. She became alarmed. She knew how angry her mother would be if she made herself sick, or how aggrieved if she died. *How stupid I've been!* She thought she should walk home quickly, but as she stood she saw that everything around her had changed.

No, on second look it was the same meadow she had visited a hundred times, still trampled and littered with cattle dung. But now the insects – the flies covering the dung – seemed to be singing, singing the praises of the delicious meal they were enjoying. She giggled at the strangeness of the thought, but truly she could hear their voices. *The flies were fattening themselves up on the droppings, preparing themselves to be happily sacrificed to the flock of red-throated fly-catchers that had arrived in the meadow and were swooping down to snap up the insects in mid-flight with their pointy black beaks. The movements of the birds were precise and perfectly timed. And the red of their necks – had she ever seen such a color as beautiful? Yes, color! Everything,* everything *was vibrant, shimmeringly beautiful. The pale fresh green of new grass was the loveliest thing she had ever seen. The edge of a single blade of grass seemed sharp enough to draw blood from her finger, and its top-heavy tip swayed a green dance in the breeze.*

The tightness in Cleatah's throat was forgotten. Her mother was forgotten. The mushrooms forgotten. She felt she was walking above the ground, her head pleasantly hollow, eyes seeing with the keenest sight. She explored the meadow for hours, hearing the voices of every living thing. Even rocks spoke to her, and the streams. The beauty of the world several times made her weep, but the weeping would turn in the next moment to laughter – watching insects working atop an ant hill, or the dance of a butterfly, which she would herself attempt to copy. While she danced she felt light as the butterfly and almost as lovely.

She did not remember gathering dozens of the mushrooms, nor the journey home. Her mother was not there, so she had sat herself down in the family hut. Better not wander through the village as she was. Finally the magic of the mushroom had begun to leave her, and Cleatah had spent the time waiting for her mother's return, trying to find words to tell her of her blissful communion with the world.

When Luna returned, all her daughter's attempts to describe it were fruitless. Luna had shrieked at Cleatah – eating a mushroom growing from a pile of cursed cattle dung! Had she lost her mind? No, her mother said, she had no interest in studying it. And her father had better not hear the silly stories of songs of flies, and plants speaking to her in the "green language." These were nothing like the spirits their tribe believed resided in the Great Mother's domain – in creatures and rock, the wind and the water. Cleatah was not to go near the mushrooms again. Ever!

But of course she did. Again and again. The mushroom, which she soon understood was as sacred a plant as any known to her tribe, became as much a teacher of the world as her mother had been. On her gathering expeditions, when she was sure to be alone, Cleatah would eat the mushroom. Then holding a medicine plant in her hand, she would listen while it spoke to her of its qualities. In this way she learned a new use for it, or how it could be mixed with another plant to increase its strength. With "mushroom sight" she watched a flock of birds pecking at the brittle rock cliffs above the river and discovered the healing properties of the mineral imbedded there. She found useful essences in sea plants and even insect venoms. The workings of her own body became clear to her, and then the bodies of others. She understood the cycle of a woman's bleeding and the flow of breath in and out of the chest. She saw, like no other man or woman in her tribe, a strange new world that lived side-by-side with the old one. Soon her mother was unable to answer her daughter's questions. Cleatah no longer asked them.

Words began to come into her head. Words for the new sights and sounds and smells and thoughts. Her head was *filled* with words, and songs that the tribe would sing in celebration, or a mother to put her child to sleep. The people were grateful for all these gifts, yet they had become fearful of her. They left her alone, thought her strange. No one, not even her mother, dreamed these gifts had arisen from the eating of a small mushroom that grew in the steaming dung of the wild herds.

This was her secret – *Ka*, which meant "the other place." And now, as Sheeva and she entered the shaded forest leading to White Waters, she would make it her business to discover Poseidon's.

NINETEEN

POSEIDON'S REPORT – The Shore Village, Day 62
    The day of the hunt has dawned ominously grey, and I find myself in a state of gloom. I've thrown open the hide that covers the door of my hut – a small but private place I've been given on the far edge of the village – to let in the feeble light, and to be sure that no one is near. Finally I'm sure no one is nearby, but to be safe I sit with my back to the door flap whispering this report.

I've had little time for close observation of the woman, Cleatah, and no luck increasing my worth among the tribesmen that would make my approach to her possible. My hunting skills have been adequate enough to deflect suspicion, but I continue to blunder in small ways and manners, sometimes causing great hilarity, especially among the women. Today we hunt again, and I find myself dreading it. I've found no perceptible good in the act of taking an animal's life. I know that if I truly enjoyed eating the flesh as the primitives do, needed the meat to survive, I would feel differently. Boah, the young man described in my last report, continues to challenge me at every turn. I walk a fine line in this competition, as I cannot make an enemy of him. But failing to best him will ruin any chance of improving my status in the tribe. Boah regularly shows sexual interest in Cleatah, though it appears she's gently but firmly rebuked his advances. I'm still convinced that she's observing me with as much interest, and secrecy, as I am her. She appears to be everything that Talya described, and more. She's respected by all and is a natural leader of men as well as women, though of course there are male roles and rituals of which she can never be a part. Her presence is powerful. Just yesterday I was waiting to be given my meal portion and became aware of someone standing behind me. Without seeing the person, I knew it to be Cleatah. I recognized her identity by her unusual scent – the smell of skin and hair baked by the sun, and flavored with a rich sweet spice – a fragrance only she bears. Perhaps it is what she washes with. I'd followed her one day to where one of the rivers meets the sea and watched as she took from her sack a brown root, smashed it against the rocks and adding water, made a white lather from it. With this she washed her long tawny hair…she is very beautiful, this woman… but I digress. I'm hoping to distinguish myself in the next several days so that I may accelerate this study.

He dressed in hide trousers, tunic and knee high boots, then began to strap on the tools and weapons he would need for the hunt.

"Poseidon!" It was Boah outside his door. His rival had recently built a small hut close by. With several other unmated men and their wolves setting up camps in the area, it was becoming known as the stags' village. Poseidon found himself bemused to be thought of in such a way. "Better hurry," called Boah, "or they'll leave without you."

"If only they would," Poseidon whispered to himself, then strode out the door into the gloomy morning.

*

The hunt had proven frustrating. While Poseidon's stamina had held up admirably on the day-long tracking of the buron herd, when the prey had been singled out and the long-handled spears hurled on the run at the fleeing beast, his weapon had missed by an embarrassingly large margin. It was found that Boah's spear had pierced the buron's neck and was proclaimed, with much backslapping, as the killing blow. Now the men in the hunting party – the wolves in a barely controlled blood frenzy – were arguing loudly about whether to take down a second buron, or simply return to the village with their kill. Wretched with disappointment, Poseidon moved away into the bush to relieve himself.

The wild thing was suddenly upon him, and before he had time to think he was fighting for his life. The beast had sprung from behind and knocked Poseidon to the ground before he saw it was a man – red-eyed and snarling, spitting flecks of white foam from his terrible mouth. And ungodly strong! They rolled and grappled and grunted – the foul stench of the creature's breath nauseating. But as the thing began to claw at Poseidon's eyes, some force – an instinct so ancient as to be primeval – welled up from the depths of him, and all that was civilized fell away, supplanted by a vicious will to survive.

Despite his strength the wildman was strangely clumsy, and once Poseidon felt the power surging in his limbs he sought to flip the man on his back. He'd almost succeeded when a knee rammed into his groin. He screamed and levitated in agony, falling back down and curling into a ball. The man sprang, but Poseidon rolled, leaving his attacker sprawled face-down in the dirt. Rallying, he leapt on the man's back, grabbing him from behind. The man struggled, writhed, bucked and with inhuman strength turned, coming up with a rock in hand that swung in an arc toward Poseidon's head. He stopped it a moment before it met its mark. The rock dropped to the ground, and Poseidon's fisted hands pummeled the man's face.

By now the hunters had found the fight and stood in a circle around them, screaming for Poseidon's victory. A terrible waking nightmare, he could hear their shouts, the wolves growling, feel the pain still throbbing between his legs, see the hideous, snarling creature pinned under him… The man's hand's suddenly clamped around Poseidon's throat, all fury, seething hatred. The grip was vice-like and in moments he was fighting for breath. Poseidon's hands found his attacker's neck, thumbs on the windpipe. He knew in that moment he not only had to kill this man, he *wanted* to kill him.

Poseidon fought for consciousness as the man squeezed harder, but saw his advantage was position. He was on top – his body's weight behind his fingers. Suddenly inspired, he rocked far back, then forward with momentum…and with a force that surprised him began crushing the man's throat. The fingers around his own neck began to relax as the man's thrashing increased. The face slowly turned from brilliant red to blue, the mouth open in a silent scream, the foam drying on the parched, bleeding lips. Then with a soft, sickening crack under his thumbs Poseidon felt the man's body fall limp. But he did not release his grip, just kept pressing and pressing and pressing. It was finally the odor of release from the dead man's bowels that brought Poseidon to his senses.

Still, it took four men to pull him off the body.

He was vaguely aware of the hunters' excited hugs, laughter, backslapping. But when several of them began examining the corpse Poseidon felt the powerful instinct that had surged through his body to save his life begin to drain out of him. His knees jellied and he staggered away so the hunters would not see him retching.

He had killed a man – killed another human being. Dressed in the skins of animals, long wild hair and beard… *What is becoming of me?* he wondered miserably. *What have I done?* He would never ever tell another person, or even record into his phaetron what he'd felt as he'd choked the life out of the poor creature who had attacked him.

It was determined by a set of telltale teeth marks festering on the man's arm that he had been bitten by an animal which carried a dreadful sickness. Once bitten, a person – no matter how healthy, no matter what medicines were given – died a gruesome, raving death. In their tribe such a person was put out of his misery before the excruciating pain began, before the madness set in, before the foaming at the mouth turned him into a monster that children ran screaming from. Once the discovery of the illness had been made Poseidon was solemnly examined to see if he had been bitten by the man, and all breathed easier when he was found to be bruised and scraped but clean of teeth marks. Before beginning the trek back the men piled dead leaves and branches on the body and set it on fire, not wishing their wolves or scavenging animals to feed on the sick man's flesh and themselves be poisoned.

In celebration of their new hunter's triumph – which though unspoken was seen as a kind of initiation – the men had decided to hunt for a second buron. They now therefore staggered cheerfully under the weight of two carcasses and were forced to stop more frequently than usual to rest. Poseidon dreaded these respites, for then he had time to think. Under the strain of shouldering the heavy pole all he could do was breathe and concentrate on putting one foot before the other without stumbling. But when he stopped he could suddenly recall the fetid stench of his attacker's breath, the fear that animated his limbs, and the violent power which had overwhelmed the civilized man he believed himself to be.

Poseidon had studied the Erthan animals, and only one fought the same of their species to the death. *Human beings*. Occasionally the lower *pithekos* might murder another, and even devour a helpless infant. But all same-species battles – usually over territory or a female – ended long before death. One individual was driven away leaving the winner dominant. No other species fought and killed in anger. Certainly no Terresian in his right mind...

Poseidon knew he must banish all such thoughts before the

hunting party returned to the village. He had defended himself against a mindless, raging creature – hardly a man. *The choice was kill or be killed, and I simply chose survival.* He decided that if he repeated the phrase again and again he would come to believe it, but was uncertain if he could muster the air of celebration that his fellow hunters were exhibiting. It was right and natural in their way of thinking that for Poseidon to have survived unscathed he must have been blessed by many benevolent spirits. Thanks and rejoicing for his life would certainly flavor their homecoming feast.

Somehow he would have to live with himself.

TWENTY

GREAT MOTHER IS *blessing our celebration this night,* Cleatah thought as she watched the raucous firelight gathering. Children were shrieking with glee and chasing each other on the outer fringes of the village. The women had cooked half a buron, and she had provided special flavorful plants ground into sea salt to season it. The men were all gathered around Poseidon, urging him to recount once again his heroic fight to the death. He smiled as he spoke, but it did not seem to Cleatah that the smile was true. A man of her tribe who had saved his own life with such bravery and accomplishment would have been basking in glory, dancing round the bonfire, drinking great quantities of kav, perhaps taking a woman to his bed.

But Poseidon only pretended joy. She was sure of it. Now Boah had taken up the story for the newcomer, demonstrating the final moments of the battle – Poseidon's hands around his opponent's throat, strangling him. In the flickering light, though no one else saw – for they all watched Boah – Poseidon's smile was frozen unnaturally on his face. *He is a strange man,* she thought, *with more differentness than what comes from a distant tribe's customs.*

With a great whoop the retelling ended, and the men returned to their family groups as the feast was served. Cleatah could see that several tribesmen invited Poseidon to their circles, but when the crowd dispersed he stood alone. She moved quickly to his side and with a few swift gestures settled herself beside him to eat the meal. He seemed surprised, though not displeased. Always before when they had been near each other he had had little to say and turned his eyes away, out of respect. But tonight Poseidon was an important man, no longer a stranger to the village. His stature had grown from that one brave act. He had earned the men's respect and the right to talk with the women if he chose to. And Cleatah had made sure it was to her this night that he would be speaking.

A bowl piled high with steaming meat and mush made from a mealy garden root was placed in front of Poseidon. He turned to her and saw that she had not yet been served. Without speaking he slid his bowl in front of her. Cleatah stiffened, looking around to see if any villager had noticed, but thankfully no one had. Despite his victory today, and increased stature among the men, what he had just done was a serious mistake in manners: a man did not serve a woman first unless he meant to mate with her. She was sure it was Poseidon's ignorance of such things. Carefully she slid the bowl back in front of him, just before the server returned, bringing another bowl and laying it down before her.

"Did I blunder?" Poseidon whispered after the server moved on.

"Not if you wish to take me to your bed." Cleatah spoke quietly and directly, but hoped he could hear the smile in her voice.

Poseidon grunted in reply, cleared his throat noisily, then crammed a piece of meat in his mouth and began chewing. She did the same and so, side by side, they ate in silence for several minutes. Finally she spoke.

"How is it your skin is so soft?"

"My skin?"

She turned and saw Poseidon staring down at his bare arm with so bewildered a look that she almost laughed. A moment later he sagged with what seemed like relief, finally understanding the question.

"My skin." He patted the front of his fur tunic. Then another look of confusion crossed his face. "My skin..." he repeated stupidly. "Soft..."

"How did you dress it?" Cleatah prompted. "What did you use? I have never seen a pelt so pliable."

"I...I..."

Was it possible he was blushing, she wondered, or was it the firelight?

"It was a gift," he finally blurted. "From my sister. She was a master tanner before...before..."

"I am sorry, " Cleatah said quietly, placing a hand on Poseidon's arm. "It hurts you to speak of your family."

"No, no," he said. "I can speak of them. They rest in Erthe's bosom, cradled by the Great Mother, no longer in pain."

"No longer in pain," Cleatah said, repeating the familiar blessing. So there *were* some rituals the two tribes shared. "What was your sister's name?"

He paused again, though for longer than seemly, then answered. "Talya."

"May the Spirit bless the memory of Talya," Cleatah echoed.

Now their eyes met and held steady, but this time it was she who turned her gaze away. She had glimpsed something beyond her understanding. A knowing that defied all of Poseidon's ignorant ways. *This* was his secret, she realized all at once. He was hiding a part of his mind! She suddenly wished she could look through his eyes into his spirit having partaken of the sacred mushroom. Surely he would be unable to hide from the clarity of vision that the mushroom provided.

All at once the thin, high sound of a reed flute pierced Cleatah's mind and brought her back to the night, the feast and the mysterious man beside her. The villagers were swaying with pleasure as the tones filled their senses with delight.

She smiled, then whispered to Poseidon, "Do you like the sounds that Sanson's instrument makes?"

"I do. I have never heard anything like it before. We played only drums in my village."

"As we did here…until I made the instrument Sanson plays."

"You *made* the instrument?"

Cleatah struggled for the right words. "I found it. It is a simple reed. I was gathering medicine by the river. I heard the wind flowing through a piece of dried reed. I picked it up. There were holes rotted through in three places. I put my mouth on one end and blew. I put my fingers over the holes and different noises came out. I brought it back to the village and showed my cousin Sanson, and he learned to make these beautiful sounds."

"You *invented* the instrument," Poseidon said.

"Invented?"

"As you invent medicinal uses for the plants you pick."

"Is this a word used in your village?" Cleatah asked. "We have no such word here."

"Yes, it is a word my tribe uses. Ones who invent are important people. The most important people."

Now it was her turn to blush. It was a relief when the servers began to clear the feast away. This man was not what he seemed to be. And as she had sought to peer into his spirit to understand him better, now she knew for certain that Poseidon was gazing into hers. *What if he learns my secret? All my secrets?* she thought but did not say.

And just as suddenly, she knew that nothing in the world would make her happier.

TWENTY-ONE

ATHENS EXPLODED IN ecstasy moments after Leanya had done the same. They fell back in the rumpled bed exhausted, each having attained mutual, enhanced satisfaction for a third time that afternoon.

"I'm starving," Athens announced, gazing out his glass wall at the pink sand of Halcyon Beach and the glittering sea beyond. "Let's call for our dinner."

"I'm not hungry yet," murmured Leanya, "at least not for food."

Athens lazily rolled his head so he could feast on the sight of the youngest and prettiest of his current bedmates. Leanya was by far the most insatiable of them, and he could only indulge in her company several times a month, on his leisure days, like today. Much more than that and he found himself becoming habituated to sensuality, a luxury he could not afford. He had an important job to do, and of late it had become his preoccupation to do it well.

There was a knock on the bedroom door, which surprised them both.

"Maybe Braccus scanned my mind," Athens said, then

called jovially through the door, "Have you brought our dinner, Braccus?"

"No Sir," came the man's voice through the door. "There's someone to see you."

"Didn't you tell him I was busy?" Athens called back, mildly annoyed.

"He says it's quite important, Governor. Otherwise I wouldn't have bothered you."

Leanya had already begun dressing and pinning up her silky dark hair. The memory of her dragging it along the length of his naked body began to arouse Athens again.

"Who is it?" he called irritably. Braccus answered, but the name sounded muffled. Athens stood up and pulling a robe around him threw open the door to find his house keeper, an older man who ran the residence with an iron fist and indulged the governor like a spoiled child. "Who is it and what does he want? It's my leisure day, Braccus."

"His name is Golde, Sir. He's the chief geologist for the mine. And he won't tell me what he wants. He insists on speaking to you."

"Do I have to put my clothes on?" said Athens, feigning petulance. Braccus answered with a stern silence. "All right." Athens closed the door and turned to find Leanya dressed and ready to leave. "Don't go," he said. "Not yet." He moved towards her and reaching out, cupped her breasts in his hands, fondling them, "I won't be long. Please."

She smiled wickedly, finding the hardness between his legs with her hand and gave it a long, slow caress. "Anything you say, Governor. Anything you say."

*

Athens was looking through the large glass door out at Halcyon Beach. His home, one of many small but lovely residences built on the coast of the Marsean Sea, was perched atop jungled cliffs overlooking a broad, pink sand shore. Life had become very sweet. The colonists had quickly adapted to the year-round day-light, with short cycles of sleep and waking. General health had improved and fertility, even without artificial assistance, was on the rise.

"So what you're telling me, Golde," said Athens to the ugly little man standing behind him, "is that you've gotten me out of bed to make a report on the waste substance of several billion bil-lion microbial creatures?"

"That's correct."

Seeing Golde again, Athens remembered he was one of those people whose every personal characteristic was rooted deep within his professional life. In this case he was a highly respected special-ist in the field of geology, and therefore must be taken seriously.

"What is so important, Sir," Golde went on, "is the nature of the substance itself, and the location of the microbes in relation to the titanum mine."

"If it's going to complicate the mining operation in any way, simply avoid it. You of all people appreciate that stockpiling the ore is the colony's most vital function."

"I think, Governor, that you should see the substance for yourself before you make any decisions. If you'll accompany me to the main laboratory…"

"To view a pile of this…excrement? On my leisure day? Forgive me if I sound a bit skeptical."

"I understand Sir, but I believe you'll have a different opinion once you see it for yourself.

*

Athens had agreed to be flown by shuttlecraft from his home to the titanum mine, processing plant and laboratories. It pleased him to be traveling not in one of the transport's utilitarian pods, but in the small silver disk he'd had designed after the *Atlantos's* shuttle crafts. Athens had brought Leanya along on the field trip, certain that once he'd seen Golde's find, he'd still have an exciting evening to look forward to with her. As the sun set the strip of creamy sand began to recede, and the shuttlecraft's pilot headed up the continent's eastern coast.

Giant tree ferns blanketed nearly every inch of the land, and pretty little satellite towns already dotted the shoreline as far as the eye could see. No one, it became clear shortly after their arrival on Mars, had any intention of building their homes anywhere but near the water. There were perhaps a dozen small villages to be found inland, but they were invariably on the shores of one of the many Marsean lakes. Though beneath the great fern forests the landscape was nearly as flat as Terres was, the lush greenery, the sun rising every morning, and the presence of water made Mars a truly exotic world.

Flying inland over the vast plain that had been phaetronically cleared in the first months after landfall, Athens could see the cultivated fields which provided the colonists with their vegetal needs, and now coming into view the enormous mining and processing complex that sprawled for miles. It employed more than eighty percent of the Terresian colonists and operated every hour of every day of the year.

Moments after the shuttle landed Athens and Leanya stood in Golde's laboratory. The place was abuzz with scientists, engineers and technicians.

"It *is* extraordinary," Athens said, turning a chunk of metal over in his hand. He moved to a lamp and held the yellow ingot under the light. "Just look at the way it glows... I swear, it's the color of the *sun*. Come here, Leanya." He pushed the girl into the lamp's halo and held the ingot up to the concavity at the base of her throat. It looked luminescent against her pale skin. "Beautiful!" He moved it higher, covering her ear as if it were an ornament. Then he smiled. "What do we know about the creatures that produce this substance?" Athens demanded of Golde.

"Let me show you something, Governor." The geologist activated his trans-screen and an image suddenly appeared in the space between the two men. Hundreds of five-inch long, oval shaped creatures undulated amidst a crystalline matrix. "The 'Golde's Organisms'— as we refer to them," he said, "have been magnified here 10,000 times. They live nearly five miles beneath the planet's surface at a temperature of one hundred and thirty degrees. Look here," he said, pointing to a budlike structure at one end of the animal. "You can see it ingesting the mineral substance surrounding it – its only food." Indeed, the enlargement was so detailed, and the creature's body so transparent, that a pale greyish substance could be seen entering through an orifice in the bud – a mouth of sorts – and its progress through the simple digestive system was actually visible to the observers.

"Have you any more samples of the ore?" inquired Athens

The over-serious geologist finally smiled. "Come this way."

He led Athens and Leanya across the workspace to a large-doored metal cabinet and without pause flung it open. A smooth slab of the substance several feet long lay on a shelf, and on another were geometric shapes – spheres, pyramids, squares, rectangles made of the shining stuff. "The deposit has apparently been building up for 2.8 billion Marsean years, Governor. There've been some very busy little microbes down there. Our sensors indicate that the vein is almost as long – if narrower – than the seam of titanum. And that, as you know, extends a substantial distance around the planet."

All right," said Athens, unable to tear his eyes from the lustrous array of magnificence spread out before him. "You have my undivided attention. Now show me what the problem is."

*

The titanum mine, a miracle of Terresian architechnos, resembled an enormous hive of robotic, web-spinning insects. On three sides the cavern rose to a height of nearly two-hundred feet, where row-atop-row of individual cells cut into the wall of solid ore. In the center of the brightly illuminated cave rose a great metallic column whose multiple purposes depended upon the functions of a massive phaetron mounted within it. From each of the cave wall cells streamed chunks of newly mined titanum, suspended in mid-air within a yellow tractor beam – the threads of the web – and were pulled into openings on the central column. The collected ore was then sucked into a thick blue elevator beam and transported up to the Marsean surface where finally it was carted off for processing.

At the mouth of each cell in the mine hung a smaller phaetronic device, sprouting six spindly legs, which allowed the insect-looking thing to creep about, directing its narrow red beam in through the orifice to gouge the ore from the rock wall. Inside, a team of four miners lifted the chunks as fast as they fell, heaving them into the tractor beam, heading – with many hundreds of such ore-laden beams – to the central column. Men, too, rode the yellow beams back and forth between their cells and the central core, waving to one another as they passed. As the mining progressed forward, cell walls would be broken down by the six-legged phaetrons, and new ones carved out. Used-up cells on the side walls were simply abandoned. In this way the mining progressed laterally through the core of Mars.

Inside the central column there was a second elevator beam paralleling the upward flow of ore. This one carried workers into the depths of the Marsean lithosphere. Athens rode this beam down with Golde and Leanya, watching with an odd sense of gratification the continuous upward-bound stream of titanum. There was the Terresian air of industriousness to the place. Though it was tedious work it was clean, efficient and safe. The undistinguished grey-brown rock promised continuing life to an entire planet, and Athens was proud of the flawless operation that provided it.

They had reached the lowest level Athens had previously visited – the floor of the cavern. But now the elevator was descending even deeper into the Marsean crust. Athens, Golde and Leanya stepped out into a sweltering, dimly lit chamber which lay directly below the titanum mine. It was perhaps a quarter as wide as the cave above it, and roughly hewn from the surrounding rock. Only the most rudimentary excavation activity, with miners using hand tools alone, was underway. The small crew of shirtless workers, their bodies glistening with sweat, chipped almost tentatively at the walls.

The miners greeted their governor with genuine pleasantness and, as usual, this warmed Athens's heart. But he was fired with curiosity about the lustrous yellow ore and impatient to see it in its raw state. In the shadowy cavern he could see nothing.

"This is an unauthorized operation, Governor," said Golde. "Very few personnel are aware of these activities, and everyone working down here has been sworn to secrecy."

"Good, good," Athens muttered impatiently. "Why don't you show me this vein you've discovered."

"Yes Sir." The geologist nodded to the foreman and the cavern was flooded with light.

The effect was mind-exploding.

The cave was completely illuminated with glittering yellow luminosity, as though the sun was afire in the walls all around them. Rather than jagged veins interspersed with the common ore it fed upon, the uneven walls appeared to have been thickly coated with a layer of the gorgeous substance.

Athens actually groaned with the sight of it and found himself speechless. He saw Leanya's eyes grow huge as she gazed around with childlike wonder. Her look was so nakedly awestruck that he laughed aloud.

"Are you laughing at me?" she asked.

"Just your expression."

"You should see your own."

Athens turned to the scientist. "Where are the Golde Organisms?"

"They lie beneath the layer of gold," he answered.

"*Gold*?" repeated Athens.

The scientist was suddenly awkward and embarrassed. "It's what the miners have begun calling the substance, Sir. We can change the name if you like…"

"No, no, it's your discovery. We'll call it 'gold'".

"Do I have your permission, then, to begin a proper extraction operation?" inquired the man, knowing what Athens' answer would undoubtedly be.

"Begin immediately. Employ as many workers and requisition all the equipment you need. We'll have to begin work on a separate processing facility."

"Yes, Sir."

"Now what's the problem you spoke of?"

"Preliminary reports indicate that for the microbes to continue metabolizing the ore, the temperature must remain at a level that is most uncomfortable to the human organism."

"Then put some men to work designing a comfortable working garment," instructed Athens.

"Secondly, none of the phaetronic frequencies we've already established can be employed to separate the gold from the microbial layer without damage," said Golde.

"Damage to the gold or to the microbes?" probed Athens.

"Both, for the moment, so we're having to work by hand. It's extremely tedious work, and there's so much we still don't understand."

"You'll begin a series of studies to find solutions. Immediately. And Golde…"

"Sir?"

"For the time being, until I can determine the importance of this...'gold' on the systems and priorities already in place, continue to restrict information to the general public. Do you think these men have kept silent so far?"

"I have no doubt of it. The stories and rumors would have been rampant all over the colony by now if they hadn't."

"That's surprising," said Athens.

"Not really. I've made the reward for their silence utterly irresistible."

"How so?" asked Athens.

"I'm paying them...in gold."

TWENTY-TWO

THE SHORE PEOPLE gathered once every year to hunt the wild bull. It was a new custom, celebrating the recent coming of the great herds onto the tribal hunting grounds. They had always killed small animals to supplement their food from the sea, but the arrival of hoards of buron, kassel and antelere had meant great abundance for everyone. The men had had to adapt to hunting larger animals, the tool and weapons-making revised, and the women learned to cook the tougher flesh. No one except Luna had complained – she had lost her medicines.

This day he joined the people in their trek up the path behind the village to the Great Plateau. It was a joyful occasion, and no one seemed to mind hauling the quantities of wood, cooking utensils and musical instruments they would need to make camp and prepare for the feast at day's end. As soon as everyone had assembled at the chosen site, the tribe's twelve strongest hunters had been blessed by the elders. Then armed only with staves and nooses, they set out to locate the buron herd. Their first task would be to cull from it a single, long-horned bull and drive it back to camp.

But before they'd taken their leave Poseidon was witness to a very public courtship display. Boah had made certain he was standing in front of Cleatah as he prepared himself for the hunt. He never took his eyes off her as he rubbed onto his muscular chest, arms and thighs the nut oil that guaranteed strength, and tied on necklaces and bracelets of tiny shells worn by all the hunters on such a day for luck. Poseidon observed Cleatah's reaction to this open display of sexuality and noted that while she did not avert her eyes from Boah altogether – for that would have signaled a humiliating insult – she never quite met his smoldering gaze.

Now the hunters had gone, and the remaining villagers began preparing for their return with the bull. A large ring was delineated with cut wooden stakes and skins hung on them. Into this the bellowing, stamping animal would be driven. It was explained to Poseidon that with all the villagers watching from the sidelines, several of the most agile boys, dressed in gaudy costumes, would join the hunters in the ring, tumbling and shouting in wild antics to distract the bull while the hunters attempted to slip their nooses around the beast's neck and all four feet. Once subdued it would not be killed outright, but tethered to four tall stakes. Only after the sun set behind the distant western mountains would the animal be ritually slaughtered as the Shore People invoked the Great Mother's blessings. The sacrifice would then be celebrated with a bonfire, music, dance and prayer in thanks for her bounty.

It wasn't until Poseidon was pounding one of the stakes for the bull ring into the ground that he recognized his feeling of satisfaction and relief that Cleatah had rebuked Boah's seduction. But this admission troubled him. Why should it matter that a tribesman pursued this woman? Surely Talya's egg harvesting – if Cleatah was finally chosen for the genomic procedure – could proceed even if she was mated with the young man.

A second unsettling thought rattled Poseidon's mind. What right did the Terresians have to tamper with these people at all? *They were human beings*, he had come to realize in the months he had lived among them. *Really no different than Terresians.* He wasn't certain when he had ceased thinking of them solely as test subjects.

Poseidon had been slowly and subtly increasing his contact with Cleatah, and he had to admit that she charmed him. Her intelligence was beyond question, but it was the easy way she dealt with him – confidently, as an equal, and with a gentle teasing about his clumsy ways – that most endeared her to him. It was wonderful to be treated as other men were. It had become tiresome being a Terresian hero. *Cleatah, beautiful Cleatah*...Poseidon stopped his hammering, suddenly shaken by the outrageous and inappropriate sentiments. He threw himself back into the task at hand and forcibly banished all renegade thoughts.

The makeshift shelters had been erected and decorated, the wood piled high for the bonfire, the ring and four-pole bull tether completed. Everyone was waiting with good-humored impatience for the thrilling moment when the bull, pursued by the hunters, would come racing across the plain and the spectacle would begin. Before they had appeared, however, thunder began rumbling, and all could see storm clouds gathered in the distance, and forked lightning striking the ground in numerous places.

As they worked the people talked about the distant storm, some of them wishing for the badly needed rain, others happy that the downpour was moving away and would not drench their celebration. No one realized until too late that the thunderous noise that slowly grew in intensity and never seemed to end was not, in fact, coming from the storm. By the time they felt the ground vibrating under their feet and saw the great cloud of dust moving in their direction, the first of the stampeding horses were upon them.

Chaos was instantaneous – shrieks and cries of pain and terror as the moving wall of wild beasts tore through the makeshift encampment. Had the horses been able to gallop past unhindered, the episode – damaging as it was – would have ended as quickly as it began. But the animals – confused by obstacles and panicking people – scattered, sending the rampage in every direction. In a frenzy they trampled cooking hearths, flattened tent poles. They reared in wild-eyed fury at the men that were stabbing at them with spears. Tribesmen shouted and waved their arms, anything to scare the animals away from the women, children and helpless elders.

Battling dust and fury Poseidon grabbed whomever he could, pushing them into larger groups, encouraging them to cling together. The bigger the human island, the more the horses avoided them. He grabbed and pushed, sidestepped panicked animals. He found himself searching desperately for sight of Cleatah. *Where was she!* He stumbled over a woman's mangled body. *Was it Cleatah?* Screams of horses, people, collapsing tents. Dust. Blood.

A child stood crying…standing in the path of an oncoming beast. No! Poseidon dashed for the boy, crossing the horse's path to tackle the child a moment before the animal thundered past, sheltering the tiny body from the barrage of pebbles thrown up from its hooves.

Poseidon lifted his head from the curled figure of the child. It was over. Dust was beginning to settle. Moans and anguished cries could be heard from all parts of the camp. He released the boy and within seconds his father, Dyon, was beside them. He embraced Poseidon in tearful thanks, then lifted the boy in his arms and moved away in a daze. Poseidon stood and began searching for Cleatah. Many villagers were injured, several appeared dead. *Where was she?*

Suddenly he stopped, feet rooted to the ground, his eyes drawn to the bullring. It had, unbelievably, been left intact during the stampede and a single horse had been trapped inside. Unable to find its way out again it now trotted round and round within the enclosure, snorting furiously, tossing its head, searching for the disappeared herd. Poseidon could not tear his gaze from the sight of the proud-headed beast so confined, its movements controlled by the ring's perimeter, its gait slowed and regulated.

Suddenly he saw, as if in a vision, *the future* illuminated before his eyes. A design began to unfold. In the next moment his vision was shattered as the trapped horse took sudden flight, leaping over the top of the ring and galloping away to his freedom. Poseidon watched it disappear in a cloud of dust…

Then he saw her – Cleatah. She stood, stunned and rigid but apparently unhurt. Sheeva, too, was unscathed but yapped about her legs in frantic confusion. Poseidon saw her reach down to calm the wolf at the very moment their eyes met. A wave of the profoundest emotion swept over him, through him. At the same moment, they heard the piteous cries of a woman. The elderly Ilato was lying in a swirl of dust. With the wolf trailing at her feet Cleatah went and knelt beside her.

As he hurried to assist a pair of bloodied tribesmen he wondered how, in so short a space of time, his perfectly ordered life of scientechnos and reason had come to this antithetical turning. Was it a new faculty he had acquired? An acceptance of instinct, impulse, intuition, a dexterity of mind. If so, he decided, it was a most glorious gift from the Great Mother. From Erthe.

Poseidon opened his heart and accepted it.

TWENTY-THREE

FROM WHERE SHE knelt tending the injured elder Cleatah recalled the moment just before she and Poseidon had found each another in the wreckage of the corral. He had been staring with what she perceived – strange as it seemed – as *longing* at the last of the creatures that had destroyed their temporary village. She tried, but could not imagine what he had been thinking.

Cleatah called one of the boys, told him to fetch her some willow branches for splits, but as she turned her attention back to Ilato's broken arm – willing herself not to search the grounds for the reassuring sight of Poseidon – she finally admitted to herself her fascination, her longing for this impenetrable stranger. She vowed silently that nothing in the world would keep her from knowing him.

*

When the hunters returned they found the ceremonial village in shambles, the women weeping for the dead. And they had come empty-handed, unable to find the buron herd, as though it had vanished from the plateau altogether. The two tragedies together were seen as a terrible omen, yet no one knew what offense they had committed against the Great Mother to exact so serious a punishment from her.

For weeks afterwards the elders sat together day and night, only emerging from their meeting for the burials of the dead. It was a solemn time for all. Children were forbidden to play and the women, normally jovial and talkative as they went about their daily chores, were largely silent. The men, every one of them, believed they had suffered a loss of their masculine powers. They had been helpless against the horses and unsuccessful as hunters. As the days went on it had become impossible for them to even look each other in the eye.

Poseidon was quiet and appeared to be brooding much as the other men were. But his mind was afire as he sought a graceful excuse to absent himself from the village and carry out his plan. On the first full moon after the terrible events he made his way to the elders' compound and humbly asked for admittance.

"I wish to leave the village for a short while," he told them. "There are rituals I need to perform at this time."

"What rituals?" demanded Heydra irritably. He was the youngest of the group, only recently having been admitted to the circle and still unsure of himself.

"It is a ceremony for the dead – the ancestors of my own tribe. But of course I will include the Shore People in my prayers. I would stay here and perform the rituals, but I am afraid I might offend someone with my ways which are... different."

"How long will you go for...if we give you leave?" asked Brannan. He was said to be one of the tribe's oldest men, but he had a sweet round face almost free of wrinkles.

Poseidon hesitated. He had no way of knowing how long he would need to accomplish his goals. This might be his only opportunity to go, but he could not be sure if he would be welcomed back if he stayed away too long.

"I will return by the half moon," he told them.

"That is a long time for rituals," Heydra said, more than a little suspicious.

Poseidon turned his palms upward in silent supplication. Further explanation would only complicate things.

The elders argued among themselves for a while longer, Heydra poking sullenly at the fire with a long stick, Elkon never taking his eyes from Poseidon, as though he was trying to pierce the outer shell that hid the stranger's secrets.

"Let him go," said Brannan finally. "Poseidon has shown himself a worthy man. We should respect his rituals."

"He should be taking part in *our* rituals," said Elkon, "if he wants to be part of this tribe."

"He saved the child's life with no thought for his own safety," argued Brannan. "I say let him go, but for one quarter of the moon's cycle."

At last a consensus was reached and Poseidon was given leave to go.

"You will come back to us in seven days then," Brannan said.

"You honor me with your trust," Poseidon replied, feeling strangely humbled before these primitive people. "This is my home now. I will return in seven days."

He searched for Cleatah, wishing to see her before his departure, but she was nowhere to be found. And though his stature had been increased further since the day of the stampede, he nevertheless felt uncomfortable asking anyone of her whereabouts.

TWENTY-FOUR

SHE COULD NOT be found because she had returned alone to the plateau in search of the mushroom. The dead had been buried, but despite the many prayers and properly made offerings, the Shore People were suffering. *What had they done to deserve such punishment from the Great Mother?* Cleatah wondered. In such times she found wisdom in the mushroom, so she'd woken before dawn and set out for the plateau.

She thought to seek Poseidon out and tell him of her plans, but hesitated for so long she abandoned the thought. He, more than the tribe's miseries, filled her mind as she made the climb, feeling the sun's first heat on her back, and set out across the plain towards the forest.

Now having eaten several of the caps she sat beside the river in utter stillness, silently calling to herself the visions and the words to give them shape. *She saw the great buron herd grazing on the distant plain. Their movements were languid and the grasses, lush and greener than she had ever seen them, swayed in rolling waves. As the enormous bellowing bull moved among the cows with their large liquid eyes, their heads turned slowly, slowly in his direction. 'No punishment,' came the words on the wind, the words as a chant. 'No punishment...' The herd was intact, the sacred bull still within the tribe's grasp. There had been no punishment intended by the spirit of Erthe. The bull lowered his head and began to feast on a stand of sacred mushrooms. His handsome head and powerful shoulders began to soften and melt, becoming the face of Poseidon, clean-shaven as Cleatah had never seen him before. It was a strong and beautiful face, the shapely lips moving, speaking her name – "Cleatah, Cleatah' – speaking her name with love. And all at once she was weeping, for the future was bright, full of promise and joy. Then the clouds swirled and parted, and there on a sunny shore she saw herself reclining, draped only in silvery seaweed, hundreds of little children at her feet, some bathing in the water, some playing in the sand. And they were all her children, beautiful children, and their eyes were grey.*

Their eyes were sparkling grey…

TWENTY-FIVE

USING HIS PHAETRON it had taken Poseidon no time at all to locate the herd of wild horses. They had moved north along the coastal plateau and stopped to graze near the low rocky mountain ridge where he'd seen them before. Climbing to the highest point he was delighted to find almost exactly the pattern of rocks necessary to begin his endeavor. A semi-circular stone canyon had been naturally carved in the range, and now using several of the device's functions he split, moved and levitated several boulders to finish enclosing the circle, all but a narrow-necked opening at the front of it.

Satisfied with his work he descended from the ridge and sat hidden in the tall grasses quietly replaying previously recorded data on the herd. He watched them with renewed interest and a certain respect, having experienced the deadliest aspect of these magnificent beasts. He knew what he wished to accomplish – *to ride on the back of a horse* – something that had never been done by any man before him. He realized, however, that he had planned only the first step: separating one of the animals from the herd and guiding it into the stone canyon.

The canyon was an approximation of the bullring in which he had seen the single horse trotting round and round, and had been inspiration for what might be the most foolhardy act of his life. He whispered into the phaetron, *"The problem I face – one that worked steadily on my mind as I traveled to this place – is whether to use the technos at my disposal in my capturing and taming of the horse, or to use my knowledge, wits and physical strength alone. I realize that if I cannot manage without the aid of ultra science, the exercise will be of no use to the Shore People. However, my time is limited. I fear if I overstay my absence from the village I will lose the advantage I have recently gained. More importantly, I cannot afford to scare the herd away with what will surely be my clumsy attempts at separating one of these beasts from the others. I think I must therefore use the phaetron, though I will use it as sparingly as possible."*

Carefully and slowly, Poseidon stepped out of the long grasses and revealed himself to the herd. Many heads were raised from their grazing, and several of the females with young ones nudged them in the opposite direction. There was some whinnying and snorting and pawing of the ground. In all, however, they seemed unperturbed and not particularly prone to aggression towards him.

Poseidon in his observations had singled out the horse he wished to use for his experiment – a youngish female, not terribly large, white with brown spots, her shaggy mane and tail solid white. She seemed spirited but not especially bold or skittish. A graceful whorl on her forehead appealed to Poseidon, and he thought the animal especially pretty. He named her Arrow. Though she grazed on the outskirts of the herd nearest him and close to a mature female – likely her mother – it appeared that Arrow had recently separated from the mare, for the elder horse was now suckling a new foal.

With a final tinge of regret that it was necessary, Poseidon set the phaetron on a mild 'narcotizing' setting and widened the beam to encompass the entire herd. At once the horses' heads that were not lowered in grazing dropped into the position of sleep. Several babies who had not yet learned the art of sleeping on their feet collapsed to the ground and rested in that position. Having no experience using this procedure in such an unusual circumstance, Poseidon could not be sure if the animal he wished to cull would become too lethargic to manipulate, and whether once Arrow was removed from the beam's influence he would be able to control her movements at all.

As he approached Poseidon recalled a scene he had observed being played out again and again within the world of the horse – mothers training their young in the art of socialization and hierarchy. It was done with the posture and angling of her body in relation to her offspring, with eyes insistent and directing, silently instructing the student in the correct behavior, and banishing the animal when it disobeyed.

He was close to the herd now, and despite the phaetron's control of them Poseidon's heart began to pound in fear. The sight of the horses and the almost overpowering smell of them reminded him of the awesome power they wielded, the deadly danger they presented. Now shifting the beam from a wide setting to a full circumference including himself for safety, Poseidon moved inside the herd's outer perimeter, just behind where Arrow stood.

In her semi-stupor she was not much alarmed by his approach. When he began the slow, careful process of separating and herding her away from the others – moving her in the direction of the canyon – she did not resist.

She walked ahead of him through the long neck leading into the rock ring. Poseidon hesitated before beginning the next phase, apprehensive about switching off the narcotizing function. Though out of range of the herd he could not know how Arrow would react to finding herself confined in the circular enclosure with a human being. But it was imperative that he release the narcotizing beam just now, as the phaetron had to be used to close off the mouth of the canyon so that Arrow could not make a dash for freedom.

Quickly, for the narcosis began to dissipate immediately, Poseidon reset the phaetron frequency and aimed it at a massive boulder near the neck of the canyon. The rock began to move slowly to cover the enclosure. Careful as Poseidon was, the sound of stone shrieking against stone brought the horse to its senses. She was suddenly altogether conscious of her unusual surroundings and confinement, and the strange creature imprisoned with her.

Arrow trotted as far away from Poseidon as she could, but found that the ring – any way she moved about in it – somehow brought her back to the man. To stay out of harm's way he stood at the center of the ring. Arrow's trot increased in speed and became a panicked gallop. Distressed and wild-eyed as the horse was, Poseidon saw only her beauty, the rippling muscles of her flank, deep chest heaving, the glorious mane flying.

And suddenly his fear ceased.

It was merely a matter of time, he told himself, before he and the horse would be joined. He stood very still and looked into Arrow's terrified eyes as she came round with every circle, like a planet revolving about its sun. Again and again she came, Poseidon's calm deepening. *He would wait an eternity to gain this animal's trust.* Her pace slowed perceptibly and finally, in exhaustion, she stopped, her tongue loose, licking her lips. He noticed her inside ear cocked toward the middle of the ring where he stood. Man and beast stared at each other with curious intensity.

Then a small rockslide spooked the horse and she bolted. Poseidon remained still. Arrow made another orbit and came around so that she fell under his gaze again. It was time to employ the technique he had observed in mother horses to elicit desired behavior from their offspring. Averting his eyes from Arrow, Poseidon took a small step towards the animal. She remained still. Another step closer, this time positioning his shoulders at a forty-five degree angle to her. The moment he did this she moved a step closer to him. His heart nearly stopped.

It had worked.

Then without warning Arrow charged Poseidon and with only a glancing blow knocked him backwards onto his rump. He had to laugh at himself, for her defiant eyes clearly said, "You seek to control me, stranger. Now I will control you."

Aware that he could ill afford to appear so weak for too long Poseidon sprang to his feet. He took several more definitive steps in Arrow's direction, angling his shoulders in the opposite direction. This time she appeared ready to bolt. He realized he had forgotten the eyes. Another step, this time with his eyes averted. She moved in concordance, then waited, he imagined, poised for his next maneuver.

It became a dance, Poseidon clearly in the lead, the partners straying closer and closer together. Sometimes it felt like a game, but one of the greatest import. Always, it felt as though the man and horse in the same ring were the only two creatures in the wide world. They were less than ten paces apart, and Arrow seemed skittish. This time after his angled step toward her he crouched down and looked away altogether, in a gesture of subordination. A few moments later he could feel the horse above him. She was sniffing his head and neck. Had she lost all fear of him? Very, very slowly Poseidon rose to standing, less than an arm's length away from her. He was not sure whether first to touch her forehead, her nose, her neck…

But before he knew what had happened she'd taken the decision from his hands – stretched out her neck and pushed at his shoulder with her nose. Poseidon gasped delightedly. He reached out for her, but his movement was too quick and she backed away, retreating to the outer perimeter of the ring and making several circuits before she slowed and stopped.

"Forgive me, Arrow," he said aloud. The sound of his voice did not appear to frighten her, so he began to vocalize as he approached her, words and nonsensical sounds as well, but all in the most soothing tones. As he stood contemplating his next move the horse nudged him again, he was sure in a teasing manner.

Knowing he was losing the day Poseidon reached out his hand and grabbed ahold of Arrow's thick mane. She pulled back her head but not out of his grasp and regarded him with one eye, waiting for his next move. It was this very move, however, which had haunted his thoughts from the moment he had seen the horse in the bullring and envisioned himself riding on its back.

How should he propel himself up there? This was the crucial question. Poseidon was strong, but he lacked leverage, and he did not know how much pressure he could place on the mane to pull himself up. And would such a bold and invasive action terrify the horse completely? The day was dying and there was anticipation of some great climax to this long dance. He knew he must move decisively and do so quickly, but found himself ambivalent about what he should next do.

He argued with himself. Since the closing of the canyon's neck with his phaeton he had proceeded within the boundaries of the natural world, and the results had been miraculous. The horse had begun to trust him. But did he trust himself? Did he really trust the natural world, naked of his technos? The last time he had done so – while in the volcanic range – it had nearly cost him his life. He must act sensibly. He needed to mount the horse and do it quickly. In the fading light he therefore again set the phaeton to the narcotizing frequency and directed it toward Arrow. She sagged at once, her head drooping nearly to the ground. Instantly Poseidon felt a pang of regret, a keen sense that he had betrayed her. But there was no time to lose.

He grabbed Arrow's mane with both hands and with a push catapulted his body to her onto her back. With a few adjustments to his posture he found himself astride her! He sighed with relief and wonder, but he had no time for self-congratulation. "May the spirit of Erthe protect me," he whispered and switched off the phaetron's narcotizing frequency.

All of Arrow's muscles instantly tightened beneath him. She lifted her head, suddenly aware of the strange weight on her back. Slowly she turned and saw the man atop her. Poseidon hardly breathed as Arrow shifted carefully on her feet. He was ecstatic. She had accepted him! The slow building of trust between them had…

Poseidon suddenly found himself flying through the air. He landed with a thump on his back and saw, to his horror, the furiously rearing horse poised above him. He rolled sideways just as Arrow's hooves came crashing down. Poseidon jumped to his feet and found himself facing the horse, now dancing in agitation, her angry eyes flashing. Summoning self-control he used his most soothing voice, whispering nonsensical words, clicks and kisses. "Whoa, whoa, shhh girl, shhh. Arrow, Arrow, beautiful girl…

The horse slowly calmed. Did he dare touch her, try to mount her again? He must. Poseidon stretched out his arm and carefully stroked her nose. She did not flinch, seemed to remember the moments of trust before the betrayal. He moved closer, grew bolder, stroked her neck and shoulders with more pressure, more assurance. Was he imagining it? Was the horse enjoying the intimacy, or at least the sensations?

Nearly all the light had gone from the sky now. Poseidon was weary from the struggle and felt the horse was weary, too. Now was the moment. Without hesitation he grabbed Arrow's mane and with all his strength swung himself up onto her back. She did not move but stood solid as he clumsily adjusted himself in the seat of living muscle and bone.

He sat as quiet and still on Arrow as he was able, the night coming up around the newly coupled pair. As the moments passed without struggle, and Poseidon's breathing slowed, the accomplishment of the deed began to dawn as something more magnificent than words could describe. His gratitude for the beast swelled and threatened to burst his heart. He leaned down and laid his cheek upon her sleek, powerful neck.

"Bless you Arrow," he whispered, overcome by an alien emotion that cracked his voice and brought stinging tears to his eyes. "Bless you my friend, sweet Arrow." Poseidon smiled in the dark and spoke as much to himself as the horse when he said, "The rest will be much, much easier."

*

If the following days were not precisely easier, they were filled with startling discoveries about the communion of men and horses, and many successes. Confined together in the ring Poseidon and Arrow worked, learned, ate and finally played together. As the bond of trust deepened, anything and everything became possible. Poseidon found that he needed a method of guiding the horse's movements. A leather thong around Arrow's neck was useless. The same thong around her forehead irritated her. The idea of placing it in her mouth at first seemed cruel, but finally worked if manipulated gently.

They walked, trotted, galloped. Poseidon took dozens of spills; the horse gazing down at him with what he began to think was amusement. He became adept at pulling himself up by her mane and seating himself in one graceful move. And the pain in his thighs caused by the constant use of previously unused muscles for gripping her sides – excruciating for the first few days – finally began to lessen.

It was time to leave for the village, and Poseidon was apprehensive. The herd had moved on, Poseidon having scared them off with a barrage of light beams radiating from his phaetron. Though this eliminated the risk of Arrow wishing to rejoin her family, he could not know how she would behave outside the confines of the rock ring. With no small regret at leaving behind the private marvel of the previous days, Poseidon levitated the large boulder at the neck of the canyon and sitting proud on the back of his horse, rode out into the world.

Free from all confines Arrow stopped of her own accord and gazed around with some confusion. Where was the herd? She stubbornly refused to move when he gave her the signal they had devised for that action – a gentle heel in her side. She became agitated and danced on the spot. Her ears were upright, listening for her family, nostrils flared, searching for their scent. Poseidon held his seat as she threw her head up and down, blowing and snorting. Then he leaned down and began murmuring comfortable words in her ear to say that *he* was her family now.

In this way man and horse remained for some time, he allowing her to mourn for her loss, her agitation by degrees lessening, and her body regaining its natural balance. Finally, without prodding, Arrow began to walk. Poseidon's heart swelled, for not only had she apparently accepted her strange future, but she had with some unfathomable instinct or unspoken communication with the man on her back, begun walking in the precise direction that would take them home.

TWENTY-SIX

WHAT SHE WAS seeing was not possible. Squatting in the sand with a group of children, teaching them how to extract the dye sack from an eight-tentacled sea creature, Cleatah had glanced up briefly and caught sight of a dark speck far in the distance, moving towards them along the northern beach. She squinted at the speck with confusion, for it appeared much larger than it should have, had it been a man approaching at that distance. The children stopped their lesson, looking up at Cleatah who had gotten to her feet and was staring in silence down the long stretch of beach.

She only became alarmed when the strange shape reached the fallen boulder. It was still far off, but she knew how big a man should appear at that distance, and this was not a man approaching. Neither was it a known beast – too tall for a buron, the largest known animal.

"Go," she said to the children. "Up to the village. Tell your parents to come down to the beach. Hurry!"

The children scrambled away and up the footpath, leaving Cleatah alone and trembling at the black shape that was coming slowly but steady towards her. Nothing about the thing made sense. Clearly it was living, an animal of some sort, but nothing she had ever seen before. And while it did not appear to be attacking, she could not be sure that it would not do so when it caught sight of her.

She was glad when the first of the villagers began clamoring down the beach steps, surrounding her and plying her with questions, then staring down the strip of sand as they followed her outstretched arm and pointing finger. Men who had rushed down to the beach without their weapons called frantically to others who were still descending to bring spears. Many spears.

The figure was becoming clearer now, though what the villagers saw made no sense to them. Cleatah could feel that even the bravest of hunters were stifling their terror, for this beast was unknown to them and it was horrible to behold.

Above, it was a man, and below a horse.

What terrible god ruled this creature? All the men had gathered, spears at the ready, into a protective mass, facing the northern beach. Still it came, with a blessed slowness, apparently lacking aggression, but many villagers were no doubt remembering the recent carnage caused by horses at the bull camp.

Then suddenly its posture changed. It seemed to be dancing excitedly in place, and the creature revealed itself to be more fearsome than before. It had two heads! That of a man *and* a horse. It turned and bucked and suddenly, as in a nightmare vision it rose up on two legs, its front legs pawing at the sky. A woman screamed and all at once the men, infused with the courage of the kill, spears poised for the throw, charged the horse-man, shouting their most fearsome war cry.

TWENTY-SEVEN

ON FIRST SIGHT of the gathered mass of villagers Arrow had panicked. It had taken all of Poseidon's strength and calm assurances to steady her. But now the men, shrieking to the heavens, were running at them, weapons raised, and he could feel the horse beneath him ready to bolt.

Poseidon began to shout. "It is Poseidon! I am Poseidon, your friend!!" He could make out some faces, but they were coming very fast. "Kalar! Boah! It is not a beast, but your friend Poseidon!!"

Several spears had already been loosed and they flew swiftly with precise aim. Poseidon ducked to narrowly avoid the first, maneuvered the terrified Arrow to avoid the next two. But the sound of his voice had so startled and confused the onrushing hunters that several had stopped in their tracks. Poseidon continued his vocalizing, calling out men's names the moment he recognized their faces. They all slowed, lowered their weapons and were staring incredulously at "Poseidon" straddling the back of a horse! Some of them shouted angrily at him, others fell to their knees weeping. The women had begun slowly to approach, curiosity overcoming their fear.

Poseidon who had managed, somehow, to calm Arrow,

continued to speak in soothing tones to the villagers who could still not believe their eyes and even less, their ears.

"Poseidon?" It was Cleatah's voice. Tentative, fearful. It occurred to him that he had never before this moment known her to show fear.

"Cleatah," he said evenly, "Come closer. I will not harm you. It is your friend, Poseidon. I am merely sitting on the back of a horse. And this horse will not harm you either."

She moved forward slowly, ignoring Boah who tried to stay her.

"How do I know it is really Poseidon, and not some man-beast from the spirit world?" she asked apprehensively.

"This way," Poseidon replied, and in a single, much practiced movement, dismounted, landing gracefully on his two feet.

There were more shouts and gasps, but now as many in delight as in terror. Cleatah had come close, very carefully, having never been so near to a horse, and not altogether believing that the man who had just separated himself from it was Poseidon. She reached out and touched him quickly, pulling her hand back, and found human flesh beneath her fingers. She touched him again, this time grasping the muscle of his forearm. Finally satisfied, her face broke out into a smile and she turned to the villagers.

"It *is* Poseidon." The onlookers were not yet convinced. "It is Poseidon, I tell you!" Cleatah turned and looked over her shoulder at Arrow, who had calmed even further. "And he has brought us…" she hesitated, hardly believing her own words, "…a very… great…gift."

*

"I wish to take a party of men to gather the herd of wild horses," Poseidon announced as he sat at the community hearth. The Shore People had not fully recovered from their first sight of him riding on the back of one of the beasts. "When they have been captured I will give you my knowledge of them. I will teach you how to ride on their backs, as I do."

There was no sound at all for a space of time, save the buzzing of night insects and the whimper of a child before being put to the breast. Then like a fire erupting in a blaze of sparks, everyone was talking at once, shouting.

"It is impossible," Elkon insisted. "How can men take control of such huge animals?"

"We have already seen one man do such a thing," offered Heydra.

"I say no." It was Elkon again. "Men will surely be injured or killed."

Poseidon remained silent, allowing the arguments to swirl around him. Someone dumped more wood on the fire, and everyone settled in to listen, or participate in the debate. Children slept in their mothers' laps. Elders scratched at their chins.

"Think," said Boah, "We could become a tribe of 'horse-men'."

"That is a bad idea," said the old woman Ilato, whose arm had been broken in the stampede. "I think the Great Mother would punish us for even thinking such thoughts."

"Why would she do that?" reasoned Brannan. "The horse is her creature and we are her creatures. If Poseidon has managed to subdue this animal, perhaps the Great Mother means for us to ride upon their backs."

Now Boah stood, as if to drive home the importance of his words. "We *must* have the horses." Demonstrating true courage, he had been the first tribesman that afternoon on the beach to accept Poseidon's frightening invitation to mount Arrow. It had only taken Boah a moment to comprehend the power of partnership with the mighty beast. Even his bristling competitiveness with the newcomer and Poseidon's increasing status within the tribe were nothing compared to the lure of the horse.

Elkon waved his walking stick at Poseidon. "You left the village on false pretenses!" he cried irritably. "You cannot be trusted!"

"Be sensible, Elkon," said Brannan, far too old to ride himself, but intrigued by the idea of the horses. "If Poseidon had told us his purpose we would never have given him leave to go."

Poseidon looked around the campfire trying to catch a glimpse of Cleatah, but she was nowhere to be found. It disturbed him that she took no part in so important a debate, and if he was honest with himself he would admit he simply missed her presence.

He rose. "I'm going to bed," he announced evenly. "I mean to sleep well, for I'm leaving at dawn for the Great Plateau. Anyone who wishes to join me should carry with him five days food, and at least one torch. The wolves must be left at home."

All were silent as Poseidon left the campfire's circle of light and disappeared into the moonless dark beyond it. The moment he was gone the voice of the tribe exploded once again into spirited cacophony, a tumultuous song that continued unabated deep into the night.

TWENTY-EIGHT

THE DAWN WAS shrouded in a thick fog from the sea, so that when Poseidon mounted his horse and rode to the edge of the village the men that had assembled to accompany him were ghostlike, their voices muted in the half-light of day. All the previous night he had contemplated the position he should take on this adventure – either as an equal comrade leading his horse on foot, which would strengthen the male bonds, or on horseback with the others walking – the group's unequivocal leader. He had finally, for better or worse, decided to stand as leader. He would ride to assert his position and to control a potentially dangerous exercise.

He therefore walked his horse slowly enough for the group – which he guessed numbered about fifty – to keep up on foot. The men were reserved, perhaps fearful of what lay ahead as they trekked north along the coast and climbed up onto the plateau, the fog only dissolving once the sun reached its noonday zenith. Occasionally a man would come forward, shyly, to speak with Poseidon, perhaps ask a question about the plan, or to study the beast that would – spirits willing – be in the tribe's control in a few day's time.

When the shadows were long and the rocky outcroppings

glowed mellow in the setting sun Poseidon saw the moving cloud of dust on the distant plain that he knew to be the wild herd – moving toward their usual night's resting place. He dismounted and gathered the men around him. They were not at all tired from the journey. Rather, they were thrumming with excitement and anticipation. He'd not yet seen all their faces, and now he addressed each one by name, welcoming and thanking him for joining the hunt. Banda, Uru, Slane, Boah. Then he stopped, startled.

He was staring into Cleatah's golden brown eyes.

He found it suddenly hard to think clearly. He had never expected her to come but she had, and none of the men were opposed. The last thing he wanted to do was put this woman in danger, but to insult her now would be a mistake. He must take his chances.

"I have never seen you hunt before."

"This is not the same," she said evenly. "This is for the horses." And with great seriousness added, "You will be glad I came."

*

Later, when night had overtaken the great plain Poseidon, on foot and still as stone, composed himself as best he could. Arrow was tied to a tree upwind of the herd. He would not ride her in the roundup, he had decided, unsure how she might react in the herd's presence, so soon after her separation from them. He knew he was endangering these men, and the woman so precious to the Terresian expedition. He'd promised them the capture of a herd of wild horses and knowledge of their taming and riding – a skill that he had only recently acquired himself. If he failed he would lose whatever stature he'd already attained.

For many reasons he had decided against using his phaetron in this endeavor, except in the most extreme emergency. It was vital that the tribesmen learn to control the horses using their natural skills alone. The roundup itself was certainly dangerous, but he believed it attainable. He tasted the cooling night air, the merest hint of fog, which would surely roll in some time before dawn. They must move now. The plan would be foiled by the thick fog.

Poseidon lit his torch. And with a magic both grand and primitive the plain was illuminated. What he saw before him was this: holding each torch aloft was one tribesman, more than fifty in all, forming a great circle around the herd. The horses, startled by so unthinkable a phenomenon were paralyzed, their eyes reflecting the blaze of lights. Straight ahead, across the plain from Poseidon, was the thin-necked canyon and its rock ring in which he had cornered Arrow only two weeks before. Though he could not see her at her designated position, he knew that at the mouth of that canyon Cleatah waited for the moment the herded horses would thunder past before throwing the heavy net he had fashioned, across the canyon's neck to imprison them. It was as good a solution as he could conceive, Poseidon thought, to give the woman an important job, but one that kept her largely out of harm's way.

Flaring out to his left was one curved line of torchmen. Six hundred feet behind them lay the eastern coast of the continent – the sea cliff with its rocky shore below. To his right was the other half-circle of light, and the wide plateau stretching out for hundreds of miles behind it.

The animals stamped and snorted nervously in a tight cluster.

With a silent prayer Poseidon signaled the men to close the circle. Stealth and slowness of motion were of utmost importance. No sudden or jerking movements... and complete silence. They must avoid the animals' panic at all costs and move them, in small increments, in the direction of the box canyon by closing in on them.

It was working smoothly, he thought. Just as he had planned it. He had counted on the element of surprise, the horses being encircled by the light – to keep them controlled. One false move would be disastrous. He had learned that his own horse responded to fear by fleeing in the opposite direction from what frightened her. Now the animals were walking, warily but calmly towards the only area of darkness – the mouth of the box canyon.

Then it happened. A man halfway down the circle on the right stumbled, and with a loud involuntary cry let go his torch which flew straight out from him into the circle of horses.

The response was instantaneous – *stampede in the opposite direction*!

The plan collapsed disastrously into chaos, and in moments the horses were racing towards the east – the sea cliffs and the jagged rocks below them – the once careful line of men frantically scrambling to avoid the oncoming herd. Horrible shrieks from the broken line of men told Poseidon the stampede had claimed human victims. Into the jumble of flickering torchlight he aimed his phaetron, but realized that if he activated the narcotizing function, men as well as animals would be disabled by its beam, perhaps causing more casualties. Instead he raced to Arrow and leapt on her back, spurring her towards the cliff edge with a wild prayer that he might somehow reach it first and turn the beasts from their deadly course.

But he was too far away, even on horseback.

The animals were galloping madly for the dark abyss, everyone watching helplessly, Poseidon closing the distance, but not fast enough. A few moments more and the horses would find nothing but air under their hooves. They would scream in terror, fall and die writhing on the razor points of stone below.

Then two torches burst brilliantly to light at the cliff's edge. They were being waved frantically, and a human voice was raised in a wild shriek meant to ward off the stampede. The sudden light and sound frightened the horses. Stopped them dead in their tracks. Now Poseidon could see the torchbearer.

It was Cleatah!

She lunged forcefully behind the confused herd, waving the flaming torches and shouting unintelligible noises. The horses, desperate to be rid of this fire-breathing, shrieking dragon, ran in the opposite direction – away from cliff's edge.

The tribesmen finally comprehended what they were seeing, and moving in pure instinct as one body regrouped to assist the woman. They gathered the herd with their torches, ever closer to the rocky foothills, tighter and tighter into a long single file. At breakneck speed and with a thunderous echo they galloped through the stone neck and into the canyon. All of them. Every horse. At the last the net was flung across the gap and suddenly it was done.

It took some time for the men to realize their success.

From his position Poseidon could hear the whoops and victorious shouts. But there was no time for celebration. He raced to the two fallen men. One was dead, mangled beyond recognition. The other, Boah, lay groaning even in his semi- consciousness. Hiding the phaetron's tiny blinking lights from any curious eyes, Poseidon worked quickly in the dark before the men now approaching reached them. He repositioned the leg with the blessed device and mended it, bone, blood vessels, nerves and sinews.

More than half the men now surrounded their fallen comrades. Boah was lifted gently and carried to the protection of the foothills where a camp was already being set. Others knelt around the body of the dead man – discovered to be Uru – closing his eyes and offering up a ritual blessing. Already two biers were being fashioned to carry each of the fallen back to the village.

A lone figure at the cliff edge drew Poseidon's eye. It was Cleatah, a torch burning at her feet lighting her figure – a strange illusion with the thick bank of fog bearing down behind her like a great wave. Riding slowly towards her Poseidon found himself savoring the sight of this woman, a tightness in his throat and a hardening beneath his tunic announcing unexpected desire.

She turned and smiled at him with quiet triumph. Silently he reached down with one arm sweeping her up behind him on his horse, and she wrapped her slender, muscled arms around his waist. In this way she rode with him back to the firelight of the makeshift camp, as though this place so warm and close – both guarded and guardian – was the right and natural order of things.

Nothing had prepared him for such a woman and nothing, for Poseidon, would ever be the same.

Twenty-Nine

THE SHUTTLECRAFT ARRIVED at Halcyon Beach early for its pickup, as Athens had requested. The sun had not yet risen when he stepped aboard the disk and it soared off soundlessly into the orange sky. The governor needed time to think before the events of this momentous day began, and nothing calmed and straightened his mind as much as a slow fly-over of his beloved colony. The moment they were airborne he looked down, as his favorite sight was Halcyon Beach itself.

Besides the deep green of the mature tree ferns, this neighborhood had been lushly planted with an array of foliage from Gaia – blooming flowers, bushes and every variety of tree. Now he could see a little girl moving toward the water line where emerging to greet her was a strange animal pulling itself along on its belly. Neither showed any fear whatsoever, for this was a "solie."

Soon after the colonists had settled themselves in towns and villages along the coast they had discovered the child-sized creatures that lived half in, half out of the sea. Warm blooded with short, stubby front feet and a single back flipper, their sleek bodies were covered with silky grey fur. Huge brown eyes and slender snouts created an expression of unutterable sweetness. Whiskers and a thick fringe of fur beneath their chins looked for all the world like a beard, and gave them a decidedly comical appearance. Theirs was a keen, almost human intelligence that they communicated through a readily understandable variety of clicking noises. But it was their affinity towards the colonists and an unabashed affection for Marseans both young and old – so strong it seemed the two species had been created one for the other – that made the solies utterly irresistible.

They had become household pets, been given names and allowed freedom to move between the sea and peoples' beachfront homes. They were naturally protective of small children and even assisted in a rudimentary education. You could leave children alone in the company of solies and be sure that no harm would come to them. With their help every colonist had learned to swim, and playing in the warm sea with the creatures had become the colonists' favorite pastime. Realizing their importance to the Marsean experience Athens had commissioned several of his top biologists to study all aspects of the animals' anatomy, physiology, behavior and mental capacity. In short measure solies had become an integral part of life, something the colonists could not imagine doing without.

The pilot skirted the coastline, then headed inland over the cultivated fields, and finally the mining complex came into view. It was eerie, thought Athens, this absence of activity in the mines, in the fields. Even the dearth of traffic in the sky – a time when the space was normally thick with airbusses shuttling colonists to work. It reminded him of the import of this special day.

"Once again to the coast," Athens instructed the pilot, " and out over the sea. I need more time."

"Yes Sir."

There was a vast continent inland, beyond the mining complex and capitol city, but Athens was rarely drawn to explore, or even contemplate it. His interest lay solely in his little part of the planet – his world. The colony.

What an amazing turn it had taken since the discovery of Golde's miraculous microbes. Everything had changed. The same emotions that had overtaken Athens on his first sight of gold had swept through the Terresian colony like a wildfire. The governor's attempts to keep the ore secret had dissolved the moment the mining operation had expanded. Workers in the "lower mine," as it came to be known, were the first to possess small amounts of the precious metal, and soon everyone was clamoring for it.

Artisans demanded supplies of it and began creating the most exquisite works of art – statues, masks, vases, dishes, goblets, eating utensils. Its low melting point, and the softness that made carving and engraving so simple encouraged the production of body ornaments. These were bought by the colonists hungry for the baubles, and paid for in raw gold. A process was developed for plating objects, and soon furniture and even whole walls were covered with it. Another process allowed it to be thinned sufficiently to coat fiber, and clothing was frequently shot through with golden threads.

As the substance began circulating into the hands of virtually every colonist, it became something of a mania. People traded it, hoarded it, and even occasionally stole it. Those who acquired large amounts of it were considered wealthy. Once, Athens had attempted to slow the production and distribution of the ore, and the people had nearly rioted. It was at first believed that people would tire of an obsession so strange to the Terresian mind. Normally they were a sensible people who found more value in the simplest of life's pleasures than in material belongings. But that had all been changed by the seductive compulsion to possess gold.

Athens himself was far from immune. Of course, in his position, access was unlimited. The geologist, Golde, only slowly came to understand the furor he had unleashed, but finally began enjoying his notoriety. Soon his humble and over-serious demeanor changed to self-importance, and his appearance became flamboyant. After all, his was a household name.

Athens's own collection of gold artifacts was staggering. Many had been gifts from his growing cadre of friends and admirers, each one outdoing the other with a more spectacular piece than the next. He procured from the gold artisans – now themselves an elite society – exquisite body ornaments that he lavished on the women who craved his company in ever increasing numbers.

Athens's dilemma had presented itself soon after gold's discovery. The colonists, so involved in the sheer enjoyment of sun-filled days, their homes on the water's edge, and more recently the gold frenzy, had all but forgotten their past lives on Terres. Federation had been told that a second ore was being mined, but Athens had failed to communicate the depth and breadth of the changed circumstances on Mars. He would have to elaborate on the subject before Terres began its long journey back into deep space. Certainly the titanum mining operation was and would always continue unabated, and the first massive shipment of ore would be sent back to the planet before it left the sun's inner orbit.

But the proliferation of gold and the cultural shifts it had engendered were less easy to explain or justify. It had become apparent through frequent communication with his colonists that they jealously guarded their possessions and had no wish to share this particular form of wealth with the home planet. Unlike titanum, it was *unnecessary* for Terresian survival – so went the conventional wisdom. Terres, it was assumed, would never miss having the gold. It might even complicate the tightly structured society. If it was all the same, the colonists would gladly keep it for themselves.

Of late, amidst the grumblings, were sentiments expressing a profound difference in values and thinking between the two worlds, and the idea of secession had actually been proposed. The "Marseans," as they now called themselves, were entirely independent of Terres, and there were few – if any – who wished to return to the old life.

Athens believed himself unqualified to come to any decisions regarding this matter on his own. He had therefore called for a referendum on the issues, each colonist allowed one vote. It was to learn of the outcome of this election that Athens was now bound.

"Sir," said the pilot, interrupting the governor's reverie. "I think you should see this."

Athens looked down at the capitol city's central plaza where the shuttlecraft was making its careful vertical descent not far from the Governor's Palace. The square and the boulevards leading away from it were mobbed with colonists – from the look of it, most of the planet's human population. Never before had Athens seen so many Marsean citizens gathered in one place. As the craft descended he could see that they were cheering his arrival.

When the shuttle door opened Athens emerged into the warmest and most enthusiastic welcome he had ever known. Many people were shouting his name, others chanting, "Keep the gold!" Still others called for an independent Mars. A little girl stepped forward and presented Athens with a bouquet of flowers fashioned of pure gold. He found himself smiling, genuinely enraptured by the encircling affection, calling out to the people, taking up their chants, laughing delightedly, waving and embracing the babies thrust into his arms. He was met at the top of the steps by Persus, herself glowing with excitement. Feeling warm and expansive, Athens pulled her into a fond hug, sending the crowd into even louder cheers. Finally he turned and signaled the assembled with a double-fisted salute. Then to roars of thunderous approval, he turned and disappeared inside the government house.

Even here were throngs of well-wishers, though most of them were Federation employees, mine officials and government representatives. Golde, in an outrageous suit of his namesake cloth, strutted around with his new bedmate, lovely and young, from whose throat, wrists and ears dripped exquisitely crafted gold ornaments.

Vice Governor Praxis took Athens's arm and steered him into a first floor meeting room where the two of them were finally alone. The sudden silence and calm within was more disconcerting to Athens now than the chaos without had been. The vice governor wasted no time with pleasantries.

"The votes have been counted and the results are in, " he said, attempting to elicit an eager response from the governor. But Athens had never cared for Praxis and turned away, deliberately peering out the window at the crowds to deny the vice governor any small pleasure from his reactions.

"On the first proposition...? asked Athens.

"Overwhelmingly to restrict the exportation of gold to Terres."

"On the second?"

"The people have voted unanimously for a gold currency."

"And the secession issue?"

"Not so clear-cut a result. Fifty-nine percent voted to secede."

"That many?" said Athens.

"Yes Sir."

"How did *you* vote, Praxis?" asked Athens, turning suddenly to confront the vice governor.

"I...I..." he stuttered. "I believe, as the majority of Marseans do, that we have no responsibility to give our gold to Terres, provided we maintain our commitment to supply them with titanum."

"And do you wish independence from the home planet?" Athens persisted.

Praxis swallowed so hard Athens was sure he'd heard a *thunk* in the man's throat. He tried hard not to smile as the squirming vice governor carefully formulated his answer.

"Well, I...you know I've always considered myself a loyal Federation man and a Terresian patriot..."

"And you voted for secession," interjected Athens.

Praxis's face flushed so instantly and deeply red that Athens was forced to bite his lip to stifle his laugh. Humiliated, the vice governor blurted out, "Yes Sir, I did. And how did *you* vote?" he demanded, hoping to turn the tables.

"Me? Why, it was a closed ballot, Praxis. I never discuss my voting record with anyone. Now, is there anything else I should know before I address the people?"

Praxis began to fume so alarmingly that Athens wondered if the vice governor would explode. He knew such treatment was dangerous – that a person so close to the high command could turn on a moment's notice, and at the worst possible time. But it pleased him to irritate the stuffy little man who looked so ridiculous in his gold ear clips and ornately carved neckband. And of course, Athens enjoyed the danger.

Praxis finally composed himself enough to rattle off a few more voting statistics, but Athens wasn't listening. He was gazing with warmest affection out his window at the plaza filled with colonists – the New Marseans – and looking towards their glorious and independent future.

THIRTY

POSEIDON SAT CROSS-LEGGED on his bed. He'd closed the hut door-flap and spoke into his device in the lowest possible tones. "It has been three moons and three days since the horses came to the Shore Village. Confused and frightened as the people were they adapted to the animals with grace and good humor. Several of the men – particularly Boah – have forged a rare partnership with them. I'm grateful the men forgave the weakness of their inexperienced teacher. In fact, delivery of the horses to the tribe has raised my stature to such a degree that I'm finally permitted all the privileges and respect of a…"

Poseidon's voice trailed off. Then, listening as he spoke the words he repeated, "It has been three moons…"A moment ago the phrase had come to mind naturally as he'd spoken. Not months, but *moons*.

When had that happened? When had his immersion into the culture reached its maximum? How had what was once alien become as natural as his heartbeat? Bloody stars, he was thinking in their language!

A long sigh of astonishment escaped him and he laid himself down to digest the idea. He would no longer record his reports.

No. He would commit pertinent data to memory. Otherwise he would just…he would live.

It had it been some time since he'd contacted the *Atlantos*. He told himself daily that his presence on the ship was not crucial. Most of the crew were engaged in their own work in far flung corners of the planet. Zalen missed his leadership. He knew that. The captain was not fooled by the quasi-scientechnic rationalizations he was offered. But he would never beg. Zalen was a stern Terresian. Nor would he ever, in his wildest dreams, imagine that the man he'd known since the Marsean mission been absorbed so seamlessly into a primitive Gaian tribe, or that the tribe completely inhabited Poseidon's thoughts.

No, let me revise that. Cleatah *inhabits my head.*

Now as a respected tribesman he was free to seek her company, even bed her. With that image before him Poseidon felt a sudden tightening in his groin. *Had a woman ever affected him this way?* Certainly Cleatah was beautiful. Brilliant. A master of the natural world. She was not shy about seeking his companionship and became his teacher as effortlessly as she accepted his teachings. He liked her. Felt *himself* in her presence. But that was no cause for the hard knot between his legs when he thought of her.

Maybe it was anticipation. Yesterday she'd invited him to go with her the next time she traveled to the Great Plateau for medicine gathering. She would only know the proper day when it came, she told him. It was childish, he knew, but he worried that she would forget the invitation and go without him. He would have to be patient. One day soon she would come before dawn and call to him through his door flap. They would walk the path up to the plateau by moonlight. She would lead the way. He would watch her strong back and long tawny legs, the soft skins hanging at her waist, imagine the smooth muscled haunches beneath…

Another long sigh. "Cleatah," he whispered.

THIRTY-ONE

THE BLOW TO the chest came as Poseidon turned and stood from the central fire. The surprise of it, as much as its power, caused him to stumble sideways and crash heavily to the ground. He looked up and saw, to his great astonishment, Boah towering above him – weaponless – but glowering with malevolent intent.

"Boah?" Poseidon said, scrambling to his feet.

"You will fight me now."

"I will not. I have no reason to fight you."

"You have taken my woman."

The others around the fire, all men who had come to talk about the coming hunt, formed a circle around the two of them. From the corner of his eye Poseidon could see women and elders streaming from their huts or moving from their home fires to the uproar in the village center.

Boah swung a fist at Poseidon who ducked to avoid it connecting with his head.

"Cleatah is not your woman," Poseidon said.

Both men and women around them began to vocalize their opinions. "She is not your woman, Boah." "Poseidon has stolen her from you." "Fight! Fight for Cleatah!"

It occurred to Poseidon then that this was an ancient custom of the Shore People: two males, one desired female. A fight would decide who mated with her.

As Boah lowered his head to ram his rival, Poseidon glimpsed Cleatah at the edge of the circle, firelight and shadow dappling her face. Poseidon crashed down onto his back with Boah straddling him, swinging with two fists at his head. Poseidon shielded himself with upraised forearms, reluctant to fight back, custom or no custom.

"Boah, stop!" Cleatah's voice rang out clear and strong. "Stop now!"

All eyes swiveled to find her, bold but impassive, balled fists at her hips.

"Let them fight!" cried Brannan. "That is the way it is done. A man chooses a woman. If two men choose one woman, they fight. He who wins the fight wins the woman."

Boah's flying fists had ceased as he listened to the elder's recitation of tribal ritual.

Now Cleatah strode to Brannan and faced him. "I am a woman and two men wish to mate with me. But I will not mate with the winner of the fight."

There was great confusion and complete silence until Elkon asked, "Then who will you mate with?"

"The man I choose. I choose Poseidon."

"A woman cannot choose!" Heydra insisted with a derisive shake of his head.

More cries of "A woman cannot choose!" rang out around the central fire.

"*This* woman chooses," Cleatah said.

Poseidon pushed a perplexed Boah off him and stood tall, unable to take his eyes from this female, brave as the fiercest hunter among them.

"And I choose Cleatah," Poseidon announced. "There will be

no fighting for her. Not now. Not ever." He looked around and saw groups of women whispering among themselves, considering the import of such outrageous sentiments.

"She chooses Poseidon!" called one bold tribeswoman. "Let Boah find another!"

Poseidon went to Cleatah then. They stood shoulder-to-shoulder, displaying less defiance than fortitude. Then joining hands they turned and sliced silently and unmolested through the crowd, a new sexual tradition burgeoning in their wake.

THIRTY-TWO

THE SPRING PLATEAU was teeming with life. Grasses were still green and un-trampled, trees bursting with new foliage, and the floor of the plain a carpet of varicolored wildflowers. They'd ridden out on Arrow just after dawn, Cleatah seated behind Poseidon, her arms linked around his waist. Sheeva, her protector, now quite accustomed to the man and the horse, trotted behind them. Sometimes Poseidon walked alongside, giving Cleatah clear sight of the world from the higher vantage point. Other times they both walked, allowing Arrow to run free, graze on the sweet grasses, or just amble companionably beside them.

More times than he could count Poseidon shouted aloud at the sight of some overwhelming magnificence, swooned at a heart-rending fragrance. He savored the lusciousness of a berry turgid with juice, delighted at the soft velvet of a flower's petal trailed along his cheek. It was not that he had never experienced such marvels, but that in this woman's company they were amplified, almost miraculous. They laughed easily together, finding humor in the same things – the antics of the furry little creatures she called lorro, the springing, back-arching dance of a young antelere.

Cleatah elucidated properties of the various medicine plants as she gathered them. She explained to him simply but beautifully the cycle of life, growth, death and rebirth of plants. Together they examined a flower inside and out, marveling at the tiny structures so perfectly formed for function as well as beauty. All of these were to Poseidon lessons memorized as a schoolboy, but now they were new again, and entirely wondrous.

He was constantly amazed at the extent of Cleatah's knowledge and natural wisdom. She had created a language all her own, though there'd been no one before now with whom to share it. Suddenly the words – descriptions of plants, their usage, their anatomy and function, effects of the weather and the seasons on them, all came forth like a great gushing river. It was as if she'd known that Poseidon would comprehend, and that her intellect would not frighten him. Her joy and excitement were infectious. She had somehow found in this stranger her equal, someone who could share all that had been unspoken and unrevealed until this day.

When the sun was at its zenith, the air shimmering with heat, Cleatah led him from the open plain to the shade of the forest. The cool on his skin felt lovely, and as he watched her stoop to carefully gather the tightly furled fronds of a fern he was struck by the odd combination of her strength and softness. There was a discernible definition to her muscles he did not see in Terresian women. Yet there was a rich female quality as well, one that made him long to touch her – any and all of her – skin, hair, face, breasts... something he had not yet dared to do. Their most physical contact had been the feel of her body pressing against his back as they rode, and that alone had set his heart racing.

Now all four of them were on foot – man, woman, horse and wolf. He glanced at Sheeva. There was hardly a moment when the wolf's eyes strayed from Cleatah. What trust the animal had accrued for Poseidon could easily be shaken by the lightest overstepping of an invisible boundary the animal had thrown up around her. By far the wolf's most astonishing olfasense was smell. Poseidon had learned his own bodily odors were changed more dramatically by emotion than by physical exertion and was keenly, if ironically, aware that it would be the beast who recognized his fears and his desires before the woman.

"You are quiet," Cleatah said. "What is in here?" She touched her temple but did not meet his eye. She'd learned that he would speak more freely if their gazes were not locked.

"I am curious about Sheeva," he finally said. Poseidon could see Cleatah's lips curl upward into a bow, as though she relished the thought of telling this particular story. She hesitated, as good storytellers do, deciding how and when to begin the tale.

"When I found her she had been badly injured, a bone broken in her foreleg. Her pack was nowhere to be found, but a buron herd grazed nearby and I thought the wolves had gone for a kill, and this unlucky one had been trampled. It did not explain her family abandoning her, but I would never know the reason for that. She was weak and in terrible pain when I found her, barely able to growl at my approach. She was young, though not a pup. Perhaps it had been her first hunt. When a young man fails in his first hunt it is shameful. If he is injured it is a disgrace. Perhaps it was so of the wolf.

"I thought I would help her somehow," Cleatah went on, "but I admit I wished her injuries had been to the hindquarters, so my head would not be within snapping distance of her jaws." Her eyes smiled, remembering. "I believed she would not hurt me, but I moved slowly. You know, Poseidon. Like it was at the first with Arrow."

He nodded and she went on.

"She whined when I touched her foot, and looked up from under her heavy lids. Then she licked my hand. I set the bone and wrapped it with vines. I brought her water and a small kill to eat. She was very quiet, very still, but I slept next to her all that night and stayed by her side the next day and night. But we could stay no longer. Her nose twitched so violently I knew something to fear was nearby – perhaps a lion. I did not help her to her feet. I knew that if she could not rise of her own accord, if she could not walk beside me, my healing had been for nothing. But she did rise, not without a pained cry, but once on her feet she found her footing quickly, though careful on the broken leg. The splint I'd made held the bone tight and straight, and we arrived at the edge of the plateau before nightfall.

"The descent for the wolf was not possible, but I wished her to shelter in the safety of the village that night. I ran down and found Boah, knowing he would not be afraid. Once night fell we carried the wolf down and hid her in my hut. She knew, somehow, knew to be perfectly still, perfectly quiet. I brought her food every day. Her leg healed well. She came to love me and I her. I gave her the name Sheeva."

The wolf's ears pricked up at the sound of her name, and she looked to Cleatah, as if for orders. Receiving none she continued her easy trot.

"How did you show her to the tribe?" Poseidon asked. "Were they not frightened?"

"One night when all were gathered at the central fire Boah went to them and said, 'Cleatah is coming now, and she brings with her a friend. No need to fear.' I came slowly from the shadows into the light of the fire with the wolf at my side. I heard Boah saying, 'You, stay down.' 'No shouting.' 'If you move, move slowly.' They heeded him and Sheeva – may the Great Mother bless her – stayed quiet and calm at my side. She didn't curl her lip or bare a fang. She sat at the edge of the fire pit. But when she grunted and lay down with her head resting on her paws there were gasps, and laughter all around. I allowed the people – one by one – to touch the wolf, telling them to gently speak her name as they did. The children wished most of all to lay their hands on this magical creature – once their enemy to be feared, now at rest, warming her fur at their fire.

"All trusted Sheeva and loved her, but it was to me that she stayed closest. She protected me as I had once protected her. She hunted small creatures and brought them home to share at our fire. So when one day she disappeared, as though she had never existed, the tribe mourned her. But no one more than me. Once again I was alone. But where before I had never known loneliness, now I did. How I had come to depend on my companion!

"Nearly a moon passed and one morning she returned, looking weary and bloated. With one look I knew her to be pregnant. In my hut that very night she birthed nine wolves so tiny they could fit in the palm of my hand. Every family wanted one, though the hunting men won out, for they argued rightly that wolves taught to hunt would bring food for the whole tribe.

"Each year Sheeva leaves us and returns with a brood in her belly. Her mate is nowhere to be seen, I think wary of the village and the tribe. After all, how can Sheeva tell him not to fear? So this is how she came to me, to the tribe, and how her children became the children of the Shore People."

Cleatah went silent, perhaps aware that she had never spoken so long or so clearly since Poseidon's coming. She stood and turned, carefully placing the ferns in her gathering bag. "Will you come with me to my bathing place?"

I would go with you anywhere, to the end of the Erthe, he thought but did not say. Instead he stood and trying to keep his composure, followed her deeper into the forest.

THIRTY-THREE

"IT'S TIME YOU bathed," she announced.

"Ha! I've bathed recently."

Cleatah could see that her remark had caused no insult but had been taken lightly, as she had meant it. "Not as you will today." Cleatah enjoyed provoking this man, for his responses were so unusual – not at all like the men of her tribe – the odd complexity of his feelings, so many of them transparent. The way he combined his words, the inflections in his voice.

She led him through paths soft with moss and hung with thick vines and brilliantly hued, cuplike flowers twining in profusion around gnarled tree trunks. Soon they could hear the rush and tumble of water and in the next moment emerged at the base of a sun-dappled waterfall. From the expression on Poseidon's face Cleatah knew it was as lovely a sight as he had ever seen. She stooped at the stream's edge and began rooting around in her bag.

"Take off your clothes and start across," she called. "It is cold. The water comes from the high mountains. Go on. I will meet you." From the corner of her eye she regarded Poseidon's naked body as he stepped into the stream. He was tall, but in the time since he had joined the tribe his muscles had thickened and firmed, especially his thighs and haunches as a result of riding the horses. Yes, he was a powerful looking man, and handsome to her eye.

She slipped off her skins and waded into the waist-deep water just as Poseidon emerged onto the far bank. He turned and watched her come across. He was staring at her naked body, her nipples hard from the icy cold. When they both stood on the opposite shore she led him downstream and away from the crashing falls to a tranquil, rock-lined pool near the river's edge. Steam rose in delicate tendrils from its dark green surface.

She wasted no time lowering herself into the water, unselfconsciously gasping and moaning in delight. Poseidon quickly clamored in after her, and she wondered if his haste was more to cover his nakedness than to experience the pleasure of the waters.

"Ah, ahhh…" Poseidon's eyes closed as he plunged in up to his neck. "Hot water," he said finally. "There is nothing in the world like it."

"You had springs like this near your village?" she asked.

"Yes, and I have missed them." He opened his eyes and looked at her. "Thank you. This is a joy."

After a while of soaking in silence she said, "Stand out of the water. There's a ledge here."

He obeyed her and found himself waist deep, steam rising off his arms and torso. When she turned to face him she had in her hands the soap root that she could knead into lather. She looked directly into Poseidon's eyes and held his gaze as she reached out and placed her soapy hands on his chest. She knew the expression she saw on his face was desire, and it did not displease her. She began to massage the lather into every part of his body above the water – arms, chest, back, neck. He stood obediently as she directed him to raise his arms so she could soap his armpits. She ignored the trembling she felt beneath her hands, and tried to ignore the thought of his male parts under the water.

"Rinse yourself," she commanded him finally, "and dunk your

head." This he did wordlessly, but as he emerged from the pool, water streaming from his head and beard and powerful body, it was Cleatah who was suddenly trembling. She wanted this man. Wanted to feel him moving inside her... But that would have to wait.

"Now sit on the ledge, Poseidon. I am going to wash your hair."

"Wash my hair?" He looked at her and laughed aloud.

"Should I not?" she asked.

"No, no. I want you to. Then will I wash yours?" he asked with a playful smile.

"Just sit down."

He obeyed her, unable to suppress his smile. She lathered the thick mane, scrubbing his scalp with her strong fingers, enjoying the feel of his head in her hands. His head, she thought, was as intimate a body part as what lay between his thighs – the sinewy tendons at the back of his neck, the gristle of his ears, the bony temples.

"Dunk and rinse," she instructed now.

When he emerged this time he saw she held a flat stone, one side sharpened to a fine edge.

"Will you let me shave your face?"

"You bathed me at your will, and washed my hair. Why do you ask permission to shave me?"

She did not answer for a long moment, forming her words only as the thoughts came to her. "You may wish to continue hiding your face from me. That is your right." She did not add, *But I wish to see it as I did in my mushroom vision.*

"Shave me," he said, his voice cracking with emotion, his eyes fastened on hers. "I do wish you to know me."

Cleatah turned away then, pretending to make a lather with her soap root, but in truth she was not prepared for Poseidon to see the tears of some unnamable emotion that were threatening to spill from her eyes.

Thirty-Four

FOLLOWING CLEATAH INTO the meadow in mid-afternoon, Poseidon reached up and touched his face. It had been nearly an Erthan year since he'd been clean-shaven, and it felt wonderful. Even more gratifying was Cleatah's expression when she'd finished shaving him and saw his hairless face. She had muttered "As I thought..." but had refused to explain herself. She'd simply washed her own hair and body, an act that Poseidon, watching her, found almost as erotic as her washing of his. But afterwards, in anointing them both with a fragrant oil – chest, forehead and temple – he sensed the entire episode was somehow a rite of purification.

In the height of the now scorching afternoon Cleatah led him through a field inhabited by a herd of grazing buron and a multitude of large black buzzing flies. She moved carefully but confidently, avoiding the several bulls that grazed with the females. Occasionally she stooped for a moment to extract a plant from what appeared to be piles of buron dung. He thought the actions strange after such vigorous bathing, but did not question Cleatah who seemed serious and intent in her gathering. When they'd left the field, however, and she was carefully stowing her recent finds in her gathering bag, Poseidon saw that she was smiling broadly, indeed looking extremely pleased with herself.

"What have you found?" he asked.

"The reason we have come out together today." She replied mysteriously.

"Show me."

"First let us go to a more comfortable place."

She took him to a shady grove of trees, a pleasant respite from the heat, and sat down facing him. The moss was very thick but dry and made for a luxuriant cushion. From her pouch Cleatah extracted her most recent find and laid it out on a bed of leaves in front of them. There were sixteen slender–stemmed mushrooms. She snipped off with her fingernails the parts that had been sunk in the dung. Then she separated them into two piles, placing each pile on a large leaf, and handed one to Poseidon. The other she held up in front of her heart. She looked directly into his eyes.

"You and I, Poseidon, we both keep secrets. You hold yours in your head. Now you hold mine… in your hands."

He looked down at the mushrooms, unable to utter an intelligible thought.

"You do not know of these mushrooms?" she asked.

"I do not."

She was struggling for words. "They are filled with powerful spirits. The most sacred plants I have ever gathered. When I eat them I see…wonders."

Certain naturally occurring life-forms on Terres were said to produce hallucinatory episodes, he knew, but for many generations the ultra-practical Terresians had shunned such experiences.

"What sort of wonders?"

"Visions…" was all she could say before tears began to form in her eyes. She seemed to be attempting to re-conjure and describe the indescribable. "I travel…to other places, though I remain here. I….see things. Everything is beautiful. Everything is…" She made a chopping gesture with her hand and her face screwed up as she groped for the word. "...sharp. I cannot explain, Poseidon. We will eat them, together, here, now. I have eaten them many times before, but never with another person. I want you to share the wonders with me, to come with me to Ka."

With that she took up the first mushroom between her thumb and forefinger. "Great Mother, bless me, bless this man, bless our journey." She placed the mushroom in her mouth and began to chew.

Without hesitation Poseidon did the same. The taste was bitter, even poisonous, he thought. But he trusted Cleatah, trusted her in a way he had trusted no other person in his life, and found that there was nothing he wished for more than to share with her a journey of wonder.

Together, one by one, they ate the rest.

*

Paralysis suffused his limbs as his mind reeled in color and light. Then in a shattering explosion of clarity Poseidon understood the sacred nature of this world. Everything was alive! *Not simply the myriad creatures and profundity of vegetation, but each and every element of the planet itself was imbued with vital, moving spirit. The mountains, rocks, sand, water, wind –* Erthe lived! *The edges of every object in his sight appeared sharp and almost painfully defined, but paradoxically, all were connected...intersected. There were no boundaries. Did the molecules of his skin not mingle with those of the oxygen surrounding them? What constituted ground, and where did the sky actually begin?*

For the first time he could feel *the spirit that animated the orange and black insect fluttering by, and questioned how it could fly. Surely muscles and aero-mechanics alone could not explain it. What mind of what creator could conceive of such a miracle? Or was it something other than mind? He stared hard at his own hand, perceived what*

169

he saw but was suddenly overwhelmed by its significance...or was it insignificance?

Into his frame of vision another hand moved to grasp his own. Smooth and slender where his was thick and work-roughened. Fingers intertwined fingers and exquisite sensations moved up his arm in tiny, pulsating waves that threatened to overwhelm him. Cleatah. The woman of Erthe who was herself made of the planet's stuff — its water, minerals, air, spirit, knowledge. This woman who cared for him, had bathed him, shaved his face to see him more clearly, trusted him with her mushroom spirits. This lovely creature whose hand now entwined his own. Was she not the greatest mystery of all?

He had refrained from turning his eyes on her face. He knew it from memory already, knew each curve, the angle of the cheekbones, the tilt of the eyes, every freckle, the fall of tawny hair that framed it. But he somehow feared looking into that face now. Feared its over-whelming beauty and its power to unhinge what was left of his precise Terresian sensibilities. Who was he now? What had he become? How could this have happened?

Her hand in his lay still and undemanding. She understood him, a man whose education and technos, whose very evolution surpassed hers by eons. A year ago he would have thought it impossible. What would happen to him if he coupled with this woman, joined his spirit with hers?

What would happen to him if he did not?

Then Cleatah slowly laid her head against Poseidon's chest, gaz-ing up into his eyes and all at once one of his myriad questions was answered. As he slowly gathered her to him and bent to kiss her mouth the movement itself seemed a destiny fulfilled. Her supple arms pull-ing him closer still, seemed to be welcoming him home. But the aston-ishing pleasure of the kiss itself took consciousness and hurled it from his mind to his senses in the space of a breath. Suddenly every nerve was inflamed — absorbing her perfect fragrance, the pleasing colors of her skin, hair, the luminescence of her eyes and unbearable softness of her skin, the ripe fruit of her mouth. He marveled at the animal way she moved in his arms, at the urgent sighs as she devoured him with her lips.

Their thin summer pelts fell away and they were naked, pressed tight along the length of their bodies. Limbs bent at angles to pull closer still. Kisses deepened. Cleatah's new-washed hair fell soft about his neck, his shoulders. His hands began searching the curves and soft mounds of her, long flanks, taut buds, moist clefts. She moaned and opened her thighs, warm and trembling, to receive him. Governed by impossible restraint he entered her slowly, gradually piercing her untouched center, liquid and sweet and tight around him. Her low moans he heard from a distance, but his own rough growls reverberated loud inside his head. Insistent fingers on his back and buttocks pulled him further inside. 'Deeper,' he heard her whisper, 'deeper, oh please...'" and the once-languid thrusts found the rhythm of a slow gallop. Then time vanished. Bodies melted boundary-less one into the other, pulsing with fierce spikes of pleasure. Spikes quickened, urgent sweetness surging, massing like a great wave cresting, higher, higher, threatening to break.

And then it did.

They came, exploding with shocked cries of pure and joyous sensation. In a vision of perfect clarity he saw the lush bodies of the woman and the Erthe as one, and knew that spirit, that single infusing spirit would now and ever after be necessary to sustain his life. And as long as she lived he would never be lonely again.

*

Once night had fallen Arrow slept on her feet near the tree where, on a soft cushion of moss, Poseidon and Cleatah had laid down side by side. Sheeva rested beside them. Cleatah's hands explored Poseidon's face, her gentle touch causing him tiny jolts of pleasure under her fingertips. He was aware that the world as he knew it before the mushroom was coming back to him: the colors beautiful, but no longer screaming their various hues. The definition and perspective of objects clear, but not abnormally sharp and ultra-dimensional. Sensations exquisite, but not overwhelming. Gently he took her hands in his and kissed them, then pulled himself up so he was resting on an elbow above her.

Somewhere in the long, miraculous stretch of the day he had come to realize that this woman would be his. But now he must reveal his secret – what he feared might turn her against him. How could she forgive him for so long and staggering a deception? Cleatah was gazing at him with wondering eyes.

"My secret..." he finally blurted, but then could not go on.

"You wish to share it with me now?"

Poseidon sat up and Cleatah, understanding the importance of the moment, sat up too. It took him a long while to speak again.

"Cleatah, I am not what I seem. I am not who you think I am, who I told you and your people I was... I do not come from an inland tribe. My people were not murdered in an attack on our village."

Poseidon could see that Cleatah was following his words, but those words were leading only to confusion. He was explaining who he was not. Now he must explain who, in fact, he was. She remained silent, choosing not to question him or urge him on but waited patiently, never taking her eyes from his face.

"You have never gone farther afield from your village than this?" he asked, and she nodded affirmatively. "But you know there is more beyond this?"

"Yes, I can see the mountains, and I have been told there is land beyond the mountains, and shores stretching very far north and south of our village. Also, the elders say the sea goes on for a long way beyond what we can see from even the highest plateau."

"They are correct. The sea is perhaps larger than any of you have imagined."

"Do you come from...beyond the sea?" she asked slowly, hardly understanding her own question.

"No, nor do I come from a village on the shore to the north or south of you."

"Then where?" Cleatah's confusion was growing into alarm, and Poseidon felt no closer to an explanation than he had when he'd started. He looked into the sky and saw that the moon had risen. It was huge and bright, and its features were clearly defined.

"How far do the elders say the moon is from the village?" he asked.

"They do not know, but think at least as far as the mountains, maybe more."

"And the sun?"

"Perhaps closer, for it gives off so much more heat and light than the moon."

"And how far are those?" He pointed to the stars, increasing by the minute in the blackness of the sky.

Cleatah smiled and shook her head helplessly. He knew she would be thinking that he was becoming harder and harder to understand. "The lights that move across the sky at night..." she said, "we do not know. They are just beautiful lights."

This woman who had but a short time ago possessed the knowledge of a great botanical scholar now seemed little more than a baffled child. This was far more difficult than Poseidon had ever imagined.

"Do you trust me, Cleatah?"

"Yes."

"If I tell you things, even if they are hard to imagine, will you try to take them as the truth?"

"I will. And I do trust you, my love." Impulsively she reached out and caressed his face with her hand, reminding them both of the extraordinary day they had shared, their intimate journey and – suddenly infusing him with the confidence to go on – the promise that she would hear him and somehow understand.

"Erthe," he began, "though you cannot see it, and therefore cannot know it, is enormous. And the land is not flat, but so large that it curves. In fact Erthe is shaped like this." With his ten fingers splayed and curved and joined at the tips, he formed a sphere.

"When I am at the highest point on the plateau," she interjected, "I can see a curve on the ocean."

"Yes, Erthe is round, like a davok seed. There are great areas of land, and even greater areas of water.

"How large is Erthe?" she asked.

"If you could walk all the way around it – if you could walk across the water – it would take you more than fifty moons."

Cleatah's mouth fell open slightly. Then she composed herself. "I am listening," she said.

"The moon is also round, the same shape as Erthe, and it is also much farther away from the village than the mountains are. It is, perhaps, as many times away from the mountains as there are buron on the entire plateau." He could see Cleatah silently calculating so extraordinary a distance, but he knew if he did not continue he would lose his confidence. "The sun, also round, is… is even farther away than the moon."

"Are you certain?" she asked, perplexed. "How can it be farther but give off so much more light and heat than the moon?"

"Because," Poseidon went on, "it is so much larger than the moon."

"I understand this," said Cleatah slowly. "The mountains appear small from a far distance, but become large as you approach them. Still, Poseidon, I do not understand where you are from, and why you talk about the moon and sun and lights in the sky to explain it."

"I know this is difficult, Cleatah. I'm afraid…it is going to become even more difficult. Where I come from, we call the lights in the sky 'stars.'"

"Stars," she repeated, gazing heavenward. "I know you can see many stars, but there are far more than can even be seen on the clearest night. These stars, small as they appear…"

"…are actually round and large, because they are so far away?" she finished for him.

"Yes, yes!" He was momentarily relieved at Cleatah's ability to comprehend such concepts, but descended immediately into desperation, knowing that his next statement would, despite her intelligence, prove completely unbelievable. Unable to go on in so teacherly a fashion, he gathered the woman into his arms and held her tightly.

"Poseidon," she said impatiently. She pushed him to arm's length and stared into his face. "You came into our village a clumsy stranger and…invented yourself a respected man. You are brave, you are kind, you are gentle. You have shared my deepest secret, accepted the visions fearlessly, joined your body and spirit with mine. I love you, Poseidon. From this day on you are my love. I want no other man, and expect that you will want no other woman. What distance your village is from mine, or how large it is, means nothing. You will still be mine."

"Do you promise me that, Cleatah?" he said. Promise that no matter what I say or do in the next moments, you will not run from me?"

"Run from you?"

"In fear. I may shock you, show you things to rival the mushroom's visions, but please, be unafraid. I will never, ever harm you."

"Tell me. Show me. Now."

Poseidon stood and presented his upturned palm to Cleatah. With his other hand he activated his wrist device. He was relieved to see that she smiled at the tiny, blinking lights of many colors under his skin – like something out of her visions.

"What is this thing?" she asked. "This thing that is inside your body?"

"It is called a 'phaetron.'"

"Fay-tron," she repeated.

"I will tell you where I'm from. It is farther away than you can imagine, but in fact, in every important way I am a man like all the men of your tribe. The only thing that makes me different is that I possess the phaetron and its secrets."

"In the same way my possessing the mushroom and its secrets make me different from anyone in my tribe?"

"Yes!" Poseidon prayed that Cleatah's experience with the mushroom would somehow make this easier. "I'm going to show you what the phaetron – my mushroom – can do. May I put Sheeva to sleep for a little while, so she isn't frightened?"

When Cleatah nodded her assent, he leveled the narcotizing function on the wolf and she fell into a deep and instant slumber. Despite the warning, when Sheeva fell unconscious Cleatah gasped and reached for her. She laid her head on the wolf's chest to assure herself the animal was breathing. She looked up at Poseidon, astonished.

But he could hesitate no longer. He activated the light source and instantly the area under the tree burst into mid-day brightness. Now Cleatah flung herself back against the trunk. A clenched fist covered her mouth and her eyes were large, darting in every direction.

Placing a gentle arm around her he said, "Let me show you something."

"You have *already* shown me something, my love."

"Come here," he said insistently and drew her back down to the ground. He cleared away a large patch of moss to expose the soil beneath it, then picked up a handful of different sized stones.

He laid the largest one – a smooth, light colored rock – in the center of the cleared patch. Around this he drew nine concentric circles, and on each of the circular lines he placed a pebble.

"I want you to imagine that this white stone is the sun. We call it Helios."

Cleatah was still trembling, but she nodded nevertheless.

"Nine worlds spin around it. This one, third from the sun, is Erthe." Poseidon took the third pebble and moved it in the dirt in a circle around the white rock. Cleatah looked confused.

"Does Erthe... do all the worlds move about in the dirt? Are they not in the sky?"

"All right. Move back," he instructed her. "Don't be afraid." Poseidon activated another of the phaetron's functions and directed it at the stones on the ground. At once they began to levitate, and with another function punched in the pebbles began to rotate in proper planetary orbits around the white rock.

Poseidon turned to find Cleatah goggle-eyed with wonder, all her fear having vanished with the miracle before her. Heartened, he picked up the tiniest pebble he could find and dropped it next to the stone representing Erthe. Instantly the little pebble fell into orbit around it.

"That is the moon," he said, "which flies around Erthe in this circle we call an 'orbit.' All of these worlds spin in an orbit."

"Orbit." Cleatah moved close as she could without disturbing the outermost stone's circuit. "What are the others called?" she demanded.

"Hermes," he said pointing to the closest stone to the sun. "Then there is Aphrodite, Erthe, Mars, Zeus, Kronos, Ouranos, Radon, Pluton."

Cleatah studied the moving configuration for a long moment, then looked up at Poseidon. "And which of these worlds are you from, my love?"

"Cleatah, you astonish me!" he cried, the worst of his fears assuaged. Suddenly he felt himself bursting with an emotion unknown to Terresians but must, he realized, be passionate love for this woman.

"I am from none of these worlds," he said, indicating the nine planets, and knelt to find one last stone. 'I am from this world. We call it 'Terres.'" He dropped the final pebble into the space between Mars and Zeus. Immediately it began whirling around the 'sun' stone, and then hurled itself far out into its elliptical orbit. So far did it travel that it moved beyond the circle of light the phaetron had created under the tree, and did not immediately come back.

"Where did it go?" she exclaimed.

"Far away. It will take a long time to complete its orbit."

"Has it gone as far away as the stars?"

"Almost as far."

Her face creased into a mask of puzzlement. 'How...how did you get here... from there?"

Poseidon laughed aloud at the thought of so ungainly an explanation and pulled Cleatah into a warm embrace. "That, my love," he said, relief flooding him, "is a story for another day, many days. For a lifetime."

THIRTY-FIVE

"STAND IN THE light, Nonae," Athens instructed the red-headed woman. As she moved to the window of the artisan's studio to allow the sun to shine down on the headdress she was modeling, it occurred to the governor that the piece – hundreds of thin gold braids hanging down from a curved diadem like a long wig – would have looked better on Leanya's black, silken hair. Still, the headdress was wonderful on Nonae, the most mature of the women Athens was currently seeing. Her slender ivory limbs were an elegant compliment to the draped and slitted gowns the colonial women had lately taken to wearing. The simply designed garments showed off to the finest effect the golden body ornaments that they all wore in great profusion.

"Would you like the headdress?" Athens asked Nonae, giving the artisan who had created the treasure a conspiratorial smile.

"You know I would," she replied, dandling her fingers sensually through the delicate gold braids. "But only if I can make you a gift as well." Nonae moved with fluid grace from the window to a display of the artisan's creations and appraised each one carefully.

"How much is it, Kedryk?" Athens asked the gold-worker quietly.

"Twelve hundred crells." But for you, Governor, I would

only require a payment in gold to replace what was used in the headdress."

"That's very kind of you," said Athens, pleased. "And of course *everyone* will see the piece. Customers will be breaking down your doors."

Kedryk smiled modestly, basking in Athens's praise.

"I think this is the one," said Nonae finally, holding a stylized golden mask over her face. "Do you like it? I think it would look lovely over your dining..."

Before she could finish, Braccus burst suddenly into the room.

"Governor, you must come quickly!

"What is it?"

"Horrible, horrible..."

"Tell me what's happened.

"The mine...both mines. They've collapsed!"

*

If the sights and sounds above ground were any indication of what lay below, Athens was sure he could not stand to see them. Lying amidst a landscape strewn with chunks of charred and steaming titanum ore, here and there scattered with pebbles of gold, the dead were – many of them – burned and mangled beyond recognition. Medics attended to the injured using phaetrons to mend tissue and bone and stop hemorrhaging. But with no one having ever conceived of so enormous a disaster, the rescue and emergency team was hopelessly small and inadequate. The screams and moans of the victims, many of them clutching at Athens's legs as he moved through their numbers, were unbearable to him.

"This way, Governor," said the shift manager, Glyss, guiding Athens toward a large jagged hole in the ground on which had once stood the mine's elevator terminal. A phaetron held in place with clamps now emitted a makeshift blue elevator beam upon which the grim-faced emergency workers were descending and the injured were continually borne to the surface. Athens and Glyss stepped into the beam and began the descent. The smell of burnt ore, seared flesh and blood was nauseating, but Athens knew he must remain strong and appear confident, his leadership the only antidote to utter panic.

They rode the blue beam down through the skin of the planet, the once perfectly vertical tunnel in some places skewed, in others studded with titanum rock and boulders vomited up from the depths. Already claustrophobic in the shaft, Athens was forced to turn his eyes away from the constant stream of mutilated and suffering miners being transported topside.

The scene in the upper mine was nightmarish, for the devastation was nearly complete. The entire cavern was destroyed. Portions of the side walls had collapsed, and there were great gaping holes where neat rows of cells had been. The central column had fallen over, crashing into the forward mine wall. The men trapped and crushed in the cells beneath it were most certainly dead, and there was a terrible resignation in the absence of rescue activity in that area.

Many of the six-legged phaetronic robots had been knocked from the mine walls and crashed to the cave floor. Others had simply gone awry, Athens could see. One of them – it's searing red beam meant to sunder rock from rock and still activated – had burnt a large gaping hole through the midsection of a dead victim hanging grotesquely from the cell opening.

When the heavy central column had fallen, all its many hundreds of yellow tractor beams had failed in an instant, releasing their endless streams of men and titanum ore in a rain of death to the cavern floor. In many places, however, Athens could see the floor itself had exploded upwards from below, leaving shards of jagged rock upon which some bodies lay impaled. In other places the upper mine's floor was gone entirely, with gaping holes that extended, he imagined, all the way down into the lower mine.

"What caused this?" Athens asked Glyss, gazing around in disbelief. "What could possibly have caused it?"

"They don't know, Sir, but perhaps an unexpected chemical reaction in the lower mine…"

"But…" Athens muttered helplessly.

"We have to make our way on foot from here, Governor," said the shift manager.

"I'm right behind you," said Athens grimly. "Glyss…"

"Yes Sir."

"Does it get worse than this?"

"I'm afraid it does, though by now they may have cleared away most of the…body parts. Watch your head here, Governor."

Athens stooped to get through a ragged hole blown in the lower end of the central column, then followed Glyss down a ladder through what was left of the shaft, now nothing more than a pile of rubble. At the sensation of liquid dripping on his cheek Athens wiped it away to find his fingers slick with blood.

"Uugth." He shuddered involuntarily and looked up. Half a man's body hung impaled on shards of the central column's metal casing.

"I'm sorry, Sir," apologized Glyss. "Be careful not to slip on the rungs. We're almost down now."

Reaching the bottom of the ladder they found themselves in the lower mine. Here men with phaetrons were clearing debris, but instead of carrying out the dead and dying they were carting away bits of human remains. The lustrous glow of gold was absent, even in the bright illumination of emergency lights.

Athens spotted a group of men, mining foremen, engineers and among them, Golde. Though they were speaking to him, questioning him and he was answering, he appeared to be somehow absent from the scene. His eyes were flat, his expression similarly flat. His newly flamboyant personality had vanished. He was drowning in remorse.

As Athens approached the group all eyes fell on him, looking for answers, encouragement, guidance, hope. He found himself, for perhaps the first time in his life, entirely lost for words.

In this terrible moment lay his greatest challenge. The colony needed him. The home world was depending upon him for its very survival. For a fleeting moment his thoughts flew to Poseidon, living somewhere on Gaia with a primitive tribe. His brother would naturally know the best course of action in such a situation. Suddenly Athens calmed. He placed an arm around the distraught Golde and looked squarely at the others.

"We can allow no panic to ensue," he said, surprised at how steady his voice sounded. "And we will stay focused, put our heads together – geologists, engineers, managers – and we'll find a solution, see this through."

Athens was gratified to feel Golde's tense body relax at his words, the faces of the others similarly soften. This was his moment. He would prove once and for all that the Terresians naysayers had been wrong about him. That he was strong and level-headed and sure and that no one – not even his brother – was better suited to lead.

*

There had been no way of knowing that the Golde organisms in the throes of metabolic process exuded a gas that, mixed in certain proportions with the oxygen pumped into the mines, produced a highly volatile condition. The report made orally to Athens by Golde himself had left them both sobered and weak with shame. The thought that something which created such joy and beauty in their world could produce so much death and suffering was difficult to fathom.

On Persus's suggestion Athens, pained and cursing the fates, had called for a general meeting of the colonists. Now he looked out over the mass of humanity assembling in the plaza outside the Governor's Palace, and with a pang remembered the last time they had gathered like this. It had been on the occasion of the independence vote, undoubtedly the happiest time in the colony's short life. Athens had been as bright and beloved as the gold ore he had gifted his people. The love they showered on him had provided him the first genuine triumph over his brother's insidious presence in his life. In fact the hero Poseidon had been all but forgotten by the colonists. If he was recalled at all it was as a quaint memory of their Terresian past, of endless dark nights and sterile cities that paled in comparison with their shining present.

Persus assured Athens that this day he could count on the strength of the people's adoration to gird them against the great loss he must announce – an insistence, for safety's sake, to cease all mining of gold ore. Golde had explained to the governor that while the explosions might be rare they could not be precisely calculated. And even a single death more was an unacceptable risk.

Athens turned to see Golde who shared the platform with him today. His was an ironic and dangerous position. While Athens had reaped as much fame for Golde's discovery as the scientist had, blame for the mining accident had been laid more often at his feet than at the governor's. Athens could see concern growing on Golde's face now as the colonists were called to silence. He would speak first, give a scientific explanation of the incident, and prepare the people for the inevitable announcement that Athens would shortly make of the mine's closing, and his rationale for the decision. There could be no more deaths or injuries under his watch, he would tell them. The colonists, whom he had come to see almost as his children, would certainly understand his concern and appreciate his care of them, even if it meant sacrifice. Persus had reinforced by constant repetition that Athens should be confident that he could convince the people that while the unlimited flow of ore would have to cease – and this would necessitate a radical shift in their economy – the existing gold would simply become a more rare and precious commodity.

A change in attitude more than anything.

True to form, Vice Governor Praxis had distanced himself from the uncomfortable public meeting, insisting that there was no need for his presence on the platform and Athens, preoccupied, barely had time to register his disgust with the cowardly man. Persus was glaring at him.

"…thus the explosion."

Athens was startled out of his thoughts, realizing that Golde was well into his presentation. He could detect in the audience a subtle but distinct shift in mood. They were very quiet, and Athens sensed they anticipated more disturbing news.

"I cannot begin to express my sorrow at the death of our friends who lost their lives in the mines," Golde went on, sincere grief creasing his features. And that is why we cannot allow such a disaster to occur again."

Athens realized the scientist had overstepped himself. This was an announcement they had agreed the governor should make. Athens was about to step forward when a woman from the audience called out in a voice whose rancor startled him into keeping silent.

"You can't mean you would shut down the gold mining operation."

"Only until a safe solution can be found," Golde replied.

"Are you sure there's a solution?" she demanded.

"No," said Golde sheepishly.

"This is unacceptable!" shouted a man in the audience.

"Unacceptable?!" cried a third colonist. "This is an outrage! Do you have any idea how many lives this will ruin!"

As more and more colonists began shouting out their opinions, most of them antagonistic, the rhetoric becoming more heated by the moment, Athens's mind began to race. He knew he should step forward – quickly – and work his personal magic to dispel the growing fury. But something held him back. Failure as the colony's leader was unconscionable. Loss of his people's love unacceptable. The germ of an idea had taken hold and was now enlarging and multiplying like the cells of a human blastula in the first moments of life. One of his genomists had recently delivered a groundbreaking report which, while rife with ethical problems, now seemed to offer Athens a viable solution.

He watched Golde trying to deflect the ever more heated barrage directed at him. The scientist finally looked back at Athens with a pleading look that said, 'Come rescue me!' Indeed, the moment had come that the governor should speak, and finally Athens moved to the podium. He walked slowly, gravely, and the crowd quieted as he approached center stage. No one could possibly know that in the crossing of that distance he had decided to sacrifice Golde at the altar of the colonists' outrage.

The scientist had stepped aside and gratefully relinquished his place to Athens. The silence of the vast multitude before him was astonishing, and he knew instinctively to use it, elongate it, enhance it for the most dramatic effect. He stared out over the sea of faces, turning slowly this way and that, as though he was caressing every one of them with his benevolent gaze. He allowed a small, pained smile to play at his lips. He opened his mouth to speak, then closed it again, as though overcome with emotion, and the effect was riveting. People strained forward towards Athens, breathless...

"Good people..." he finally began in the warmest of voices. "...we together have suffered a great tragedy in the mining accident. There's not one among you who did not lose a family member or a friend on that terrible day." He paused again, as though gathering strength for what he was about to say. "Like you," he finally continued, "I believed our operations – both titanum and gold – were safe. Never once was it explained to me that there was the remotest possibility of danger in either mine."

Athens kept his eyes straight ahead, and it appeared that he was restraining himself from turning to glare accusingly at Golde. *Do not think of him* Athens commanded himself. *Someone must be sacrificed.* It could not possibly be himself. He was the colony's leader. Adored. Trusted. He could never let them down. "The easy thing," he finally continued aloud, "would be to shut down the gold mining operation indefinitely, perhaps permanently. Simply restructure our society and economy to function without free flow of the ore. Certainly we would survive, because we are strong. But why, my friends, should we go without the thing that brings so much joy into our lives when there is a solution at hand?!" He knew that Persus would be wondering what he was about to say, but he refused to look down and meet her eye.

As the crowd stirred with interest and excitement Athens silenced himself again. He was formulating his thoughts in the moments just before the words flowed from his lips. He felt inspired, alive. "We will have our gold!" he cried, lifting his voice to be heard over the crowd. "We will have our gold and no human life or limb will be lost for it again!"

The colonists came to their feet, cheering. They were shouting encouragement, though no one yet understood how such a thing was possible.

"Today is not the day for lengthy explanations about how this will be accomplished, but it is a day for promises to be made!"

The crowd roared it approval.

"Do you trust me?!" Athens shouted.

"Yes!" came the mass reply.

"And you know that I am a man of my word?!"

"Yes!!"

The sound of their voices was shaking the air.

"Then you have my promise that if you can survive for three

Marsean years with the gold that exists, the mines will be re-opened and not another human life will be forfeited!!"

As the cheering became wilder Athens leapt down from the platform and moved out among the crowd. He wished to bathe in their adulation. It excited him, strengthened him…and it allowed him to forget, if only for the moment, the wreckage of a man who stood on the stage, arms hanging limply at his sides. Athens never wished to do Golde harm.

There had simply been no other way.

THIRTY-SIX

THEY RAN THROUGH the driving rain, a downpour that had turned the plateau into a vast bog. It was farther afield than Cleatah had ever traveled in her gathering forays, far enough from the village, Poseidon had calculated, so that the villagers would never be aware of the shuttlecraft's arrival.

He had prepared Cleatah as best he could in the past two moons, teaching her the Terresian language and customs. She had proven an astonishing linguistic student – learning vocabulary, syntax and grammar almost instantaneously. Customs, behavior and technos had been more of a struggle. It was not so much a matter of comprehension as disbelief, and occasionally disapproval. She thought the Terresian ways cold and callous, especially with regard to the rearing of children. Where was the affection, the physical bond when young ones were taken from their parents' homes to be schooled in large institutions? How could people live inside their houses so much of the time and not outdoors in the natural world? And why were the houses so large?

Neither could Cleatah fathom the lack of passionate love and commitment between men and women, something her tribe took for granted. How could males and females simply bed each other throughout their lives, changing partners at will? That was behavior for youngsters. Poseidon explained that for many thousands of years his people had, in fact, practiced such passions and customs as the Shore People now did, but that these had been discarded by their advanced society.

To live without the sun so much of the time, to sleep through their long winters, and to live without ties of love and affection seemed impossible to Cleatah, though because it was Poseidon insisting that these were the facts, she tried her hardest to accept them. As for the technos itself, Poseidon had withheld from Cleatah many details of Terresian mastery over the physical world. He had discouraged her curiosity about the phaetron, avoided demonstrating the cloaking function and the healing function, worried that too many 'wonders' might frighten and confuse even an intellect as impressive as hers. Lately, however, he himself had begun to think that such advanced technos – miracles really – were unnecessary, even slightly ridiculous. He would catch himself in such thoughts more and more frequently as the day of his re-uniting with the Atlantos's crew approached.

Now they were hurrying through the storm to meet the shuttle that would deliver them both into his world, and he believed he was far more apprehensive about this meeting than was Cleatah. He had prepared her for the idea of a flying machine that would take them high into the air and far past the mountains in no time at all. He had described the *Atlantos*, its crew, what they would wear, what they would eat. He explained their expectations of her.

But nothing, he mused, could prepare his associates for Poseidon himself – for what he planned to say to them, for what he had become. A quick check of his wrist device revealed that they were nearing the coordinates for landing.

"Poseidon!" he heard Cleatah exclaim over the howling wind. "There!"

He looked up and saw what was an extraordinary sight, even to his sophisticated eye. Cleatah must be thinking she'd stumbled into one of her mushroom visions. In front of them, five semi-circular rainbows sprouted equidistant around a thirty foot diameter of ground, looking like a gargantuan spider with an invisible body and multicolored legs. Within the circle, it appeared that no rain at all was falling.

Before he could stop her Cleatah broke from him and ran for the fantastic cluster of prisms. When he reached her she was standing awestruck in the center of the circle, gazing up at the sky above her, which was mysteriously dry. The five half-circular prisms glowed with a soft, subtly pulsing brilliance. She twirled around and around in place like a wonderstruck child.

Suddenly the prisms vanished. The sky over Cleatah's and Poseidon's heads disappeared as the circular, silver shuttle disk, its five equidistant lights pulsing, uncloaked and materialized, hovering above them.

Cleatah gasped and Poseidon, protective arms quickly encircling her, pulled her close. An instant later the blue elevator beam shot downward from the center of the disk. Poseidon slowly moved her toward the beam.

"I won't let you go, my love," he whispered. "I'll never let you go."

In the next moment the blue beam enveloped them and whisked them upward. They disappeared into the circular door and it silently shut behind them. The beam winked out of existence and a moment later the shuttlecraft disappeared entirely from the rain-swept plateau.

THIRTY-SEVEN

THE CREW – scientists, technoists and flight specialists alike – sat dumbstruck at the circular table, eyes fixed on their commander...or what had become of the man who had once been their commander. The Terresian garments Poseidon had immediately donned upon his return could not disguise the bulky musculature beneath. His long unruly mane, the sun-bronzed complexion and work-rough hands were an affront to their sensibilities. And the wild glint in his eyes belied the normalcy of Poseidon's modulated voice. Only Talya lacked the bewildered expression of her crewmates. Poseidon had sought her out first, privately in her quarters, to apprise her of his much-changed circumstances. He'd stayed but briefly, preventing the inevitable angry confrontation. She'd kept to her rooms since then, but Poseidon had insisted on her presence at this meeting. Now having admitted to his associates only the broadest truth – that the female subject Talya had discovered on her first field study – name of "Cleatah" – would not, in fact, be employed in either the genomic cross-fertilization or cultural stimulation protocol as planned, and, more shockingly, that he would be remaining on Gaia after the crew's departure for Terres. Poseidon waited uneasily for the expected response.

"So you are suggesting an extended experimental program," said Cairns, finally breaking the silence.

"Actually, I prefer to think of it as my *life*," Poseidon said, his features set in a state of mild repose. "I have no intention of returning to Terres with this or any future expeditions."

"He will be mating with the subject, 'Cleatah...'" Talya spoke the name pointedly, "...*himself.*" She sat directly across from Poseidon, furious and dry-eyed.

"But why, Sir?" asks Phypps. "Forgive me, but I don't understand the decision. None of us do."

Poseidon looked around the table at the faces of his crew. Each was dear to him. Their intelligence, courage and dedication to their fields of study, as well as their unspoken commitment to progress and Terresian values had always provided common ground between them. Science had been all the fulfillment any of them had ever needed.

How... Poseidon thought...*how am I ever to explain love?*

"My friends," he began," I came to this world as you all did – to serve the humanity which peoples both Terres and Gaia...and with every intention of returning home. But in my explorations I discovered a simplicity that pleases me more than I could ever have dreamed. A mate with whom I wish to spend my life. This existence...*feeds* me...indescribably."

"But they are primitives," argued Ables. "What kind of stimulation, mental or otherwise, could you possibly be 'fed' for the rest of your life? And it will be a very, very long life at that. I don't have to tell you that one of our years is many times multiplied on Gaia. The Terresian metabolism lived-out here will make you appear immortal."

"I know that, Ables."

"Your...woman," the geologist continued, unable to hide his disapproval, "will age normally for her species. She'll become ancient while you remain..."

"Ables…"

"Sir?"

"I mean to stay, whatever the consequences," Poseidon said in the gentlest tone. He looked at his cohorts, stiff with shock and betrayal. "Your window for reconnection with Terres before she heads back into deep orbit is very brief, and will be upon us in less than six months. Preparations need to proceed in good time, but adjusted for my absence. I'm granting Captain Zalen my command. I'll be notifying Federation shortly. I wanted you all to know first." Poseidon stood. "I'll be in my quarters if anyone wishes to speak to me privately. I welcome you all to come and meet Cleatah." He avoided Talya's eyes, but hard as he tried he was unable to keep his lips from twisting into a smile as he added, "She is a most extraordinary woman."

THIRTY-EIGHT

ONCE SHE HAD assessed that the woman was elsewhere occupied Talya went to Poseidon's quarters. She'd decided she would see him in a place where they could be private and she could quickly, gracefully exit if the need arose. And she would need to escape, she was certain of that. She was about to face the bedmate that had publicly rejected her for a primitive Gaian tribeswoman. She must override her humiliation, remain calm and altogether rational, she reminded herself for the dozenth time since she'd left her own quarters. She knew the eyes of every crewmember followed her as she passed – no doubt wondering what she was thinking, what she would say to Poseidon. *They were pitying her.* One thing she knew: she could not countenance their pity!

Arriving at his rooms she knocked, and thankfully the door opened at once. He stood there, as if he'd known she was coming just then, though she'd not alerted him. Her spine rigid she pushed into the room without invitation, refusing to meet his eye. She moved directly to the dining table under the window where but a short while ago they had sat with Athens and Korber, the marvelous expeditions to Gaia and Mars and her plans for an auspicious pairing with Poseidon ahead of them. Talya laid both hands on the table to steady herself. She hoped to scathe him, flay his calm exterior, cause him to feel as diminished as she herself now felt.

"I thought more of you than this," she finally said. Her voice sounded oddly hollow, echoing in her skull. "You are a well-bred Terresian man. How can you abandon your ancestry and succumb to these unhealthy... hungers?"

"There is no way I can explain it or apologize, Talya," he said, taking her hands.

She controlled her urge to rip them angrily from his grip. "You disgust me. I think you've taken on quite a bit more of the aboriginals' ways than you realize. You've lost all objectivity and grown unpleasantly emotional." This last had been meant as an insult, but she could see in Poseidon's face not a whit of embarrassment, instead the beginnings of a slow, almost shy smile. It was all she could bear. Talya pulled her hands from his.

"How can you do this?" she hissed.

"I did it..." Poseidon said, but paused for a long moment to put the words together carefully..." because I could not *not* do it."

"So I'm to understand that you are compelled to sacrifice everything – the knowledge, the resources and the beauty of our culture...for this *primitive*?"

She saw Poseidon gazing mildly about his quarters. "I used to think this beautiful," he said, annoyingly unperturbed by her comments. "But my perception of beauty has changed. And my perception of knowledge hasn't diminished. It has *expanded*. The indigenous peoples of Erthe do lack all but the most rudimentary technos. It's true, their culture is still stunningly simple, but their lives are rich! They're connected, Talya – heart and mind – with this astonishing planet."

"Oh spare me your hyperbole! I can see that the surroundings are lovely on Gaia. I'm not blind. But you don't belong here." Talya's frustration was escalating, "You are our planet's most distinguished scientist, our most respected leader. Will you simply desert us all for this ridiculous delusion?"

"I already have."

Talya turned away, her eyes stinging. She wondered briefly if she should go now, spare herself any further unpleasantness, but she had to know.

"So you 'love' this woman?" She could not keep the sarcasm from tainting her voice. "Next I suppose you'll want to father her children."

"I do want a family."

Talya sniffed derisively.

"I've decided that I'll give the crew members a choice – they can go if they wish, but any who want to remain here can stay, carry on in a personal capacity. Make a different sort of life for themselves."

"Really? And what of the Terresian projects? With this one irresponsible act you'll dismantle a hundred thousand years of evolutionary progress."

"Not at all," he replied in a maddeningly even tone. "Certainly it will proceed on a smaller scale, but the mixing of my genomic materials with Cleatah's, and our children's with other natives will, after a number of generations, have a significant effect on Erthe's human evolution."

Talya was suddenly silent. She was considering Poseidon's words, extrapolating from them an idea of her own making. Surely it was a mad scheme and not a little perverse, but the more she considered it the more feasible it became.

"I think perhaps I'll stay," she said finally.

Poseidon's expression of shock and confusion gave Talya some grim satisfaction, seeing on his face and in his posture the dismay she had wished for, but until this moment had been unable to elicit.

"If you don't wish to carry on with the Terresian objectives, so be it," she continued. "But I'm sure you wouldn't prevent me from proceeding with them if I chose to stay."

"Well I...I..." he stammered, but she could see his mind rushing, attempting to decipher the consequences of her continued presence on Gaia on his personal fantasy.

"It sounds as if you've already begun animal domestication with the collection and training of horses," she continued, "and we will introduce grain cultivation as planned. There's no reason we shouldn't initiate the linguistics and written language initiatives as well."

She smiled coldly, certain he realized her bold suggestion had nothing at all to do with civic duty. Poseidon was right. The interbreeding of a specimen such as himself with the extraordinarily evolved Gaian female would eventually produce a unique and magnificent race of human beings – indeed, the Terresian expedition's original objective. It was simply that she believed her bedmate's sexual preoccupation with the woman would be short-lived. No matter Cleatah's qualities, she must eventually bore a man of such complexity and intellect. And of the new emotions he was feeling, well, he would soon revert to the deeply ingrained instincts natural to a Terresian – coolheaded reason. His "love" for the woman was merely a fanciful whim, a temporary derangement of Poseidon's mind. Further, the female would grow old and ugly very quickly, while she and Poseidon would remain vital. When his insanity passed, Talya – her dignity, equanimity and beauty intact – would be there waiting for him. In their unnaturally extended lifetimes the two of them would have completed an extraordinary amount of genomic research and restructuring of the population. She and Poseidon made a brilliant team. They would be remembered on Terres together...heroes.

"So it's decided then," Talya said in a voice she found surprisingly dispassionate. "We'll have to revise your plans, of course. I can't possibly carry on without equipment. And others may choose to stay. Of course I'll talk to Zalen and make sure, but I believe that when Terres comes back around, it will be close enough during the 'window' that the crew can fly one of the shuttles back home. We'll keep the *Atlantos* here as a base of operations. The library and laboratories will be essential to our operations, don't you agree?"

It was difficult to keep from smiling, and before Poseidon could answer or object Talya decided the moment had come to terminate the meeting. She never dreamed the outcome would be so gratifying, and suddenly she found herself brimming with confidence and genuine excitement. She did enjoy a challenge. She started for the door, then turned back to Poseidon with a pleasant expression. "When will you make the announcement?"

"Tonight, at the evening meal," he said, subdued.

She could see he was pulling himself together, but it no longer mattered. She had unnerved him, bested him. And it felt wonderful. She executed her coolest and most attractive smile from the doorway.

"Till this evening," she said.

THIRTY-NINE

NOT SURPRISINGLY, NONE of the other crewmembers opted to stay.

Cleatah, however, charmed everyone before the first week was out. All who had labeled her a 'primitive' were astonished at her intellect and mastery of the Terresian language in so short a time. But it was her warmth and directness that beguiled them, much as it had Poseidon. He watched her interaction with Chronell, holding his hand in hers and examining his face as she correctly diagnosed an as-yet untreated condition, then prescribing a potion made of a native plant to cure it. After that Chronell privately approached his commander and shyly inquired if there were any other women in Cleatah's village who were anything like her. Poseidon was sorry to say that while the warmth was common to the entire tribe, this woman's level of intellect was not. In the end Chronell – as all the others – decided to return to Terres.

Word that Talya would remain on Gaia to carry out the genomic directives was met with almost as much disbelief as Poseidon's announcement. It was whispered that the planet had a strange effect on some Terresians, causing them to act in a most peculiar and dangerous fashion, and as plans progressed for the crew's reconnection with Terres it was with a sense of nervous anticipation that they longed to be gone, lest they fall prey to these untoward emotions themselves.

*

Since Talya's private visit Poseidon's mind had been churning almost out of control. At first her suggestion that she stay on had rocked him as violently as an Erthan land tremor. But as the days passed a notion sprang into his consciousness and took hold. He would lie awake at night, Cleatah long asleep, and ponder the plan. It grew complex and unruly, and when he finally slept his well-developed Terresian dream-state allowed for still wilder and more grandiose machinations to emerge.

But this day as the shuttle disk left Erthe's atmosphere – the daytime blue sky becoming black-flecked with brilliantly glittering stars and the boggling sight of Erthe receding into a small, blue-green disk – Poseidon could think of nothing but the look of wonder on Cleatah's face. They were alone, as he'd insisted on piloting the shuttle himself. He wanted to demonstrate the magic of Terresian technos in a way that Cleatah could truly grasp. She stood very still at the shuttle's largest window watching the moon grow larger and brighter by the moment. Certainly she had believed him when he'd explained the nature of the solar system to her, understood conceptually the moving pebbles representing the spherical sun and planets. But now here she stood, unmoving, yet flying through the air, with day turning to night – not slowly as the sun set, but in an instant. And here was Erthe's moon taking up more of the black sky as every moment passed, the details of its craters and mountains distinct and frightening.

All of this Poseidon could clearly read in his lover's expression, much as she could be awakened merely by his thoughts. They were becoming – two separate individuals – attuned in a way he had never considered possible.

"Once, soon after I met you," she began, "I had a vision, and

I have never forgotten it. I was sitting alone on the shore near the village with water lapping at my feet, colorful fishes nibbling at my toes. And I was surrounded by children playing happily there. There were hundreds of them. I remember thinking that they were, every one of them, my children, and they were all *your* children as well."

"How did you know they were mine?"

"Because they had your eyes. Your grey eyes…and I knew they were yours because I could never imagine – even then – having anyone else's children."

Poseidon moved behind her and clasped her around the waist. She covered his arms with her hands, fingers absently caressing the fine fabric of his jacket. "I've been thinking, Cleatah…"

"Your favorite occupation," she said, still unable to pull her gaze from the sight of the moon.

He began to speak – quietly, commanding himself to control his fervor which, together with the strangeness of his ideas, might frighten her. "I've had a vision of my own…"

"Tell me."

"A great joining. A bringing together of our two peoples, our two cultures. It's already begun with you and me, of course, but I've been imagining all the ways Terres and Erthe might be co-mingled."

Finally Cleatah pulled her gaze from the moon and turned to face him. "Explain this. Tell me what you see. I don't understand."

"I see a city. You remember from our lessons – places where a great many people come together to live and work, learn and play."

She nodded with understanding. "Where is this city that you see?"

"Close to where the Shore Village now stands."

She smiled, amused. "But where do these 'great many' people come from? Our village is small."

"We would gather them from every part of this continent,

which is very large. Many tribes inhabit it, and though each of them is small, together they would make a great many."

"But why? Are we not happy as we are?"

Now he looked away, staring at the Erthan moon looming brightly before them. This was the most difficult of all to explain.

"When I first decided I would stay I believed I'd be content with a life of simplicity, living with you, loved by you. And if you don't agree with my vision I'll be content. I promise you that. But now I'm constantly visited by this vision of something more. I'm asking for your consent, for your participation. Without it I cannot possibly carry out my plan. But forgive me. I haven't yet answered why." He paused one last time, then plunged into his explanation.

"When I think of the bounty of Erthe I'm nearly as overcome by joy as I am when I think of you. Shortly after I arrived here I found – much to my surprise – that I had fallen in love with a *place*. It is unimaginably more beautiful than my home world." Poseidon stopped for a moment, silently comparing the land-scapes of the two planets. "But you've seen the diffractor images of Terres. You know what I'm saying is true." He didn't wait for her affirmation, just went on. "And the people here…they pos-sess a quality that we Terresians have lost, lost so long ago that we don't even miss it. But we *should* miss the feeling, the passion, the love…"

"We are also jealous, Poseidon. Sometimes hateful. Sometimes violent. And we are so…" she looked around her at the shuttle's gleaming control console, "…ignorant beside you."

"I don't agree! And this is my point. What we lack, you pos-sess. What you lack, we possess. Your knowledge of Erthe is as rich and detailed as mine is of Terres. Certainly with my technos I could come to an understanding of this world and its people, but it could never be as fine and brilliant as what you could teach me. Conversely, certain uses of Terresian technos focused upon the natural resources of Erthe would produce..." In his excitement he became lost for words.

"A city?" Cleatah finished for him.

"Yes! A city, a civilization. A culture of extraordinary magnificence! The arts would flourish. Terresian design forged into Erthan stone. Natural sciences would blossom. The whole continent would become a fabulous garden with animals in abundance. It would boggle the senses!"

"And the people?" she asked. "How would they come to know what is necessary to build this...'civilization'?"

"With your help," Poseidon answered, clasping her hands in his. "In the beginning you would teach them to never be afraid – of me, of what is new, what is different. Later, our children and their children's children will share our blood, our essences. It is in these offspring that I see the most shining aspect of our future. The mixture of Terresian levelheadedness and Erthan passion would create a splendid human being, an ideal society, a great and fair government."

Cleatah was filled with wonder at the things Poseidon described, but he could see she was uncertain...even afraid.

"We would begin slowly," he continued. "I won't frighten the people with the kind of sights and sounds and knowledge that I shared with you. We would start with education, sharing a common language, learning to grow foods that will sustain a larger population. Mining the stone and minerals necessary for building. The rest will follow naturally. You and I, Cleatah, we can create this! But I can't do it without you. I can't do it alone."

He could see in her faraway gaze that ideas of which he spoke, the visions he conjured, were at once far too vast for her to grasp...and altogether clear. She was silent, unable to find words to express herself. When she began to tremble she turned away from Poseidon. But the sight that greeted her caused her to gasp aloud.

The pale, mottled surface of the moon – that sacred orb that she had wondered at and worshipped her whole life – now filled her vision. Poseidon's arms encircled her from behind, and tears began to gather in her eyes. This man, this stranger from another world, had given her the very moon…and now he wanted her help.

She would, of course, deny him nothing.

FORTY

"A GOOD DAY TO you!" Athens cried a moment after his diffracted image appeared in the *Atlantos's* library. He was in as cheerful a mood as Poseidon had ever seen him. This called greeting – "A good day to you!" – had become the Marsean's most common one, as the rising of the sun every day was cause for great celebration.

"Good day to *you*, brother. You sound as if the female company you keep is satisfying you well."

"To the greatest degree. And the mines are booming. What reason do I have to feel anything but glorious?"

Poseidon grew silent, and stayed silent till Athens said, finally, "What is it? Is something wrong?"

"Nothing's wrong. Nothing at all. However, I have decided… to stay on Erthe."

"Erthe. What is Erthe?"

Poseidon realized then how long it had been since he and Athens had seen one another. Spoken. Shared their thoughts. It might have been a hundred years that had passed, so much had changed. How to explain any of it?

"Erthe is Gaia."

Athens laughed. *"You?* You are staying behind on Gaia?"

"Yes."

"And the crew?"

"All are leaving during the window, except Talya.

"You devil!" Athens barked.

"It's not what you think."

"What I *think*?" I can't think at all. I'm phazed entirely…Tell me your plan."

"This is bound to be as much a shock to you as it's been to everyone I've told." Poseidon exhaled a contented sight. "I have come to love a woman of Erthe. Her name is Cleatah."

"From the Shore Village you've been living in for all this time." It was not a question. Athens was slowly making sense of it all. "But staying?" he said. "For what purpose? Are you becoming a tribesman?"

Poseidon could hear derision in the word. Yet he could not help smiling when he answered, "No. I have *been* a tribesman for all of this time."

"And you're sending your crew home without you?" Athens was disbelieving and not a little scornful. "At least when you left Aeros without Elgin Mars you came back with titanum. Now the Terresians' favorite hero is staying behind on a primordial world, keeping with him the greatest genomist of her time. And for what? Rutting with an aboriginal?"

Poseidon was certain nothing he could say would make Athens understand. Instead he said, "We are building something here."

"What, a race of monkey people?…Sorry, that was uncalled for and rude."

"All that and more," Poseidon replied evenly.

Athens reined in his flaring temper. "I imagine to do such a thing you'd have to have good cause."

Much better than you think."

"Well, I suppose it will be good to have my brother in close orbit."

"But not *too* close," Poseidon said.

Athens laughed. "Perhaps I'll like this brother better than the old one."

"Perhaps you will."

"He will have a beautiful native at his side. I assume she's beautiful. But he will have – and for this I do not envy you, brother – incurred the unbridled Wrath of Talya."

FORTY-ONE

TIME GREW SHORT for the crew's departure. In less than a week the window would open and the crew would be departing for home. It was an orderly protocol, but in their faces Poseidon could see confusion and loss. When Federation had first learned of their commander's willing defection and finally believed it a certainty, all they'd managed to broadcast in their visual transmissions over the endless miles of space were long mournful silences and expressions of abject stupefaction. They were deeply shocked at Poseidon's decision, and helpless to counter his incomprehensible reasoning. Convincing Federation to send the crew home in a shuttle with the data gleaned from the Gaian expedition was far easier than gaining permission to keep the *Atlantos* with he and Talya on Erthe. In the end they'd relented, with the stipulation that they would be readying the planet for possible colonization during subsequent close orbits.

Poseidon's fellow scientists and technos crew would face returning home without their beloved leader. Commander Mars had at least been lost to an heroic death. When it was learned that Poseidon had abandoned his world and his family for the love of a single woman, the Terresian people would at best be dismayed and shaken by word from Gaia, and at worst coolly derisive.

Talya Horus's motives would be even harder to decipher.

Zalen had taken the news in stride, himself drawn to Gaia, but his occupation was entirely phaetron-based. Without technos the man had no function. No purpose. Ables had attempted briefly to dissuade Poseidon from staying, but he could see in his commander's eyes the sheer, unconquerable determination of love, if not the concept. That was still a mystery to the Terresian psyche.

No one in the crew dared speak to Talya about her decision to stay. She was considered by all as a paragon of steadiness and restraint, but these days she doubled her reserve, lengthened her silences.

*

There was one transmission to Terres that Poseidon dreaded nearly as much as he joyfully anticipated it. When Manya materialized before him she quietly regarded her son's startling transformation – his tanned and muscular physique, the long wild mane.

"It appears that you've found something on your voyage that 'surprised' you," she finally said with tender indulgence.

"I have."

"And what is her name?"

"Am I so transparent?"

I'm your mother, Poseidon. You are meant to be transparent to me."

"Cleatah. She is called Cleatah."

"Is she as beautiful as her name?"

"She's something more than beautiful. There is a whole world within her." Poseidon's voice broke. "She loves me, Mother."

Manya's features relaxed into a smile, and her eyes closed. "I've seen the images of Gaia. So many times I've imagined you in those magnificent landscapes. And now I can envision you there with a woman who loves you." She continued, her voice fanciful, "You know, I often wish I could be there on the planet myself."

"But you *are* here. I've named a mountain after you. She's very majestic, Manya. Very fiery. She nearly killed me."

His mother's eyes flew open and she laughed a throaty laugh. Poseidon could see in her a more profound serenity than he had ever remembered.

"You know, of course, I won't be seeing you again," she said, never taking her eyes from his. "There's little chance I'll survive this PseudoMort. It will be strange going to sleep knowing I'll never wake."

"Have you said your goodbyes to Athens?"

"He wept like a child. But he is so happy in his world. My life will end knowing both my boys are content. What more could I ask for?"

Poseidon thought on this for a long moment. "A splendid final dream," he finally suggested.

"Perhaps I'll dream of my namesake – Manya erupting in a fiery spasm."

"A fitting end, Mother," he said, smiling at the thought. Then seriousness overwhelmed him. "I love you very much. Thank you for my life…and for a heart that can feel."

Tears were streaming down Manya's cheeks, and Poseidon reached out across the miles, in vain, to wipe them away.

"Sweet dreams, Poseidon," she whispered, "and a long, joyful life."

FORTY-TWO

TWO DAUNTING TASKS still lay ahead. The *Atlantos* needed a hiding place, as did the two shuttle disks that would be left behind. Zalen and the technos crew were consulted. Talya rightly insisted that a location central to the planned city, provisionally called "Atlantos," was crucial. Of course the Shore Village must be preserved intact, and Cleatah requested its close proximity to the city. Zalen suggested entombment of the ship under the crust of the Great Plateau. Poseidon rejected this. He wished for closer proximity to the ocean.

They settled on burial of the larger craft at sea-level, south of the Shore Village, where the plateau curved naturally into a massive amphitheater, the ground at its base layered with black sand that covered lavic rock hundreds of feet deep. The shuttles – so they would be more readily available for flight – would be hidden in two horizontal caves high up on the plateau's palisades.

Till now the Shore People knew nothing of Poseidon's true home, or that he possessed tools or weapons beyond a spear, blade or arrow. He had been accepted as the mate of Cleatah, and he'd proven himself courageous and worthy as a tribesman. But the greatest obstacle required Cleatah's counsel. "Should the tribe," he asked her, "be allowed to see the *Atlantos* fly? To hover and vaporize rock and sand? To watch as it lowers itself down beneath the ground, and the disks settled into the cliff face?"

"It is too soon," she replied. "There's no way to prepare them for such a sight. They'll die of fear." It was just as Poseidon had suspected.

"Before I came to the village, when I found the horses, I put them to sleep so I could safely separate Arrow from the herd. You remember I did the same to Sheeva while we ate the mushroom."

"You want to do this with the tribe?"

"It may be best."

And afterwards?"

"We'll cover the vessels completely so no one will suspect it had happened. My worry," Poseidon said slowly, measuring his words, "is what they will think when they lay eyes on the great ertheworks necessary to build the city."

She thought silently for a long moment, as though gazing into the months and years ahead. "By such a time they'll know you to be far more than a Shore Tribesman." She caressed his cheek with her hand. "You must not worry. Put the people to sleep. Bury your ships. We still have to gather the tribes and bring them across the continent, teach them to speak one language. Surely that's enough for now."

So it was done.

With the Shore People narcotized, Zalen flew the ship to the seaside, found the center of the miles-wide amphitheater, and directed the phaetron's beam downward. Black sand was blown away into a low circular mound below the craft's perimeter. The highest frequency boring function then vaporized the lavic rock, carving out a tremendous space to a depth capable of hiding the vessel completely. Zalen skillfully maneuvered the *Atlantos* into the manmade cavern, and the sand was re-deposited atop it. The disks were slotted into their horizontal caves, stone doors set in place to camouflage them.

When the Shore People awoke from their sleep, no one, save Cleatah, was the wiser. And the heart of Atlantos was once and forever set in stone.

ENTERPRISE

…of the inhabitants of the mountains and
of the rest of the country there was also a
vast multitude…

I will now describe the plain, as it was fashioned
by nature and by the labors of many generations
of kings through long ages. It was for the most
part rectangular and oblong, and where falling out
of the straight line followed the circular ditch…
it was carried round the whole of the plain, and
was ten thousand stadia in length. It received the
streams which came down from the mountains,
and winding round the plain and meeting at the
city, was there let off into the sea. Further inland,
likewise, straight canals of a hundred feet in width
were cut from it through the plain, and again let
off into the ditch leading to the sea: these canals
were at intervals of a hundred stadia, and by them
they brought down the wood from the mountains
to the city, and conveyed the fruits of the earth in
ships, cutting transverse passages from one canal
into another, and to the city…

Plato's *Critias,* 4th Century B.C.

FORTY-THREE

"I AM MOTHER TO not a single child," Cleatah said in the teasing lilt she employed so often these days, "and now you wish me to birth a civilization."

Poseidon watched as she rose from their bed and plucked up a shirt to cover her morning nakedness.

"Why would anyone from the gathered tribes listen to me? Elder men, wise women? I am young. They will have their own ways."

"I believe they'll follow you. They will love and revere you."

His eyes lingered on her sleepwarm body, and he wished she would be slow covering it. He never tired of the sight her – the tall, supple form and graceful movements, the full breasts and prettily muscled limbs. That thick tawny mane never failed to thrill him. Cleatah was, to his greedy eyes, as much a wild animal as a woman, eliciting sensations and primal instincts that he'd never known he possessed. At night when he reached for her, even in half-sleep, she came willingly. She curled and wove tendril-like around him, nestling her face with short, fragrant breaths into the curve of his neck. If Poseidon kissed her – anywhere – she came slowly awake in his arms, always glad to have been roused, then commencing to rouse *him* to extents he could never have imagined possible. Only an hour before Cleatah had been strad-dling Poseidon, riding him, moving in voluptuous rhythm to pleasure herself, having learned there was no better way than this to pleasure him.

But today he needed to bring his Terresian sensibilities to the fore and, with Cleatah, to direct their thoughts and efforts to the "Great Undertaking." The months ahead promised to kindle all manner of creation, from the grandest to the minutest scales. Some would provoke and foment fanciful, even inconceivable notions, then inflame their spirits to follow these extravagances through every impediment and hardship...to consummation.

What was yet unspoken – and uneasy – was Talya's part in all of it. In the ship's kitchen she had blanched when he and Cleatah announced their intentions to gather the tribes from the farthest reaches of the continent in order to found their new society. He observed the two women standing side-by-side. They were equal in height and both slender, yet they couldn't have differed more. Cleatah's posture was unselfconsciously lithe, agile, her limbs fuller, more muscular. Talya stood ramrod straight and seemed to wear her skin and clothing as an armor. She ever-so-slightly recoiled at Cleatah's nearness.

Talya had spluttered at the idea of a new civilization, her nor-mally frosty skin flushing pink with one of the rogue emotions to which she'd lately fallen victim.

"Can you hear yourself, Poseidon? You've gone completely mad." She'd turned away from them to retrieve her meal from the diner-window, but he knew she was only hiding the embarrass-ment of her emotion. "I won't have anything to do with it."

"It was your choice to stay," he said. 'Like it or not, this is the future of Erthe. You can do what's necessary to help us, or you can stand by as an observer. You need to decide quickly, though. We're moving ahead at once."

Poseidon had seen the subtle trembling, the sighing breaths

she was using to calm herself. Then she'd swiveled to face them again. "I suppose you expect me to start an exponential breeding protocol with this 'gathered tribe' while you build your city."

"No breeding program," Cleatah had unhesitatingly corrected Talya. "Once the tribes have come, they will mate among themselves as we in the Shore Village have always done."

Cleatah's quiet assurance never failed to astonish Poseidon. But it infuriated Talya who continued to believe herself, in every way, superior to this decidedly bright, yet wholly aboriginal, woman.

Talya had turned to Poseidon then, her eyes flashing dangerously, assured that he would take her side against this unreasonable argument. She'd been mistaken.

"In every way possible," he told her, "we'll proceed according to natural laws. Erthe's laws."

Talya gaped at him disbelievingly. "You want me to put aside the genomic protocols laid out by Federation? Had I known that..." she spluttered but could not finish.

Had you known, would you not have stayed? Poseidon thought, but did not say.

"I'd like to speak to you alone." Talya hissed at him.

"There's nothing you can say to me that Cleatah should not hear."

Talya's closed-lipped mouth worked in silence as she chose her words carefully. "This is anarchy," she finally said, calm and steady. "You've commandeered a world, Poseidon. A Terresian world."

"Erthe is its own world. Our interventions have brought evolution far enough. We have to stop playing God."

Talya laughed bitterly. "And what are you doing, if not playing God?"

"Call it what you will. The decision has been made. The city's infrastructure will be laid down with the phaetron – erthe-moving, primarily, to spare the people back-breaking work. I imagine this will 'elevate' me in the people's eyes."

I would say so." Her tone was caustic.

"You know very well there's a difference between using tech-nos to move stone, and using it to manipulate the species at a cellular level," he said.

"We have always done it. Do you presume to be the single man who unilaterally derails so crucial a Terresian program?"

I do." He spoke in an unmistakable directive. "Human genomic interventions stop now. The population will reproduce as it always has, at a rate and with mutations determined by natural circumstances alone. There will be no more tampering."

"You call my *work* tampering!" Her skin glowed red with rage.

"It is tampering," he replied, with a calm that could only incite further fury. "And it stops now."

That had ended the conversation, and Talya had avoided them for several days. Today had been set aside for their meeting in order to begin the physical plan for Atlantos City and its environs. As Poseidon and Cleatah walked side-by-side through the deserted ship from their quarters to the hub, turning down the hall of laboratories, he wondered if working long hours in Talya's space, amidst the highest levels of technos, Terresian thought forms, and the silent but omnipresent phaetronic vibrus that permeated the body of the craft, would rattle his mate.

It was the vibrus Cleatah despised above all else.

She always longed to have her feet planted in the soil and sand, rock and vegetation, to hear only natural sounds and feel only Erthely energies pulsing beneath and around her. She'd reluctantly agreed to sleep in Poseidon's quarters while their creation took form. But it had become her habit before every day broke to slip from bed, and fearlessly riding the blue beam to the surface emerge into her own world. Poseidon imagined that first inhaled breath, the joy and relief of sipping the smells of her beloved planet. There too, waiting patiently for her mistress, was Sheeva. All attempts to bring the wolf into the *Atlantos* had failed, and even her fearlessness and devotion to Cleatah could not surmount the animal's revulsion and dread of the unnatural and claustrophobic interior. On most days the pair of them would descend the cliff face and walk the beach north to the Shore Village. Cleatah visited with her people, speaking to them of the world-shaking changes that were coming. She spoke to them of *the future.*

It was difficult for me to understand 'future,'" she'd told Poseidon. "How will I explain it to them? Every day is the same as the day before, and the same as the day after. Only the shaking of the ground or the most terrible storms with winds that blow down our huts make us think of past times. 'That was the day before the great shaking that killed Boah's father,' someone might say. But they will never consider a storm or a quake in the *future.*"

When they entered Talya's laboratory they found her standing in front of a diffracted rendering of the Great Plateau, its fertile plains laid out in a neat grid of farms and lushly planted fields, irrigated by a massive system of canals. Far in the distance was the volcanic range, Manya still and peaceful, towering above the other peaks. It was clear that Talya had no intention of revisiting their last conversation about human genomic manipulation, and had decided to move forward. Contribute in some other way.

"What are we seeing here?" Poseidon asked.

I've devised a system to maximize food productivity."

"What is this?" Cleatah demanded, pointing to the center of the Great Plateau, slashing her two middle fingers first horizontally, then vertically, indicating the unnaturally organized crosshatched pattern of farmland and canals.

"It makes best use of the land," Talya answered, unable to keep the condescension from her voice. "More food can be grown this way. Rivers that twist and turn back on themselves maybe pretty, but they're wasteful. The canals distribute water to farms with the greatest efficiency."

"You would change the course of a river?" Cleatah glanced

back to Poseidon. "You would not permit that." It was a statement more than a question.

I might." He knew his answer would evoke Cleatah's displeasure, but Talya's ideas were sound. "We must think first about feeding a great many people. We can't bring the tribes here only to let them starve."

Cleatah returned her gaze to the projected likeness of the Great Plateau. "I don't understand. How did it come to look this way?"

"Let me show you," Talya replied, wiping the "finished image" of the farmlands away with a swipe of her fingers over the trans-screen. What was left was the plateau as it existed before the *Atlantos* had arrived, its two graceful blue rivers descending from the mountains and flanking each side of the broad plain. The first superimposition Talya now produced showed the crisscrossed grid of canals dug into the plateau which was devoid of its grasslands. The next superimposed image showed the re-directing of the rivers into the canals, leaving the natural waterways arid and lifeless. Another image overlaid the patchwork of fields, their circles and squares inscribed with planting rows in the brown soil. Finally the dry grid was superimposed with green plantings, looking very much like a vast fertile garden, one that would have been envied by Terresians, its proportions and fecundity almost too extravagant to believe.

Cleatah stepped back. While she now understood the process of terraforming her world, she clearly disapproved. Yet she remained silent. She'd won the argument over the unnatural breeding program that Talya had wanted to adopt. Cleatah was supremely sensible, even-tempered, Poseidon thought. While she had quickly learned the idea of standing firm on her most cherished principles, she had also mastered the equally critical concept of compromise.

Poseidon came to Cleatah's side now. "This is a good plan. What you can tell us is the kind of food that will best nourish and please the gathered tribes. You cannot know what those of the farthest villages eat, but perhaps you can speak to us of the foods favored by the Shore People – aside from what comes from the sea. We can't be certain all people will like to eat those creatures. Then we'll show you what we've brought from Terres and from other continents on Erthe. Let you taste it. Together, the three of us will decide what to plant in the fields."

"And the men will no longer hunt?" Cleatah asked then, remembering an earlier conversation with Poseidon, one that had disturbed her profoundly.

"Not in the way they have been doing," Talya answered, enlarging the image of an area of grassland enclosed by sturdy wooden fences. With a flick of her fingers thousands of buron appeared, grazing contentedly inside the vast pens. "The herds will no longer roam freely. They'll be contained so that they can quickly and easily be slaughtered for food."

"Some buron of both sexes will always have free range," Poseidon told Cleatah.

"So we will continue the Ceremony of the Bull?" she asked him.

He nodded, pleased to be pleasing her. He knew she worried that without the natural grazing of large hooved animals the sacred mushroom would be more difficult to find, though she would never have said so within Talya's hearing. Poseidon could see by the glint in Cleatah's eye and the thin line of her lips that even the assurances of some free-ranging buron had not placated her entirely.

"Come with me to the plateau," Cleatah said suddenly, her tone commanding. "Both of you. We'll stand there, look out over the plain, not here in front of this…this…"

"Diffracted imaged," Talya finished for her.

Cleatah closed her eyes and Poseidon saw she was willing herself to calm. He guessed the word she'd sought to describe the plateau but did not yet have in her vocabulary was "abomination." Poseidon could see that his mate dearly wished to give Talya a sharp swat, as one might chastise an irritating child. But more than anything she wanted to be free from the confines of the ship, striding along with the wolf at her heels.

"I agree," Poseidon said. "We'll walk the plateau and you can show us the places of greatest fertility. You know what grows there now. That will help us know what to plant in the future. You can show us where the herds normally roam."

"They will need to drink. All the animals as well," she said and glanced at Talya. "You will leave one of the rivers running freely."

"Ridiculous," Talya said. "That destroys the entire agri-grid."

Cleatah faced Talya squarely. "You will do as I say."

Without another word Cleatah strode from the laboratory. Poseidon and Talya locked eyes but said nothing. He could see color rising from her neck to her cheeks to the top of her ears. Then he turned and followed his mate out the door.

FORTY-FOUR

COUNTLESS DAYS AND endless nights were devoured by dreams and imaginings of the first civilization on Erthe. The Great Undertaking had been conceived in Poseidon's love of Erthe, and nurtured in his love of Cleatah and the people and creatures of the planet. The two of them talked of nothing else. He related memories of Terres and brought her into the *Atlantos* library so she could learn the history of the universe and the solar system of Helios. When they ate the mushroom together ideas flew out of their heads like great flocks of birds exploding from the surface of a lake in noisy clouds of color and movement.

Cleatah often said her greatest pleasure, aside from the presence of Poseidon's company, was to learn something new, then devise questions from that learning. What she enjoyed even more was Poseidon's delight in those questions – both their complexity and all that he learned in creating perfect answers for them. He himself was full of questions. Questions about Erthe. As Cleatah's student he drank in knowledge that flowed like a river from her whole being. She spoke volubly of a plant's qualities, or the healing minerals to be found in a rock. For the physical joy of it she mimicked the movements of a bird slowly stretching a wing, or a wolf its back.

He realized, though, that so alien a sight as a city would be impossible for Cleatah to conjure unless she had experienced it herself. Poseidon held her hand tightly as he slid the cylinder into the *Atlantos* library's diffractor. As the metropolis materialized around them he heard a sharp intake of breath, and Cleatah snatched her hand away to draw it to her throat. She was silent as she turned in a full circle to view the wide boulevards, the massive public edifices and many-storied residences towering on both sides of her. As she looked up at the cloud-dappled blue sky of the contour dome, a family chariot buzzed overhead, causing her to duck. Then she laughed, remembering it was all an illusion, and she took up his hand again. She was unable to tear her eyes from the sleekly dressed Terresians they passed as they "strolled" down the street together. Poseidon could only smile to imagine the ecstatic chaos taking place inside her head.

"It's all too close," she finally said. "And too big."

We can build the homes smaller, and place them farther apart."

"But where are the trees and the grasses?" she lamented. "And water. Where is the water? I don't wish to live in a city – even with you, my love – if I cannot sit in the shade of a tree or put my feet in moving water."

"What we have on Terres are 'gardens,'" he'd explained, and led her to the Central Plaza, walking her through the carefully manicured beds of flowers, shrubs, and trees in perfectly ordered rows.

She stopped, and he could see her thought turning inward, the wheels turning. Then she said, "Could we not put a garden on the roof of a house?"

"I suppose we could."

"With trees and flowers, medicine plants and hanging vines? So that birds and insects would surely visit."

Poseidon closed his eyes and conjured a street with a row of such dwellings. "Will these houses not need water to nourish their 'hanging gardens?'"

"They would." She sighed, sounding thwarted.

"There is a way," he insisted. Then beginning with the need to water Cleatah's imagined roof garden, he conceived first of a system of pipes to every home and building in the city, and expanded it outward to an aqueduct – perhaps two – that would be fed by the rivers roaring down over the Great Plateau from the far mountains.

That was how it continued – the creation of their city, their society. A germ of a notion conceived of by one, fueled by the ideas of the other, spun out, built upon and extrapolated to proportions previously inconceivable and fantastic. Why, asked Cleatah, should not hot as well as cold water be piped down from the plateau, a place where many people could enjoy bathing in a warm pool? And how wonderful would it be, Poseidon asked, to build a permanent track for racing horses, a stadium where the whole population of the city could gather for celebrations?

The actual shape of their new city came to them one warm afternoon as they sat in the sand of the Shore Village beach, gazing south to the site of their anticipated metropolis, under which the *Atlantos* was now buried.

Cleatah began tentatively. "Remember when you showed me – with pebbles flying in the air – our sun and the planets twirling around them?" With her finger she etched a small circle in the sand. "Helios," she named it, then drew orbit after orbit around that, each larger than the last. "Can our city have this shape?"

Poseidon stared for a long while at the ring of concentric circles, then slowly traced a finger between two of the rings. "Let this be a waterway." He pulled his finger around within the next two orbits. "Let this one be land. Here…water again. And see, buried under 'Helios' – the central island – lies our vessel. With a short straight slash of his finger from the central isle across all the ring islands and waterways to the sea, he said, "This will connect all the island to the ocean, a 'harbor' where our vessels can shelter from storms. What do you think of it?"

"It is very beautiful…" Cleatah concluded with a playful grin, "…for a city."

*

A serious void remained in their planning. The most formidable mission of their endeavor was the gathering of all the aboriginal peoples of the continent. Only Cleatah, a single native female, and Poseidon would be shouldering the entire burden. Despite his integration into the society of the Shore People he knew himself to be an inauthentic man of Erthe.

"Boah will help us," Cleatah told Poseidon with great authority.

"But he knows nothing of who I am, where I'm from…and what I'm capable of doing. He's strong and fearless, but I think it will frighten him."

"You do not know Boah," she said simply.

Cleatah went to the village alone. She came riding back with Boah on his horse Kato to the Great Plateau, where Poseidon waited. The young tribesman seemed shy as he came to face his hunting mate, the man who had healed his shattered leg at the horse roundup and mysteriously won Cleatah without a fight.

"I've told Boah that the world will be different now, by your hand and mine," she said. "That many changes are coming, and that if he wishes, he will help us. I told him that you are a man from a village far, very far away, and that you and your kind can do many things that men of our tribe, or nearby tribes, could never dream of doing. He doesn't believe me. He says you are a good enough hunter, and you did bring the horse to our people, but that is all. I said you would show him that there is much more that he should know about you."

Boah glared at Poseidon, much as he had the night of the

challenge for Cleatah – respectful yet distrustful, and supremely confident as a hunter of his skill should be. "Show me," Boah said simply. "Show me now."

"Look at Kato," Poseidon replied. "I am going to make your horse sleep. I will not hurt him. You know I would never harm a horse. Watch."

Poseidon directed his wrist device at Boah's mount, his head high, strong jaws working the sweet grass he had just grazed upon. Instantly the horse stopped chewing. His head drooped and a moment later the powerful legs folded under him. He fell into a deep stupor. Boah ran to Kato and examined him, saw that he was breathing normally and in no distress. He stared wordlessly at Poseidon, unable to form a question to ask.

"You tell me when to wake him," Poseidon told Boah. "You decide."

Boah glanced at Cleatah. He thought hard and decided to wait. He paced about, displaying admirable self-control for a man whose horse had just collapsed into an unaccountable sleep. Several minutes passed before Boah strode back to Poseidon and, eye-to-eye, demanded. "Now. Wake him now!"

Poseidon deactivated the narcotizing function and instantly the horse began to stir. Kato lifted his head and shook it, then scrambling to his feet snorted and pawed the ground, as if impatient to be on his way. Boah was breathing hard. The muscles in his arms, shoulders and neck tightened. His hands balled into fists. But he was silent.

"There is more that I can do, more that I can show you," Poseidon offered.

"This is all you need to do," Boah replied. "I know now that you are more than a man. You are a god."

"No, Boah. We are the same in our bodies in every way. But I possess what I call 'technos.' This is hard to explain. Perhaps Cleatah can make you understand it."

"Poseidon is just a man with a tool," she said without hesitation. "He carries it under the skin of his arm."

Boah shook his head slowly from side to side.

Cleatah went on. "Think of a spear. It is *your* tool. With it you can change something – change a living buron to a dead one. With a rock-grinding stone tool you can change loto root into food. Poseidon's tool is a powerful one. It can heal. It can put living things to sleep. It can move heavy things without touching them. It can make you learn things, see things. Not one of the people of the shore or the plateau have this tool. It is one that comes from Poseidon's people…" She gazed at Poseidon for permission to say, "…and they are not the people he told us were his tribe when he came to us. We can explain that to you later, but now you must believe us when we tell you that Poseidon is simply a man with a very great tool."

While Cleatah spoke, the tension in Boah's muscles began to dissipate. His breathing became slow and easy. He thought for a long time, his forehead creasing into a spider web of lines. Then he said, "Is a horse a tool?"

"Yes!" Poseidon cried, his face erupting into a smile. He threw both arms around Boah. "Yes, my friend, a horse is a very powerful tool." He beamed at Cleatah.

She embraced Boah, too, her heart surging with joy and relief. She said to Poseidon, "What you cannot show or teach the people, I will show and teach them. What I cannot do, Boah will do."

*

His dream was of flying above the Great Plateau, over vast plains, mountains and rivers, down to the far shores of the continent. But it was not Poseidon flying. It was instead a shiny metallic object in the shape of a long-hafted, triple-headed spear. His mother's voice portentously announced this weapon was a "trident." Its handle and each of its three sharp-tipped prongs had names – the shaft was Poseidon, the trio of tines Cleatah, Boah and Talya. The trident flew amidst the puffery of white clouds and pierced whirling black cyclones, but never strayed from its true course till finally it focalized its target and descended with increasing speed towards Erthe. When it slammed into the soil, throwing up a cloud of dust that coalesced into a fabulous city of concentric circles, Poseidon awoke.

*

The four of them had gathered around a fire the night before their departure to ride out into the villages. Cleatah poked at the embers with a stick, watching Talya and Boah across the fire, talking together.

She leaned over and whispered in Poseidon's ear. "She wants him in her bed."

He laughed quietly and shook his head. It was impossible, he thought. Talya's revulsion for intimate contact between Terresians and "the primitives" was too deeply embedded in her psyche to allow such a thing. Boah was no stranger to Talya. She had observed him, while cloaked, during her early field work in the Shore Village, though on their first official meeting Boah had been struck speechless by the sight of her. Never had he laid eyes on such a creature – the fine yellow-white hair, delicate features and long, pale limbs. He'd been paralyzed and could hardly utter a greeting.

Since that time Talya had emerged from the *Atlantos* several times to meet with the others to discuss their formidable endeavor. Clearly ill-equipped for interaction with the tribes, it was agreed that her tasks were best accomplished at the ship's home base. This night it seemed that Talya's initial condescending amusement at Boah's inclusion in the team had transmuted into respect for his native intelligence.

"We should all get some sleep," Poseidon suggested. "We'll

leave before dawn. Will you make your prayers to the Great Mother tonight?" he asked Cleatah and Boah.

"We will," Cleatah said, smiling at Poseidon. Then she turned her gaze on Talya. "And what prayers will you be offering tonight for our great undertaking?"

Talya was taken off guard. "I…I wish for every…success, and that you all return safely from the journey."

Poseidon struggled to remain straight-faced as Talya stood and abruptly left the campfire, but he was reminded once again that the two women in his life were far more evenly matched than he could have ever thought possible.

FORTY-FIVE

THEY WARILY APPROACHED the village of the Foothill People – miners of flint, quartz and obsydion – as they were known to be a fierce and stubborn lot. Their settlement was laid out along a river, and their houses were built into stone cliffs. Their men were known as masters at fashioning the best and sharpest tools, ones they traded with nearby tribes.

The men and elders who came out to meet the approaching strangers could see they were well-armed, but their posture seemed in no way belligerent. Cleatah and Boah on horseback stayed at the edge of the village, with Sheeva sitting attentively at their feet. Poseidon went forward alone, on foot. In their language he told them their offer in the simplest terms possible. They laughed at him. Why, they wanted to know, should they leave their home for 'a very large village on the eastern shore where the sun rises?' They had lived here always. Food was plentiful, and few dared attack them by virtue of their weapons. But they listened intently as he spoke. He showed them a large blade made of honed steel – a material that fascinated them, having never seen it before. But even as Poseidon demonstrated cutting rock with his blade he could see that some of them had their eyes fastened on Boah and Cleatah, more specifically their horses.

At first Poseidon ignored their blatant stares, tempting them with the secret of his steel implement and a promise to show them the mines where the ores that made them could be found. Some of the headmen were fascinated, but their attention was finally drawn away by several younger men who were moving cautiously towards the horses and Boah, and to Cleatah who had slipped to the ground and, with spoken words, was giving the wolf instructions to remain motionless.

Boah began to speak in an open way to the young tribesmen, showing them that the horses were harmless, even friendly. He was offering rides, causing nervous laughter. With that the elders left Poseidon to watch this curiosity. A demonstration of Cleatah mounting her horse with the help of a foot in Boah's clasped hands was all it took. The bravest of them was hefted into the saddle behind her. A walk, a trot, and a few moments of galloping, and the man was whooping with joy and terror.

The three of them were asked to share a meal in the headman's magnificent stone dwelling with its soaring natural arched ceiling – sweet white-fleshed fish from the river and rich meat of the oryx cut into thin slices with their razor sharp blades. Poseidon asked them again if they'd leave their village and come with them. He promised them steel tools and horses. He also promised peace and safety, though he added that they would have to live among many more people than they did now – a great many more, and far away from their settlement and houses in the cliffs. Some of the elders sat back, talking among themselves and glaring at the strangers suspiciously.

Then Boah spoke quietly to Poseidon. "I think just a few wish to come," he said. "They want the horse. The elders do not want to leave their stone village, their mines and their forests, as I would not. So let them who wish to stay, stay, and those who wish to go, go. Later those who leave with us might come back here and tell others to join them."

It was decided that Boah, with this wise strategy, should be the one to speak further to the elders. In the end more than half of the men, women and children agreed to leave their village to follow the trio.

The gathering of the tribes had begun.

*

They visited a village that had survived a long drought. Its people were little more than skin-on-bone, their children's stomachs' bloated with starvation. With all of the tribe gathered Poseidon showed them a sapling, and with a wave of his hand over the tree caused it to grow before their eyes. Its trunk thickened, its leaves sprouted and tiny buds of fruit expanded and ripened to wholeness. Mothers wept when he handed the fruit to them and they fed their children. Every man, woman and child from that village left their home behind and followed.

*

In another mid-continent settlement far from lush vegetation the women suffered terribly in childbirth without the medicines of the plateau and forest, and many infants were dying. During the trident's time there a woman gave birth, and with the medicines Cleatah had brought with her she saved the life of her child and also eased the mother's suffering. With the urgings of the women this tribe, too, deserted their village down to the last elder.

*

While moved by Poseidon's healing of a pustulant leg wound, Arak – headman of a western tribe that was steeped in dark superstitions – became angry at the "miracle." Unwilling to relinquish leadership, he stood eye-to-eye with Poseidon and growled menacingly, "A man cannot be a god. We will be punished for this!" Every one of his followers refused to leave with their village to go with the demonic horse beasts and a wolf that obeyed the commands of a woman.

FORTY-SIX

"TALYA, I'M SPEECHLESS!"

"I doubt that very much."

Standing in the circular library of the *Atlantos* she could see Athens's image before her. He appeared to be sitting oceanside under the spreading canopy of a giant fern, a golden goblet – she supposed filled with jog – held lightly in a be-ringed hand. On an ornate table at his side was a plate of some unrecognizable food, slippery and glistening and raw, probably from the sea. *He must have diffractors everywhere*, she thought, then said, "Working hard, I see."

"To what do I owe the pleasure of this visit?" he replied, ignoring her sarcasm.

"We haven't seen each other since we parted ways on Gaia. I simply thought it would be neighborly."

Athens drank deeply from the goblet. "You are many things, Talya, but neighborly is not one of them. You need someone civilized to talk to, and the best you can do is me."

"Do you mind?"

"No, no! I'm delighted to share your company, whatever the circumstances. You're looking very…"

The pause was so protracted that Talya found herself annoyed, in the way she was always annoyed by Athens's insolence. But he was right. She was desperate for someone to commiserate with.

"So you think I look old and haggard?"

He laughed aloud. "No. You're still the most beautiful woman I've ever known. What you do look is *furious*. Rage is radiating from every pore. It's rising from you like…"

"That's enough. You're enjoying this far too much. I think I've made a mistake calling on you. Why don't we just…"

"No. You need me to say these things for you. You're incapable of saying them yourself. But you're feeling them, and that alone – feeling emotion at all – must make you think you're losing your mind."

With the stinging truth of his words she felt hot tears welling up. But she was still not disposed to lay herself entirely bare. "Poseidon's made a catastrophic blunder," she said.

"I couldn't agree more."

"Everything he's worked for – his science, his reputation…"

"You. Throwing you away was his biggest mistake."

She swallowed hard and felt a single pathetic tear escape from her eye.

"What of this great undertaking of his? This civilization of brutes?" Athens pinched one of the gelatinous morsels between thumb and forefinger and popped it in his mouth. He smacked his lips and licked both fingers, slowly and with purposeful sensuality.

Talya stifled her revulsion. "He's very determined. As far as he's concerned, it's progressing according to plan. I will admit…" she began, but hesitated before continuing.

"What will you admit?" Athens wheedled, sitting forward in his chair.

"They're an interesting species. Genomically they're nearly identical to Terresians. I've discovered several small anomalies – quite inexplicable. But for all intents and purposes, they are *us*, though woefully lacking culture."

"And culture is what my brother intends to offer them?"

236

"Not precisely."

"What then?"

"He plans to take bits of their 'culture' – from all the scattered tribes – and introduce only certain motes of Terresian knowledge, then meld them into something altogether new, but 'natural' to the planet."

"'Certain motes'? What does that mean? What about our technos?"

Now Talya laughed. She knew how bitter it must sound. "He expects to use it very sparingly, if at all. Your brother is so inflamed, so inspired by 'the native accomplishments' that he raves on and on in his transmissions from the field. I *try* to show enthusiasm, offer suggestions. 'Could the night sky gazers be taught navigation by the stars in the vessels built by the future adepts of ship building? Might the textile weavers bring with them not only their looms and designs, but seeds of the plants from which they've harvested their fibers, ones that I can propagate genomically and grow in great profusion?'" Talya sighed despairingly.

"So even once his brilliant new society is a reality, you will still be living among savages."

"I don't know, Athens!" she shouted, then groaned with defeat, "I don't know."

His voice grew uncharacteristically gentle. "Why did you stay? What possessed you?"

"I know he's going to change his mind eventually."

"That's true enough, but still…this 'Cleatah' – what does he see in her that he could do such a thing? All I can imagine is pure animal lust," he went on, "which surprises me, really. I didn't think he had it in him."

"Unlike you."

"Quite right." Athens was unperturbed by the jab.

"Well, I suppose I should ask you about yourself," she said.

"To be neighborly?" he teased.

"Just tell me your news. Not women."

"Why not women? Isn't that news? Or does it make you jealous?"

"Athens!" she snapped threateningly.

"All right, all right. Well, you know we've had our own catastrophe here."

"The collapse of the mines. I heard."

"I'm happy to say we're on the way to full recovery – a massive improvement in efficiency and safety. And I have one of your own to thank for it."

"One of my own?"

"A genomist. Gifted man…"

And then Athens, all arrogance dissipated, all mockery dispelled, began to speak in the most glowing terms of his own beloved Mars and its radiant, limitless future. His talk of a society in which Talya could live most comfortably was quite soothing. She found herself fully engaged in the conversation, plying this once-irritating buffoon with questions and opinions of technos and alternative scientific approaches. All of them were cordially welcomed or intelligently rebutted. He was enjoying their conversation, too.

Only once, very briefly, did this fleeting thought cross her mind: the grandiose dreams of the brothers Ra were not so very different at all.

*

"Let me see you," Talya demanded.

"Not now," Poseidon said quietly. "I'm in the middle of the encampment. It's dark – just a sliver of a moon – and I haven't got long. There's a birth we're attending."

She was momentarily annoyed, but then thought it better this way. She would hate to have him see her overly avid as she described her newest protocol.

"I'm going to begin the horse breeding program immediately," she said.

There was silence on his end, though she could hear the clamor around him. His precious "Gathered Tribe" had become a seething mass of humanity, and Talya wondered what was keeping it from becoming a rabble.

"I realize I wasn't to start until you returned, but you've promised the arrivals 'many horses,' and I think it's wise to begin multiplying the herd now. When I go into the Shore Village to collect materials I'll remain cloaked."

"Talya, it's dangerous to work with animals that large. You've had no experience around them."

She found herself enjoying the alarm in his voice, so she calmed and flattened her own even more. "I'm perfectly capable of learning their anatomy and behavior. If necessary I'll use the narcotizing function when I work." She waited a moment more while he tried and failed to invent rationale to dissuade her, then added, "You have no need to be concerned. I'll be perfectly fine."

"Of course you will," he finally agreed.

Am I hearing relief in his tone? she wondered with a sudden flare of irritation. *The more busy and contented I am, the less Poseidon will have to think about me.*

"Please transmit your expedition times, and let me hear from you once you're back on the ship."

"I told you not to worry."

"And I'm ordering you to report as specified."

"Yes, sir."

She heard him sigh.

"Talya, let's not fight."

"We're not fighting. Not at all. I hope the birth is successful. Good night."

She clicked him off before he could say any more. She smiled, pleased at having unsettled him. And pleased, too, at her fascinating new endeavor.

FORTY-SEVEN

THE FOREST OF the North was already known to Poseidon, he'd told Cleatah. With the diffractor he had explored it many times. But what he knew of it concerned him. It was hot and dense and wet and crawling with life, both miraculous and dangerous. Talya's anthros summary revealed a large tribe – the Arran – spread like tentacles throughout it. He had described the place to Cleatah, and now as they left behind those already gathered who were camped on the open plain with Boah overseeing them and neared the forest, she could feel her desire to walk its verdant, slippery paths, seek its medicines, grow into a fever. Poseidon set his wrist devise to locate the fastest, safest route to the main village.

"I haven't journeyed alone with you since our voyage to the moon," she said as they regarded the dark tangle of trees looming before them.

"I can think of nowhere more different from that as this place we're going. But remember, we're here for the tribe. Much as you want to investigate every medicine plant you see, we simply cannot take the time."

"If we find the people, we will find the medicine," she said, disappointed but understanding.

It took only hours tramping through the crush of greenery to make contact with the first small encampment of the Arran people, a dark-skinned race despite the dearth of sunlight through the thick canopy of leaves. It would be three further days of hard trekking to locate the central village, a sprawling compound of stick and thatch houses carved from the forest, surrounded by a wall made of thick branches.

They were greeted with curious stares. No Arran had ever seen such pale skin. They were made welcome nevertheless and shortly discovered who led and who was most trusted among the tribe. A headman named Kull made decisions of daily life, but when the invitation to leave the forest was made to him it became clear that "Ta'at" the spirit doctor would need to be convinced.

Cleatah followed behind Poseidon, and he behind Kull, as they made their way through the crowded village, hundreds of pairs of eyes watching them pass. Ta'at stood at the large-leaf door of his hut, stooped nearly in half, fingers clutching a staff as gnarled as his fingers, but his skin was as unlined as a child's. Next to him, straight and tall as the ancient one was hunched was a young man of Cleatah's age, his forehead high and broad, the thick black hair straight and falling to his shoulders.

They were led inside and invited to sit. The young man, Thoth, did the talking, though prompted frequently by his father. When the offer had been laid before them Ta'at had conferred with his son.

Thoth said, "My father would like the people of the village to go with you to the new land by the water. But there is something to stop us going. Plants that cannot be left behind."

"Are they food, Ta'at?" Cleatah replied. "We promise there will be food enough for everyone."

"It is not food to eat," the old man said, surprising them.

Cleatah and Poseidon fixed their eyes straight ahead, though she wished desperately to confer with her mate.

Finally Cleatah spoke. "Are these spirit foods?"

The old man had to peer up from his stooped head, but his gaze was steady. His silence endured for what seemed an eternity. Then he nodded.

"There are two vines that twist around the sagron tree," said Thoth "and they must always be moist."

Now Cleatah spoke to Poseidon in Terresian. "Can you not promise him that their vines will grow on the Great Plateau? They may survive in our small wood, where the hot and cold springs flow. You must promise them. The phaetron – I've seen it do wonders."

"You wish me to use technos?" he asked incredulously.

"For this, yes. Ta'at is a green teacher. We must have him."

"All right. Promise him."

She turned back to father and son and said, "If you bring the vines, they will grow."

Ta'at inclined his head towards his son again and whispered to him.

"Something else," said Thoth. "We cannot leave our ancestors behind." He turned his body to reveal two mottled human skulls in the center of a small altar. "Many others, all the bones of our tribe, lie in a cave nearby. Many, many bones."

Cleatah saw Poseidon silently calculating, imagining a compromise. Ta'at and Thoth never took their eyes from his face.

Finally Poseidon touched his forehead with two fingers. "Let them know they may take as many bones as they can carry."

Once the answer was given Cleatah and Poseidon were shown out and allowed to sleep in an empty hut, creeping insects that lived in the thatch falling on them all through the night. In the morning they were called back to Ta'at's hut where the old man, his son and Kull were waiting. No one spoke but Ta'at.

"Erthe and the Great Mother choose the Gods," he said regarding Cleatah with a warm gaze. "I see they have chosen you.

The Arran will follow you, every one of us, from the forest. We will bring only the skulls of our ancestors." She felt Ta'at boring into her mind, like the tree beetle who tunneled far into the bark of the yew. "And we will bring our vines. You have promised me they will grow."

"I will keep that promise."

"You have been to Ur," Ta'at said. His words were uttered as a question...and a truth. "I see it in your eyes."

Cleatah hesitated before she spoke. She believed she knew what he was saying, and it excited her. "I have been to...another world, but your 'Ur' and mine may not be the same place."

She saw confusion on Ta'at's face, and it was much the same as hers. Surely his vines took him to another world, but how could she think that it was the same as Ka? Did different plant medicines not provide different healings? Why would the juice of two deep forest vines deposit its drinkers into the same world as eaters of mushrooms? Was there one Ka, or were there two?

"You have met the uth-cray?" Ta'at said. This time it was a question, proffered cautiously, suspiciously.

Now Cleatah was tongue-tied. That was a word Poseidon had taught her, one she liked. She had to think how to untie it. In Ka there were only creatures of the daily world that were brighter or bolder or spoke to her in clear voices. "Who are the uth-cray?" she finally said.

Ta'at laughed. Really laughed. From the belly. He laughed long and hard. "I cannot explain," Ta'at said, wiping tears from his dusky cheeks. "But one day I will take you to meet them."

Cleatah took Ta'at's hands in hers and smiled broadly. Then she and Poseidon stood. What was left for Kull and Thoth was the plan for an orderly retreat from the forest. Thoth held open the leaf door, stopping Cleatah with a hand on her arm.

"My father is old, very old. I fear the journey will kill him."

Cleatah nodded.

"I have been taught the making of spirit vines into juice."

"Good," she said, "then you will carry on for him when he dies."

But Thoth's forehead was knotted with worry. "There is much I do not yet know about Ur and the uth-cray. I cannot learn it all before he dies."

"I see much life left in your father. He may live for a very long time."

Thoth grinned and Cleatah saw that he was a beautiful man.

"He would be very pleased *never* to die. He says he dreamed of your gathering, the many people for us to live among – 'the more to share the spirit vine with,' he told me."

She smiled inwardly at that. Lately she had dreamed of giving the mushroom to the people as well.

"If my father dies…"

"There is no need for worry, Thoth. I will not leave you alone in this or any other world. It is my promise." Tears glittered in his eyes.

"We will be waiting with the others on the southern edge of the forest," she said.

FORTY-EIGHT

TALYA HAD LANDED the shuttle on a broad beach north of the Shore Village and walked south, activating the cloaking function only when their boats and nets spread out on the sand came into sight. The beach was deserted, everyone having climbed the beach stairs to the village in time for the evening meal. There was plenty of daylight left for this – her sixth foray of the horse breeding protocol. She was no longer surprised at her pounding heart and the sense that her neural network was firing at maximum levels. Annoying and enflaming Poseidon with the announcement of her mission had been immensely satisfying, but execution of the program was, surprisingly, proving to be its own reward. She'd always found her research in human genomic revisioning enjoyable, and never expected that applying the Molecular Sequence Reorganization principles to the Gaian horse population to be so challenging. She saw the role that the horse played in even the simplest human society. Those Shore People who had mastery over horses were thought to be elevated, potent individuals. Therefore, in Poseidon's experimental civilization, whomever controlled horses at their elemental level would possess limitless influence.

As Talya climbed the empty steps the smells of charred meat

and fish assailed and mildly nauseated her. She'd never gotten used to the idea of eating flesh and thought it amusing that Poseidon now relished the taste of it. Invisible to everyone, she sidestepped the families sitting around their cookfires. A small child running in a wild circle came careening into her legs and was knocked back by a solid but unseen barrier. She moved past quickly, heading for the corral at the base of the plateau.

Talya remembered the growing intoxication during her initial cloaked missions – recording the horses as they grazed, hunted, raced and mated – and recalled the unexpected disappointment she felt once the collected images had been phaetronically assembled, integrated, and recreated in her laboratory. While her detailed study of the three-dimensional bio-facsimiles – the muscular, skeletal, vascular, digestive, nervous and reproduction systems – was fascinating, she found herself longing for the physical presence of the living animals.

The next series of data collections were, as Poseidon had warned, more potentially hazardous, and had indeed required separating out and narcotizing each animal in the herd. Testicular sperm aspiration and egg harvesting with phaetronic devices she had designed and fabricated had proven daunting at first, but in the process Talya reaffirmed her admiration of these magnificent beasts, and she found herself strangely gratified and humbled to be probing them in so intimate a manner.

Then once again she had found herself back in the laboratory, in the tedious process of preserving and storing the samples. Colors, markings, temperament, relative strength and speed of each individual had been recorded. But it was the subsequent genomic re-sequencing, necessitating long weeks in front of her trans-screen, that grated on her the most intensely after the stimulation of field work.

In multiple transmissions with Poseidon, Cleatah and Boah she'd discussed the role of horses in the culture. Some would be needed for simple transportation, and for this a smooth amble was preferable. Large, heavy horses would be required for plowing and pulling ore wagons; lighter, faster and nimble mounts for hunting and racing. She had then chosen pairings of mares and sires, and at the genome level reshaped complexes of preferred characteristics. Finally she injected a single chosen sperm directly into the chosen oocyte, fertilizing it.

Today – finally – she would be depositing the first of the embryos into the mares. She approached the corral with its heavy scents of grassy dung, sweat and musk, with what was perhaps unjustifiable confidence. There was no way of telling if the intra-fallopian implantations would take hold and generate a live birth.

She entered the enclosure. The horses had grown used to her presence, and she walked among them, stroking a flank or a muzzle. She located the first mare and spoke calmly to her. Within moments the animal was following Talya to an empty corner of the corral. Slowly she lifted her wrist device to the female's head and activated the narcotizing function.

It was, she realized, as the animal dropped first to her knees and came to rest on her side, the first completely satisfying moment Talya had experienced since arriving on the planet.

FORTY-NINE

Yazman, birth doctor of the Ladoon, stood at Poseidon's and Cleatah's fire in the center of the encampment. Shadows danced on her wizened face.

"Ta'at is dying," she said.

As they followed her through the field of slumbering humanity and fires burning down to embers, Cleatah watched Yazman's skinny, rod-straight back as she made her way to a camp on the edge of the gathering. There they found Kull and dozens of Arrans, and many Green Teaches clustered silently around two campfires side-by-side where they watched as Thoth squatted, stirring two bowls of dark liquid. Nearby a roofless enclosure of skins and weavings had been erected, and Cleatah suspected that inside it Ta'at lay dying.

She squatted down beside Thoth. At once she could feel the fear in him.

He looked up at her. "What if my mixture is wrong?" he whispered.

"It is not wrong," she soothed. "You have done it correctly many times before."

"But never to give to Ta'at before he dies." Thoth look down at the bowls again, perhaps to avoid her eyes. "He wants only you and me with him. Kull is angry."

"Why?"

"In all his years Kull has never drunk the spirit juice or met the uth-cray. He is a fierce a hunter, but he does not like the sound of the uth-cray."

Cleatah knew that when The Gathered were settled on the Great Plateau she would journey to Ur. She had looked forward to it with all her heart, but now she would be forced to go unaccompanied by Ta'at. Thoth would have to suffice as her guide. Thoth, who lacked surety in himself in almost all things.

Leaving Poseidon to sit vigil with the Arran men she and Thoth entered the enclosure. She was glad they had not roofed it over. The luminous stars filled her with confidence that this death would be overseen, as all were, by the Great Mother, but also by the special gods Ta'at worshipped. And by the uth-cray. Before long the nearly-full moon would be overhead, a further comfort.

Ta'at was sitting up, propped on both sides and around his shoulders with soft bedclothes, and he looked to Cleatah not at all like a man about to leave this world. He waved a happy greeting at her, and she sat herself on one side of him. Thoth kneeled on the other. Now displaying none of the hesitation or self-pity she knew he was feeling he handed the single bowl of spirit juice to his father.

In their many conversations Ta'at had attempted to describe Ur. Sometimes it sounded like her mushroom visions – a world of brilliant lights with stars throbbing and colors dancing together. But there were differences. In Ur giant snakes would speak to him, there were bird-headed men, and a great wind took him sailing through the sky and under the water. It was, Ta'at said, "a place where death is known." Of the creatures he called the uth-cray the old man reported, "They are slim-limbed, their skin the color of ashes, and their eyes – very large – are as black as the space between stars." He found them gentle beings and smiled when he spoke of them.

But Thoth had no such comfort in their company. Silently they threatened him with their small slit mouths closed, as if speaking from their minds directly to his.

"What do they say to you?" Cleatah had asked.

"They warn me."

"Of what do they warn you?"

He shook his head in confusion, unable to answer. When Ta'at would suggest that he, too, had initially feared and distrusted the uth-cray, Thoth grew agitated, arguing, "No-no, you just say that to calm me."

But now Thoth showed great restraint, unwilling to delay or hinder his father's passage to Ur in any way. Ta'at closed his eyes and whispered something unintelligible before he put the bowl to his lips and drank.

Cleatah and Thoth sat with him as the time passed and the nearly-full moon took its place in the sky above them. Ta'at spoke of the stars as though they were old friends and told his son that he would miss seeing his beautiful face. He would be waiting in Ur – he swore this – for the time Thoth would join him there.

But when Ta'at stopped in mid-sentence to raise his hand in greeting to someone unseen, and his mouth curled into a beaming smile, they knew he had found his way to the other world and that the uth-cray had been there to welcome him.

FIFTY

I T HAD FALLEN to Talya to ready the Great Plateau for the many thousands arriving any day now. At first in her solitary endeavors after the Trident's departure she had been lonely, and angry at herself for missing Poseidon's company so keenly. But after occupying herself in the world of horses it had slowly insinuated itself into every sinew, every corner of her brain. It was work, still, but now it was passionately explored and rendered.

The subject was suddenly beautiful to her eyes and made her heart pound. Genomes were no longer hard numbers, but living things. The very *essences* of living things. The sparks of life. Inspirations came floating from behind her shoulder as elemental wisps and whispers – elegant solutions to formulae, inventions of technique, the urge to preserve the biological forms as art. Talya's wait for Poseidon to tire of Cleatah might be long, but she'd found a way to make the best use of her time on this planet.

The plain above the village had proven more fertile than even she had expected it to be. Its volcanic soil crisscrossed with her network of canals was already a paradise of fruited trees and vegetal crops. "Tools," like buron-driven plows, had been fashioned by Poseidon's direction and design and were waiting to be used by the first generation of farmers. Corrals were in place for the tremendous herd of buron that had been driven across the plain with the Gathered Tribes. This infrastructure remained cloaked from the Shore People's sight, and a vibrus perimeter subtly steered them away from developed areas to their hunting grounds and bull ring.

The many cloaked visits she made to the Shore Village horse corral had proven exhilarating. She delighted in both the plethora of healthy mares and foals she'd produced and the tribe's astonishment and joy. Of course they credited the Great Mother for these gifts and made generous offering to her. Everywhere Talya walked in the village she saw flower-covered altars. It amused her to think that the offerings had, in fact, been made to herself.

Finally on this Spring afternoon gazing out at the Great Plateau a thin veil of dust began billowing on the horizon, and she had her first sight of Poseidon's 'Gathered Tribes.' As they came she could only marvel at their numbers, far exceeding his original expectations. The act of delivering them, even to Talya's critical eye, was a triumph of organization, sheer will and faultless vision. No one would ever know it, but the roiling mass of humanity excited her.

There were, she decided with a self-contented smile, countless opportunities afoot.

FIFTY-ONE

ON ONE HORSE Cleatah and Boah had ridden ahead to the Shore Village with news of the coming. Everyone had been told of this venture before their departure three years ago. But even then the trio knew they had failed in their attempts to explain the magnitude of the event when Brannan asked if the gathering was like Poseidon's much-celebrated horse round-up.

Now as they slid from their mounts shouts of joy and embraces warmed Cleatah heart. She'd lived for so long among masses of strangers. Home to her had never seemed so sweet.

A gathering in the village center quickly became a noisy throng with children darting like insects between the people. It took some time before tribesmen and women settled themselves to hear a report of their unfathomable future.

Cleatah beheld the assembled, and she looked at Boah one last time before she spoke. "Honored elders, friends. Boah, Poseidon and I have brought home with us what you may see as a great herd of tribes."

There was talking and shouting. Nervous laughter. An infant began to cry.

"We hope that when you climb to the plateau," Boah told them, "what you see you will understand is not an invasion of enemies, but a blessing of new friends and tomorrow's families bestowed by the Great Mother herself."

Everyone quieted and Cleatah thought – hoped – that his words had managed to sooth them. But suddenly erupting from the stone path leading to the plateau came shouts, fevered and fearful. She turned to see a hunting party – some on foot, some on horses – descending not as ordered and self-satisfied men normally returned from the hunt, but terrified. Agitated. Their eyes wide and showing their whites. Children fled to their parents' arms, and a cry went up among the villagers.

"What have you done, Cleatah, Boah! Where is Poseidon?"

"We've done as we said we would," Cleatah answered calmly. "Poseidon is at the head of a great many tribesmen and women and children."

"Where will they live?!" Hydra called out. "How will they be fed?"

"We have brought with us a herd of buron larger than you have ever seen," Boah said. "These can be eaten. They will build a village on the Great Plateau. And they will sustain themselves with no harm to the Shore Village."

There was more shouting.

"You will like these people!" Boah cried above the uproar. "I have made many friends among them." He smiled his winning smile. "Some of the women are very pretty."

There was male laughter at that, and the heat of the moment began to cool.

Cleatah said, "All of them have left their homes to come here."

"Why have you done such a thing?" Elkon demanded.

She swallowed hard, the answer sure to sound like the ravings of someone bitten by a rabid animal. "In great numbers there is great strength." She was silent as she gazed around her at the familiar faces. "If you choose you can join with them, live among them, mate with them. There are many ways you can help them, and they will be very, very grateful. Or you may want to stay here in the Shore Village instead. See them little. It is only as you wish it to be."

"Now if you like you should come and meet your new neighbors," Boah said, swinging up on his horse's back and pulling Cleatah up behind him. "They are the Gathered Tribes," he added with some pride, "and they are eager to meet you."

FIFTY-TWO

IT WAS CELEBRATION day in Itopia.

Poseidon gazed out at the sprawling settlement. Night had fallen and fires were lit. Musicians were making fantastic sounds. Drumming rhythms moved women in their cloth garment to dance and sway in the firelight, their long hair flying, their ornaments clicking. He was always awed that Itopia – a Terresian word that meant "good place" – had materialized in little more than three years since the Gathered Tribes' arrival on the Great Plateau. The village had been built, mines dug and fields cultivated with startling cooperation and ease. Even the concept of foods stored for use in leaner seasons had been quickly accepted.

Of course none of it would have been possible without a common language. The phaetron had synthesized a basic tongue from Terresian and all the languages on the continent – a language called "Terrerthe" – and it fell to Cleatah to teach it. People were unwilling at first to abandon their tribe's languages, even angry at her attempts to force on them something as primal as the way they made themselves understood. But little by little the many diverse languages fell into disuse, only clung to by the oldest and most stubborn.

From their pounded mud hut in the center of the village

Poseidon and Cleatah oversaw the miraculous creation of a people. He used technos sparingly, if at all – not wishing to appear godlike, but hoping to free the men from grueling labor. Perhaps their greatest joy was watching a class of artisans emerge. The weavers, potters, basket-makers, painters and sculptors of stone were pleasantly shocked to know they'd not be forced to hunt, cook or garden in order to survive.

Poseidon knew that for any civilization to grow or evolve hard metals were necessary. Those who had previously engaged in mining commenced digging for iron and carbon ore, and the first smelting furnaces on Erthe began producing steel. Too, the phaetron had located shallow veins of a reddish metal the miners named "orich," and this was dug from the ground and fashioned into artifacts of great beauty. Granite cut from the cliffs with steel tools were worked into large rectangular blocks by a small army of stone masons and rolled on tree-trunks to be piled on the headlands of the Great Plateau.

New tools were invented. Introducing a flat "sledge" to the top of the wooden rollers led to a wheel, and then to a cart using wheels-on-axles. The principles of mathematics, the laws of gravity and simple physics were taught to the cleverest of the inventors leading to the development of winches, levers and pulleys.

Those with a passion for horses became, with Boah's leadership, herders of the buron. It was hard, dirty and sometimes dangerous work, but the magnificent beasts allowed them to ride on their backs for work as well as the delightful pastime of racing. The men of this "brotherhood" secretly believed themselves the luckiest men alive.

Hunters continued their traditional ways, hunting the wild buron, antelere, lyox and wild turkeys on foot, and even the tusked elephants that were discovered in a large herd on the far northern coast.

Those with a passion for the sea began building sturdy vessels that used rudders for steering and were safe in the sea beyond the waves. Islands off the shore that had never been visited by the Shore People became a frequent destination. The invention of the first sails to catch the wind caused great excitement. Everyone had crowded onto the beach one night to gaze out at the black ocean. They could hear the roar of waves and saw only glimpses of moonlight on the wavering foam. Then all at once the sea was illuminated before them, as though the stars had fallen onto the surface of the water. It was a parade of newly built vessels, each carrying a firepot that lit up its sails and sailors, a spectacle of movement and light from north to south and far out into the waves.

A fellowship of enthusiastic "star-gazers" was born. Using their knowledge they began calculating the best seasons for planting, harvesting and fishing, and celebration days to worship the seasons. When they'd begun discovering the planets Poseidon had gifted them with their first lenses, made from a hot phaetronic beam directed into beach sand and minerals to turn the silicon into glass. He taught them the art of lens polishing, and they began a rapturous exploration of the night sky, observing planets and moon and stars that were farther away than they'd ever dreamed.

The Gathered Tribes had become the One Tribe and earlier this day, after a bountiful harvest had been gathered from the land, sky and ocean, they had celebrated their new society. This morning, with the greatest solemnity, the men of the Shore Tribe had performed their ancient Ritual of the Bull. The sacrificed animal's sacred blood was divided and dispersed to the fields, the orchards, the corrals and the sea in hopes of continued abundance. For the feast, the one hundred buron that had been slaughtered were prepared in one hundred different ways. Mountains of grain were ground into flour and thousands of loaves of bread were baked. Everywhere were piles of ripe, succulent fruit that people could eat at their pleasure. People wearing woven garments and ornaments of quartz and orich, and beads made of seashells, wandered through Itopia visiting with neighbors and friends, showing off their healthy infants and prettiest handicrafts.

At midday there were games – running, wrestling and jumping. They threw thin iron disks to great distances. But nothing caused greater excitement than the horse races. With ceremonial pomp Heydra had come forward to announce the significance of the horse to their tribe. He recounted the now-mythic legend of Poseidon's roundup, and Cleatah's part in saving the first herd from a terrible death. In the races Poseidon competed alongside Boah, the Shore People and the new brotherhood of horsemen as an equal. Race after race was called for, *insisted* upon, and run with unflagging courage and endurance. The shouts and laughter left the people hoarse and happily exhausted and the winners – suddenly heroes – were hoisted upon the shoulders of the crowd.

But now the full moon was at its height in the night sky. Cleatah came quietly to Poseidon's side and placed her hand in his. He could feel her trembling.

"I know," he said.

"I can hardly believe the time has come."

"Do you think they're ready?" he asked.

"I think they trust you. Some of them have already seen your 'godlike powers.'"

"But this…"

She stood before him and kissed him on the mouth, lingering there sweetly, unrushed, as though the moments to come were no more significant than their daily intimacies.

"I'll be with you," she said, then smiled. "The worst that can happen is that they all run away screaming."

He laughed at that, held her close for a moment more, then together they went to gather the One Tribe at the headlands of the Great Plateau.

FIFTY-THREE

POSEIDON LOOKED OUT over the assembled. They stood in a great mass a way back from the settlement. Cleatah and Boah flanked him, wearing expressions of the greatest solemnity. Realizing that their leader, their teacher – the one whom some believed a god – was about to speak, everyone grew very quiet. They never realized their silence was unnecessary, as Poseidon was even now programming the voice projection function of his phaetron so that he would be heard clearly by all.

"My friends," he began in Terrerthe, "I'm going to show you something that you have never before seen. It may be frightening, but I swear to you that what you see and hear now will not harm you in any way. Anyone who doesn't wish to witness this vision should turn away, but if you do watch, you must promise not to move from where you stand, and you must remain calm. What I will show you…is a very large village, what is called a 'city.' The huts will be made not of pounded mud and grass, but of stone." He smiled broadly. "It is the granite that the miners and stonemasons have been taking from the mountain and cutting into blocks these three years.

"Now we live on the Great Plateau, but this city will be built on the side of the sea – just there." He pointed to the headlands behind them. "Small waterways from the sea, and rivers from the far mountains will flow into the city and all around us, but a mighty wall will protect it from the dangers of giant waves. While you on the Great Plateau have been learning to plant, harvest, herd and mine, our friends the Shore People and others who made their homes on the water's edge have learned to build sailing ships. These will become a part of your daily lives.

"All of this I'll show you, and more. When you see the place, know that it is *your* place. You will – with my help, the help of Cleatah and Boah, and the leaders of the One Tribe – climb down from the Great Plateau and build this city. Then it will be yours to live in. Let anyone leave now who does not wish to witness a vision of their new city."

Among the many thousands of tribesmen, women and children, it seemed not a single muscled twitched. Not a person turned away. The silence was absolute. Even the birds ceased their calls. The wind, as if Poseidon had sent a request, suddenly died. He could hear blood pounding behind his ears. He turned and gazed at Cleatah and saw with the greatest surprise that Talya stood beside her. Talya, who had never before set an uncloaked foot in Itopia. Poseidon heaved a grateful sigh to see there was an ease between the two women. Boah moved to stand at Cleatah's side and the two clutched hands. Three pairs of eyes gazed back at Poseidon with hope, love and the pride of accomplishment.

He had synchronized his wrist phaetron with the ship's more powerful device to insure the image was immense, razor sharp and sparkling with the truest colors.

Now he turned back to the people and began to speak. "Behold a new world. Your world, your home. Atlantos!"

Then with the merest touch to his wrist he engaged the diffractor. At once the air began to crackle and spark. A moment later the Great Plateau was no more, the firelights of Itopia disappeared altogether. Even the low stars above the horizon were gone.

In their place stood a fantastical metropolis of several concentric rings – both land and water. As though staring down upon the spectacle from the edge of the headlands in daylight, all could see the rounded amphitheater of the plateau's cliff-face enclosing three quarters of the circular city. A towering seawall high enough to hold back the greatest sea waves completed the span.

Water-filled canals glittered in the sun. Upon them hundreds of vessels, their white sails and bright flags snapping in a crisp breeze, moved in and out through a massive sluice gate – itself carved with the symbol of the Trident – to the ocean beyond. On the outermost "ring island" could be seen the tiny figures of men loading and unloading cargoes onto docks and into warehouses. A marketplace filled with stalls teemed with women in colorful shifts.

Another canal separated the outermost ring island from a middle ring isle. On this were built grand public buildings, pretty white, red and black stone residences amidst lush trees and flowering gardens where children were playing. Plazas, roadways and bridges spanning the canals like spokes of a wheel were crowded with carts and horses. A massive system of aqueducts connected every part of the city.

Poseidon chanced a look at the peoples' faces and saw their transfixed gazes and slack-jawed astonishment. Women held their children tightly to them, and the fiercest of hunters unashamedly clutched one another. He sagged with relief. They had not run screaming in fear. Shown a glimpse of their inconceivable future the One Tribe had, in a moment of remarkable trust, accepted a wondrous vision born of the most impossible of dreams.

Poseidon turned to find Cleatah. Her face was wet with tears.

ATLANTOS

And beginning from the sea they bored a canal
of three hundred feet in width and one hundred
feet in depth and fifty stadia in length, which they
carried through to the outermost zone, making a
passage from the sea up to this, which became a
harbor, and leaving an opening sufficient to enable
the largest vessels to find ingress. Moreover, they
divided at the bridges the zones of land which
parted the zones of sea, leaving room for a single
trireme to pass out of one zone into another,

— Plato's *Critias,* 4th Century B.C.

FIFTY-FOUR

HOW COULD IT be, Poseidon wondered, that they had arrived at this singular morning less than fifteen years since his team returned to Terres? It was nothing less than miraculous. He and Cleatah stood atop the massive seawall. In moments they would give the signal to open the Harbor Gate and begin filling the city's system of canals. He found he couldn't take his eyes off her, wind whipping the long tawny hair against a sun-touched cheek of almost the same color. She was radiant, regal in the white tunic that grazed her ankles, though the strong sinewy feet appeared misplaced in her fine worked-leather sandals.

From this vantage Poseidon could see thousands of pretty residences and stately public buildings on the Middle Ring Isle with its tree-lined roads and neighborhood plazas. Warehouses were still in mid-construction on the Outer Ring Isle. Standing along both sides of the still-empty Great Harbor and Circular Canals, and on the arched bridges that gracefully spanned them were all the citizens of Atlantos. Poseidon knew he was not imagining a thrumming human vibrus in the crowd, the air of high expectation for this moment of communal triumph.

All those years ago he had begun with the wall, a structure necessary to complete a tremendous circle – a three-quarters-round natural amphitheater in the cliff-face of the Great Plateau, just south of the Shore Village. With every member of the One Tribe watching from above he had employed the ship's larger device to "magically" lift giant granite blocks that had been quarried by stone miners and cut by masons into mid-air. They were stacked precisely in place along the seaside. Row after row of blocks were set, several deep, till the wall was a hundred feet high, twenty feet thick. Ore miners, smelters and metal smiths had worked night and day for months to fashion a solid steel sluice gate for the center of the seawall. Engineers had invented a mechanism of vertical rails, winches and chains to raise and lower it.

Despite the displays of Terresian technos that Cleatah had previously witnessed, at the building of the wall Poseidon felt her trembling at the sheer power of the phaetron. To be honest he'd never before employed the device in a building project of this magnitude, and even he was awed by the display. He'd refused to dwell on the fear such feats would surely instill in the people, or their certitude that he was a god. There'd simply been no other way.

With the wall and sluice gate in place the next step was carving out the canals. Like a master artist at a vast blank slate he projected the city's round template, illuminating it in sharp concentric circles of light. Then with its "vaporize" frequency the device had begun churning up the volcanic rock beneath the amphitheater's black sand. It dug the canals, with a broad, straight harbor bisecting them. This left two wide ring-shaped islands. A round island at the center perfectly overlaid the body of the *Atlantos*.

Poseidon had marveled at the stonemasons' quick study of cement mortar, and their designs for sturdy aqueducts and elegant bridges that connected the ring islands. These had been put forward and executed by men who less than ten years before could build nothing but simple mud huts. On the islands themselves homes began springing up along with public bath houses. On

Cleatah's urgings hot as well as cold water had been piped into the baths to create a luxury that none had ever before enjoyed.

Along the circular canals hundreds of docks had been built, ready for the day that water would fill them and the ships – from fishing boats, to cargo vessels to small family pleasure crafts – would be set down in them. The stonemasons had scratched their heads at Poseidon's instructions to build large empty structures along the far edge of the outer ring island – warehouses – with long stone piers jutting out into the canals. They could not yet conceive of a "future" in which these buildings would be filled with goods traded from across the sea in three-masted ships on continents yet undiscovered by sailors.

Out of sight but critical to this new society was the terra-formed Great Plateau, now connected to the city below by two massive bridge ramps. There the buron herds grazed within a vast fenced pastureland, and the horses used to manage them were kept and bred. Fields and orchards, watered by Talya's precise and efficient irrigation system were thriving and abundant. Itopia was still a bustling settlement, occupied by farmers and herders who wished to be near their work but also maintained houses for their families in the city below.

Farther across the plains were the mines – orich, quartz, granite, iron, carbon, shale and salt. The miners were an independent breed. Most chose to live where they worked, wishing only to visit the city on occasion. They and their families had taken up the architecture of fabulous cliff dwellings, living in the very mountains they mined. Thus the first Atlan colony had been born.

Finally, from the northern end of the seawall were steps leading down to the beach and Shore Village. Only the elders still called it their home, though family and friends regularly made the short journey into the past to visit with them or remind themselves of their old lives and place of origin.

"Well…"

Cleatah's voice snapped Poseidon from his reverie. There was an edge to it. Something new. The merest hit of reticence. Resistance. Or was it defiance? But there was no time to question it now. He inhaled a long deep breath of sea air and steadied himself.

"My friends," he began, the phaetron amplifying his voice throughout the entire city, "you were once many tribes with many languages. You joined together to become the Gathered Tribes, then arriving on the Great Plateau transformed yourselves again into the One Tribe of Itopia. Here today, surrounding you are the magnificent fruits of your labor. Know that each and every one of you holds a place in Cleatah's heart, and in mine, for you brought our dream into being. So it is to you, the people of Atlantos, that on this glorious morning we dedicate this city."

With a nod of his head the signal was given. Two hundred men heaving chains through a massive winch set into the seawall slowly lifted the gargantuan sluice gate. Millions of tons of seawater began cascading through portal, filling the harbor and spreading sideways into the curving canals. A great roaring cheer could be heard rising from all parts of the city.

It was then, in the moment of their greatest triumph, that Poseidon felt a tightening in his gut. Brief, but sharp enough to be noticed. It was a clutch of some distant, nameless foreboding. But how could it be so? This was a marvelous day. Sunlit and overbrimming with hope and promise. He dared to glance sideways at Cleatah who was gazing out over the city and the people – now "Atlans" – citizens of their new civilization. He moved to reach for her hand, something to assuage his fear. But he could read her thoughts and the language of her body, and this is what she was thinking:

What have we done? There is no turning back now. It was what he was thinking!

Then he saw her shoulders settling ever-so-slightly and heard a long sigh shudder past her lips.

No reassurances here, Poseidon thought and pulled back his hand.

Let's go down and walk along the canals," she finally said. "I want to visit Boah's house."

She turned and started down, but Poseidon hesitated so he could take one last look at the city from the wall. Cleatah stopped and turned back to gaze at it with him. The harbor and all the canals, while only inches deep in water, were nevertheless rippling and glittering in the sunshine. Already one could appreciate the full magnificent symmetry of the alternating rings of water and land.

"It's beautiful," she said and smiled, but she didn't linger.

What have we done? There is no turning back now.

FIFTY-FIVE

THEY CHOSE TO traverse the Middle Ring Isle – the one that boasted the majority of private residences – on foot. It was a day of celebration and of hard work as well, for once the harbor and canals had been filled everyone who had built a water craft – and there were almost as many varieties of design as there were designers – was eager to set the boats into the water. Nearly every home on the Middle Ring Isle had its own wooden dock. The canals quickly filled with vessels and happy families sailing or rowing about, enjoying the sights of their city from this new vantage point. There were larger ships manned by the new "navigators" as well. Those from the inland tribes who had never been on boats allowed themselves, terrified and giddy, to be taken on their first water journeys. Others stayed on the banks of the canals and watched the astonishing flotilla drifting past. Laughter could be heard echoing down the waterways, and there came over the city a slow easy grace born as much of the population's contentment with their lives as with the unique design of their new city.

As they walked Cleatah and Poseidon were greeted with affection by everyone. They enjoyed the sight of the many new homes, some of quarried black, white and red stone, others of rammed-erthe. Some were yet unfinished. Atlans were gathered with their families and neighbors admiring a black-and-white patterned wall here, a roof of layered slate there, a hanging garden blooming with lush vegetation. They sat at long wooden tables, large enough for a family of ten to recline among soft cushions of colorful textiles. Something as simple as a wooden table instilled pride, as the idea of furniture was a wholly new one for a people who'd previously known the simplest of beds in rough huts, and nothing more.

They found Boah's home on the inner rim of the Middle Ring Isle, close to one of the two bridges that connected the Middle Ring to the Central Isle. A crowd was mingling there. Boah was a popular man for the help he had given to so many since the gathering of the tribes. He had friends from every sector of Atlan society.

On the dockside of the lovely but modest erthan house, in the shade of a long vine-covered portico he had proudly set his table of finely polished cedar wood – a gift from one of the city's finest woodworkers. A simple rowing vessel that paid homage to the boatcraft of the Shore People was tied to Boah's dock. While there was fruit and bread and fish aplenty the table groaned particularly with succulent cuts of meat, tribute from the faithful Brotherhood of horsemen. These were men whose lives as hunters and herders had been blessed by Boah's generously shared knowledge of the beloved beast.

Tanned and muscular, his limbs fairly bursting from the short, sleeveless shift of nubby cream cotton, Boah beamed a broad white-toothed smile at the sight of his two best friends.

"Poseidon, look," Cleatah said quietly in his ear. She was staring at the back of a tall slender woman speaking to several Atlans near the table.

The woman wore a long, finely woven azure shift nearly to her sandaled feet, and a matching shawl that gracefully wove round her head and shoulders. When she turned slightly her face was revealed in profile.

It was Talya.

"Look at that," Poseidon whispered, as pleased as he was astonished. Since her brief, anonymous appearance at the visioning of the city to the One Tribe Talya had remained as sequestered from the people as she had during the great gathering and the years at Itopia. The one exception, it suddenly occurred to Poseidon, was Boah, whom she had seen sporadically as she carried on with her work.

Now as Boah came to Talya's side he placed an arm around her shoulder, and she smiled up at him with a radiance Poseidon had never seen in her. They were clearly more than friends and work mates.

"Friends, neighbors, Brothers of the Horse," Boah began, speaking to the assembled with confidence and authority. "This woman is called Talya. You do not yet know her, but you *do* know her brother...our beloved Poseidon."

A gasp caught in Poseidon's throat, and he felt Cleatah clutching at his hand. From the corner of his eye he could see she was barely controlling her expression, one that outwardly exuded placidity and happiness. Then he caught Talya's eye. Her look – unrecognizable to anyone but himself – begged him to support her lie. *What harm will it do,* he thought suddenly, *if it makes her life more pleasant to be known as my sister?*

Now everyone followed Talya's gaze, and they were smiling at Poseidon with the warmth and affection he had come to depend on for his own contentedness. There was so much happiness around them. So much good...

He smiled back at Talya and intoned simply, with a respectful nod, "Sister."

Boah puffed further with pride as he went on. "You have not known her, but she knows you. With the magical tools of her family's tribe she has made our fields and orchards fertile and abundant, and grown buron with the tenderest and sweetest flesh. And brothers," he continued, gazing at the horsemen, "if you wonder why, year after year, our horses run faster and longer, wonder no more. Give thanks to Talya."

With that, Boah lifted from a basket on the table a fabulous necklace of cut quartz stones and shimmering mother-of-pearl shell beads. Talya's mouth fell open with shock and delight.

"With Erthe's offerings," Boah said, slipping the strand over her head and around her milk-white neck, "I honor our sister... Talya."

The horsemen began first, with their signal of brotherhood, a closed-fist slapping into a cupped palm. Then one by one the Atlan women came and embraced her. Small children tugged playfully at her azure shift and suddenly Talya laughed, loudly and uninhibitedly – a sound, thought Poseidon, that he had never ever heard her make before.

It pleased him, he realized with a swelling heart, beyond measure.

FIFTY-SIX

"THERE WAS A fire between Boah and Talya today," Poseidon said as they reached the bridge to the Central Isle. "I know you saw it, too."

"Everyone who was not blind could see it," Cleatah replied with a smile. "And those without eyes could smell it."

Poseidon laughed.

"I was just then thinking of Talya as well," she said.

"Introducing her to the Green Teachers?" He knew her so well, Cleatah realized, that he did not read her thoughts so much as *share* them.

Now he was referring to the men and women she had discovered during the gathering of the tribes, ones that possessed knowledge both great and mysterious. Who lived in the vegetal world. The Green Teachers' combined influence was the greatest of all in Atlantos. Plants for food, medicine, oils, soaps, plants for weaving and dying were of supreme importance to the people. And then there were the plants for visioning. No one but she had eaten the mushroom, but others had experienced the erthe mysteries by drinking bitter potions – like her friend Thoth – and others still by smoking the leaves of a bush that grew in great profusion along the foothills of Manya and her sister mountains.

She and Talya had worked together in her laboratory to find constant and plentiful sources of food. Too much time spent in the ship's confines sickened Cleatah, made her weak. She even struggled with her studies in the *Atlantos* library, always feeling when she emerged onto Erthe's surface that she had somehow escaped with her life. And the two of them argued, rubbed each other raw.

Talya and her unnatural growth programs! It seemed wrong to tamper with the Great Mother's plants and animals. You might grow and eat them, hunt, corral and slaughter them for food. But to *change* them? Talya could transform the essence of living things, reshape the way they grew. More seeds on a stalk of grain. A flower petal's deeper shade of red. A horse with the size of its father but the markings of its mother. This frightened Cleatah. Made her angry. How many times had Poseidon defended Talya, reminding Cleatah that this was Talya's work? Her greatest delight.

Then one year a swarm of locusts the size of a storm cloud had destroyed an entire planting of grain just before harvest. The people protested loudly. When they'd lived in their own villages there was always enough to eat. But here, with so many mouths to feed, a failed harvest of the grain they had come to depend on was frightening. But their greatest fear was that they had angered the Great Mother by leaving their homes and putting their lives in the hands of Poseidon, a creature who was neither a man nor a god. Loss of the entire crop was a sure sign that she was mightily displeased.

There seemed to be no calming them. It was then that Talya – ever-calm as she was – revealed Protocol 9. A fast-growing variety of grain was sown, and increased watering by way of her irrigation canals avoided a dreaded famine. No one ever knew that "Poseidon's sister," working with phaetron technos in her laboratory deep underground had saved them. In the peoples' minds the Great Mother had taken the Atlans back into her favor.

But that single act had earned Talya Cleatah's undying gratitude and respect.

She had invited Talya to meet the Green Teachers then, but she had refused, still preferring her lonely laboratory. Today, having seen her at Boah's house out among the people Cleatah had decided she would invite Talya again.

Poseidon and Cleatah had arrived at the bridge to the Central Isle and paused to gaze out over the canal. They'd crossed this bridge so many times during the city's construction, but water had never coursed in the curved channel before.

"Did you know that Talya and Boah were working with the horses together?" she asked.

"I did not. I've been…preoccupied."

It was Cleatah's turn to laugh.

Poseidon had recently taught her that word – "preoccupied." He liked to tease her, accusing her of being preoccupied almost every day. And indeed she was. Sometimes she would even forget to answer him when he spoke. She would gaze far into the distance and see things. Things that were not yet there. Things that would be there in the future. Her work at the Academy. Teaching Atlans to speak, read and write the common language filled whatever time she was not spending with the Green Teachers and Talya.

Crossing over onto the Central Isle they passed its "navel" where behind a towering circle of hedge hid the portal to the *Atlantos* – a place that had come to be known as 'Poseidon's Grove." She'd learned to activate the blue elevator beam that would suddenly wink on and whisk her into the vessel below. These days Cleatah was able to effortlessly navigate Poseidon's technos. It never failed to surprise her.

But beyond the grove on the Central Isle was a green landscape, lush with ancient trees, grasses and flowering shrubs. She recalled the first time Poseidon had brought her here. She'd stood staring around wonderingly at what he'd built – a meandering rock-and-boulder-lined stream that cut through the center of the green, utterly wild meadow. And then suddenly her wolves Araba and Sky – daughter and son of Sheeva – had come bounding towards them. They halted, panting and whining at their feet, pushing themselves under Poseidon's and her hands for caresses.

Cleatah stood staring around her, wonderstruck.

"What *is* this place?" she'd whispered. "And how are the wolves not afraid to be here?" Many times she'd attempted to bring them from Itopia to wait for her in Poseidon's Grove while she worked in the *Atlantos* with Talya. They'd refused to even cross the bridge to the island, ears flattened against their heads, eyes downcast in embarrassment of their fear. She'd long ago ceased trying to bring them.

He'd told her it was their home. "If the wolves can be happy here, so can you."

But she was already moving in long strides behind a thick row of ancient-looking trees.

"Those will be residences and stables," he'd called after her. "Some of your favorite Green Teachers and their families will live there. Some horsemen." She saw houses there, made in the new fashion out of stone. They were still unfinished. Roofed shells with large window holes that she could see would let in light from every direction.

"I want my horses near me," Poseidon had said. "And you know how preoccupied you are, busy at the Academy. Someone will need to tend the medicine garden."

She'd turned to him wide-eyed. "What have you done?"

He gestured to a small red footbridge that crossed the stream. Cleatah ran on ahead to a low thicket of flowering shrubs. On the other side she'd found an expansive garden. She walked its narrow footpaths, ecstatically counting dozens of varieties of medicine plants, inhaling the familiar sweet and pungent fragrances. Some of the plants had been laid out in neat rows, others spread in natural patches. Clusters of leafy vines hung from trees that shaded the whole perimeter of the garden.

"You've brought everything I could ever need from the Great Plateau!"

"And from other villages as well. More are arriving every day. This way you'll have medicine from all corners of the continent."

She'd thrown her arms around his neck and kissed him then. But he'd begun pulling her from the garden with a teasing smile. She knew he was bringing her to their future home, a residence Poseidon had himself designed and built for her. He was very proud, almost shy about it. The place was a long and graceful structure, not overlarge but lovely in its combining of rock, erthe, whole timber and slate. The length of it undulated with the soft contours of nature. Not a single straight line could be seen, as though to the builder they would have been an affront. At the structure's center there was no door. Instead was a tall, wide entryway framed in gnarled tree trunks, finished to a burnished glow.

"You don't like closed spaces," Poseidon had told her as they passed through the arch, "so I made the outside and inside one."

They had entered a spacious, high-ceilinged chamber nearly as bright as the day itself. She'd angled her face upward and saw the sky above her through a thin transparency of glass. It was the gathering room. On the walls were textiles of every color and design. Arranged on the floor below them sat intricately woven baskets and shapely pots, some as large as a person. Gifts from every tribe. An enormous stone hearth had been built into an entire wall. She'd marveled at the immensely long polished stone table overlooking a wide window archway. Beyond this was the Great Harbor canal lined with granite blocks that stretched in a perfectly straight line from their new home, past the Middle and Outer Isles, all the way to the seawall. Even from this distance she'd been able to see the still-lowered sluice gate.

Cleatah had given Poseidon a helpless smile. "How can we live here? It's so big."

"Think of all the things you've learned. Will learning to live here be so hard?" He'd taken her hand. "Come, let me show you." He pulled her through a smaller doorway to be greeted first by the sound of crashing water, then by a warm mist that, when passed through, revealed a tall irregular chamber, its walls made all of white granite boulders. He turned her to see the corner behind them.

There, painstakingly recreated, was their secret waterfall from the Great Plateau. Two streams of water gushed down in a continuous flow – one cold, one hot. The waterfall was decorated with clusters of glittering quartz stones and long flowering vines. There was even a supply of the root Cleatah used for lathering soap.

It was then she'd felt a tightening in her throat. She was unsure how this "bathing room" made her feel. As Talya changed nature, Poseidon – with his technos – had *re-created* nature.

"You don't like it?" Poseidon asked, astonished.

"I do. Of course I do. I just…"

"Shhh. Come on." He'd led her through a final doorway.

This room's light was dim and soft, and here the torches were ablaze. There were no walls to be seen – only rich red patterned textile panels hanging from the high ceiling to the floor. Cleatah's nostrils were touched by familiar sweetness. She'd followed the scent and to her delight found her altar to the Great Mother. Her old oil lamp burned before the carving of the goddess she had worshipped since childhood.

"You brought my altar from Itopia?"

"It wouldn't be your home without it."

Then she saw the bed. Between the broad expanse of gorgeously carved posts were arranged a profusion of furred pelts, woven coverlets and cushions. And laying across it was a white shift. At its waist had been laid a red belt of an intricate weave – one of the western tribes, she guessed.

"Will you put it on?" he asked her.

Cleatah fell silent. She had not yet relinquished her skins. She raised her hands in front of her.

"I'm not going to force you, love," he said with a crooked smile. "I don't know…"

He'd held the garment up to her cheek. It was soft – a very fine weave, she thought. And it was fragrant – as though it had been imbued with mattock and elsin. She imagined how the shift would feel against the skin of her breasts and belly, her thighs and haunches.

She'd pulled off her vest and the pelt that covered her from waist to knee. She stood naked before Poseidon.

"Lift your arms," he'd commanded her. She did as she was told and he slipped the dress over her head, pulling it down along her torso. It tickled her side and she'd laughed nervously, feeling like a silly young girl.

But when Poseidon carefully tied the belt around her waist and stood back his face was lit with delight and not a little surprise.

"What?" she said. "What do I look like?"

He could see she was at a loss. "I don't have a mirror. You have to trust me, Cleatah. You look amazing. Like the Great Mother… in human form."

She grew suddenly alarmed. "You shouldn't say such a thing!" She'd started pulling the shift over her hips.

"No, please. Leave it on." He'd pulled her to him. Held her long body against his own. Buried his face in her hair.

"You like it better than my skins," she said.

"Maybe."

"Because I look Terresian?"

"No! You could never look Terresian. You're just…beautiful."

It *had* felt wonderful against her skin, so light, with it's flowery fragrance. She took a step, expecting her limbs to be imprisoned by the narrow lines of the dress, but the seams ended at the top of her thighs. She could stride in this garment as well as she could in her outfit of pelts.

"I'll wear it again on the First Day," she'd promised him. The day they would open the sluice gate and fill the canals.

"Then shall we take it off now?" he said with a sly grin. "Mustn't get it dirty."

She'd raised her arms and closed her eyes as he'd dragged it slowly up her torso and over her up-stretched arms. She felt his warm lips on her breasts, and her knees faltered. With a low laugh in his throat he'd caught her up and pushed her back on the bed. Its thickly furred coverlet had felt so soft and cushioned behind her back. *If this is civilization,* she'd thought, *if the gifts of the ship's library were hers for the taking and the wonders of Talya's technos could feed the people, then she did like it. She liked it very much.*

But here, now, on the First Day as they approached the residence again and Cleatah remembered the avalanche of water as the sluice gate opened and the huge canals began to fill she felt a claw at her belly, a brief tightening of her throat. It was not just the thought of herself giving up her skins for a pretty white shift, but that the whole populace of Atlantos was now at the mercy of Terresians and their technos.

What have we done? she thought. *There is no going back. There is no going back...*

Poseidon led the way through the arch to the gathering room where a fire roaring in the stone hearth was the only sound to be heard. He sat her down on the wooly white rug and took her into his gaze. "Do you know what you've done, Cleatah? You've birthed a civilization. You've become the mother of a people." He ran his fingers down the curve of her cheek, and his voice grew husky. "Do you think it might be time you became the mother of our children?"

She was startled by the question. For so long she'd put it out of her mind – the painful longing that tore at her every time she saw a baby at its mother's breast. Now she remembered her dream of Poseidon at the water's edge and the many grey-eyed little boys and girls who played at her feet. All of them hers. All of them his.

"Yes, my love," she said as she untied the red belt and lifted the dress above her head. Worry scattered like wisps of clouds on a windy day. "It's time we made a child."

FIFTY-SEVEN

EVERYONE HAD GONE, leaving just the two of them alone together. Talya and Boah lay stretched out face-to-face amidst a long nest of cushions in his fire-lit garden. Kav had loosened their limbs and voices. She remembered the evening, how she'd laughed more frequently the more intoxicated she'd become. Now she found herself staring at this man, this primitive she had come to know, her eyes fixed immodestly on all parts of his body.

His thick forearms with a feathering of sun-bleached hair.

His obsydion eyes with firelight dancing in them.

His mouth, lips and teeth. *What will be the effect*, she wondered languidly, *when these are applied to parts of* my *body?*

Not a word had been spoken of it, not a touch of skin on skin, yet she'd been certain that she and Boah would couple this night. Perhaps soon. She hoped soon.

She discovered to her surprise that she had been leaning in closer and closer to him. His scent – Erthan, clearly not Terresian – was mildly salty, mildly sweet. Not as pungent as he was after a hard ride. In this moment his smell was altogether pleasing. Arousing. This surprised her. Olfaction had never before played a part in coupling. She wondered when he would first touch her.

How? Where? But he did not reach out across the small space between them. *Is he going to touch me at all?* she thought with the merest touch of panic. *Have I only imagined his intentions?*

Such speculation was forgotten with the next laugh.

It was then she realized he had been waiting for her to move first. Not so long ago she'd disparagingly thought Boah nothing more than a primal man. Now it was apparent that he was cerebral as well…and very much in command. *All right, I will be the first to move.* She leaned in and laid her fingers on the back of his hand. With a slow smile he grasped her fingers and turned the hand over exposing her palm, then sank his lips into it as though it was a luscious half-fruit.

In that instant her soft gynae flesh pulsed sharply, twice, then a third time. She felt warmth spreading to her belly, her pubis and thighs. As Boah moved his slightly opened mouth across her palm and fingers, sucking on their tips Talya closed her eyes and felt her heart racing. The insistent thump startled her, but no more than the warmth between her legs turning to wet. With her other hand she buried her fingers in his long, thick black hair. She heard him sigh with deep satisfaction.

Suddenly he was lying full-length right beside her, pushing away cushions and lifting his tunic over his head. She startled again at the nearness of him, the expanse of naked skin, tawny and taut. His hands, perfectly strong and perfectly tender, touched her everywhere, moved her this way and that, lifted a forearm overhead so his lips could explore the cup of her underarm. He pulled her blue shift up to her hips, and more slowly still, spread her thighs wide apart.

Her hands were busy, too. The pleasure at the simple touch of them on his flesh surprised her. She sought and found his soft double sack. She felt his flesh-and-steel rod grow slippery under her fingers. But far from relaxing into her hand he took her body and lifted it with ridiculous ease, placing her astride him, pulling her down on him. With that she lost all sense of time and reason. All the places on her body she'd imagined him taking in his mouth, he did. She heard herself crying out, whimpering joyfully, begging for more of this, more that, *There, there! Please, oh please!*

Then with another turn she was on her back. He was inside her, stroking with a slow intentional rhythm, pulling her legs higher, then pushing them apart. She was groaning loudly. Never in her life had such a sound escaped her lips. The sound brought her a moment of sanity. *I should engage the enhancer, pace the crescendo, intensify the climax.* But the moment ended with a sudden flurry of arms and legs and a swift sweeping spin of her body that set her onto bent knees. The enhancer controls were out of reach, both wrists pinioned above her head in Boah's large sinuous hands.

His face burrowed in wet silky hair at her neck.

He was thrusting deep, galloping joyously.

She was his ride.

The rhythm began to coax from the deepest place in her a sweet sensation that with every stroke redoubled, strove, magnified, redoubled again. *Slower,* she told him, *slower. Barely move.* Then, like the points of a thousand-petaled flower opening at once Talya blossomed with a fury so sharp and so sweet that a braying cry burst from her throat. The sound was not pleasure. Not really. It was pleading, praying, beseeching.

Let it never stop. Please, please, please...

*

Talya came lazily awake in a warm tangle of limbs and strong sexual scents. There was moonlight enough to see Boah's beautiful face next to hers, and cushions strewn about them round the fire that had long ago burned itself out. She was altogether naked, her shift lying in a careless heap just out of reach. Some of her muscles had begun to ache and she was deliciously sore between her legs. At this thought memories and sensations flooded through her, threatening to once again swamp her, rock her like a small vessel in a rough sea, just as they had done before.

Before, when she'd lost every last shred of inhibition or control. Before, when she'd been laid bare, rutting for hours like a wild animal with Boah.

It had seemed perfectly natural as it was happening. Then she remembered: she had never engaged the enhancer. Yet the coupling had been...*what had it been? Prolonged. Frighteningly raw. Primal. Insanely satisfying.*

Nevertheless, the desire to separate from the man was growing into an urgent need. She knew any attempt at disentangling their bodies would wake him, so with a few taps at her wrist he was narcotized. As she wrestled out of his sleep-heavy arms and legs she felt the spell of the evening lifting. She paused once to smooth back a dark thatch of hair from Boah's brow, and a pang of some unspeakable emotion – *yes, it was emotion* – fluttered briefly in her chest.

Talya stood and slipped the rumpled blue shift over her head. The shawl was nowhere to be found, but the necklace he had presented her was at her feet, the quartz stones glowing dully in the moonlight. She picked it up but hesitated, resisting the urge to put it around her neck, keenly aware that she was drowning in sentiment.

I really must get a hold of myself. I must.

Tying the leather sandal straps around her ankles she stood erect, took in the remains of the celebratory feast on the cedar table and moon-dappled water in the canal, and wondered at her own appearance. Was she ravaged, like the carcass of roasted buron, or as serene as the tiny waves lapping against Boah's dock? She gazed down one last time at his sleeping form, so peaceful and sated, then turned and started back to the *Atlantos*.

*

It was the first time the ship had felt deserted and the hum of the vibrus so unnaturally loud to her ears. The monotone grey metal surfaces contrasted sharply with the colors and textures still impressed in her mind's eye from the evening before. She felt a surge of familiarity and relief as she reached her laboratory, but as the door slid open a sharp and unexpected stab of longing assailed her.

Poseidon.

How had it happened that the source of her fulfillment was someone other than her chosen mate? A sudden startling epiphany stopped Talya in the doorway. She stood, overtaken by the understanding of Poseidon's unquenchable passion for Cleatah. He had lost himself in the sensual realms and had no intention of finding his way out. Now she comprehended that for a Terresian such sensations, once allowed a foothold, could be permanently desired. Addictive.

She would not allow them to control her. No. It was unthinkable. Irrational. Embarrassing. She moved from the doorway into her laboratory, as though the intentional step was a reclaiming of her sanity. She went directly to the cabinet where an array of devices were stored, and with a clatter she set the necklace on a counter and reached for the small gynae phaetron. Without hesitation Talya set it to the "abort" function. She was nowhere near the fertility phase of her cycle. Nevertheless she lifted her shift and slipped it inside herself. *No sense in taking any chances.* Perhaps it was a symbolic act. No matter. She would not, under any circumstance, become a slave to her desires or emotions.

But later in her quarters, steam rising from the shower stall, Talya hesitated before stepping naked into the water. She wiped an open hand across her shoulder and chest and brought it to her nostrils. Faint but definite – what was left of Boah on her skin. She let the hand drop to her side, then angled it up to caress her belly and slowly snake lower to her pale silky triangle. She let a single finger discover the moist cleft and closed her eyes at the shock of pleasure it produced. A moment later she was setting her wrist device to "Orgasm – Strong."

Then she stepped into the pounding shower and let the phaetron do its work.

FIFTY-EIGHT

"I'M PREGNANT."

Joya rolled off Athens, allowing her long fragrant hair to sweep across his face and neck. She lay next to him so that her face was close to his.

"Mine?" he asked, mildly surprised.

"Yes."

Athens pulled back so that he could see the whole of her lovely face. "Will you carry it to term?"

"I haven't decided. Probably not."

The fetus, he knew, would gestate quite as well – and more safely – in the breeding laboratory, and it would save Joya the discomfort and bodily distortion of pregnancy. Still, the idea of offspring was curiously appealing.

"Is it a boy?" he asked, stroking Joya's belly. It was flat and perfectly toned.

"A girl. She'll have my hair and eye color."

This cheered Athens. Joya's silky black hair and eyes were her nicest features.

"But the gene-scan gives facial bone structure predominantly to you." She ran her fingers over his angular jaw, rough with stubble. "She'd be better off looking like me," Joya teased.

"I agree. We'll modify any parts you don't like."

She lowered her head and twirled her tongue around his nipple, bringing him almost instantly to arousal.

A child, he thought, and was reminded suddenly, warmly, of his own mother. He remembered snuggling in her arms, having the top of his head kissed. "What if I told you I wanted you to carry it to term?"

"What if I told *you* you were being ridiculously sentimental?" She bit down playfully on his tender flesh.

Athens grimaced in pained pleasure. "I'd say you were acting impertinently to your governor and needed to be punished." In the next moment he decided his tumescence was far too delicious to waste on such pointless babble and slid his fingers into the warm, wet folds of her. He paused for a moment to decide exactly how he wanted to take Joya this time, but found himself instead to be thinking, *A daughter, a beautiful daughter...*

*

Athens knew he was dreaming. Not the regimented working dreams of PseudoMort, but one of the sweet, lazy dreams of Mars. He was in his bed at the beach house gazing through the large glass doors of the upper deck, to the sea. But there were no blue crashing waves, no cloud-dappled skies, no birds soaring and diving. It was night, and all he could discern out the glass was deep blackness and glittering stars. He might have been looking out the window of the transport that had brought them to Mars, the stars were so bright, so close.

He felt a warm hand grasp his hard sex and turning his head slowly saw Joya smiling that pouty-lipped smile he loved so much. He looked down to see her fingers, long and soft and white moving slowly, rhythmically over its shaft, caressing the head. He heard his breathing quicken and felt the pleasure rising, beginning to intensify. I should tell her to slow her stroking, he thought. I don't want this to be over so quickly. *But now he noticed something odd — the acrid smell of burning rock.*

The smell of deep space.

Fear gripped him, unreasonable and chilling, though the pleasure in his loins continued to build and build quickly, paralyzing him. It is all right, I'm dreaming, *he thought,* things are always odd in dreams. *Slowly he lifted his eyes to the glass doors. Just beyond them, hovering above the deck, were three plasma spheres, glowing orange and pulsing to the rhythm of Joya's strokes.*

What are they doing on my deck? *he thought, panic rising.* What are they doing on my deck!

He felt he should look down again, though he knew it was not what he wanted to do. He did not want to look down to where the raw pleasure was growing, growing... Not with the amber spheres suspended ominously outside the glass. He should really not take his gaze from the orbs. But his eyes defeated him. He felt the slow creak of the lids as they lowered, his gaze lingering on his chest, then to his belly and past it, where the hand was working him.

But the hand was not Joya's. The fingers were long, far, far too long, with boney knuckles, lacking fingernails. The hand's color was grey. Grey! And it moved in terrible rhythm at the end of a spindly grey arm.

Athens shrieked in terror and insane pleasure as he came and came and came...

FIFTY-NINE

RISING NAKED FROM bed in the thin dawn light Talya found a heel of bread and a fat crumble of white cheese on Boah's table and downed them ravenously. Their nightly exercises always left her hungry – for food and more copulation. He was always obliging though more and more – to her great irritation – he spoke of children. She would share his bed gladly but children were out of the question. She'd recently had to say it aloud, and watched him flinch at the words. Nevertheless he continued to bed her, pleasure her…and himself…most nights of the month. People spoke of Boah and Talya as though they fit naturally together. *We do fit together 'naturally,'* she thought with a twitch deep inside her, and smiled. In that way she could not get enough of him.

She pulled on her shift, unsurprised by his absence in the house. There was some horse business to be seen to at the city stables. He would meet her later in High Atlantos. She stepped out into the sea-crisp morning and saw that he'd tethered the horse to the cart so that it would be ready for her. Her tool cases were laid out neatly side by side with Boah's things – horse blankets and bridles, several shifts and a pair of sandals – all he would need for his extended stays in Itopia. The Brotherhood had lately been objecting to his life in the city, so far from the buron grazing pastures and the grasslands where the horses ranged and bred. Boah had told her it would please them if he stayed in the settlement more. She had not objected. They would still have their trysts at his home on the canal, but now when she went to High Atlantos for work she would stay a night or two in the old village with him.

From Boah's house on the Middle Ring Isle Talya crossed the bridge to the Outer Ring. She sat on the seat at the front of the wagon, the horse pulling it. She'd never enjoyed riding. Though the rhythmic gait stimulated her pleasantly, she felt vulnerable with her legs spread wide over the beast's back. Clopping along past the South Market she could see it coming to life even before the rising sun peeked over the seawall. Vendors called out friendly greetings to her, and she called back to them. Talya still marveled at the ease with which she had been accepted into Atlan society once she'd emerged from her solitude.

She turned the cart onto the South Ramp that rose in a sweeping curve to the headlands of the plateau. The cobbled surface of the long ramp caused the cart to clatter noisily, rattling Talya's bones and setting her teeth on edge. Like so many aspects of the city its construction – though an amazing feat of engineering – was rough. It was even beautiful in its way, though lacking refinement.

Not unlike Boah, she thought. There was always a whiff of the savage about him – though now he was famous as the First Man of the Great Plateau.

Above the city stretched "High Atlantos." It was home to many who saw the fields and orchards, mines and herds and the Itopia settlement as more their domain than the circular isles, canals, bridges and houses enclosed behind the seawall. Where would the city be without the food the plateau provided? The water? The horses?

The horse still held a power over men like no other. The

beasts made them stronger, more fearless. Better hunters. If you were a horseman a woman would smile at you before she would another man. There was strength in the Brotherhood. Strength that came from loyalty and a shared love of the animal. The men rode together, ate together, bantered comfortably, laughed rowdily, competed good-naturedly. Without effort men from many distant tribes had forged themselves into a single sub-tribe with unbreakable bonds.

They toiled happily to keep the pastures green with sweet grasses, assisted at the birth of foals, improved their herding, and raced for the simple joy of it. Their women wove them blankets and short tunics of a pattern and color all their own. They were keenly aware that they'd been blessed by the Great Mother, and gifted the horse by Poseidon.

They were the proud men of High Atlantos.

Boah led them by virtue of his knowledge, something so strong and inborn that no one questioned it. He was generous, humble and soft-spoken. He'd told her that when he was young he'd been loud and sometimes bullying. Now he found that the quieter he spoke to men and horses the harder they listened. Only when a buron herd ran amok, or a brother was endangered did Boah's shouts shatter the peaceful plateau. They were commanding. Surprising. Frightening. Some claimed he could turn a stampeding herd back on itself just with the sound of his voice.

Talya thought of him and smiled.

Close to the lip of the plateau ledge the view of the city was complete. She always stopped her cart here to gaze down at it, never failing to marvel at its perfect symmetry, a virtue she much admired. It had been a stroke of genius – the concentric circles – making such excellent use of the water and the land. Whenever she took in the sight she mused ironically that Poseidon was a geologist, not an architect. The talent must have been latent in him.

Seeing she was alone on this part of the ramp Talya quickly activated the bio-locate function on her wrist device. The triangulation complete, a small diffracted image materialized in front of her showing Poseidon on the Outer Ring Isle at the proposed site of the Horse Race Stadium. This was another of his wild schemes, all of which were meant solely for the pleasure of "his people," as he so quaintly referred to them now.

She could see him gesturing broadly over a vast as yet unbuilt-upon area just west of the city stables – a sprawling complex of stalls and grazing lands that lodged all the animals employed in the metropolis. Still under construction nearby was an extravagant and improbable indulgence conceived by Poseidon himself – a bath house for the horses.

The greatest proportion of male Atlan horses lived in the city, with only the breeding stallions living in High Atlantos, stabled with the females and their offspring. The city's horses were seen by many as the society's greatest resource, available to all as needed. No one "owned" a horse and, though common property, each of them was equally cherished and pampered.

Talya was content to view the image without sound. When she secretly observed Poseidon like this – an activity she knew he would despise – she preferred him to be silent, as so many of his actions and sentiments irritated her. Some, like his surgically removing the phaetron from his wrist, she found quite ridiculous.

Then into the picture walked Boah, his eyes following Poseidon's grand gesticulations, the two men certainly imagining what would become the city's most magnificent structure. Now Boah pointed "there" and "there." Poseidon nodded and smiled, seemingly pleased with his friend's ideas.

The sudden clattering of cart wheels on the ramp above Talya took her by surprise. She deactivated the phaetronic image and it winked out instantly. It was time she moved on. This was too important a day to be late. She tapped the horse's rump with a long slender stick and it trotted on.

As all who traveled to the top of the South Ramp Talya was greeted by the immediate sight, sound and smell of the great buron herd that grazed unhurriedly and uncrowded, enclosed by fences and gates. The shaggy pelts on their backs suffused the pastures with a rich musk that floated wherever the wind took it. As she traversed the long well-constructed road beside the pasture there was time to consider the Brotherhood and horses – the reason for this day's visit to the plateau.

Her stature among the Brotherhood had been increasing with each of her genomic progressions – a larger horse to carry a heavier load, a faster mount to win races, a thicker foreleg for endurance, a gentler breed for women to manage them more easily. Each success raised her higher in the Brotherhood's eyes and increased the men's solicitousness. Though she dealt with horsemen very naturally – speaking without pretention, eating and laughing with them at their campfires – it was whispered that this milk-skinned, sun-haired woman and sister to their beloved Poseidon possessed strong magic. That she was herself a goddess.

The grasslands were a place of bucolic loveliness – rolling green pastures and ponds dotted with tall, luxuriant trees and the graceful mares grazing there with their young. The stables were ahead, and the horse pulling her cart picked up speed, eager for the company of other horses and the men with steady hands. The ones who knew the words to whisper in their twitching ears to calm them.

When Talya arrived at the birthing barn it appeared by the size of the crowd that the entire Brotherhood was in attendance, all of them milling excitedly near the barn's wide-open door. Two of them helped her down from the cart. Her equipment was taken down and the horse and trap were led away. She could feel men's eyes burning into her, admiring and undressing her. Of course she was aware – and Boah lost no opportunity to remind her – that while their respect was sincere every one of them wished to bed her. They all envied Boah his possession of her affections. She strode to the far stall where a gathering of horsemen as large as the one at the door announced the day's grand event.

"Boah has not come?" It was the man called Joss who'd spoken, his gravelly voice tinged with disapproval. He was kneeling at the side of a brown and white mare that lay in the straw in the final moments of her labor. Talya could see the deeply tanned, muscled back and long sinewy arms of Boah's second-in-command, and found she could not tear her eyes from the tensed, naked haunches showing out the sides of his leather loincloth.

"He will be here, perhaps not before the birth," she said.

"A most important birth," Joss said pointedly.

Talya went to his side and knelt beside him.

"Will the foal be pure white?" he asked. There was a rough challenge in his words.

"White, as I promised. And a female."

Joss turned and fixed her in his gaze. There was something feral about him. Dangerous. The glittering black eyes, the tightly pulled skin over lean cheekbones. A single crooked incisor might as well have been a fang.

"This is one promise that should not be broken," he said.

"Have I ever disappointed the Brotherhood?"

The mare was laboring hard now. Her side, lathered in sweat, heaved with every contraction. Joss moved quickly, reaching up inside her and ruptured the grey amniotic sac. A foot dislodged, then a second. The foal's muzzle appeared. Joss spoke gently to the mare, rubbing her flank with an open palm. Now a head and neck appeared, wrapped in the sac. Joss peeled it away as it came.

Talya hardly breathed as the shoulder, abdomen and hips emerged. Finally the hind legs. With all of the sac peeled away it was clear that the horse was pure white.

But it was limp. Lifeless.

Talya could hear agitated murmuring around her. What good would her promise of the first pure white horse born of two brown-and-white parents be if the thing was born dead?

Joss worked quickly, clearing the infant's nasal passages. He leaned down, placing his mouth over the foal's nose and began to breath. Another man knelt beside the small body and rubbed it briskly with a rough cloth.

With a sudden jerking spasm the foal kicked all four hooves. Everyone fell back, giving it space. *Giving* her *space.* Talya noticed with a small thrill – it was a female. A moment later the horse scrambled to an awkward stance on gangly legs.

Joss helped Talya to her feet and they turned to face the assembled Brotherhood, now crowded outside the stall door.

"A healthy white female, as Talya promised!" Joss cried, his voice trembling with pride.

The Horsemen came crowding around them chanting, "Talya! Talya! Talya!" She liked the feel of all that male flesh so close, the salty scent of them, the husky voices celebrating her name. Then in the crush she felt it – unmistakable. It was Joss's arm snaking around her waist, his wiry fingers caressing the small of her back. Talya's heart lurched for a single perilous moment.

Then she leaned back into his fingers…and smiled.

There was no warning of the first jolt or the colossal roar of the erthe grinding against itself. When the barn's vaulted ceiling began moving and groaning, sending dust down on the horsemen's heads they fled towards the door shouting in terror.

With inconceivable strength Joss lifted the white foal in his arms while two horsemen covered Talya's body with their own and made their way over the convulsing floor towards the light of day.

What greeted them was a scene beyond imagining. The grazing meadow was a bright green sea of angry rolling waves. Mares and their foals had stumbled instinctively towards each other, and now in a large disorganized herd were running in panicked circles.

Then in a moment that would be seared forever into their memory Talya and the Brotherhood watched as a wide gash ripped open the ground beneath the herd's feet. She would remember the moment as altogether silent – though of course there would have been crashing and rumbling as the quake continued to batter the erthe as the horses screamed and died.

She did not hear the horsemen's openmouthed wails, but saw them falling to their knees, covering their faces with their hands.

Neither did she hear the sound of her own bleating, helpless cries.

SIXTY

THEY HAD BOTH been thrown to the ground, but as Boah staggered to his feet and began running as best he could on the convulsing erthe towards the stables Poseidon found himself paralyzed, cursing himself for having sectioned-out his wrist phaetron. Without its seismic triangulation function all he could do was guess at the quake's epicenter and depth. From its severity and direction he believed it to be the nine-hundred-mile long vertical fault in the ocean nearly one hundred fifty miles from their shore. The probability was great that a drop in the sea floor to the west of the fault had occurred in the first moment of the rupture, and that a vast displacement of water was sending a seismic sea wave in their direction. He could guess at the calculated time of its arrival. What he could not know without the diffractor was whether the quake had triggered an undersea landslide. In any case he could wait no longer.

Poseidon pulled himself to his feet and ran to join Boah. One of the stable walls had collapsed, trapping a stableman and a horse under the rubble. Boah and several men were finding it impossible to lift the giant blocks from their friend. Again Poseidon cursed himself. If he'd had his wrist phaetron helping the men and animals would have been possible.

He ran into the crumbling stables, quickly pulling uninjured but wild-eyed animals from their stalls. There were few inside – the rest at work at various sites on the ring islands. Poseidon mounted one, herding the others out before him.

"Help us!" Boah cried from the collapsed wall, his hands covered in blood.

"I've got to get to the seawall! Poseidon shouted back. "Something worse is coming!" He raced away, galloping past the line of Outer Ring docks and warehouses still being built on the canal where workers were struggling with fallen walls and gravely injured men. Across the Outer Isle he could faintly hear screams of distress from the North Market.

As he crossed the canal bridge he saw to his relief that the seawall had been unscathed by the shaking and the men of the Wall Watch, though unnerved, stood faithfully at their posts. They were gazing nervously inland towards the city, concerned for the damage and injuries of families and friends. They saw Poseidon riding hellbent towards the wall.

"There is a wave coming! A great wave! Look for it! When you see a white line of foam from north to south, come down from the wall and run inland! Gather any you find and take them with you!"

Poseidon leapt from his mount, summoning the four ground-level Wall Watchmen and ran to the massive mechanism that, but a year before, had required two hundred men and heavy chains to winch the monolithic sluice gate open. Its design for emergency closure was different, needing just three men and the force of gravity to close it. Once the lever was released the metal behemoth would slice down through its vertical grooves in the seawall and in moments seal both the tall decorative portal and the deep channel below it.

"Heave!" Poseidon cried, and he and two of the Wall Watch threw their weight behind the giant release lever.

It did not budge.

"Heave!"

The second attempt was as futile as the first. Something was jammed, but there was no time for further diagnosis.

Poseidon shouted up to the wall guard, "What do you see?"

There was ominous silence from above.

"What do you see!"

But when, before his eyes, water in the Great Harbor began to fall away Poseidon knew with certainty what terrible sight was before the Wall Watchmen's eyes.

"The sea has gone!" one called down in bewilderment. "There is no more water in the sea!"

With that Poseidon was done with human labor. Abandoning the lever he dashed to his horse and mounted it in a single swift move. With sharp kicks to the beast's sides and frantic shouts in its ear they raced back over the First Canal Bridge and across the Outer Ring Isle. He refused to stop for the people wailing in fear at the canal water's disappearance, or even for the injured. The Second Canal Bridge was crowded with Atlans gawking at the fast-emptying channel, but Poseidon's "Make way! Make way!" scattered them. He traversed the Middle Ring Isle swiftly.

On the Central Isle he ran for the Grove and rode the beam down into the ship, his heart pounding, the blistering inner reproaches for his stupidity coming one after another like blows to the head. It took but a moment to secure a small phaetron, then to retrace his steps and – on horseback again – his path across the bridges and ring islands.

As Atlantos blurred around him he saw in his mind's eye the catastrophe unfolding. The swell of water surging through the open seawall gate, the canals refilling quickly with the force of the seismic wave and with its extraordinary wave length overflowing and finally flooding the city so carefully enclosed behind the sea-wall and by the cliffs of the plateau.

A great bowl of water drowning every living thing!

As Poseidon approached the seawall he saw to his horror the Watchmen racing down the steps. The great wave was near. There was no time. The gate must be shut or all was lost. Now he could hear the awful roar. There was no need to see the thing to know its white foaming crest would stretch from the north horizon to the south.

The ground guards were waiting loyally at the winch but as Poseidon approached he shouted for them to run, to stay away from the harbor and canals. To climb to the highest rooftop.

Then he turned to the frozen winch and fighting panic activated the imaging function, allowing him to see inside the mechanism. There it was — a rock lodged firmly within the gears! But the sound was growing louder as the great wave crashed in on itself not a mile from the wall.

Frequency set, he directed a pulverize emission at the stony impediment and held steady – aware of the danger posed if the metal winch itself was damaged, or fragments of the shattered stone further obstructed the gears.

With a fracturing blast the rock shattered into fine dust. Poseidon sagged with relief…but the expected mechanical release did not occur. For a moment that seemed an eternity the sluice gate remained impossibly, steadfastly, aloft. *What more could he do?!*

An imperceptible metallic creak…*had he really heard it?* Yes, another! All at once the gate started its screeching descent, first slowly as the winch began to turn and finally – overburdened by weight and gravity – fell precipitously and heavily, and with a resounding thud crashed onto the channel floor.

Then the wave struck.

The seawall shuddered once with its explosive impact. Poseidon could hear the mass of water coming and coming, but the light spray from above told him its height would not overwhelm the structure. His knees buckled and he sank to the ground, his back against the wall that had saved the city. In a moment, when he had recovered his senses, he would turn the phaetron out to sea and determine if a second wave was charging toward their shore.

But for now he would simply breathe – one blessed breath at a time – and give thanks to the Terresian technos that had saved them all.

SIXTY-ONE

WITH DOOM DARKENING their sights Cleatah and Boah led the searchers down the north seawall steps to what had, before the wave, been the beach of the old Shore Village. The killer tide had scoured away much of the fine black sand, leaving a hard crust of lavic rock – points of the shallow water reef now sadly shorn of its colorful living skin – poking up above the water's surface, and dead sea creatures rotting in the sun.

All in the party knew what lay before them, for in the two days since the catastrophic quake naked bodies, and parts of bodies of the Shore Village elders, had come crashing pitifully up against the seawall. Then as the tide receded it took its gruesome cargo with it.

On that terrible day, after the sluice gate had slammed shut the Shore People who lived in the city had rushed to the top of the seawall to watch in dread the seething black ocean that had risen nearly to its ramparts.

Nearly, but not quite.

The wave had topped seventy feet. Though the Shore Village itself was raised on its own tiny plateau above the black sand beach it could not have been spared the water's fury. Poseidon had tried to prepare the villagers for the inevitable findings – the men and women whose fathers and mothers, aunts and uncles had chosen to stay in the only home they had ever known. The elders had showed little interest in leaving the ocean's edge for the city that had sprung up behind a strange man-made mountain of stone – ironically, a mountain that would have saved them from the sea rising up in a towering wall of death.

What must they have thought as the thing approached? Had they known what they were seeing? Or would they have gazed in curiosity at the receding water and the frothy white line stretching north to south? And if, in the final moments, had they apprehended the impending disaster would they have sought to flee up the footpath to the safety of the Great Plateau?

The people of the city, except for the Wall Watch, had been spared the nightmarish vision, but those guards – now set apart forever – would become famous with the telling and re-telling of what they had seen. The ocean disappearing, laying bare the sea floor for miles. The reefs on the shallow continental shelf and the previously hidden precipice where the sea bottom could not even be seen. It was here, the watchmen would say, that the wave – little more than a raised line of onrushing white foam – had suddenly reared up like a thousand horses on their hind legs and become the hideous towering breaker that had sent them fleeing down the wall like terrified children.

As the search party approached the village plateau it tore at Poseidon's heart to see the ancient stone steps he had climbed the day of his first coming washed entirely away. They were forced to scramble on hands and knees up the unforgiving cliff face and were met with the sight of what had been the Shore Village…now scoured entirely clean. Not a hut, not a tree, not even the low rock wall that delineated the settlement's boundaries had been spared the water's onslaught. It was bare ground all the way inland to the steep footpath that led to the headlands of the Great Plateau.

It might have appeared as if nothing at all had happened on this sandy shelf above a black sand beach near a blue sea and its dainty waves. Only the battered carcass of a giant grey shark with flies buzzing round its sunken eyes and feasting on the wide expanse of gum above several rows of razor teeth told a tale of the wave that had, in a terrible roaring instant, obliterated the noble elders and the age-old village of the Shore People.

The searchers wept quietly where they stood, trying in vain to conjure the village, to fathom the loss of what they had once been and everything they had known. They did not say so but Poseidon guessed they were giving bitter thanks for the city they had chosen for their home. The city that had saved them.

"There is nothing here," Cleatah murmured, slowly shaking her head. "Even their spirits have been swept away. All we have left of them is in our hearts."

She turned and walked back the way she'd come. One by one those who had been the Shore People followed her down the cliff and back to Atlantos.

SIXTY-TWO

ALL THE PEOPLE of the city and all the people of the Great Plateau were gathered in the morning shadow of the High Atlantos stables. The streets and houses and markets of the metropolis were abandoned, and Itopia was once again overflowing with members of the One Tribe who had assembled for a celebration of life and memorial for the dead.

There was much to mourn. The elders of the Shore Village were gone and hundreds had been killed by falling stone in Atlantos City. In the mountain settlements workers had died when mines collapsed on them. More than half the mares and their young had been swallowed up in a single horrible instant by Erthe herself.

Yet the city and its people had been saved from the wave's wrath by Poseidon's seawall. And of profoundest importance on that otherwise tragic day, a pure white foal had been born and survived the devastation. In the weeks following, this horse had become a symbol of the Brotherhood's hopes and all Atlans' future dreams. The Great Mother, it was often repeated, would never have spared the foal had she wished to curse their new society. The little creature was her blessing and her promise, and it was not lost on the horsemen that Talya was the Great Mother's helper in bringing it into the world. Once viewed merely with lust and jealous fever, the beautiful woman who held the secrets of life in her smooth white hands was these days venerated and adored like no other female, save Cleatah.

This morning at the Grave of the Horses – the ominous abyss that now rent the grazing meadow in two – everyone was gathered. They were listening to Boah who stood high on a rock platform to be better seen and heard by the congregation.

"…so while the loss is great and we honor our dead and will never forget them," he called out in Terrerthe, "…we have no more time for mourning. The Brotherhood has promised horses to the mountain settlements whose mines must produce ever more ore to build our city. To the docks for our ships and the warehouses for the cargoes they will soon bring from across the sea. A 'Stadium' will be built where the horses will race for your pleasure."

At this there was happy murmuring in every part of the crowd.

"The time for spilled tears is past. There is no time to waste. We look to Poseidon's beloved sister Talya, who brought forth the white foal with her life-giving tools, and who promises in the coming years to increase our herd tenfold!"

The morning rang with shouts and Talya's chanted name, and clenched fists punched the air. Now Poseidon climbed up to join Boah on the platform, placing an arm around his friend's shoulder.

"So begin the games," he called cheerfully. "Light the cookfires. Set the tables with the bounty of our fields and pastures. We – the people of the far mountains and the city, horsemen, orchardmen and farmers of the Great Plateau – we are all Atlans, and we are here to banish thoughts of death and destruction. To celebrate life – all that the Great Mother has provided us – and the promise of a shining future!"

SIXTY-THREE

TALYA HEARD THE cheers going up around her, composed in equal measure of true elation and faith in the peoples' beloved leaders. When the crowd began to disperse Poseidon and Boah stepped down from the platform where she and Cleatah met and embraced them. When the family of Brannan came and pulled Boah and Cleatah away to show them a stone tribute for their grandfather she found herself standing side-by-side with Poseidon. They gazed out at the milling assembly – men and women talking with animation, laughing at each other's jokes, children chasing each other and shouting happily, and wolves mingling comfortably among them all.

She was loathe to spoil so fine a moment, but there were things that needed to be said.

"Do you ever think how close you came to losing this?" she began. "All of this?"

"Every day. Many times a day. I'm haunted by the men at the stables whose lives I couldn't save."

After this admission Poseidon's protracted silence began to gall her. *Was this all he would admit to?* "Then do you plan to reactivate your phaetron?" She was aware her voice was sharp as a metal probe.

"I've thought about it."

"*Thought* about it? Why haven't you done it? What more has to happen to prove you cannot simply abandon our technos on a whim?"

"It was not a whim, Talya. I thought long and hard before I removed it."

"I suppose Cleatah applauded it when you did."

"She was pleased, of course she was."

"And was she pleased when its absence nearly drowned Atlantos and killed every living thing in the city?"

Talya was sure the silence that followed was Poseidon's refusal to dignify her harsh and quite ridiculous question with an answer.

Finally he spoke. "When she was consoling me..."

Talya cringed inwardly at the thought of this tender intimacy between them.

"...she reminded me as she often does that I am not a god."

"But you *are*, Poseidon. And so am I. What powers do gods have that we do not? The difference between you and me is that I choose to use everything at my disposal to help these people. You've let sentimentality overtake reason. No matter how much you wish to be an Erthan, you will never be one. You are a Terresian born and bred, and you will *die* one."

He turned and faced her. "What makes you so bitter? You have everything you could possibly want here – much, much more than you could have had on Terres. You are respected. No, let me correct that. You are revered. Famous. You have two lovers..."

Talya found herself reddening at the thought that her sexual habits were so commonly known and so easily accepted.

"...and every horseman who doesn't share your bed wishes he did. But I would argue that, all this considered, you are no goddess. You're simply a woman with advanced technos. A woman who refuses to be satisfied with an embarrassment of riches."

Talya felt her cheeks stinging with the rebuke.

"All that said," he went on before she could speak, "I concur with your logic about my device. I'd planned to ask for your help re-activating it."

Desired as they were, his words shocked Talya to the core. How could she feel so humbled by Poseidon's concession? This was one emotion she would never reveal to him. To anyone.

"I'm glad you've come to your senses," she said in the gentlest tone she could manage. "When we return to the city…"

"Much appreciated," he said, cutting her off.

Finished with her judgment and criticism Poseidon turned and disappeared into the crowd.

SIXTY-FOUR

THOUSANDS OF FIRES blazed in the dark of the winding footpaths of Itopia Village. After a long day of games and feasting, celebration was still in the air. The rude mud dwellings of the Gathered Tribes' first settlement were largely unfamiliar to Talya as she walked among them, as her visits to Boah's new quarters here were few and far between. Even her recent encounters with Joss took place at odd moments in dangerous settings outside the encampment.

Thoughts of Joss never failed to arouse her, particularly the latest experiments with her enhancer to augment the already-explosive climaxes she'd been enjoying. Still, at this moment Talya was craving the attentions of Boah. She noticed a kind of desperation in her search for him tonight, and while this irritated her mildly it made the hunt for him more exciting. She'd only caught glimpses of Boah during the day's celebration. She'd cheered for him in the races and refused to intrude at a somber gathering of the Shore People to privately memorialize their elders. Boah's preeminence in Atlantos, second only to Poseidon's, had become unequivocal today, and the urge for his company was proving irresistible.

His cool reserve in the face of the rivalry with Joss had proven almost Terresian. While her bedding with the two of them had caused an uproar within the ranks of the horsemen Boah himself had remained utterly composed – affectionate and desiring her company, but lacking the smallest hint of possessiveness or jealousy. He had been heard saying, "Talya is my woman. She is not my mate." And to her great relief in recent weeks he had finally stopped suggesting she bear his child.

Everywhere Talya stopped to ask at Boah's whereabouts people had been welcoming and kind. Many offered her food and drink, and spoke of the honor they felt with her presence at their table.

He was close now. She could feel it. Several horsemen who knew him well had recently seen him on foot, traveling in the direction of a group of dwellings on the outskirts of the settlement. She would enjoy sex with him tonight – less savage, less excessive than what she had with Joss. More refined. Well, perhaps that was an exaggeration. Boah had proven a good student, but he had retained enough of the animal quality that set Erthan men apart from Terresians.

Then she heard his unmistakable laugh – warm and deep and booming. It surprised her to feel, at the sound of it, a sudden twitch between her thighs. Perhaps tonight she would let him know how much she missed him in her bed. Talya rounded a corner and stayed just beyond the light of a fire between a cluster of huts, now crowded with people. She recognized the textiles of a shore people from across the continent, with vary-colored shells woven into their designs. There was more laughter. She sensed they were members of a large family – and there again was Boah's laugh.

She stepped into the firelight as the crowd parted and there he was, his black eyes flashing, smiling his brilliant smile...at a pretty, small-boned woman whose belly was swollen with pregnancy. She gazed up at him adoringly, and he kissed her cheek with the gentlest touch of his lips.

Talya's heart began crashing against her ribcage. She fought paralysis and stepped back into the shadows before she could be seen. She stumbled away on the dark footpath and steadied herself against a mud wall. Her discipline proved stronger than her pain. She rebuked herself for such maudlin emotions and pulled her thoughts together. *Of course Boah would expect offspring. It was a wonder he hadn't any children already. And the woman he'd chosen was timid and subservient – exactly what he would desire in a mate.*

A "mate." The word stung her unexpectedly. *Talya is my woman. She is not my mate.* She sniffed sharply and straightening her spine pulled herself tall. She composed her features into a semblance of tranquility and began retracing her steps back to the center of Itopia. She would waste not a single moment more on such preposterous Erthan self-indulgences. She was better than this. A proud Terresian.

Her heart rate slowed. With every step Talya felt the forced smile she had plastered on softening. She willed her equilibrium to return. *I will be fine*, she told herself.

I will be fine.

SIXTY-FIVE

CLEATAH WAS SITTING among the ones she loved the best, her nearest and dearest in all the world – Poseidon and the Green Teachers. Nothing could make her happier. They had gathered for a quiet counsel around her dear friend Thoth's gently burning fire, and talk had been of fertility.

Yazman spoke of the moon's cycle and the fecundity of crops. There was no arguing with Yazman. She was old and had watched the growth of countless plantings long before Talya and her tools had increased the size of the Atlan harvest.

Zane asked why certain female wolves filled their dens with pups season after season, and others were barren.

"Those females who are fertile have a scent that only male wolves can smell that draws them like a bee to a sweet flower," was Tolmak's answer. He was a master of healing potions, one from whom Cleatah had learned much since their meeting. She trusted all the Green Teachers, but none so deeply as Tolmak. He absently folded a large leaf between his long bony fingers.

Cleatah asked him – all the time holding Poseidon's eyes with her own, "Why do I not conceive?"

Tolmak stared down at the once-large leaf, now a small pile of squares, then tossed it into the fire where it slowly browned and crinkled into nothing. "You ate silphan for many years. How many years?"

Cleatah counted in her head. "Nine," she answered, suddenly alarmed at the implication. *Have I eaten the preventative seed for too long?*

"No, you haven't erred," Tolmak said, reading her thoughts, or perhaps her expression. "It will take the tarax and ackil you are eating now a little time to overcome the silphan, which is very strong."

Cleatah saw Yazman slip something into Poseidon's hand. She was very fond of him and enjoyed giving him advice, even when it had not been requested. He always indulged her.

"What have you given him, Yazman?" Cleatah said with a grin.

"She's given me a smooth red quartz stone," he told Cleatah. "You must hold it in your right hand when we make love."

Yazman leaned in to whisper to Poseidon again.

"When we make love in the moon's *crescent* phase," he said, then turned to Yazman with a teasing smile. "What if I wish to make love to her in the full moon, or in the new moon or in the half-moon?"

"Make love to her enough," Zane remarked, "and you will need neither the tarax, the stone *or* the moon to get her pregnant!"

Everyone laughed at that, all but Poseidon who gazed at Cleatah with such naked desire that she blushed. But as she held his eyes she saw, over his shoulder, Talya standing behind him, still as a stone.

"Join us, Talya," Cleatah said.

"Poseidon turned. "Yes, come sit with us."

Zane and Yazman moved to make room for her.

"No. Thank you. I'm…I'm meeting Joss," she replied, unmistakably flustered. "I'm meeting Joss," she mumbled again and turned, disappearing into the shadows.

SIXTY-SIX

SHE DID MEET Joss. To a chorus of lewd shouts she pulled him from a bonfire circle of raucously celebrating horsemen. They found a darkened path and he took her roughly – the way she demanded it – her hands and face pressed up against a hard mud wall. When he finished, leaving her unsatisfied – as she had wished – Talya dropped her shift and straightened. Refusing to meet his eye she left him behind her and walked away, feeling the scrapes on her hot red cheek with trembling fingers.

With a few touches to her wrist device she cloaked herself, and blessedly invisible to the still celebrating Atlans she found her way through the dark, fire-dappled settlement to the deserted city below.

*

Alone in the echoing silence of the ship Talya drank herself into a frenzy. The jog, never meant to be imbibed so extravagantly, sent her brain spiraling to unheralded heights of imagination, only to crash through the floor of consciousness into a raw abyss of confusion and pain.

A day passed. Two. She drank. She seethed. Tore off her clothes and tossed in bed for hours, pulse racing, nerves firing, heat seeming to flare from her pores. She was sure sleep had permanently evaded her. She leapt up and pulled on her shift, despising its primitive weave, and donned a fine Terresian garment. Then light-headed and weak-kneed she reeled down the deserted corridors of the *Atlantos* reviling her weakness and praying to rid herself of such violent sensations. But the mind reeled, too:

How have I come to this? How? I'm Terresian, calm and rational. And now I've succumbed to the same fever that possesses Poseidon. No, not the same. His is a passion of 'love.' Mine...mine is of fury.

What a fool I've been!

Why did I not leave with the others? How could I have so badly miscalculated the passage of time? The Terresian constitution should have caused the months and years here to speed forward, easing the wait for Poseidon to regain reason. But no. My execrable bio-rhythms slowed! Time drags. I might as well be an Erthan! Boah and Joss... drowning in sensual pleasures...even the horsemen's worship...nothing fills the void of this life – cold and silent and black as space. And now there'll be children to bind Poseidon and that smug, devious thief closer still. Imagine how he'll react to offspring! *Fatherhood will catapult him into paroxysms of emotion.*

Wait. She stopped and stood, holding the wall to stop her swaying. *A thought came to her – random – the germ of an idea, a seed.* The warm, quiet hallway was a perfect medium for growth. *Close your eyes and see it.... There it is, the seed, the seed, warm and throbbing with the imperative to grow, bursting its shell. Sprouting. Breaking ground. Snaking and curling upward. Flowering. Oh!... it is a dark and twisted thing. An appalling scheme. Not like me! Treacherous and rotten and glutted with passions I despise.*

No going back. Not now – not to Terres nor the safety of moral ground. If...I...must...exist endlessly *in this place, I will mold it, redefine it, suit it to* my *desires. I will behave immoderately – as the primitives do. Twice humiliated is entirely enough.*

I will never suffer like that again.

*

Still drunk and giddy Talya stepped from the pillar of blue light and emerged from Poseidon's Grove, at once activating her cloaking device. Invisible to members of the household who had now returned from High Atlantos she crossed the stream and passed the darkened homes of the Green Teachers and horsemen that lived within the environs of the Central Isle. She approached the residence.

Moving through the open entryway she was struck, as she always was, by the palpable peace and quiet of Poseidon's home. *Irritatingly peaceful,* she thought. It was as though a tranquil existence had become the single focus of his life. *How pathetic.* Talya reached the couple's bedchamber, but before entering she scanned through the wall to be sure they were there and sleeping. When she saw that they were she moved cautiously to the doorway. Pointing the phaetron at the pair of them she activated its narcotizing function.

She moved to the bed. There were the two bodies curled comfortably together, already in the deepest sleep state possible. The sight of them was wrenching but she steeled herself and went to Cleatah's side. Quickly she pulled down the light coverlet. They were both naked. Talya could not help but stare at Cleatah. She was lovely – perfectly formed and softly rounded in the womanly places. Her face in repose was undeniably exquisite. Talya glanced at Poseidon's nakedness, once so familiar to her, and her anger flared again.

Then a cold efficiency overtook her. There was no more hiding behind intoxication, no reasonable excuse for this. She knew precisely what she was about to do. Talya rolled Cleatah on her back. Fully narcotized the woman's head and limbs fell into unnaturally limp positions. She was utterly helpless, and for perhaps the first time in her life Talya assumed complete control. She opened the small metal case that held her gynae phaetron and extraction tools.

And then, casting all doubt and all honor aside, she set to work.

SIXTY-SEVEN

"YOU'RE LOOKING BEAUTIFUL as ever," said Athens to Cleatah's diffracted image. "And keeping my brother very happy, I see." He was in his Marsean bedroom overlooking the sea.

Poseidon thought that aside from a dark weariness around his eyes Athens looked well, if ostentatiously outfitted in a short tunic of spun gold. The handsomely defined muscles of his arms were encircled with fine-worked bracelets of the sun yellow ore. He held at his hip his little girl Athena – not yet two – her short black ringlets matching her huge sparkling black eyes.

"We thank you for the gold, " Poseidon said. "A generous gift, considering how short a time it's been since the mines have been operable."

Talya, Poseidon and a hugely pregnant Cleatah had gathered in the *Atlantos's* library for the meeting. Via the phaetron Athens had been sending to Erthe a great quantity of artifacts and magnificent jewelry. At their feet was the day's offering – three raw bars of his precious metal.

"I'm happy to say both the mines are within weeks of opening again." Athena whispered something in her father's ear and he set her down on the floor where she fixed immediately on the gold clasps on Athens's shoes. The child seemed unaware of the Erthe family in front of her. "And much improved as well," Athens continued. "We expect the titanum output to triple, at the least."

"Triple?" Poseidon was incredulous. "You won't be sacrificing safety for increased productivity, I hope."

"Not at all." Athens' smile was confident, self-satisfied. "Talya, come here. Let me look at you."

She stepped forward and raised her hand, palm facing him. He raised his palm to hers, and though millions of miles separated them their hands appeared to touch.

"Is it possible," he said, "that you're more luscious than when we last spoke?"

"Anything is possible," she replied with a teasing smile.

"I wish this blasted device could transport you to Mars." Athens held her eyes for a long moment, then turned to his brother. "And how is the great city of Atlantos progressing?" he inquired, pacing about the bedroom.

"Slowly but steadily," Poseidon replied. "The artisans are still learning their crafts. And some of the stone work is laborious and time consuming."

"You're mad to deny them the phaetron."

"You know where I stand on that. If we're to thrive as a great society the people must learn industriousness. But as long as it's work they enjoy and they reap the rewards of their labor they have no complaints about working hard."

"I've found myself another solution to the problem of hard work," announced Athens matter-of-factly.

"And that is?" Poseidon asked.

"Drones."

"What do you mean?"

"You know what a drone is, Talya. Tell my brother."

"In the laboratory we can genomically produce large numbers of organisms that are identical to each other," she explained.

"What form do these drones take?" Poseidon asked.

"Human. Well, *almost* human. Actually, sub-human and super-human."

Poseidon was growing alarmed. Cleatah was altogether confused. Only Talya remained sanguine. It was clear this was no surprise to her.

"You remember I said we'd be tripling production in the gold and titanum mines?" Athens continued, not waiting for a reply, "Well, we will accomplish our goal using these creatures. They're extraordinarily strong and incredibly stupid. We've bred males only, and they entirely lack aggressive or sexual tendencies." Athens grinned with self-satisfaction. "They're perfect working machines." My colonists will never have to put themselves in danger again."

"You can't be serious." Poseidon was slack-jawed. "What you're describing are humanoid slaves."

"Why was I so sure this would be your reaction?" Athens's look turned suddenly sour. "Talya, tell him why this is a brilliant idea."

"It does have its merits," she said evenly, "provided the drones are well-treated."

"Of course they will be. They'll be fed the best food, receive the best medical care... and they'll do a little hard work underground." He fixed Poseidon with a wicked smile. "Even *you* believe in hard work, brother. Of course the colonists are ecstatic. I've created an ideal world for them. A life, more or less, of pure pleasure." He regarded Poseidon petulantly. "You don't approve. Well, it can't be helped. Anyway, it's done."

"Done?" Poseidon was confused.

"We've been incubating them for three years. There are growth-accelerating chemicals... "he smiled at Talya, "We so appreciated your help." He held Poseidon's eye. "The drones are fully developed in every way necessary. They've been learning their skills. They're ready to go into the mines."

"This defies every humane principle we've ever learned!"

"I won't lose another colonist in the pursuit of gold," Athens said.

"Then lose the pursuit of gold!"

"I don't have that option."

"Of course you do. You have a choice. How can you even consider so contemptible a decision?"

An ugly expression marred Athens's handsome features. "Because if I don't give the people what they want they'll find someone else who will." He looked away. "Everything comes so easily to you. I've worked hard for what I have. No one, nothing, *nothing* will take it from me." He faced Poseidon again with a sour expression. "I wish you could have been happy for me. But I suppose that would have been too much to ask." He turned to Cleatah. "Good health to you in your delivery." He nodded straight-faced at Talya.

In the next moment the image of Athens and his tiny daughter dematerialized. All that was left of their presence were three golden bars glittering on the library floor.

SIXTY-EIGHT

WITHIN THE RED stone birthing house a warm herbal mist hung above the women who'd gathered for this unrivaled occasion. Cleatah's hands rested lightly on the mountain of her belly that rose above the warm saltwater tub. She was grateful to see kneeling around her the most adept of the Green Teachers murmuring with quiet concern about the twins they all knew were about to be born. Many of the tribes believed a double birth to be a dangerous omen, but now one of their own – their much-revered teacher – was giving birth to twins. She was certain they would find their fears groundless after all. To her surprise Talya was among the women, listening and watching closely to learn what she might do to help.

When the next violent contraction seized her Cleatah shrieked and clutched the sides of the tub. She was vaguely aware of a warm hand atop her own, and a fragrant cloth wiping her brow. When the spasm passed her eyes fluttered open and she found that Talya was her comforter. She had changed somehow, emanating a new warmth and kindness. She had even taken Boah's fathering of Zeta's child with good grace, and had mourned with them when the boy was born dead.

Another contraction gripped Cleatah and all thoughts

dissolved into fierce sensation. Zane began whispering encouragement and instructions as the first infant thrust itself into the world. Cleatah's head rolled from side to side, but as another pain ripped through her, her gaze fell on Talya. Her eyes were gleaming, her lips curling upward. It seemed a smile of pleasure, but there was something more.

Something strange about it.

Cleatah suddenly recognized the expression…but then with a final, resolute push her second son came wailing into his life. All else was forgotten.

All was forgotten but joy.

*

Later Cleatah lay on a wide couch in an adjoining room of the birthing house, one son suckling as the other was rocked by Yazman. The doors swung open and Poseidon stood at the threshold. He didn't move to enter, simply stared at the scene, enthralled.

"Poseidon, come see your sons," Cleatah said.

Only then did he move to her side and kneel so that his face was close to hers and he could see the milksweet features of the infant. "He was the firstborn," she told him, "and so, as we decided, he is named Atlas."

Poseidon first caressed her face, then with a touch as delicate as the fluttering of a butterfly's wing he laid his fingers on the infant's cheek. His expression was utterly wonderstruck.

She gestured for Yazman to bring Atlas's twin to the couch. "This is Geo," Cleatah told him.

Poseidon looked up and saw the younger boy being held out to him. He hesitated – this man who was as fearless as any she had ever known – trembling apprehensively.

"Take him, Poseidon. He's yours."

He stood and took the child into his arms, gathering him to his heart. He seemed unable to take his eyes from the infant's features. The boy was identical in every aspect to his brother. A small cry escaped his throat and suddenly tears began spilling from his eyes.

Cleatah clutched his hand and held it to her lips. "Do I take it you like your sons?"

"Almost as much as I like their mother. Thank you for this gift, my love. Thank you…"

A noisy crowd of Shore People burst into the room. As was the custom some bore flowers, others food and jugs of kav. The new parents were instantly surrounded with everyone crowding around to see the infants. The celebration had begun that would go on for many days and many nights. The sound of flute and drum burst forth, a song of thanksgiving raised in the newborns' names.

*

Night fell and the music and celebration spread to all parts of the city. Joyful sounds echoed down the waterways and the sparkling, twirling fireshow in the sky that Poseidon had launched left everyone shouting and awestruck.

Cleatah and the twins had been moved in a spirited procession from the birthing house on the Middle Ring Isle across the arched bridge to the Central Isle, and now the three were resting within the main residence. People were feasting and dancing outside around a roaring bonfire in the courtyard. Their songs were ancient chants in praise of the Great Mother and the gods of Erthe, but they sang new ones as well – songs of their city, of the horse and brave horsemen, and the deeds of their beloved Poseidon and Cleatah.

Poseidon watched as men and women moved in sensual rhythm to the drums, their faces glowing in the firelight.

"You must be very pleased." Talya's voice came from behind.

He turned to find her standing so close he could feel her

breath on his face. There was a genuine pleasantness to her smile, and her eyes appeared unnaturally bright, he thought. Perhaps it was the reflection of the fire.

"You know that I am," he said, unable to withhold a grin.

A tribesman and a young woman came to dance before them, gyrating and thrusting suggestively. Her eyes were closed, his face ecstatic.

"I'm pregnant, Poseidon," Talya said.

"That's wonderful news!" Impulsively he embraced her, then pushed her to arm's length. "Who is the father?"

Before she could answer Boah emerged from the dancers and swept Talya into his embrace. As Poseidon watched they began to move together rhythmically, sensually, never taking their eyes from one another's faces. It was extraordinary. He'd never seen Talya move like that. Never seen such passion in her. Boah's hands encircled Talya's waist, and his hips and muscular thighs pushed closer to hers. *Thank the stars*, Poseidon thought, *she has allowed the true gifts of this planet – these people – to soften her, heal her wounds*. And now she was pregnant with a Erthan man's child. It was the final gift of this blessed day.

All at once Poseidon was seized by a rogue emotion so fierce it rocked him on his feet. Though he was surrounded by friends and well-wishers he was overwhelmed with emptiness. But he knew the remedy. In the next moment he turned from the fire, the music and the revelers, and walked through the archway into to the residence. There awaited all that would fulfill him.

There awaited his family.

SIXTY-NINE

66 "TALYA IS HAVING my baby!"

Boah had waited to shout out his announcement till the horsemen had settled down in the shade to eat their morning meal. He happily accepted the backslapping and even some crude jokes about riding the queen mare.

"About time," muttered Tork.

"Is that why your eyes are red?" Patak said.

"We did drink a fair amount of kav," Boah admitted.

There was raucous laughter at that.

Talya had, in fact, waited until he was very drunk to tell him she was carrying his child. Thankfully he'd been sober enough to make love to her.

"So you'll lifemate with her?" Elkon asked. He was a fellow Shoreman, and this was the way of their tribe.

"Of course. She's having my baby."

"Joss fixed him with a playful grin. "The first of many?" His old rival for Talya's affections looked genuinely pleased.

"If the Great Mother allows it."

"Remember the time in the village when you fought with Poseidon to mate with Cleatah?" Elkon teased.

Boah felt himself flushing with mortification at the

memory. "Back then we thought him a puny stranger who could barely hunt."

"And now," Tork said, "he will be uncle to your children. His children and yours will be cousins."

Boah grew serious. "Our two families will be joined by blood." He gazed around at his friends. "I'm very proud."

"Look at him," Joss teased, "he's puffed as wide as the feathers on a wild turkey's breast."

Everyone laughed at that.

"Enough!" Boah cried with mock severity. "Let's eat. We've got horses to attend."

Joss nodded a sincere affirmation to his friend before he bit into his bread. Tears sprang to Boah's eyes. Here he was surrounded by his horse brothers, knowing that the luminescent being they all so admired, even desired, was finally and truly his own. A child was on the way, and kinship with Poseidon's family was secured.

His happiness was boundless. There was nothing more that he wanted. Not a single thing on Erthe.

SEVENTY

THEY SAT IN rows at tables the length of the enormous hall – two thousand of them outfitted in simple blue coveralls. They could barely be considered men, so young and tender were their hairless faces, but their bodies under the thin fabric were hard, muscular and mature. Brown-haired and blue-eyed, each and every one of them was identical in every way, even the same vaguely triangular birthmark in the center of their left cheek. They might have been considered handsome had their jaws, in repose, not sagged so prominently as they did, or had the light in their eyes not been so dim.

They ate their meals – large plates of hearty grain and vegetable stew – in a silence punctuated only by grunts, chewing, and the clink of utensils against bowls. The drones had been carefully seated so that no one sat directly across from another, for although the creatures had shown little interest in communication or even eye contact, these were the experiment's early days, and it was best to be cautious. No one knew what mutations of intellect or aggression lay dormant in them.

A series of three loud metallic beeps signaled the drones that there was a minute remaining to finish what was in their bowls. At the sound of another long beep they stood, pushing their chairs back. Then they turned, all of them to the right, and in a calm and orderly fashion filed out.

One drone remained seated at the far end of each table. When the hall had cleared completely they rose in unison, and without a sound or a word of direction from the overseers began moving down the line stacking the dishes. In the course of the morning meal not a word had been spoken nor a rule broken. It was Athens Ra's great Marsean workforce.

And it was, indeed, perfect.

*

The newly reconstructed titanum mine once again hummed with activity. The central column's descending and ascending blue elevator beams delivered workers down to the cavernous chamber and chunks of ore to the surface. A new and improved generation of six-legged ore-cutting robots climbed the vertical walls tearing chunks of titanum from the cells, and yellow tractor beams drew the bounty into the central column. And while miners rode the yellow beams across the chasm to and from the cells as they once had, now there was no cheerful camaraderie, waves or work songs to make the time pass more pleasantly. There was only silent, mindless labor, the hum of phaetronic beams, the crunch and crack of rock shorn from the two hundred-foot high seam of titanum.

A small crew of overseers – Marsean colonists paid handsomely for electing to spend their working hours in the mine – had little to do, as the drones, while subnormal intellectually, were more than capable of learning the rote tasks necessary for their jobs.

Far below in the baking heat of the gold mines the overseers moved about in air-cooled protective garments. Scientists had never discovered a way to improve working conditions without jeopardizing the gold extraction but it had been unnecessary. The workforce was able to survive the stifling heat unperturbed.

Inside a cell at the titanum mine's 15th level four of the brawny drones stood in silence as the robot's red beam gouged huge chunks from the leading wall. When the twenty-second burst of intense energy ceased they began to lift the rocks out of the cell opening and heave them into the yellow tractor beam. Productivity had increased due to the size of the ore chunks freed. The colonists had been able to lift boulders only a third of the size and move them at a fraction of the speed than the drones now could. With another burst from the robot's red beam the ore-releasing process began again.

Suddenly the worker closest to the cell opening turned sharply and ducked reflexively as a large jagged slice of the wall collapsed above him. His swift reaction saved him from receiving any injuries to his head and torso. The other three waiting patiently for the twenty-second burst to cease made no comment, hardly acknowledging that the accident had occurred. A moment later the quartet began lifting the released ore from the newly-made pile and throwing it into the yellow tractor beam.

It was only when the drone closest to the cell opening reached to retrieve a boulder that he noticed his left arm below the elbow was missing. He and the others stared at it in silence. It was a clean, bloodless severance, the wound obviously cauterized by the slicing red beam in the instant the arm passed through it. The hand and half the forearm lay at the drone's feet. He picked it up with his remaining hand and looked to the others with a quizzical expression.

He was impervious to pain, as his creators had consciously excised from his and the other drones' genomic structuring all pain and temperature sensory sites. It was the same bio-mechanism that allowed his identical brothers toiling in the gold mines below to move about unprotected and unperturbed in near-scalding temperatures.

The armless man, as though suddenly recalling a learned

instruction, turned from his work-mates and climbed out the cell opening. Still clutching his severed arm he straddled the ever-moving yellow beam and rode it across the abyss to the central column. Once inside he sought an overseer, the nearest one having his back to the drone. He tapped the colonist's shoulder and when the man turned to see the creature holding the arm in front of him the overseer's eyes widened in momentary surprise. Then he called for assistance. A supervisor and a medic were there in moments. They examined both the severed forearm and the stump which had finally begun to breach the cauterization and was now oozing blood.

It was quickly decided which of the two overseers would escort the drone topside, and before they stepped into the blue elevator beam the colonist discarded the severed arm, tossing it into the ore elevator where it was quickly pulverized.

*

The drone's bleeding had become profuse by the time they reached the medical facility. While he still showed no signs of pain or panic he was pale from the loss of blood and shock, and needed support to walk the final steps to the treatment room.

A young, pretty female tech sat scanning a report. She looked up and saw the overseer and the injured drone. "Another one?" she asked unperturbed.

"We're still working things out down there. One wrong step and 'thwap!' Good thing they don't know the difference."

"Let's get him on the table." She looked up and smiled, "Myles, isn't it?"

"You remembered," the overseer said, pleased. It occurred to him that the attractive gold earbobs he'd seen the other day at his artisan friend's studio would look lovely on the young woman, but she was all business.

Together they lowered the worker down and strapped him to

the table. He didn't struggle and seemed to be getting weaker by the moment. The tech, unperturbed by the patient's blood that pooled at her feet, chose an instrument from the shiny counter. She centered the device on the bloody stump and activated it. Instantly a film began forming over the open wound stanching the crimson flow. The film thickened. It was first grey, and one could see tiny lines beginning to form. A moment later the lines could be recognized as blood vessels which quickly filled, and suddenly the layer of new skin was pink and healthy. Its edges knit so perfectly with the severed forearm that no seam was apparent. Color returned to the worker's face. His breathing evened and normalized.

The tech relinquished the first tool and moved to a shelf on which stood a row of instruments. They were all similar in that one end consisted of a small phaetronic device. Each was adapted on the other end with a soft, transparent receptacle of a different size and shape. The tech chose the one she deemed suitable and began to fit its see-through sock-end over the drone's newly healed stump, leaving the long sheath empty.

"Accelerator," she said offhandedly, naming the device. "This is the part I like the best." She smiled as she switched the device on.

"It just takes a minute," she said. She used the time to clean the bloody floor with a quick sweep of her wrist phaetron, then turned back in anticipation. "There!" she said, pointing at the drone's stump.

The change was noticeable. Two small bumps had appeared in the center of the new skin and were growing larger at an astonishing rate.

"Those are the arm bones. They're two of them, but they grow so close together at first they kind of look like..." she smiled, this time rather coyly. Indeed, what had been two bumps now merged into one, and this protruded outward, straining against the stump's derma looking ever more phallic.

"Will it bust through the skin?" Myles asked.

"No, no. See there." The tech pointed. "New skin is being produced to keep up. Tiny muscles have already started developing inside. And nerves... Well, that's it." She was dismissing the overseer, but the flirtation was obvious. "See you next time," she said.

Myles was suddenly shy. "Next time."

As the door whooshed closed the tech was already helping the drone to his feet. She led him through another door that opened into a medical ward of sorts. It was a spare dormitory where nearly a dozen drones reclined quietly on tables. To each was attached one of the devices, the transparent film covering a different body part. The distal end of a thigh bulged out where a knee joint was slowly rebuilding itself. The right side of a drone's face under the accelerator was regenerating a cheek and ear.

The tech found an empty table at the end of the room and carefully laid the drone down on it, speaking to him absently – more out of habit – knowing that he barely understood her words. The colonists who worked the mines had all been instructed to treat the drones gently, though overt kindness was unnecessary.

"We'll just put you here next to your friend. He lost an arm, too." She strapped him on the table, placing a small cushion under his neck. "You'll be out of here in no time."

The tech moved away, not even glancing at the other patients, and exited the otherwise unattended ward. The drone turned his head to look at his identical brother lying next to him, just staring mindlessly at the ceiling. If he had looked more closely he would have seen beneath the transparent sheath a forearm, in miniature, lengthening and developing at a slow but perceptible rate.

On its end was the bud of a perfect embryonic hand.

SEVENTY-ONE

"IT'S A GIRL, a *girl!*" Cleatah cried, unable to conceal her pleasure. Today it was Talya reclining in the warm salt-water birthing tub and Cleatah kneeling between her friend's knees. Cleatah held the partially submerged infant in one hand and cleaned the tiny body with the other as the women in attendance bathed Talya's face, neck and breasts with damp herb-fragrant cloths. Someone murmured that the new mother looked serene, nothing like a woman who had labored for eighteen hours and delivered her first child moments before. Cleatah guessed, but did not say, that Talya had employed the pain-suppressing function of her wrist device.

Yazman tied the umbilical cord in two places several inches apart. Then with a brief, silent blessing Cleatah took up a small sharp knife and severed it. She gently floated the infant to Talya's side and slid the baby under her mother's arm, helping it find a breast. She began to suckle immediately.

With a pang, Cleatah thought how much she hoped for a daughter next time.

There was low whispering and relieved laughter as Yazman and the other women began tidying up the birthing chamber.

They could hear the men who'd gathered outside to wait for the moment when they would be allowed to enter.

"This is Boah's first living child," Cleatah told Talya, "so his celebrations may go on for weeks." She smiled down at Talya who remained silent and contented, completely consumed with the little creature cradled in her arms.

*

Later, when Talya was resting in the adjoining chamber Boah was shown in. He was wide-eyed, his face puffed with emotion. Cleatah watched as he fell unselfconsciously to his knees at their side and kissed the tender, sleeping bundle, then kissed Talya.

"I've been waiting at home with my brothers," he said. "I put in a good supply of kav, but we all stayed sober till we heard that you, that...*she* was all right." He swallowed hard, unable to take his eyes off the child.

"Here, hold her," Talya said, and he lifted the delicate girl from her arms. "Get your fill. I'm going to take her back to the ship for a little while."

He started to object, alarm creasing his handsome face.

"I need some time alone with her."

"The two of you must come live at my house."

"I'll send word to you."

"You'll call for me soon?"

"I will. I promise."

Boah stood and reluctantly moved to the door where Cleatah stood. He embraced her and departed.

"Why don't you give her the other breast?" Cleatah said, coming back to Talya's side.

She moved the infant carefully, first laying the girl on her back between Talya's breasts. It was Cleatah's first sight of the child's face. She could see its head was perfectly formed, the cheeks already pink and glowing, the lips a pretty bud-shape whose corners turned up as if in a smile. Then she opened her eyes to the world for the first time. Cleatah's breath caught in her throat as a gasp. She stared disbelieving.

The child's eyes were grey.

SEVENTY-TWO

DESPITE THE ACHING exhaustion Talya had clearly seen Cleatah's recognition of Poseidon's own daughter in her child, and for a moment regretted the searing bolt of agony and confusion in her rival's eye. But the emotion was short-lived, nothing more than Talya's own vulnerability in that moment. She was barely aware of Cleatah rising to her feet and fleeing the birthing chamber. The regret had quickly evaporated and was supplanted by an equally foreign and unexpected sentiment. It was directed at the tiny, squirming infant at her breast who, with uncanny instinct, had begun suckling hungrily.

Is this what is meant by human 'love'? This jumbled upwelling of warmth and joy and fierce possessiveness? Talya experienced a moment of disquiet, even panic. She attempted to reconcile who she'd been just minutes before with the person she had suddenly become. All rational thought seemed to recede along with her calculated reasons for creating this child – the lust for an inviolable bond with Poseidon. The pleasure of reprisal for Cleatah's theft of Talya's chosen mate.

Now suddenly there was only this grey-eyed, velvet soft creature lying in her arms, feeding on her body. Someone of her own that no one could steal from her. Ever. One that nobody else could possess or control. If this was what it meant to be Erthan, she thought, a slow smile creasing her features, she would have no trouble living with it.

None at all.

SEVENTY-THREE

POSEIDON STORMED INTO Talya's quarters to find her leaning over Isis who lay sleeping on the bed.

His face was twisted with fury. "How did you do it!"

"Isn't it obvious?" she answered, aware that the familiar Terresian chill had returned to her voice. "I harvested your sperm."

"When?"

She'd never seen him so angry. In fact it looked as if he might strike her. *There was so little Terresian left in him*, she mused. *A pity...* "Does it matter when?"

"Just tell me."

"Soon after I learned Cleatah was trying to conceive, but before she actually had."

Poseidon looked as though he had stopped breathing.

"She'll never have the daughters she wants so badly," Talya added. They'll all be boys... and they'll all be twins." This had been an extra small cruelty she'd devised that night she'd performed her genomic modifications. The superstitious regarded multiple births as abominations.

Poseidon turned away suddenly, as though he couldn't bear to look at her.

"I went to your rooms with only the thought to direct the

outcome of your children. I extracted Cleatah's ovum and made the changes in them to produce the 'twin effect' before reintroducing them into her body. Of course men are responsible for the sex of their children. I made certain the necessary genome for females would never again be produced in your sperm."

"*Why* Talya! Why did you do such a thing? If I thought for a thousand years I could never imagine a more obscene violation, such a senseless act."

"It made perfect sense to me." Talya came deliberately around Poseidon to confront him. Her eyes were blazing. "I didn't want her to have any female children – girls who would grow up to look like their mother whom you so adore. When Cleatah begins to age – as she soon will – you would have had her daughters to remind you of her, when she was still young and beautiful…"

"What you're saying is *insane*. Something inside you has twisted horribly…"

His words had no effect on her. Now she moved to the bed and picked up the child who had awakened and was crying hungrily. Talya looked back at Poseidon and smiled, pleased with herself.

"Funny, I didn't conceive of the idea of impregnating myself until I was already working on you. It was a sudden revelation, and I thought it rather brilliant. Cleatah would never have a girl, but *I* could… Oh, don't look at me that way."

"I'm not sure I can look at you ever again."

"Perhaps," said Talya, a wicked glint in her eyes, "but you *will* have to look at our daughter." She held Isis out for him to hold.

He stared at the helpless creature, the pale gold hair and delicate features that already resembled her mother's.

And the grey eyes.

She watched him take the placid infant into his arms. He looked down at his daughter, his features roiling, then moved to Talya's door.

"What are you doing? Where are you taking her!"

Poseidon was silent as he strode from the living quarters towards the ship's hub and down the science corridor. Talya was helpless, her fists clenched as she followed behind him. Only when they stood together in her laboratory did he speak.

"Change her eyes."

"What?"

"The color. Change them to brown."

"I will do no such thing."

"Yes. You will. You will do it now, while I watch. Bloody stars, Talya, have you no sense at all of what you've done!?"

Her face hardened defiantly.

"I want you out of here. In a week you'll pack your things and move to Boah's house. For now you're confined to the ship. Don't show your face on the surface. And access to your laboratory…" He shook his head.

"We are not going to live with Boah. My work is here."

"You're not listening to me. Your work here is done. When you leave the *Atlantos* it will be for the last time."

"You wouldn't dare…" She looked at Isis who seemed to be gazing at her mother trustingly.

"Change her eyes. Now."

"I won't do it."

Poseidon impaled Talya with a glare so murderous that finally she faltered.

"No one is ever going to know she's mine," Poseidon said. "*She* will never know. You will not use the technos of your wrist device, and I swear to you that if I learn you have – for any purpose – I will cut it out of your arm!" He inhaled a ragged breath, trying to calm himself. "I'll hold her while you gather your tools."

She turned to her instrument cabinet. Even in defeat Talya stood tall, her spine rigid. "Bring her here," she said quietly, her back to Poseidon. "Bring me our daughter."

SEVENTY-FOUR

THE MEMORY OF Cleatah's face when she'd come from the birthing house tore at Poseidon's heart as he raced on Arrow's back up the South Ramp. Though she'd readily accepted Talya's pregnancy without his knowing participation, she was yet a wounded animal, all bared fangs and claws. He had never seen her like that, and it frightened him.

When he'd returned from the ship – his daughter's eyes now dark brown, like Boah's – he believed he'd find Cleatah still at the residence. But she was gone. He found the twins with Yazman at her house. One of the horses was missing from the stable.

He chose Arrow to ride. No longer young, she was the steadiest of all the mounts. And she knew his mind like no other animal. The moment they'd left the Central Isle stable the aged mare had with no physical direction from her rider headed west, making her way across both ring islands and their bridges, up the ramp to the Great Plateau.

Though most of the old paths had been obliterated by the patchwork of cropland and grazing fields, and those that led into the forest were mostly overgrown Arrow plodded confidently on. They left the dirt path to follow a rocky stream for a short time, only to return to one that resumed on the stream's far side.

Poseidon never uttered a sound as they traveled, letting the animal lead, for if they were of one mind as Poseidon believed, they were of one heart as well.

That heart sought and would surely find Cleatah.

*

In a green glade they found her horse, and Arrow joined him to graze on a lush patch of sweet grass. Poseidon dismounted. Even after so many years' absence he quickly found the path in the thicket that Cleatah and he had taken to the waterfall so many times.

Though he was certain he would find her there the first sight of her – naked and waist-deep in the river, bathed in the fall's violent spray – jellied Poseidon's knees. For some time he did not make his presence known, as just the act of watching her in the old place steadied him. What he would soon be forced to reveal would open new wounds and try her spirit, even as she attempted in the purifying waters to heal the ones she'd already suffered.

Poseidon removed his clothes and waded into the river. When he was halfway to Cleatah she turned and saw him. His heart sank. The crashing waters had done little to calm the raging animal inside. Even the sight of him did not move her. She turned her face away. He closed the distance between them and with the thundering cascade a chaos around them he pulled her to him. Her body was stiff, unyielding. Steeling himself, he took her hand and led her to the shore to a place where the falls would not drown out their words.

She was silent as he spoke, he desperately searching for the least punishing words. But there was no gentle way to convey Talya's cruelest cuts of all. As the poisoned words fell from his mouth he watched Cleatah's face distort in horror, then fury.

"It wasn't enough that she took your seed to make your child together? She had to give us nothing but twins and steal from us any hope of having daughters as well?" She spoke as if the truth was just then dawning on her. "There will be no women of our line, Poseidon. *No women!*"

"I know," he said with a helpless wave of his hands.

"You *know?*" She trembled, outraged. "So now that you know, what will you do?"

"I don't know how to undo what she's done."

"Then punish her."

"How? What is the punishment for this...this crime?"

Cleatah skewered Poseidon with her eyes. "What is the punishment for murder?"

"Cleatah..."

"She murdered our daughters!"

"You know I cannot harm her physically. It flies in the face of thousands of years of Terresian evolution. What we've built here on Erthe. This is a peaceful society. I told you, she's changed the girl's eyes..."

"Not enough."

"The two of them will be leaving the Central Isle soon. You won't ever have to see them. And I've locked her out of her laboratory."

Cleatah laughed bitterly.

"Keeping Talya from her work, from technos – there's no more terrible punishment than that. You must believe me."

She seemed to be considering his words.

Poseidon struggled to hide his relief. "This is my fault," he went on. "I was blinded by my own happiness. I couldn't see how sick with jealousy she'd become."

"I don't blame you," Cleatah said, her voice flattened, remote. The fire behind her eyes was suddenly, inexplicably extinguished. Without a word she stood and slipped her dress on, belting it with the woven tie.

"Will you come home?" he said. "Please, love."

346

She nodded and let him lead her to the horses.

Everything will be all right, he heard himself silently repeating. *It will be all right.* But the strong, sinewy fingers that were painfully squeezing his heart told him otherwise. He had fathered Talya's child. She had tricked them, betrayed them, and gotten away largely unscathed. His pathetic ignorance had shattered the illusion of their beautiful, perfect world.

Nothing would ever be the same again.

SEVENTY-FIVE

FROM THE DECK of his majestic new home Athens gazed down the length of Halcyon Beach and found himself very pleased. The broad ribbon of fine pink sand – flanked on one side by the sparkling blue-green sea and on the other by palatial residences built since the re-institution of the gold currency – had become the colony's favorite playground. And today, on the yearly anniversary of their arrival on Mars, a holiday colonists had named "Landfall," it seemed as if every last soul had come out to celebrate.

His latest companion, Patrice, a truly marvelous specimen of female beauty, moved to his side taking one hand, little Athena taking the other. Together they started down the long steps to the beach. Patrice wore a spare costume designed to expose much of her flesh to the solar rays. Like so many of the colonists she had become devoted to bathing in the sun's health-giving emissions, a pastime that had had the effect of somehow softening the naturally rigid Terresian demeanor. They'd hardly stepped foot on the sand when Athena broke away to romp with some neighbor children and their pet solies at the water's edge. Knowing she was perfectly safe he and Patrice moved along the beach crowded with carefree families lounging on the sand and playing in the gentle surf with their whiskered companions.

Watching the scene Athens contemplated the importance of the drone workforce to the general contentedness of their society. They really could not be underestimated. Those few colonists who still worked in the mines were supervisors. This was on a strictly volunteer basis, and the colonial mine workers were among the best-paid individuals on Mars. Farming and manufacturing were technologically and robotically performed, and each person was only required to work one or two days out of every ten. It was a perfect arrangement. Those few genomists who opposed Athens's labor force on moral grounds had long ago been transferred to other projects. While he still privately chafed at the memory of Poseidon's disapproval he had come to believe it was the best decision he had ever made since their arrival on Mars.

Vice Governor Praxis had been, and was still the project's most vocal opponent. Athens believed the opposition was simply a measure of Praxis's personal dislike for the much-loved Governor. He continually threatened to alert the home world of Athens's "slave labor force" which, Praxis said, was contrary to every ethical Terresian principle. But the threat was laughable. There could be no meaningful communication with Terres for thousands of Marsean years, as it had finally flung itself into its deep space orbit and PseudoMort had been initiated. For most of the colony the home planet had become a dim and rather unpleasant memory. Athens therefore allowed Praxis to keep his post. It wouldn't do for the colonists to perceive their governor as a tyrant who brooked no dissenting opinions. The vice governor had become nothing more than a pesky insect that Athens would occasionally swat away. He took great pleasure in humiliating him, the more publicly the better.

The colonists were therefore free to pursue the process of real civilization on Mars. Perhaps it was not the lush paradise that

Gaia was, but his people had created a fabulous land of leisure, decorated by artistic wonders created in abundant gold. While the filthy and dangerous work of mining went on out of sight and mind, they enjoyed lives of contentment with time enough to pursue any and all interests… and of course, plenty of time for recreation. Adults devised toys, sports and games – from simple physical competitions to intricate mind challenges. Children who, on the home planet had spent most of their waking moments in serious education, now discovered the world of play. They were delirious with it, abandoning themselves to all manner of natural pleasure. It was a perfect arrangement.

That was why, thought Athens as he surveyed the happy scene at Halcyon Beach on Landfall Day, he had chosen not to alarm his people with the disturbing reports of solies found dead on some of the more remote beaches to the north. Actually the solies themselves had not been found. Rather it was bits of them strewn among the rocks, or a horrible mash of bone, muscle and fur that appeared to have been chewed up, digested and spat out again. Too, there was a growing number of the creatures gone missing from colonists' households. Athens had authoritatively announced that these disappearances were simply the natural habit of the animals. As much as the people loved their solies they were wild creatures whose impulse was to periodically return to the deep.

He had quietly decided he would commission an investigation into the deaths and get to the bottom of it. He would do it soon. Just now he was a bit preoccupied. His nightmares had grown more frequent – the amber plasma spheres, glimpses of odd triangle-faced creatures with bulbous black eyes. But it was too magnificent a day to be worrying about such things. All of it could wait.

Colonists saw the honored couple walking up the beach and cleared a choice spot for Athens and Patrice in the shade of an overhanging tree fern. Many approached to pay their respects to the governor and brought offerings from their family's picnics. Athens warmed with pleasure, knowing that the beachgoers felt a sense of completeness and contentment that their leader was among them in their celebration.

He was thinking that he should call Athena to sit and eat with them when the first scream shattered the idyll as surely as a hammer blow to delicate crystal. A woman stood – rigid in the sand – her arm outstretched, finger pointing to a monstrous head so recently emerged from the waves that seawater still cascaded down its hideous, scaly snout. A solie struggled frantically in the beast's fanged jaws.

Worse than the sight itself was the creature's inexorable movement – unperturbed by the hordes of people before it, it advanced from the sea through the shallows toward the beach. Colonists scattered, shrieking in panic. Some had enough presence of mind to grab their children. Others desperately splashed into the surf to snatch their youngsters from the horror that had appeared in the suddenly treacherous ocean.

Like an unfolding nightmare three more heads appeared and began following the first monster that had emerged from the water onto the sand. Even on their short front legs they stood twelve feet high with long sleek bodies and a single posterior flipper. Their dark green, scaly torsos were dotted with dozens of large raised patches of an undulating, jellylike substance. Here the skin was a transparent membrane, and beneath it a colorful network of red and blue blood vessels could be seen. From the beasts' shoulders protruded six heavily muscled tentacles, several of which were independently searching out and snatching up solies, now making a desperate dash for the waves. The first unlucky solie had already been devoured, and a second in a tentacle's crushing embrace was being delivered to the creature's razor-toothed maw.

The other three amphibious monsters had in the next moment come ashore, hungrily eyeing and picking off their chosen meals.

By accident – or perhaps curiosity – one of the beast's huge tentacles wrapped itself around a man trying to rescue his little girl. His scream of agony caused every colonist to look back at the scene they were fleeing. And now disbelief mingled with horror and repulsion as they watched the creature take its first taste of human flesh. By some small grace the man had lost consciousness, or perhaps died, before his limp body was devoured.

For an instant Athens's senses failed him, panicked and paralyzed by the magnitude of the atrocity before him. Then a terrible high-pitched trill from the man-eater alerted the other three amphibians that this new warm-blooded prey was good eating and they, too, began scanning the beach for humans.

The sound also thrust Athens into action. He looked back frantically for Athena but saw she had been swept up by a neighbor and was being carried under his arm off the sand. Then Athens took off running down the beach toward the living nightmare.

Unbelievably, the events had not yet completed their horrible unfolding. More than twenty colonists had set their phaetrons to the rarely employed "kill" frequency and were attempting to clear the beach of humans previous to initiating their counter-attack. But before this was accomplished the four amphibians began a strange metamorphosis. It appeared as if large chunks of skin were being sloughed from their bodies. In fact it was the veined, jelly-like areas that were disengaging themselves from their hosts – dozens of independent, parasitic creatures who now skittered across the pink sand with such speed and agility that many had found solie and human victims before anyone had had time to aim their weapons or flee.

The result was instantaneous and sickening. Attaching themselves leech-like to any area of open skin, the jelly creatures began extracting bodily fluids at so accelerated a rate that the person was incapacitated before defense was possible. As the lucky scattered to safety victims fell writhing to the ground, seeming to shrivel before everyone's eyes, with the parasites ballooning into large blood-filled sacs so overloaded they were barely able to make their way back to their host creatures.

Now on the front line of men with phaetrons Athens picked off several dozen of the parasitic jelly creatures. He and a few others had a straight shot at the amphibians. They took aim and fired. Two of them were felled instantly, crashing to the ground and dying with shrill, ear-splitting screams. The other two, reacting with a speed not imagined in such large cumbersome creatures, disappeared into the waves before another phaetron round could be fired off.

Weary and sick with revulsion Athens and his shooters now moved among the remaining parasites, vaporizing their turgid, struggling bodies to spare witnesses the grisly sight of exploded bloody membranes.

Finally it was done.

Dazed colonists straggled back onto Halcyon Beach to retrieve the bodies of their loved ones. Wondering briefly if his refusal to alert the Terresians of the earlier killed solies would come back to haunt him, he suddenly and painfully realized the Martian idyll was over and that a terrible kind of night had settled over Paradise.

SEVENTY-SIX

CLEATAH WAS SUDDENLY gone.

It had not taken Poseidon long to realize that she had not simply left the residence for an early walk to the Academy. There was an eeriness, an emptiness about the Central Isle. Something somber to the point of doom. With terrible trepidation he went below into the ship.

Neither Talya nor the child was there.

Fear seized him. What had Talya done? He knew her to be capable of the most despicable acts, but violent abduction? Cleatah was strong, but she was no match for the phaetron. She'd been so troubled in the last week. He'd tried and failed to make amends for Talya's betrayal, but she had been distant and largely silent. When she did speak aloud to him and the twins it was tenderly, but in increments the telepathic conversations that they frequently shared had become harder to hear. They finally ceased altogether. This unnatural silence between them explained how he'd had no warning at all, no call for help.

A terrible thought gripped him. *Could he not hear her because she was dead? How had he allowed any of this to happen? Talya's crime. His beloved woman gone without a trace. His fault. His fault…*

SEVENTY-SEVEN

I T WAS UNCLEAR what had woken her from a sleep like death. Before she opened her eyes all was utter blackness, but she could feel a bone-rattling shake beneath her supine body, and her arms – *how peculiar* – were pinned tightly to her sides. There was a dull ache in her right arm, and the dampness at her chest could be nothing other than her breasts leaking milk. Then she heard Isis crying in a place behind her head. Talya tried without success to open her eyes. The sound of her child's cries clawed at her insides, and warm liquid came rushing forth in two small floods.

"Isis," Talya cried weakly, aware that her voice was cracked and feeble. "Isis!" With all her strength she lifted her eyelids. Her head swam in the daylight, though she was shaded from the sun by a plain woven cloth. Her back, flattened along the bottom of a cart, was jounced violently by what must certainly be uneven ground beneath the wooden wheels. *This could not be an Atlan road.* Now she understood she was bound tightly, pinioned within the confines of a length of cloth, immobile.

Talya could see nothing to her right or left, as the arched shade cloth touched the high sides of the cart. But the rear of the cart was open. Lifting her head from the cocoon and looking straight ahead she could see out the back. What stretched before her was as terrible a sight as she had ever seen.

Wilderness. Vast grassy expanses of the Great Plateau with snow-capped Manya and her sister-mountains nothing but tiny mounds in the distance from where this wagon had traveled. Atlantos, she calculated with a sinking in her gut, was far, far behind her.

Isis had stopped her wailing. Instead were wet sucking noises and the soft, satisfied grunts Talya knew so well. Someone was feeding her child!

"Where am I?" she cried, finally finding a voice loud enough to be heard. Yes, she had been heard. Isis was crying again. *Crying for her!* "Who is there? Where are you taking me?" She felt the cart rumble to a stop and heard the driver climbing down from the seat behind her head. Talya's heart pounded chokingly in her throat. The vision that appeared at the cart's opening could not have been more stunning.

It was the strident figure of a long-forgotten Cleatah, a wild-haired female attired in ragged-edged, rough-sewn animals pelts. Her posture was that of a hunter, though where a spear would have been held diagonally across her chest was instead strung a soft cloth sling. Inside it hung Talya's tiny child, red-faced and bawling.

"Give her to me," Talya demanded, her voice hoarse with longing.

Cleatah stood silent and still, unmoved by the baby's cries or its mother's commands.

"What are you *doing*, Cleatah? Where are you taking us? Tell me now."

Without a word Cleatah climbed into the wagon bed and laid Isis down at Talya's bound feet. Again the infant stopped crying, perhaps at the sight of her mother's face or a whiff of her familiar scent. Cleatah came on her knees to the front of the wagon and with one hand lifted Talya's head. With the other she held a water flask to her prisoner's parched lips. Talya wished to resist the gesture without receiving some answers but her thirst was unbearable and she greedily drank till she was sated. Before she could resume her questioning Cleatah backed away, climbed from the wagon and lifted Isis out, again placing her in the sling.

"No, don't take her!"

To Talya's dismay her daughter quieted and began suckling at Cleatah's milk-heavy breast.

"Please, give her to me. And tell me what's happening!"

Cleatah stared impassively at Talya as though she was trying to make sense of the scene before her – a scene that Cleatah had herself created.

"At least let me feed her," Talya begged.

"If you did she would sleep and never wake up," Cleatah said, breaking the silence. "For now, Poseidon's daughter will drink my milk."

"What did you give me? How…?" A stinging pain shot suddenly up from Talya's right wrist, shocking her into silence. When she attempted to move it inside the binding the whole arm ached. Her blood froze with the realization of the pain's origin. "What have you done? My phaetron…" she said with growing horror.

"Nothing you haven't done to me. To Poseidon. You can never hurt us again."

Talya's rage crashed violently inside her skull and chest. "You will let me out of here! Immediately!" she shouted. "Give me my child!"

Cleatah's expression might have been pity, or revulsion. "That's enough. We have a long way to go." Gently rearranging Isis' little limbs in the sling so the feeding was easier Talya's captor turned to go.

"Cleatah, wait! Wait! Does Poseidon know what you've done?"

Talya heard the Gaian primitive who had bested her in every conceivable way climb back into the seat and take up the horse's reins. She heard Cleatah click her cheek twice, and with a sharp lurch the cart began to move.

SEVENTY-EIGHT

BOAH HAD BEEN waiting – though no one would have said patiently – for Talya's summons. No woman treated a man like she did, yet no man would dare to command her. His brothers refrained from comment, though at the city stables where he worked these days to be close to her and the child he could see them watching him differently. They wondered why he'd been kept from seeing his daughter until Talya called for him, yet they'd stayed blessedly silent about it. But this day as he and Joss delivered a gangly-legged foal Boah knew he had waited long enough.

"Clean him?" he said to Joss.

A moment later he was out the stable door and trotting down the stone roadway without having met a single horseman's eye. All he could think of was his daughter, the flower-petal skin, the delicately arched features that he knew upon first sight resembled her mother's. When he reached the Outer Ring baths he couldn't remember how he'd gotten there.

He stripped off his sticky tunic and at the warm fountain washed the blood from his arms and face. Then he stepped into the pool where thankfully few were bathing. He soaked only long enough to achieve the cleanliness needed to visit his family. He smiled to himself as he toweled off, silently repeating the words in his head.

His family.

He needed desperately to see them. Talya and the child. His daughter. As he took a fresh tunic and started for his house he allowed himself to venture future thoughts. *What name would they give her?* – pretty little filly with a sun-yellow mane. He would teach her to ride. No matter that Talya never got on the back of a horse. The girl would very naturally ride. All the Brotherhood would love her like their own child.

At home he paused only long enough to tie his long hair back into a tail and to grab the fine blue and yellow blanket woven respectfully by the horsemen's women, and dash out again. He reminded himself to walk and not run so he wouldn't be sweat-covered and disheveled to see his women.

When Boah finally crossed the Central Canal bridge and neared the circular hedge that now hid the ship's entrance he saw Poseidon standing there. His tall frame seemed strangely stooped. Boah could see his features were torn with anguish.

"What is it? Is it Talya? The child?" He tried to move around Poseidon, but he blocked the way with his body.

"Tell me what's happened!"

Boah could see Poseidon trying to rearrange his features. He opened his mouth, then closed it again. Then he leveled his gaze on Boah and with much difficulty held steady. "You're a man who speaks only the truth, Boah, and you speak it from the heart," Poseidon began. "Now I have to tell you a truth...that will break your heart." He waited before he went on, composing himself as best he could. "They're both healthy." He fell silent again, this time for so long that Boah thought he would not speak again.

Boah shook his arm. "Tell me!"

"At the High Atlantos stables..." Poseidon finally continued, though haltingly, as though each word was poisoning his mouth,

"…you've seen Talya choose a particular sire for a particular mare." As Boah nodded his understanding Poseidon exhaled several times, pushing his fingers through the thick thatch of hair above his forehead. "In that same way…she chose a sire for her own child."

Boah nodded, certain that Poseidon was speaking of him. But his friend's expression had grown even more desperate.

"She led us all to believe it was you. It was not…I am the sire."

The muscles in Boah's body clenched reflexively. Poseidon raised and opened his hands before him in an attitude of surrender.

"She stole my seed while I slept. I *promise* you this. She stole it with technos, and impregnated herself with it."

Boah suddenly understood how it must have been for the mares and foals when the abyss had opened in the High Atlantos pasture during the great quake…tumbling and falling, limbs flailing helplessly

"Cleatah has taken her and the child away from the city," Poseidon went on.

"Cleatah…?" Boah's head spun, envisioning the consequences of Talya's deed upon his oldest friend. He replayed the words "taken her and the child" several times over in his head. It meant they were gone already. Vanished from his life, like one of Poseidon's Terresian cloaking tricks.

"We'll tell everyone that Talya has been called away on urgent family matters," Poseidon said, eyes glassy. Boah could clearly see that the man was as stunned at Cleatah's actions – her abduction of Talya – as he himself was. "No one will question a mother taking so young an infant with her. No one has reason to question the story."

"The child…" Boah said aloud – the only spoken words of his lament. The muddled confusion inside his head gave way to sudden clarity. He was crashing headlong into one of Talya's merciless betrayals after another. Theft. Cunning. Lies. Physical violation.

And the stinging truths: Talya was no sister to Poseidon, but a jealous lover. The daughter he believed his was another man's child. His own seed had been spurned, regarded as unworthy.

An invisible hand squeezed Boah's guts, forcing him to turn from Poseidon. He blindly retraced his steps home. His family was no more. It had, in fact, never been at all.

Once in his door he collapsed as though physically beaten and lay on the floor, motionless. His future visions began to fade. His bright-haired daughter riding low on the back of a fast pony. Gone. Talya, beautiful and wild, feeding wood into the blazing hearth of their home. The light banter he and the horsemen shared dwindling to whispered pity. Misery supplanted misery. Cleatah, his dearest friend on Erthe, suffering horribly at Talya's hand. Now Cleatah, in reprisal, had exacted a terrible punishment on all of them.

And the child, like a length of delicate cloth, would forever be torn between so many angry hands. *The girl.* He captured a small sob in his throat.

He had never even learned her name.

Seventy-Nine

T HEY HAD TRAVELED nine days, stopping only to sleep and eat. Each night Cleatah would free Talya's legs and right arm, allowing her to feed herself, walk about so her muscles would not shrivel from disuse, and void her bladder and bowels. She would make a bed for herself and Isis next to Talya in the cart.

Many times Cleatah saw Talya stare disbelievingly at the cut-and-sewn flesh at her wrist. She wondered if Talya thought that Boah or Poseidon might still be coming to rescue her, bring her and her child back to the city. Cleatah knew that Talya was "seething." Poseidon had taught her that word. *A quiet agitation.* She had known it described the sea or the clouds, but now Cleatah knew seething could describe a person as well.

After a few days Cleatah's rage had softened enough so that she could give Isis to her mother for feeding. She found she missed the baby's suckling. She missed her sons. Her breasts ached for them. They were only eight months old, and she hadn't wished to leave them. There was nothing in the world she had wished to do more than be with them.

But she had to be rid of this woman.

It was still unfathomable, the act that Talya had committed. It was hard to know what inflamed Cleatah more – that Isis was

Poseidon's child, or that she would never give birth to a daughter. The latter was worse, she finally concluded – the fate of bearing no female children in all of her life. It was a punishment she could hardly comprehend. Poseidon had taken blame for his ignorance of Talya's monstrous assault. But now Cleatah wondered if she herself had grown so soft in her new "civilized" existence that she no longer sensed danger as it approached.

Saying nothing to Poseidon she had carried out her plan, asking no help from anyone. At the last, once Talya's bound and inert body rested in the cart with the horses stamping and snorting impatiently to be off in the crisp night air, she had gone to Yazman – who with her family shared the Central Isle – and told her their destination. The only one Yazman might tell was Poseidon, when he came looking for her. She did regret the moments of fear he would certainly experience when he found them missing. Yazman might also relay the message to him that she did not wish to be followed. The decision would of course be his.

Cleatah prayed day and night to the Great Mother that he would not follow. As they crossed the continent she spoke to him silently, hoping that the distance between them would not prevent his hearing her. She was used to this unspoken conversation that flowed endlessly between them. For all these years it had been soothing to know he was with her inside her head, even if he was out of her sight. It had made her feel safe, always. Now she worried that in the last days she had silenced the conversation to accomplish her plan without him knowing. Perhaps she had silenced it forever. *Please, Great Mother,* she prayed, *let him hear me again. Let him hear me with all these miles between us.*

As each day passed she worried less that Poseidon would pursue them, but she was unsure of Boah. He would know nothing of why Talya and his daughter had gone, under what circumstances, or where. Would Poseidon tell him what he knew? What, if anything, would he reveal?

It was not her concern, she'd finally decided. Her task was to remove the woman from their lives. Poseidon might object to his daughter's absence. In fact, this was Cleatah's only regret. The child was blameless. Isis was a dear and beautiful baby. Suckling the girl had afforded Cleatah a different sort of pleasure than she experienced with her boys. And Cleatah would without question protect the child with her life. She was, after all, Poseidon's blood.

Her mother – if Cleatah was entirely honest with herself – she wished dead.

EIGHTY

THEY REACHED THE Taug Village at dusk on the twelfth day out. Behind it a wide river meandered by its lightly wooded shores. Isis was crying as they approached, and Cleatah hoped this would gentle the spirits of the Taug people who now watched a wagon pulled by two horses cross the settlement's boundary.

This was one of the tribes that had scorned the strangers and their four-legged beasts ten years before during the gathering of the tribes. The Taug whispered suspiciously among themselves for days after Boah's demonstrations with the large devil animals and Poseidon's impossible feats. Today Cleatah had a young baby hanging at her breast, and called out a peaceful greeting as she approached.

They allowed the cart to roll up next to the just-lit central fire where the women were handing out the nightly meal – a boiled knot of meat and a whitish mush in a small gourd bowl. The men, as she had remembered them, looked strong, bright-eyed and healthy. The women were well-fed and contented, the children lively and playful.

The headmen approached her, and several elder women crowded in behind them. Cleatah began to speak imperfect Taug.

It was understandable enough. She had practiced her speech and worked to make a complicated request sound simple and understandable.

She wished for the village to take in this woman and her child. Cleatah had brought gifts to exchange for the favor, but if the woman and baby could be given a hut of their own she would work as the other women did and become a member of the tribe.

She told how, when her own tribe – the Shore People – had allowed a stranger into their midst, it had proved a blessing. Under no circumstance should the woman be allowed to leave the Taug village. Cleatah remembered that this inland tribe fished from the river's edge with nets and had only the simplest of boats. If Talya had visions of escaping it would be on foot with an infant across the vastness of the continent.

The headman consulted with the elder women and turned back to Cleatah. *Was this woman very ugly or deformed?* they wanted to know. *Was she sick or crazy?* Cleatah assured them Talya was none of these. In fact she was a much-revered woman, but now she was being punished for an ill deed, and the tribe did not wish to have her in their presence. *Would this woman treat the Taug ill?* They asked.

Cleatah had thought long and hard about this and had concluded that the tribe was in no danger from Talya. Without her wrist device she would be entirely helpless. Of necessity, her days would be spent learning how to survive in this place and how to keep her daughter safe.

Talya would at first be unhappy, she told the headmen and elder women, but she would harm no one.

It was finally agreed that the Taug would take her.

Cleatah returned to the covered cart and lay Isis down. She freed Talya from all her bindings. "Make yourself presentable," she said.

Talya ran her fingers through the pale hair, now stringy with sweat and grime, and tucked the fabric that had imprisoned her arms into a semblance of a garment.

"You will be careful what you tell the child," Cleatah told her, her voice laced with threat. Talya was silent, trembling. "Her father is Boah. Poseidon and Athens are your brothers, her uncles. They, like you, come from 'a place very far away.' Poseidon and his family, and Boah, live across the plateau in Atlantos. Athens lives 'across a very great ocean.'" Cleatah climbed out of the cart. "Now come out. Bring the child."

Desperation shook Talya. "Are you coming back for me?"

She watched Talya gather Isis into her arms.

"Will you come back?" It was a pleading whisper.

Cleatah said nothing. Then she turned away.

Eighty-One

THE FIRST INDIGNITY of her banishment had been a bath in the icy river. As soon as Cleatah, the cart and two horses had disappeared out of sight the women had surrounded Talya, one of them taking Isis from her arms. The rest laughed and poked curiously at her unnaturally pale skin, bruised in places from the hard wooden cart under her back and buttocks, and her filthy yellow hair. She could tell from their expressions that they thought her unpleasantly thin, and next to their plump curves and ruddy cheeks she must have appeared freakish. But she stank, so even the icy water that made her prickle all over was a relief of sorts. She allowed the women to scrub her, though never taking her eyes off the girl who dandled Isis on her lap. Surely relieved to be done with constant jouncing travel the child was giggling and patting the girl's face with her fat little fingers.

How could this have happened? How could she have so underestimated Cleatah, her passion and her fury. In her wildest dreams Talya could never have foreseen so brilliant a revenge brought down on her head. Not only were the Taug hundreds of miles from Atlantos, they were one of very few tribes who had shown no interest in joining the others in a new society. They were unimpressed by horses. They shunned the very idea of cultural evolvement. They were as backward a tribe as existed on the continent. Without her phaetron Talya was paralyzed, at these people's mercy for every necessity.

There was irony in her gratitude towards Cleatah who, in her unceremonious farewell, had announced coldly that she hoped never to set eyes on Isis or Talya again. Talya had worried on that terrible journey that her punishment would be losing her child as well as her place in Atlan society. But thankfully Isis had been returned to her.

She would keep to herself until she could make a plan. At least these women were kind. She'd make herself unattractive to the men who – watching her bathing ordeal from a distance – seemed more curious than aroused. Perhaps Boah was already on the way to save them. Certainly he would want her back, want his child – no one would tell him the truth of her parentage. What of Joss and the Brotherhood? Would they not demand to know her whereabouts? And Poseidon – he could never have agreed to such rough justice. She was confident that this hideous village was in no way her destiny, or that her daughter must be raised among savages.

Talya gazed riverward and saw the morning light blinking like a thousand tiny suns on the rippled surface. She heard Isis' shriek of laughter from the shore and thought of how far from her home on Terres she had come…and how much farther she would have to travel before she was through.

EIGHTY-TWO

THE GREAT PLATEAU was all but behind her. Cleatah had already passed the mining villages never making the slightest detour, so eager to be back that even the necessary stops were an annoyance. Her body craved her babies. Atlas and Geo would be little boys soon, rough and tumbling and seeking the company of older boys and men who would harden them, teach them the manly arts. But for now they were hers, seeking the softest parts of her, nestling in the curves of her body as they fed, making sounds like the sweetest birds, fragrant from hair and feet, tiny fingers tangling in her hair as their budlike mouths pulled and sucked at her breasts.

She summoned thoughts of Poseidon. He was her love, the pleasure between her thighs, her teacher of all things marvelous, the deep well of her trust in the goodness of this life. Every day of this miserable journey she had fixed him in her mind's eye – at the Academy Tower with the star-gazers sweeping his hand across the glittering fires in the night sky. With the stone masons at the site of the Horse Stadium urging them on to feats of artistry in their burgeoning craft. With the boat builders igniting their dreams of voyages across the distant sea.

But her happiest visions – the ones that had eased the

loneliness of empty plains and endless mountain chains – were those of Poseidon at the residence. In the gardens. Always Poseidon with the boys. His capacity for the emotions of love and caring had swelled with the birth of their sons. He was prone to fits of helpless laughter and bouts of sudden weeping. Despite his never-ending labors in the city he spent every possible moment with his children, riding them on his back, composing chirping little songs for the simple pleasure of making them laugh.

He would be waiting for her return. He might be angry at her outrageous actions, but he had honored her judgment and her punishment for Talya. He'd chosen not to follow them nor allowed Boah to follow either. He would forgive her. She was certain of it.

The horses were straining against their traces, drawn by the scent of a familiar sea. Cleatah clicked twice in her cheek, but they needed no urging. They were taking her home. To her love and her family.

They were taking her home to Atlantos.

EIGHTY-THREE

THE BROTHERHOOD WAS well-aware of the two women's absence from their lives. Talya's was perhaps more keenly felt, as Cleatah – having retired to the residence on the Central Isle with the birth of her twins – was less a public figure than before. No one even noticed she was gone. But the horsemen's questions to Boah about their patron and mother of his newborn daughter were met with genuine bafflement. Even if he'd wished to, there was simply no way to explain the web of Talya's treachery and lies, or Cleatah's unexpected revenge. Only Joss dug at him with questions, suspicions, but these, too, went unanswered.

Boah had fallen into an unnatural silence among his friends and suffered alone in an impenetrable gloom. The days grew into weeks and the torment seemed endless. This day at the High Atlantos stables he was tending to a boil on a mare's hoof when shouts began echoing through the rafters: "She comes!"

Boah dropped the horse's foot. He ran for the door. In the distance, approaching from the south was a solitary cart and solitary driver. He leapt on the nearest mount and galloped off, riding west for a distance to avoid the Grave of the Horses. The cart was in his sight but with a sinking heart he discovered it was occupied by Cleatah alone. *What had he expected?* he thought miserably. *That Cleatah would have had a change of heart and brought them home?*

When his horse met the team she continued driving them, her face and posture rigid. He rode alongside, but found himself bereft of words. The obvious question – the only question – hung in the silence between them.

Finally she said, "They are well, Boah. Far from here, but safe and cared-for."

They approached the chasm outside the grazing pasture.

"Cleatah. Stop. Talk to me!"

She drew the team to a halt and climbed down as Boah dismounted. He went to her but refused to embrace her until questions were answered.

She peered down into the darkness of the abyss. "I took them twelve days ride to the south. To the Taug." She spoke in hushed tones, never meeting his gaze. "They're fishermen and weavers. A prosperous village on a river. They're traders. We visited them during the great gathering. They refused to join us in Atlantos. Remember?"

"I remember," he said. His lips were set in a grim line.

"Why are you telling me where they are?"

"I tell you because you deserve to know."

"You're certain that I won't go after them?"

"I can't be certain. But I ask that you do not."

"And Poseidon?" he demanded, but he already knew the answer.

Now his shoulders slumped and his arms hung down like broken tree limbs. "I've tried to remember the words she used to deceive me," Boah said, eyes downcast with shame, "but I cannot. I'd drunk too much. Perhaps she never said the child was mine. Perhaps I only assumed it. Then it would not be a lie."

"She did nothing to correct you," Cleatah added in a hoarse whisper. "That made it a lie. She extracted Poseidon's seed while he slept. That is worse than a lie."

"I've been such a fool."

"Don't torment yourself." Cleatah laid a gentle hand on his arm. "How could anyone have foreseen so outrageous an act? I believed she was my friend. Poseidon's too. None of us can be held accountable for our ignorance."

He was searching for words to beg for Talya's return. For the child.

"She couldn't stay here any longer, Boah. If I'd had to look at her...I might have killed her." An icy tone crept into Cleatah's voice, and he thought he saw a hint of a dark smile. "So I devised a 'protocol' to rid us of her."

Boah startled at this. Here was a Cleatah he had never known in all his life. Like the wolf she'd brought into the Shore Village those many years before she was utterly fearless, quietly commanding by virtue of her strength and ferocity.

"I'm sad that it's come to this," she said, "but I'm not sorry."

He turned to his horse and laid his head on its broad flank, as though he might find comfort there. Courage. But his voice when it came was weak and helpless. "For a long time I saw Talya as my woman, but never my mate...not until she conceived the child. She bore her as if she was mine." He hoped he did not sound pitiful. "Everyone believes this child is mine."

"Isis," Cleatah said in a whisper. "Her name is Isis."

Boah rubbed his hands over his face. "Isis..." He tested the name on his tongue. "She may not be the seed of my body. Yet she *is* my daughter." He looked pleadingly at Cleatah. "My heart tells me she's mine."

Cleatah's face prickled with tears and the brisk breeze.

"They cannot come home?" he said in the quietest voice.

"They cannot, Boah. They cannot."

She wrapped her arms around him and held him as he shook. In weary silence they contemplated what these strange and beloved creatures from another world had wrought upon their own...and wept.

EIGHTY-FOUR

FOR ALL OF Cleatah's absence the boys had fussed and cried, even rejecting the breast of the two young mothers kind enough to share their milk. He could hear Sanja now, trying to sing Atlas one of Cleatah's lullabies, but nothing was quieting the wails. Then Geo joined in.

Poseidon found the three of them in the gathering room. The woman's own infant lay contentedly in the pillows while Geo, sitting up beside the baby girl, was squalling. His face was an alarming shade of crimson that matched the tear-streaked cheeks of Atlas who was cradled in Sanja's arms. She just shook her head helplessly. Poseidon swept his young son up and slung him onto his shoulder, nearly deafened by the screams in his ear.

Then all at once the crying stopped. In an instant. Both boys at once. There was nothing from them, not even a whimper. Poseidon could see their heads swiveling slowly from side-to-side, as though they were looking for something. Sanja gazed at Poseidon, puzzled. Then her own child began to bawl, and they laughed at the strangeness of it all.

"Take her," he said of Sanja's daughter. "I'll hold the boys." He lowered himself into the cushions setting Geo onto one knee. Then Sanja handed Atlas down onto the other.

Their silence continued. They uttered none of the new words they had recently learned and loved to repeat endlessly. Then one at a time Poseidon turned them to his chest and held one on each shoulder near to his heart, and closed his eyes.

"What is it?" he whispered. "What do you hear?"

He thought how he missed their mother's voice, both words and songs, and the voice that was unspoken.

Then, with the merest shimmer behind Poseidon's eyes a vision began to materialize. It was so clear it might have been a diffracted image. *Cleatah alone, sitting straight-backed on the seat of their wagon traversing the Great Plateau. She was wearing skins, and her honey hair was loose about her shoulders.*

Is this what had quieted the boys? Bloody stars, she was thinking of them! *I hear you, love. I see you! We all see you coming!*

Now Poseidon noticed Manya far in the distance, and before the cart Cleatah's destination. He thought his heart would burst with the relief of it – just a few miles ahead were the headlands of High Atlantos.

*

On foot Poseidon traversed the bridges and ring isles, never stopping for the many greetings, nor to admire the gorgeously carved stone pillars of the city's newest bath house or accept the warm meat pies held out to him by vendors in the South Market Square. His sights were set squarely on the South Ramp – the gracefully curved roadway running from the market to the High Atlantos Stables. But when a crone with a bright toothless smile waved her arm above a great bucket of tall-stemmed flowers in whites and yellows and purples he slowed, turned and backtracked.

Recognizing the urgency on his face she wordlessly scooped an armload of her beautiful bounty and laid it in Poseidon's arms, whispering, "She will like them."

He nodded his thanks and ran the rest of the way to the base of the ramp where he stopped, feeling suddenly foolish. What made him so sure she was coming? A mysterious vision he had conjured in the gathering room? It was just as likely wishful thinking as anything. But the boys had stopped their crying so suddenly. He wasn't imagining it. Even Cleatah's protracted silence couldn't last forever. *She is thinking of me...and she is near!*

But what if his fears were real? What if she could never forgive him for what he'd allowed to happen? It had been his leniency with Talya that encouraged such audacity in the first place. Against Cleatah's wishes she had meddled with nature and altered the course of a great river. Now Talya had tampered with Cleatah's very body and changed the course of her life. Much as she loved him, surely some part of Cleatah's affection had been sullied forever. He was almost afraid to look up at the curving roadway. Afraid that she'd not be coming. Afraid that she would. He lifted his eyes and prepared to wait. Forever if he had to.

There, halfway to the bottom...was that the side of their cart? Was it a woman in profile? *Cleatah!* His heart leapt to his throat, nearly choking him, and he forced himself to breathe. She had not seen him yet. There was more of the curved ramp to descend. Poseidon felt the weight of his future in the next moments – endless pain...or forgiveness.

The clopping of the hooves on the cobbles was louder now. The horses' heads emerged first, and finally the whole team and cart and the driver were before him. He was stuck to the ground, feet made of stone. His voice caught in his throat, dry and rasping. All he could do was lift his arms high in a wild waved greeting. The forgotten flowers were falling in a shower around him at the instant Cleatah clapped eyes on him.

In the next moment she was running down the curved ramp, her hair flying behind her. Their collision was sudden and shocking and sweet. His raised arms lowered slowly down around her pulling her into him, closer and tighter, and tighter still.

"You heard me calling you," she whispered.

"No. I *saw* you. Our sons heard you."

"And you brought me flowers."

"Yes."

He began to laugh at the thought of it and bent to gather them. She stooped and took some up in her arms as well. The horses and their driverless cart clopped to a halt beside them.

"Shall we go home, my love?" she said. "I want to see my boys."

He nodded, unable to utter a sound.

Side-touching-side, blossoms festooning her lap, they drove through their city of circles, marveling at all they had conjured out of thin air, with countless shouted blessings and the cries of seabirds following them all the way home.

EIGHTY-FIVE

THIS WAS TERRESIAN science at its best. The sharpest minds contemplating the inexplicable and making a civilization-altering discovery. The solution was so simple and elegant that there was only celebration within the small cadre of scientechnoists who laid claim to it.

Then why do I feel so desperate? Persus wondered. *Why am I terrified to bring the findings of the physics men to Athens?* Governor Athens. She found it harder all the time to keep her distance. To keep perspective. He was like luscious food to her, always a finger-length out of reach.

The Governor.

There had been a blackness hanging over him since the phibions' attack on Halcyon Beach. The hastily made plan to move the entire colony inland was a dismal alternative to their idyllic existence. People told themselves that the solies were lovely creatures but there'd be plenty to enjoy without them. Without the beach.

Gold. Games. Technos. Bed.

She knew Athens would not take well to the report. He already looked ill. Haunted. These days he muttered about bad dreams, huge black eyes... *Black eyes?* When she'd asked if he meant Athena's eyes he'd nearly snapped her head off. But she was sure that today, for Governor Athens, would mark the boundary to a darker place still.

Of course she had no choice. She herself had commissioned the study, though the physics men had been arguing the problem since the accident in space – a mystery too delicious to ignore. And with titanum and gold production reaching an all-time high there was much leisure time for contemplation. Long nights together in someone's laboratory. Every trans-screen lit. Fingers flying over the equations. Fat, juicy formulas. Many shouted suggestions but only one perfect solution. These men played at science like a game.

Their joy will be Athens's destruction, she thought many times a day. She needed to steel herself. *No, it will be all right. He is stronger than he appears. Of course he is.* She stepped through his office door. Arranged a pleasant look on her face.

"May I accompany you to the meeting?" she said to the back of his chair that was turned to the window. He was silent, still, as though screwing up the nerve to speak. "Sir?"

"Yes, I'm coming."

A moment later he was beside her. He towered over her, and for the hundredth time she bemoaned her pathetic stature and short, heavy legs. Then she admonished herself – this was no time for such selfish and petty considerations.

Very soon Athens would be needing her help.

Eighty-Six

"BUT WE'VE *ALWAYS* suspected alternate dimensions," Athens said, annoyed and quite relieved. He'd been vaguely dreading this physics report, but here nothing was new. "In our whole scientechnic history we haven't been able to find any proof of them."

"What we're saying, Governor, is that we *have* found proof."

Athens looked at Persus with an incredulous smirk. "This is the team you commissioned?"

"Yes, well, not exactly. I never realized when I put the question to them that they'd been quietly studying it since our accident in space."

Athens startled at the reference.

"The evidence of an alternate dimension is also our problem," Callas said, putting an irritating emphasis on "problem."

Athens had enough problems already, he thought.

"You see, there's a thin fabric, a membrane that separates our known dimension from the other. By our physical assaults on Mars…"

"'Physical assaults?'"

"Drilling, Sir," said Clax. "We are quite certain that drilling has had more than a superficial effect on the planet's mantle. We've also been tearing holes in the…fabric."

Dark dread began to settle over him. "What do you mean, 'The evidence is also our problem?'"

Monus finished for the others. "The tears can *grow* from the point of origination. Or possibly multiply. Some of them are in and above the ocean." He waited to collect himself before he continued. "We believe the phibions are coming through the tears, Sir. When we first postulated it we had sensors installed along the coast. Every time the sensors detected a new tear occurring, the incidence of incursions escalated dramatically."

"Haaa…" It was less Athens's word than a blown-out breath. "The solies?" he whispered.

"They're a new food source for the phibions, not an ancient one as we all believed. That's why the poor little things have no defenses."

The implication was ghastly. He, the colony's governor, was directly responsible for the solies' demise. "What does this…" he felt himself ripping the words out of himself "…have to do…with the accident in space?"

"What the data shows," said Callas, trembling with triumph, oblivious to the effect of his words, "is that, like the small rending in the dimensional membrane from drilling, a larger tear was made by our transport and the *Atlantos* at the approximate location of the accident."

"How much larger?"

"We don't know. But this is where the plasma spheres…"

"What?!" Athens cried.

"You do remember the plasma spheres?" said Clax.

"Of course I remember them!" Athens snapped. *They are in my dreams!* he thought but did not say. "Which is it then?" His voice was shaking. "Holes where we drilled? Holes in the ocean? Holes in *space*! And how are you so sure it was made during this mission? What about the previous Mars mission – my brother's expedition? They were drilling in the crust…"

"It could have been, yes…"

"Then why are you blaming *me?*"

"We're not laying blame on anyone, Sir."

Athens knew he sounded frenzied. Even he could hear the whine in his voice. He felt himself shrinking. *Oh why hadn't Persus minded her own business?* He stared at the physics men. He'd made them uneasy. There they all stood, larynxes bobbing up and down in their skinny throats.

Clax swallowed hard. He looked at the others who were waiting for him to finish the rendition of their findings. What all of them in the room now knew was that the answer would be a blow to the governor.

"We have reason to believe a tear now extends at least from the planetary orbits to Mars."

"*At least?!*" Athens shouted.

"It may encompass the entire solar system…and farther out into deep space. We just don't know yet. We're continuing to study it."

"Yes, you do that," Athens said, turning to go. *Poseidon had known all along what happened to Elgin Mars. This was his reason for insisting on the Gaian expedition for himself and leaving this murderous planet to his fool of a brother. He'd been betrayed. Betrayed!* "And in the future you, Persus…" Athens spat her name, "You will ask for my personal commission of any scientechnic studies of this magnitude. Is that clear?"

"Of course, sir."

As he made his exit he knew his composure was as thin as the blasted interdimensional fabric. He hoped it would hold steady until he was safely behind his office door.

CHILDREN OF RA

He also begat and brought up five pairs of twin male children…And he named them all; the eldest, who was the first king, he named Atlas…

— Plato's *Critias,* 4th Century B.C.

EIGHTY-SEVEN

POSEIDON WAS DREAMING.

Astride his horse Arrow, outstretched along the beast's muscular neck, they flew unfettered through a cloud-littered sky. Cumulous puffs caressed his face and soft curls of white soothed his eyes, soothed every molecule of his being. They emerged into the expected cool blue to the sight of a tempest in the far distance. A boiling black mountain rose precipitously, rose to the edge of the atmosphere. "There is a dangerous storm ahead," he whispered in Arrow's twitching ear, but the words seems to spur the horse on, speeding fast and straight as her name, closing the distance between them and the storm. There were streaks of lightning flung from the clouds to the Erthe's surface below, and there and again ghostly electric bolts like statues of light shot upwards to the edge of space. He felt himself straining against his mount, trying in vain to slow his inexorable forward flight. The dire rumbling echoed in his every cavity, multiplying a whispered warning of doom, and the black thunderheads closed around them, blotting out all light.

Poseidon awoke dream-addled in the dark, a pale glow from the Great Mother's altar fire reassuring him of his whereabouts. Cleatah stirred beside him in their bed. Now he could smell the sweet breath of an infant and reached out to touch the tender flesh of the child curled between them.

The foreboding dream slipped from memory with every muscle he moved and every waking sensation registered – the comfort of the nightclothes in a loose tangle about his limbs, his woman warm and safe an arm's length away, the child between them with his brother in a wooden crib at the foot of the bed.

All was right with the world as the last of the night made way for the morning.

On solstice days like this Poseidon rose well before dawn. He would bathe, then walk – not ride – up to the Great Plateau to stand on the headlands in time for sunrise over the eastern horizon. A private ritual. He had said his goodbyes the night before to Cleatah, to Atlas and Geo who at six were old enough to remember his absence of several day at the last Winter Solstice. Ammon and Evemon – nearly three – would miss him, but the youngest, Thoth and Siris were four months old and would never know he was gone.

Last night Poseidon had embraced the youngest twins for a very long time. Logic told him they were safe with Cleatah and Yazman's family on the Central Isle, but the thought of leaving these two had pained and worried him. He felt them, body and spirit, barely tethered to the Erthe.

But of course it was the near-loss of Siris at birth, Poseidon reasoned. It must be the memory rattling him – a rare blockage deep in Sirus's throat. With Cleatah weak and helpless with delivery of the twins just moments before Poseidon had taken the bloody, squirming bundle from the midwife and run from the residence, through the gardens, across the footbridge, blotting out the sounds of choking, his own heart crashing against his ribs, to the circular grove of trees in the middle of the Central Isle. He'd descended on a beam of blue light into the mothership *Atlantos*. Had run down the long corridor to the medical bay and laid the baby down. The blessed scan. The blockage discovered. The procedure called up on the trans-screen. He had taken up the surgical phaetron with shaky hands that he willed into stillness, and began.

The memory still had the power to fill him with terror.

Now he managed to slip from the bed without waking Cleatah or Thoth and in the bathing chamber washed himself under the warm fountain of water. Clothed in a clean tunic he padded quietly out the front arch of the residence into the misty morning, stopping once to look back at his home. Everything most dear to him resided here. He felt them safe, as safe as they could be on a wild planet at the mercy of the unknown.

His many thoughts had taken him on foot across the Inner Canal Bridge as well as the whole breadth of the Middle Ring Isle where Atlans in their homes were beginning to stir. The first of them were finding their way into the neighborhood public baths. So foggy was it on the torch-lit Middle Canal that he could hear but not see the skifes loaded with fruits and grains, vegetables, buron carcasses and cages of live turkeys, all making for the docks of the North and South Market squares of the Outer Ring Isle.

At the base of the South Ramp Poseidon began to climb at a brisk pace, the steep angle of the long curved bridge rising to the lip of the Great Plateau burning the muscles of his thighs and calves. Already the ramp was alive with foot traffic and carts. Those who recognized the "Father of Atlantos" in the flickering torchlight greeted him with friendly shouts that he returned with a wave and a smile. He was always chagrinned at how many faces he remembered and how few the names.

At the ramp's summit Poseidon paused amidst the growing clamor of horses and riders, carts of foodstuffs, and ore from the mountain's mines and villages. These days most of the Central Range of volcanic peaks were dormant, though he knew them to be unpredictable. Only Manya belched an occasional plume of smoke, reminding Poseidon of the fiery eruption that had killed his crew.

He turned from the ramp's summit and walked south along a little-used dirt track that skirted the headlands looking far over the sea. Just below him he could see in the budding light Atlantos spread out in its three colossal rings of land and water, the city whose very bones he had hewn out of solid rock.

Near the cliff's edge Poseidon entered the stone chamber that hid a portal to the shuttle disk and allowed the blue elevator beam to transport him to its interior. He wished Cleatah could be with him for this Solstice journey, but the twins were too young for her to leave them. He would make the exploration of Erthe's far reaches and populations himself this time, but it would be the last, he promised himself. Cleatah relished their expeditions of the planet too much to be left behind.

The controls responded silently under Poseidon's hands – first the cloaking device for the craft, and then the careful horizontal emergence from its stony crypt beneath the headlands. As the first beams of sunlight kindled the clouds into radiant color, and with a phaetronic burst of speed that never failed to thrill him, Poseidon sped across the sprawl of Atlantos City heading seaward for the far horizon.

EIGHTY-EIGHT

CLEATAH LOVED SPRING Solstice. She would have liked to be with Poseidon roaming the planet, standing amidst the most thrilling glories of Erthe. But to be honest she was more than content to be home. With her children. Tending her garden. Watching over the people, offering counsel when necessary.

Abundance was everywhere – in the fields and orchards, in the city and High Atlantos. With the lessening of seasonal storms their ships, laden with salted fish, had begun sailing to the shores of other lands to seek trading partners. The Academy was nurturing the minds of men and women to inspiring effect. It was mating season, and here on the Central Isle she'd watched birds as they claimed their darkened hollows, fashioning twigs, bark fibers and down into comfortable nests.

She found herself watching a pretty blue-dappled bunting. It was a small broad-chested creature who, most trustingly, had woven her nest in the crotch of a tree not far above the level of Cleatah's eyes. On tiptoes she could peer in when the mother had gone to feed, or watch as one tiny egg appeared after another till four had accrued, stippled and leaning comfortably one against the other.

Cleatah found it made her unaccountably happy to watch this fatherless family, this fearless little female. She waited with eager anticipation for the hatching to begin. One day after the mother had flown off a red-backed snipe – twice as large a bird as the bunting – landed on the rim of the nest and stood glaring down at the eggs. Cleatah moved quickly thinking to shoo it away, then stopped, scolding herself. *Who am I to interfere with the natural order of things?* Heart pounding she watched as the snipe stepped into the nest and covered it with its generous bulk. The snipe lowered its head, seeming to strain, then settled. Softened. A few moments later it flew away.

Cleatah walked quickly to the tree crotch and looked down to see a fifth egg in the nest, pure white and twice as large as the bunting's. She found herself annoyed at how it crowded the little eggs, disrupted the symmetry of the four. She was outraged at the snipe mother's act itself, one for which she did not have a name. Cleatah stepped back, retreating to the garden with one eye fixed on the nest.

When the bunting returned she stared down with beady black eyes at the egg that was not her own. She tapped it with her beak, cocking her head, listening for the sound of life within. She pushed it gently. Large as it was she could have rolled it from the nest.

Cleatah found herself silently urging the bunting, *Throw it out! Rid yourself of the intruder!* But the bird – perhaps confused, perhaps resigned – spread herself wide and with fluffed feathers nestled down on all five of her charges for the long sitting.

In the days that followed – and to Cleatah's delight – first one then another and another of the bunting chicks came forth from the stippled eggs, their demanding beaks opened comically for their feedings. She found herself praying that the snipe chick had died in its shell, and refused to feel remorse for such base instincts. She wasted no sympathy on the abandoned creature and harbored great indignation for its mother.

Then one morning a great commotion rocked the nest. The snipe chick was breaking through its shell. Though she was desperate to get nearer Cleatah forced herself to keep her distance. What she could see was that once freed of the egg the sharp-beaked birdling tossed the pieces over the edge and with its long wax-tipped pinfeathers sat as a giant among the four bunting chicks. It crowded the brood, and Cleatah could imagine the intruder bruising their bodies with the sharp elbow of its too-large wing. From the first morning it demanded feeding, day and night, the mouth yawing wide. Nothing satisfied its hunger. The bunting mother was run ragged, till her chest bones poked through her faded blue feathers.

Cleatah's rage grew with every passing day. She found herself distracted, distraught with worry over the state of the nest. She dreamed about the birds and woke up calling out a warning in the night. And then one day with the mother gone hunting for the endless feast of beetles and oily white pupae to satiate her family, the snipe began its assault. The smallest of the bunting chicks was pushed out of the nest. Before she could save it, it was snatched up and devoured by a stalking raven.

Cleatah's heart broke to see the mother return each day to find another of her babies gone. Finally only one of her own remained sitting side-by-side with the monster child. The bunting chick grew, feathered out, and one day fled the nest and his mother, never looking back.

Cleatah could not tear her eyes from the sight of the mother bunting now standing on the nest's edge looking down at the snipe. It was not yet full-grown, yet as large as she was, its mouth open, still clamoring for its meal.

Cleatah heard herself whispering aloud, "Fly away! Abandon

the creature that murdered your children. You are free to fly. Let the snipe die!"

But with its head swiveling and black eyes blinking the bunting stepped carefully into the nest and, outstretching a wing, covered the body of the chick who had never known another mother than she. It shut its demanding beak, satisfied for the moment with the comfort offered.

Tears sprang suddenly to Cleatah's eyes and words flowed into her head uninvited. *I am witness to forgiveness. Forgiveness for an outrageous act. Forgiveness for the innocent struggling only to live.* She sat down in the grass, allowing her eyes to close, allowing her thoughts – this teaching – to envelop her. Clearly it was a gift from the Great Mother. It had been shown her for a reason. *Can I also forgive? Have I lost a single child? Am I not replete with beautiful sons?* Cleatah could suddenly see that perhaps – in the natural order of things, under any circumstances – she would never have had any daughters, even without Talya's mischief. Isis, poor child, was an innocent.

And she was Poseidon's blood.

Cleatah stood on shaky legs and went into her medicine garden. She chose the youngest, sweetest curling ferns and took them to her bedroom altar. With shaking hands she made an offering. She spoke in earnest to the Great Mother asking for an answer to the greatest trouble she had ever known.

Next morning she woke in the dark knowing that something inside of her had turned, like the wind's direction on a blustery day. *I am the mother of sons,* she heard ringing in her head. She rose from her solitary bed and went to see her children where they slept in peace and safety. The sex of her children no longer mattered. She was content with the multiplicity of lovely little boys, each of whom was a tiny whirling world of pleasure. No daughter could give her more than her boys did. She would find comfort in the mates they would one day take, and contentment in her grandchildren. Some of them would surely be girls.

Suddenly she was longing for Poseidon's return. It was only days away but she wondered if she could bear the wait. She needed so badly to talk to him, to tell him these things. Tell him about the bunting and the snipe. Talk of forgiveness. There would be rules and conditions, conduct that would govern the exiles' return. But the family would be joined. All of the children shared Poseidon's blood. How could she keep them from one another?

One of the babies stirred – Sirus, the youngest. She caught up his squirming, sleepwarm body in her arms before his mewling became a cry and put him to her breast. Comforted at once he grew placid, with the tiny wet sounds of pleasure she loved so dearly. The world was suddenly complete, perfect. There was nothing more that she wanted or could even imagine that she did not already possess.

I am the mother of sons, Cleatah whispered into the dark.

EIGHTY-NINE

DURING THE WHOLE of his overland journey south to the Taug village Boah had struggled to control the warring gods in his head. Had he not been so distracted he might have seen the masses of flowers painted in broad strokes across the never-ending meadowlands of the Great Plateau. He would have smiled at the pairs of mating birds in their comical dances, smelled the air, rich with the essences of life. But here he was, on his way to bring Talya and her daughter Isis out of their long exile and back to Atlantos, trying to quell his rage and a wrenching worry that their meeting after five years would break his heart all over again.

He and Kato – the favorite of all his mounts – had been tramping across the plateau for ten days now, and the beast was frequently lured away from the path by a pool of clear water or an enticing patch of sweetgrass. The pair of work horses tethered behind them pulling a covered cart followed after Kato for these lazy interludes, and Boah hadn't the heart to hurry them along. Days ago he had admitted to himself the relief he felt at the delays.

He'd become well-practiced at concealing his fury at Talya's "misdeeds" – as Poseidon and Cleatah called her appalling decep- tion, when they spoke of it all. During the days and months that followed their going he'd sought soothing companionship within the Brotherhood, but solace was found nowhere more completely than in the company of horses. Talya's betrayal had cut deep. Into his manhood. Into his heart. He had been lied to, but worse he had been compelled to cultivate and preserve the lie with everyone around him. The Shore People had no word for this kind of falsehood. It was a Terresian word. Because of this woman Boah had been set adrift in a sea of lies.

Yet – and this bewildered and confused him – he missed Talya in his life. Despite everything he sometimes hungered so powerfully for her that he woke from dreams of their coupling with an ache in his loins that forced him to finish with his own hand. When months of her and Isis' absence passed into a year, then two, sympathy for him grew. His horse brothers were curious, wanting to know how long he would wait to take up with other women, sire other children. He was silent on the matter, but in truth he'd been too raw to desire anyone at all. Only recently had he put aside the worst of the pain. Taken a woman to bed.

With Talya gone so, too, dissolved the promise of her horse breeding wonders – the speedy regeneration of a full herd to replace those lost in the Great Quake. This responsibility had fallen to Boah. He used what natural technos he had learned from Talya, and employed the knowledgeable hands and stout heart of Joss. The two struggled side-by-side to breed from the pure white mare a white male, which eventually succeeded. But when they sired him on his mother hoping for a female and fully expecting the first in a long line of white foals, the Brotherhood – assembled for the momentous birth – had groaned in dismay when the offspring emerged male and black as a moonless night. "She shared her bed with us," Joss murmured with frustration as he'd wiped down the dark foal and helped it stand on its thin wobbly legs, "but not her most important secrets."

How many times in these last years had Boah's longing and

defiance overwhelmed him? Cursing his promise to Cleatah he'd saddled his horse and raced out across the plains in a lathered fury. But he'd always returned, staying the storm of feelings until reason could take hold.

Then at the last half-moon Cleatah had come to him. In the past five years the lifelong bond they shared had become as strained as pulled leather. He could see she was trying to speak but tears were trembling on her lower lid, threatening to fall. "It's time for Talya to come home. And Isis," she told him. "Poseidon misses his daughter. I can't keep them apart forever. I'm the one who took them away. Call me a coward, but I don't want to be the one to fetch them home. Nor should Poseidon be."

He'd been silent for a long while. Paralyzed. Speechless. "Everyone will expect us to live as a family," he'd finally said in a hoarse whisper. "Your kin."

"This is how it will be," Cleatah said. "Talya will forever be known as Poseidon's sister. Isis is your daughter, my niece. But whether you take them to live with you…whether that is Talya's desire…is a matter for the two of you to decide. Poseidon has made a small house ready for them on the Middle Ring Isle if you decide to live apart. Talya is forbidden entrance into the *Atlantos*. Her technos, even for the horses, will no longer be available to her."

"I understand." It was all Boah had managed, so turbulent were his thoughts, how frantic the pounding of his heart.

"Will you do it? Will you bring them back?" Cleatah asked, unaware her fists were clenched into tight balls. She looked away then. "I have so much to learn about forgiveness."

The rest had been left for him to decide. When he would go. How many horses to take. What he would say when he saw Talya. How he would answer her questions. Whether, indeed, he would ask her and Isis to live with him. The Brotherhood would expect him to be overjoyed at their return, expect them to share his house, to raise Isis together, and other children that would surely come in the future.

But now after twelve days in the silence of the Great Plateau and the confusion of loud arguing inside his head he was no closer to knowing what he would do when he laid eyes on Talya than when he'd set out from the city – whether anger would prevail... or good sense.

Ahead Boah was surprised to see rows of neatly planted crops, fields that had not been there during the Gathering of the Tribes. On second thought it should be no surprise at all. Talya had lived among the Taug for more than five years now. Of course she would teach them the craft of plant cultivation. Who knew what other schemes and mischief she had gotten up to. He passed a few Taug men bent over the field rows and received curious stares. Some of them put down their hand tools and followed the stranger towards the village.

In a clearing outside the low wall near its entrance Boah saw a small knot of children huddled over something on the ground. They suddenly jumped back in surprise and giggled as the baby hare they'd been watching sprang straight up in the air with a squeak. Only then did the children look up and see the stranger and his trappings. With their small faces turned in his direction Boah instantly identified the oddity among them.

She was tall for her five years, and straight as an arrow shaft. Her pale hair and milky skin – even darkened as they were with dust and smudges of dried mud – were her mother's, and her gaze more piercing and more question-filled than the other youngsters' were.

When his horse came abreast of the children he slipped down to the ground. They surrounded him, tugging at his tunic, gently slapping his mount's flank and side and gabbling excitedly in the Taug language. He had learned enough of it with Poseidon's wrist device to finally say with a friendly smile, "My name is Boah."

In all the commotion he'd kept one eye on Isis and now watched as she startled. She faced him fully and stared. He could see now that she was an exceedingly lovely little girl. Her once-grey eyes, turned brown by Poseidon's technos to hide her identity as the child of her grey-eyed father twinkled with an intelligence far older than her years.

"My father's name is Boah," she said.

Of all the words the child could have uttered these were somehow the most unexpected. The most cheerful and warming. At once the phrase explained much about the years of Talya's absence from Atlantos and, too, answered the single question that was most important.

Boah bent down on one knee before Isis and regarded her every feature. She was looking into his eyes so steadily that his own gaze was pulled away from the dimpled cheek, the straight fall of golden hair, the sweet upward curve of the lip, to fasten onto her unwavering stare.

"Will you take me to your mother?" he said.

She didn't answer. She didn't smile. She simply pivoted where she stood and began to walk towards the cluster of Taug huts. Boah picked up Kato's reins and with a clattering of the team and trap and an excited babble of children's voices, prepared as best he could for the meeting that for five long and confounding years he had quietly dreaded and fervently craved.

NINETY

THE PATTERN OF the weave was pleasing to her eye, a lovely symmetry – the red, purple and green in perfect balance. Talya stepped back from her loom for a different perspective. Yes, she liked it very much.

"Zanza, come here and see what you think."

The woman whose face was a ruin of wrinkles, whose weaving house was the most esteemed in Taug, came to Talya's side and silently appraised the cloth. She used her one long fingernail to push aside the warp and assess the color – or perhaps it was the thickness – of the woof.

"You will teach the pattern to the others?" she said in the rasp that was her voice.

Talya nodded, pleased at this. It was the closest thing to praise she would ever receive from Zanza. Curious, how Talya's grasp of mathematics applied to weaving had proven the most valuable tool in her acceptance by the tribe, by the women at least. The women had been her lifeline to survival during her early days in the village. Then she'd been a pale, skinny curiosity speaking a strange tongue, abandoned with her equally pale infant on the threshold of the settlement. They'd been little more than a burden. Two extra mouths to feed. The females had been wary at the outset.

Desperate at first, struggling to learn the Taug language without benefit of the phaetron and clutching at any safety or comfort in her new and terrifying circumstances Talya had quickly recognized that the first glimmer of acceptance and trustworthiness might be found in her fierce protectiveness of her child. She sought the counsel of other mothers breast-feeding their children, silently thanking the stars that her own lactation had not failed her as it had so many Terresians in recent generations. She shamelessly flaunted her sincere affection for Isis, a most beautiful and charming child. Still, motherhood would never have sufficed to win her a place in village society.

It was Talya's intuitive grasp of Taug weaving and her ingenious innovations of the craft that did. Her technos-inspired patterns had set the women on fire, ruffled feathers to be sure, but ultimately set the river trade of their textiles humming. More boats arrived from settlements farther up and down the river. Word began to spread.

Talya had at first dyed her hair brown with burr nuts. She had smeared a powder of fine ochre and mud on her body and on Isis to avoid the stares of villagers and traders alike. Slowly the Taug men had grown used to her presence.

The outrage at her and Isis' abduction and banishment at Cleatah's hand had threatened to swamp the early days of her abandonment. But her very survival hung in the balance, so Talya had resolved to calm herself and entertain only rational thought. When she did this she discovered to her surprise that Cleatah, her tormenter, must have given abundant thought to their place of exile.

The Taug were peace-loving, finding no enemies among the people who trolled the river on boats seeking only to trade.

What the Taug traded was woven cloth. The tribes' weavers – all women – were therefore valued highly. They were treated well. Kept happy and productive and well-enough fed to provide many happy babies. The Taug's circumstances, Talya surmised soon after her otherwise inauspicious arrival, were well known to Cleatah, who had visited the them in the years of the Gathering of the Tribes. So contented were the villagers with their lives that they had refused to travel across the land to take up residence in a very great village called a "city." Cleatah – Talya cursed and praised her in equal measure – had chosen wisely and well, even if she'd done it less for Talya's benefit than for the only daughter of Poseidon.

To her chagrin Talya realized that she had vastly underestimated her rival's capacity for wrath. But how could she have known? While never docile, and oftentimes defiant in her defense of "the natural order of things" Cleatah - "Subject 4251 - in all the years since Talya's discovery of her in an aboriginal village on the coast of the continent, had never once bared her fangs. Of course the protocols, the outrageous violations Talya carried out in a desperate fugue, had been utterly immoral. They could never be excused on any reasonable grounds. Worse, impregnating herself with Poseidon's sperm to bear the only daughter he would ever father, and limiting Cleatah's own capacity for childbearing to twin sons – were unforgivable, irreparable acts.

Still – and Talya had considered this thought every day since her abandonment in the Taug village – her exile had not been too high a price to pay. If she had not behaved so despicably, the only child on Gaia with purely Terresian blood would never have been born.

And Isis adored her.

Spirited as she was she obeyed her mother. Thought her weaving beautiful. Isis was proud of her. Standing among the women at tribal gatherings she would slip her small hand into Talya's and gaze up at her as though she was The Great Mother herself. When they snuggled together in their crude bed, the girl exuding the fragrance of flowers and grasses in which she had tumbled and rolled that day, she would hang on Talya's every word. Ask to hear ever more stories of "Atlantos – the great village where I was born."

She was a clever little thing, learning Terrerthe and Taug with equal facility. She had been willful and wild from the start. Talya had often wondered what force was strongest in the child – the Terresian blood or her Taug upbringing. She was physical, and even at five years old won footraces with boys who were bigger than her. Like other Taug children she was immoderate in her speech, her voice clear and open and sometimes – to Talya's dismay – rather loud. She was openly affectionate and readily gave and accepted the embraces of other children, tribesmen and women. She was exceedingly tender to small living things. Talya never knew if her daughter's disposition was the natural resurgence of ancient genomes, as in her Uncle Athens's constitution, or the force of the Erthe's insuppressible influence on so malleable a being.

But now Isis had reached the age where her days were spent not at her mother's knee, but rousting about with other children. There was no denying that with every passing day her daughter was becoming a little Taug savage. It was believed a girl or boy of five was meant to freely roam the village with other children, to swim in the river, engage in rough play, learn by trial and error. She must understand and begin to commune with the gods and goddesses that resided in the sun and the moon, in the wind and the water and everything that lived and breathed in the world around them. The children might be injured. They might be bitten. They might be killed, but the bonds of parenthood *must* be loosened, lest the child become afraid of everything. This could not be tolerated. It was, in fact, the greatest of the Taug anathemas.

In the first years she'd found the Taug men entirely unappealing. The thought of their rough hands on her flesh, their coarse unrefined manners made her skin crawl. Boah and Joss were highly civilized next to these tribal males. But for some time Talya had allowed her sexual, sensual, even emotional impulses free reign in Atlantos. Finally the torrid gazes of her many young, muscular Taug admirers had breached her defenses.

Two years after her arrival a feast that lasted far into the night saw her drunk and dancing in the firelight with men and women alike. One of them – a tall wiry fisherman who reminded her of Joss – had pulled her out of the circle of light and into the shadows. She'd quickly come to her senses but had still allowed him to take her there on the ground, hoping to quench the cravings that had lately assailed her. But she'd felt nothing in the deep rhythmic thrusts or the probing fingers. Though the man had ejaculated with gruff moans of pleasure he had quickly decoupled, and refused to meet her eye or speak to her as they returned to the firelit celebration.

He never approached her again, and from that night on the Taug men showed no carnal interest in the pale stranger. Clearly their intercourse had been lacking in some way, and he'd spoken of it to the other men. Perhaps they thought her a demon of some sort – harmless in the everyday sense, but dangerous to masculine energies.

More interestingly, a short while after the ill-fated coupling the headman named Pulat had come to her almost shyly to ask for her help. Among the offerings Cleatah had brought to the Taug Village with her captives were bags of seeds. Pulat and the other men – hunters and fishermen – had no knowledge of agriculture, and wondered if she did.

It had proven the most auspicious of Cleatah's gifts. With Talya's help the Taug had planted rows of enkorn and emmer and pulse. The grains proved pleasing to the tribe's palates and provided nourishment, and even some colorful dyes for the weaving women's looms. Taug stature among the river traders had risen, everyone thinking them a most clever people who could fish, hunt, weave *and* plant.

Once again the strange woman had made herself useful, just as her abductress had promised them five years before.

Talya's life, therefore, while far less than ideal had at least become tolerable.

"Mother," she heard Isis call loudly from the doorway of Zanza's weaving house. She spoke the word in Terrerthe, not the "Muta" of Taug, and there was excitement in her voice.

Talya found she could not tear her eyes away from the new geometric design on her loom. Her heart was crashing against her ribs. She had wished, even prayed every day of her exile for a single event. She had schooled her daughter with the promise of its eventuality. One day, *one day...*

Talya steadied herself, then turned to face her hard-won future.

NINETY-ONE

THE ANGRY MAN inside Boah's head hoped that Talya would look worn and haggard from years of village work, that the stiffness and arrogance would be scoured from her spirit. But there had been something about the child as she led him by the hand through the Taug settlement, fresh and sweet and unspoiled, that abolished the thought and prepared him for his first sight of Talya.

That she was still as exquisite and graceful as she had been the last time he'd seen her shocked him less than her dress and posture. Like all other Taug women she was bare-breasted, wearing only a wrap skirt of the famous tribal textile down nearly to her ankles, and she knelt on the erthan floor at what was certainly her own loom. Only her head had swiveled to the doorway at the sound of Isis calling her. Boah found himself trembling, and heard Isis whispering up to him sympathetically.

"It's all right. You don't have to be afraid."

He laughed at himself then and Talya, seeing the broad smile, assumed it was intended for her. She stood quickly and without a word rushed over, throwing her arms around him. Isis hugged their knees, locking them together tightly and Boah, who had never planned such a warm or public display, found his arms encircling the woman who had in the cruelest way taught him the meaning of betrayal.

Finally Talya pulled out of the embrace. Smiling triumphantly at her daughter she turned to the weaving women. "This is Isis' father, Boah. The man from Atlantos that I spoke of."

"Well, he's as good to look at as you said he was," Zanza remarked without the hint of a smile. But all the women broke into laughter, and Isis tugged at Boah's tunic, demanding to be picked up. This he did, as much to cover his embarrassment as for a chance to hold the child in his arms. In the time it had taken to walk the length of the Taug village listening to her unending chatter he had been dazzled by Isis. The raw edges of his pain were soothed, as though with one of Cleatah's healing salves.

He saw Talya move to the wrinkled crone who had spoken, asking for permission to leave. He noticed the old woman acquiesce with a lascivious leer unexpected in someone her age. Boah was relieved to be out of the weaving house and away from the stares and misconceptions. He put Isis down as Talya came after him through the cloth door and wordlessly led the way through the village.

But here, too, blatant curiosity followed their every move. There was not a single eye – male, female, young, old – that was not fixed on the strange little trio, the tall pale woman, the muscular horseman, and the mud-streaked little girl who was grinning from ear to ear, skipping along behind them.

Boah came to Talya's side and spoke quietly. "That was a chance you took, telling them that Isis' father would return for you one day. What if I'd never come?"

"It was impossible for me to think that way. If I'd believed we'd be left here forever I would have gone mad."

Boah marveled at how unselfconsciously Talya strode among the tanned, voluptuous Taug. Not simply that her small white breasts were exposed, but the sureness with which she held herself

– head high, meeting the gazes – *respectful* gazes – and greeting everyone who called out to her by name. How had she managed it? Charmed the Taug as she had charmed himself and the Brotherhood down to the man?

She was holding open the door to a mud and stick-built hut on the edge of the village. Isis scooted in before them. Boah felt a stab in his knotted stomach. He was not yet prepared to confront Talya's rage in private. But as he stepped across the threshold into the darkened hut he felt Isis tugging at his hand again.

"Come see my altar," Isis said, more a command than an invitation.

She is her mother's daughter, he thought incredulously, yet strangely unsurprised. She pulled him to kneeling in front of a wooden shelf upon which were arranged a clay chimney and small clay figurine of the Great Mother like the ones worshipped by the Shore People. There was a crude rendition of a horse and the skull of a tiny rodent, all surrounded by a mass of yesterday's wilted flowers.

"Muta and I spoke to her every day, asking if we could go home to Atlantos and see the horses. Muta made the horse out of clay. It's not very good." She giggled.

Boah looked up at Talya, whose expression was indulgent and embarrassed in equal measures.

"Well, *I* spoke to the Goddess," Isis corrected herself. "Muta said the Great Mother hears the prayers of children first and loudest." She looked up at her mother with a wonderstruck smile. "You were right, Muta." She stood up. "I'll get some sticks for the fire and some new belly flowers for offerings."

"Belly flowers?" Boah said. "I've never heard of them."

"They're so little you have to lay on your belly to see them." She stood respectfully at Talya's feet. "May I go, Muta?"

"Yes, my sweet. You may go."

Isis darted away like a small animal, leaving the hut door swinging.

"Terresian. Atlan. Taug. She is all three," Boah observed. "She looks like you in many ways. But the high brow, the square chin… that is Poseidon."

Talya seemed surprised that he knew. "She once had his eyes as well," she said, bitterness creeping into her voice.

This took Boah aback. Did Talya dare begrudge the phaetronic change in eye color? But he was unwilling to quarrel with her – for now at least. Isis might return at any moment.

"We've had great success with the herd," he said instead.

"I'm happy to hear that."

"We've recovered nearly the number of all the females and foals lost in the quake."

She nodded, genuinely pleased.

"But the line of white mares has been a problem. Only the males are pure white."

"It's something I can remedy when we return," she said with a faraway smile, as though she was imagining herself at the High Atlantos stables. She must have seen him stiffen. Alarmed, she placed a hand on his arm. Her fingers were cold. "You *are* taking us back?"

"Yes. Both of you."

"What then?"

"There are…conditions."

"I should have known." She sighed and looked away. "Let me guess. I've no access to the breeding program."

His nod confirmed this.

"I'm not a welcome guest at the residence."

"On some feast days, if you bring Isis to visit her 'cousins,' you will be invited."

"So I'm just to keep to myself and work, then?"

"No."

"No?"

"No work. You may never go into the ship or any laboratory. I'm sure they won't object to your weaving…"

"What?!"

"No use of technos. Ever."

Her pale skin flushed, and her mouth compressed into a thin, tight line. "Whose conditions?" she whispered.

Boah refused to answer. In truth he could not be sure. He guessed they were Cleatah's rules, but how could Poseidon object? Perhaps they were his as well.

"You may come and live with me as my lifemate. We'll bring up Isis as our own," Boah continued, trying to flatten all emotion from his voice. "Or you may tell a story – if you like – a reason you wish for you and Isis to live apart from me. There is a house on the Middle Ring Is…"

"No phaetron…" Talya murmured. "Perhaps if I speak to them…"

"I would not."

Her expression was raw with despair. She had for these five years believed in her restoration to life in Atlantos. Promised it to her daughter. Perpetuated the lie of Boah's paternity. She must never have dreamed such harsh conditions and constraints would be imposed upon her.

"There is life without technos, Talya. A good life. When I saw you there at your loom I thought, "She has learned something here."

"I *have* learned something," she snapped, "that the woman who…" Talya stopped herself.

He could see that she'd thought better of ranting to him about her ills. "It was Cleatah who chose to bring you home," he added. "She who you should thank." He knew instantly, even before Talya's eyes flashed furiously, that this would further goad and not soothe her, and wondered if this was part of his own punishment for her.

"Mother!" Isis cried as she burst through the door, her hands piled with sticks and tiny points of green and red and yellow. "I found the yellow ones. The ones that Great Mother likes." The little girl knelt before her altar and brushed away dead flowers to make room for the living. "I almost let the fire go out," she said, "and Muta forgets, too." She smiled up at Talya whose anger seemed to evaporate in the child's presence. "But we mustn't let the fire go out. Great Mother has brought us my father, and he's taking us home to Altantos." Then Isis turned her smile on Boah. "May I ride on the horse with you?"

In that instant he found that his wish that Isis was his own child had entirely vanished. It had been supplanted by the conviction that from this day forward she *was* his child. She was his to protect and guide, to teach and be taught. Even if they shared a home, he knew, Talya would never be his. Not truly.

But Isis – to this precious flower sent to him by the goddess – he would devote his life and all the love in his heart.

NINETY-TWO

CLEATAH WAS GATHERING kindling for her bedroom altar – twigs and thick lengths of bark that fell at the base of the yew tree in her medicine garden. She wondered if the bark had cured long enough. Too green and it would not catch. The fire would smoke. Unfortunate for that day's prayers.

To be honest there had been times since Boah's departure for Taug that she regretted her decision, worried that Talya might return as she had gone – jealous, selfish, cruel. One morning when Cleatah woke from a frightening dream she had railed nonsensically at Poseidon for having brought such a terrible woman to Erthe and, worse, the technos that had allowed for such irreversible harm. He'd held her quietly in his arms as she'd raged, claiming no defense. Then he suggested she seek counsel with the mushroom. He could see that the Great Mother's guidance did not suffice. Cleatah had gone alone to a quiet place on the Great Plateau and eaten the sacred fruit. The mushroom had spoken gently to her, pleased at her forgiveness. The spirits assured her that the future of Atlantos could only be elevated by her kindness.

Now she added one last piece of yew bark to her gathering basket. If Boah had followed the route she'd taken with Talya and Isis he would be arriving at the riverside village this very day. She was aware of how badly he'd suffered in the past five years. Cleatah had burdened him with lies, as well as her own anger, and for this she was regretful.

Talya, if she was sensible – and wasn't this the central trait of the woman? – would choose to share a household with Boah and Isis on their return. To live as a family. Boah might find a way to set the wrongs aside and even rekindle the fire between them. It had once burned bright as the sun. Perhaps it could again.

Surely there is good in this undertaking, Cleatah told herself for the hundredth time. *Even joy.* She wanted desperately to believe the mushrooms' message – that blessings would come from forgiveness. In any event it was done. The arrow had been loosed and was even now finding its mark.

Her basket full Cleatah entered the residence and passed into the bedroom. She crossed to the altar kneeling before it, concerned at how low she'd allowed the fire in the small clay chimney to burn. Quickly she set some of the bark on the faltering blaze. It refused to catch. *Too green,* she thought. *Not enough time to cure.* Or was this a sign? *Not enough time for Talya to change. Have I erred on the side of mercy? Have I made a terrible mistake?*

She blew long, even breaths into the chimney and redoubled her prayers. "Oh Great Mother," she whispered, "let me have a sign..."

A moment later the kindling burst into flame.

NINETY-THREE

"IF YOU ARE expecting an apology..." Talya began, but Boah's rueful laugh cut her short.

"From you?" he said, and turned his gaze from the campfire to the stars. "As much as I would expect you to sprout wings and fly."

"How can I apologize for what I've done?" she said. "My rewards are so much greater than my punishments. I have Isis. And I know, I *know*, you see what I see in her."

Boah had no argument for that, so he said nothing. His thoughts strayed to the little girl asleep in his wagon.

"I did it as much out of weakness as strength," Talya said, "and you may believe this or not but it was never my purpose to harm you or Cleatah or Poseidon. It was selfish desire, with no thought for anyone else. That's all it was. Those who meant the most to me, I hurt nevertheless. I had to do it, Boah. I needed someone for myself."

Again, he said nothing. He'd always known that Talya had wanted him, but never needed him. She'd risked his hurt and wrath, all to give birth to Poseidon's daughter.

"She was my greatest idea and my greatest creation..." Now Talya laughed at herself. "...conceived while drunk." She spread the red coals with a long stick and stoked the blaze. "How could I know the magnificent creature she would become?"

Boah tore his eyes from the night sky to see Talya's face, welling tears reflected in the firelight. "She is the best thing you have ever done," he agreed.

Boah remembered these last days of their journey home. Isis had ridden in front of him on the saddle rug, chattering ceaselessly in a voice that lilted in his ears. The sound was sweet beyond imagining. *If a flower had a voice...* Isis' very thoughts delighted him with their spritely leaps, one to another and another. *Mother tells me all the time about the beautiful city, and I can* see *it, Patu, when I close my eyes. What do you see when you close* your *eyes? What I like the best, I think, are the horses. I like* this *horse.* She patted Kato's side. *Is he your friend? I have friends that are animals. They let me feed them. I can touch them. Did you ever touch a hare? I speak to hares, oh, and they are very* very *soft.* She shrieked with sudden laughter. *But their noses are cold! And the great huts in the city...* Isis outlined a large square in the air in front of them. *Mother tells me, but I don't know. She says they are bigger than all the village huts gathered together and put in one place. Is this true? It* must *be true, or why else would she say it? The water in circles in Atlantos... I see* that. *It is like our river, only round.* Isis used the tip of her finger to draw three circles inside each other on Kato's neck. *I will like that very, very much – the water in circles.*

"What have you told her about Poseidon and Cleatah?" Boah said to Talya.

She held his eyes with that self-assurance he knew so well. "That he is my brother, and she is his mate. They have sons. The sons are her cousins. She understands these things."

"Does she know why you have been living in the Taug village?"

"No. And she hasn't asked."

"Will she understand why her family will not fully embrace her when you return?"

"I don't know. Taug families stay very close. All the children belong to all the adults. I've told her every truth that I could. She'll learn for herself the breadth and depth of Cleatah's harshness." Talya looked away. "Do you want me to live with you...?" she asked. There was not a hint of pleading in her voice.

Boah found himself wishing that there had been.

"...or is it just Isis you want under your roof?"

He thought about that. "I cannot have one without the other," he finally replied.

"At least you're honest," Talya said, then muttered – though loud enough for him to hear – "more than I can say for myself."

"I still find you beautiful." There were other words he might have used to describe what he felt for her – the warmth in his belly, in his loins. "I would have you in my bed again...gladly," was all he said.

Her mouth curled slowly into a smile. "Good," she whispered with a husky quaver. "Then all is not lost."

Contentment washed over him then, like the gentlest of waves. In the space of that moment Boah had regained a family, one he believed he'd lost. He wondered if this woman would dare to do such a thing again. Had the years changed her? If not, then the child certainly had. He wanted to know.

Boah reached for Talya's hand. Even in the firelight he could see the stains of the weaver's dye on her fingers, feel a roughness of the skin never there before. He slid his palm under her night wrap and over her shoulder, then down to cup a breast. She closed her eyes and exhaled with slow satisfaction. He bent, pulled aside the cloth and took the suddenly erect nipple in his mouth. She ran her fingers through his hair like she had done the first night of their coupling, then laid herself back, slow as a snake, pulling him atop her.

Her arms were stronger now, the sinewy arms of a tribeswoman. But something about her as she opened herself to him above and below was softer, more slippery, like the delicate muscle of oyster. But with the first of his insistent thrusts a snarl replaced her low groans and now she was *alive* under him, scalding him, clawing at his back.

It was the Talya he remembered, the Talya he desperately desired.

Fear of future betrayals bloomed suddenly like dark flowers at the edges of his mind, threatening the pleasure of their thrashing bodies. But he banished the fear, forcefully, as Talya had been banished from the city, clinging only to the good in the circle of his campfire's light. That was what mattered, and only that – the sweet little girl asleep in his wagon, and the promise of riding this hot-blooded, pure white mare till the very end of his days.

NINETY-FOUR

"AM I WRONG to fear she hasn't changed?" Atlas heard his mother say, the words carrying across the inner meadow of the Central Isle to her medicine garden where he'd been passing to the stable.

"If Talya has changed, are you willing to treat her accordingly?" This was his father uttering a word Atlas, now six, had never heard before as Poseidon came walking into view beside Cleatah. He stopped to face her.

Straining to listen Atlas stepped back behind the maze-like walls of the garden that had grown taller than his head. He sought an opening in the greenery so he could continue to watch them.

"I'm willing. In order to bring her here with Isis I've had to forgive her. But I can never forget what she's done."

"Nor should you." Atlas could see his father looking away as he said, "Nor should I."

Father wore this same expression as when someone repeated the oft-told tale of how Poseidon had saved the city by shutting the ocean gate before the great wave hit the seawall. Yes, it was exactly the same. His mouth turned down and his large frame seemed, for just a moment, to grow smaller. Atlas had always thought Father held a secret about the gate and the wave, and it was not a happy one.

"Well, I guess we will know soon enough," his mother said. "When is Boah bringing them?"

"They're coming from his house at high Helios."

"What shall we tell the boys?" she asked, taking Poseidon's hand in hers. But before he could answer they strolled away, back to the residence arm-in-arm.

Atlas considered this slyly overheard conversation. His mother feared something and sounded angry. She never sounded angry, or hardly ever. His Aunt Talya was coming with Isis. This, he knew, was his *cousin* Isis. And Atlas was certain that his father had an unhappy secret. *What could all this mean?*

He ran for the stable where he knew his brother would be found. But instead he saw Geo just now exiting the house of Yazman, the Green Teacher he loved the most.

The twin boys came face-to-face.

"Yazman made honey cakes. I ate two," Geo said and licked his fingers as if to prove it."

"I don't want honey cakes. Boah is coming back. He's bringing Aunt Talya and cousin Isis here, at high Helios." Was his brother's expression puzzled or was Geo simply uninterested? Since Boah's sudden and mysterious journey had removed their horse-master from their daily lessons Atlas had thought continuously about the happenings that had upset their routines, and now had disturbed their parents. Geo had shown nothing but calm about it, as he did about so many things. He was less fascinated by horses than Atlas, and curious mostly about trees and flowers and the medicines their mother grew in her garden.

"Don't you remember Boah saying he would come back with our aunt and our cousin?" Atlas asked.

"Yes!" Geo said irritably, then "No!" sounding sorry at his lack of interest in such matters, or maybe forgetfulness.

"Well, come to the residence if you want to meet them."

"I *do* want to meet them. Should I make them flower wreaths for their hair?"

"Yes." Geo was full of good ideas. Atlas turned to go, then turned back abruptly. "Make one for Mother, too. She looks pretty with flowers in her hair."

"Where are you going?" Geo called.

"To Boah's house to see them secretly first, before they come here."

"You have to do everything first," said Geo accusingly.

It was true. Atlas's need to be first in everything – from first out of their mother's belly, to first out of their beds in the morning, to first across the finish line in a foot race – described him perfectly. Happily, Geo's mild temper and differing pleasures from his brother's meant the twins were rarely at odds.

"High Helios at home," Geo called after Atlas.

"High Helios!" he called back and raced for the bridge to the Middle Ring Isle.

NINETY-FIVE

SHE'D BROUGHT THE family together – Poseidon and all six boys – to the gathering room when the sun shone the brightest. Cleatah wished for the meeting to be bathed in light to forestall any darkness that Talya and the child might bring. She had put on a simple white tunic belted with a thick textile sash from the youngest of the Academy weavers, her hair freshly washed and curling round her face and shoulders. She felt strong and sure, as though she fit perfectly within her skin. The boys gathered about their father with smiles and rough-housing on the floor added further to her confidence.

Yet when Boah led the pair of golden-haired females into the room to stand beneath the skylight Cleatah was forced to plant her feet with extra firmness to absorb the shock of them. Behind her she heard Poseidon rise. Without being asked Atlas and Geo picked up the smaller boys, Ammon and Evenor, in their arms. Thoth and Siris toddled to their mother's side, hanging on her skirt to gaze at the peculiar sight.

There was no one in all of Atlantos that looked remotely like Talya or Isis.

Their bodies were long and very slender, and their skin shone in the sunlight an unerthely white. It was the hair, thought Cleatah watching her sons' wide-eyed expressions, straight and fine – the daughter's worn long, the mother's in many braids – that inspired fascination. It seemed on fire as they stood quite still with Boah behind them. He himself was motionless.

Then all at once Isis exploded from Talya's side, her arms outstretched. Crossing the room she threw them about Cleatah and her three-year-olds.

"I am your cousin Isis," she explained in perfect Terrerthe. Then she tilted her head and gazed, smiling, into Cleatah's eyes. "You are my aunt."

This was the custom of the Taug – warmth and open affection between family members – one that Talya had permitted Isis to learn.

"Welcome, Isis," Cleatah said, swept by emotions of every sort. She tore her gaze from the child to the mother. "Welcome, Talya."

The delicately angular features that all men thought beautiful seemed frozen on her face. Then Poseidon stepped forward and made the few strides that took him to her. He embraced her awkwardly and spoke the word "Sister" loudly and insistently for all the children's sakes.

With that Atlas and Geo joined the scintillating clutch of new family members, speaking excitedly to Isis who though a year younger was taller by two fingers than they. In unison they put the infants down to crawl at their mother's feet and followed Isis who was exploring the room, appearing as easy and carefree as a child who had grown up in the residence.

When she reached an intricately woven tribal hanging she turned to Talya. "Mother, look! It is Taug! I think it is Zanza's!"

Talya extricated herself from the stiff circle of Poseidon's arms and joined the children who stood gazing at the hanging. She lowered into a wide-legged squat till her face was level with the children's. It astonished Cleatah how easily and unselfconsciously the woman moved, even squatted – a position she had never once seen Talya assume.

"It *is* Zanza's," she said, stroking Isis' head with easy tenderness. Talya spoke to Cleatah and Poseidon, her first words. "Zanza is the mother of my weaving house. Indeed, the Mother Weaver of Taug."

"Talya herself makes beautiful cloth," Boah added, hoping to ease things further.

"Tell us how you knew this was Zanza's weaving," Talya instructed her daughter.

"Well…" Isis began, hesitating only briefly, "you see how the red crosses the blue at the corners over and over again? And the triangles of yellow that sit one on top of the other? These are Zanza's marks, and no one else in the village makes them."

Cleatah saw that Atlas and Geo were enthralled by the girl's clever recital. The girl herself. In fact the talkative eldest twins seemed tongue-tied.

"I rode here on a horse with my father," she continued, undaunted by the unnatural lull in conversation. "He says there are many horses in Atlantos."

"Would you like to see them?" It was Atlas. He had finally found his voice.

"Oh yes! Mother, may I go and see the horses?"

She nodded and watched with mild astonishment as the three children tripped happily and comfortably out the front arch. Once they had gone Talya crossed the room to face Cleatah.

"I understand the conditions of my return. I hope you won't punish Isis for my misbehavior. She's just a child. A very sweet child, as you've seen. She believes herself part of this family." Talya glanced at Poseidon. "She *is* part of this family, even if I am not."

Cleatah startled at the defiance in Talya's voice and demeanor.

"What of her education?" Talya continued. "What about your boys?" She gazed at Poseidon. "Do they know your origins?"

"Not yet."

"They haven't been taken into the ship? Met their Uncle Athens? The one who lives 'far away across a great ocean?'" There was the merest bite in Talya's voice as she repeated the myth she had been instructed by Cleatah to disclose to her daughter about their offworld ancestry and Athens's home on Mars.

"He's seen them," Cleatah offered. "When they were small. Too small to remember."

"When do you plan to reveal it all? Terres? Our technos?" Talya asked insistently.

"A year. Two years, maybe three," Poseidon answered. "When we see fit."

"Will you allow Isis…?"

Talya had gone too far. Boah moved behind her placing a hand on her hip. He must have seen the anger beginning to flare in Cleatah's eyes. "Talya and Isis will be coming to live with me. They'll be my family," he said, glowing with pride.

Poseidon laughed with pleasure and not a little relief. Even Cleatah managed a smile. Perhaps Talya saw the sense in giving ground just then. As she snaked her arm around Boah's waist Cleatah saw the scar at her inner wrist where in a state of barely controlled rage she had relieved Talya of her phaetron five years before. Unexpected tears stung Cleatah's eyes.

"Your sons are beautiful," Talya said. There seemed to be nothing more than sincerity behind the words.

Cleatah nodded her acknowledgment, but it was still too raw, still beyond her capacity to utter to the woman who had denied her daughters the words "Thank you." With the dreaded moment behind her Cleatah nodded cordially to the reunited "Trident" and strode from the gathering room.

A new day had dawned in Atlantos.

NINETY-SIX

"THIS IS MY mother's medicine garden," Geo told their fair-haired cousin as they skirted the outside wall of the maze. It looked to Atlas – though he could not be sure – that Isis was only being polite as she stooped to examine the petals of his brother's favorite red and white rodendron. Yes, there it was! Her eyes were darting to the Central Isle stable where a horse was being led out for exercise.

Geo noticed too and said, "But we can go to the racetrack if you like. And the Outer Isle Stables."

"I would like to see the *buto mota*, also," said Isis.

"We don't know what that is," Atlas told her.

She screwed up her features as she considered the translation. "River circles," she finally announced, looking pleased with herself.

Geo looked blankly at her, but Atlas smiled. "The canals," he explained to his brother.

She was odd, Atlas thought, with her strange language and woven skirt that looked something like what the elder women of some tribes that lived in Itopia wore. Yet he seemed somehow to *know* Isis, understand her. Even though she was eager to see and hear and smell and touch everything in her new home it seemed to Atlas that she *knew* things. Things he didn't. And this was unnerving. No child in Atlantos, besides Geo, knew more than Atlas did.

"Why did you not grow up with us in Atlantos?" Atlas finally blurted.

"I don't know," she replied playfully. "Why did you not grow up in Taug?"

This made them all giggle.

"Here is your *"buto mota,"* Geo announced as they reached the center of the bridge to the Middle Isle.

They stopped to gaze over the canal.

"I lived on a river," Isis said. "It started in the mountains and ended in the sea."

Atlas thought for a long moment. "We have water, too, sweet water that starts in the mountains and ends in the sea, but we capture it in the aqueducts and it flows into homes and baths before running into the canals and the ocean."

"What are baths?" she asked. But before either boy could answer she cried, "Oh look! There is a boat like the ones that stop to trade in my village!" She pointed to a simple skife with a single sail and a crew of two men. "We trade our weaving, and now our grain that mother helped grow, for wood and the flowers for blue dye."

"We trade with boats, too," Geo offered. "Look there." He pointed down the length of the Great Harbor where a large three-masted ship was turning into it from the Outer Canal. Even from the Central Isle bridge they could see nearly fifty men on its deck.

Atlas watched as Isis' mouth fell open in amazement.

"It's very big," Atlas told her, hoping not to sound like a braggart – something his father had taught him never to be. "We call it a tri-reme, a ship with three masts and three sails. It travels far across the sea."

Isis thought for a long moment, puzzled. "What is across the sea?"

"I'll tell you that tomorrow," Atlas said. "Let's hurry now, so we can see the horses while they train."

As they traversed the cross streets of the Middle Isle and the bridge to the Outer Ring Isle, Isis' eyes grew wider and wider with astonishment. She and her parents had entered the city that morning before dawn, so this was her first true sight of Atlantos.

But Atlas noticed there were many curious eyes following the little girl as well, she dressed in tribal garb, her hair glinting white-gold in the sun. He thought he saw expressions that bespoke of recognition. He even heard a startled whisper here or there. "Talya…" "Doesn't she look like Talya?"

The boys took Isis through the North Market. Her head swiveled from side-to-side to see throngs of Atlans milling about the gaily colored stalls and collecting water that spurted in four directions from the central fountain of carved red stone. There were mounds of cabbages, barrels of grass peas and broad beans. A pyramid of pomegranates. Huge baskets were piled with dried figs, dates and chestnuts. A beautiful dark-skinned girl and her beautiful mother called in a sing-song voice, enticing people to come and taste their special confections – yellow cakes dripping with orange honey, and pan-cakes topped with figs and sweet curdled cheese. Standing in front of the next stall the children's mouths watered to smell the fragrant onion pies and thick soups that were ladled from a giant pot into peoples' smaller ones.

Nearby were every sort of dried fish hanging on strings, and living squid in a great vat, pulled from the water when an Atlan housewife commanded it be put in her basket. There were mountains of bread, some crusty round loaves, others braided into fantastical shapes, dusted with bee pollen and sugar. They saw caged rooks and rows of their eggs snuggled in beds of down to keep them from breaking. They watched as half a buron was taken down from its hook to be butchered.

"*Et lunta beg centa plat,*" Isis murmured.

"What does that mean?" Atlas asked.

"Guess," she ordered him.

He smiled at the game, having no idea whatsoever what she'd said. "Those are very large buron's balls," he replied with a straight face, and was pleased when she shrieked with laughter.

"I said…" she giggled again, "…'I am very glad to be in the big village.' We have no word for 'city' in Taug."

They came to the edge of the market and moved on.

"I'm glad you're here, too," Atlas said, feeling warm in his cheeks, suddenly and unaccountably shy. "We're almost there," he added quickly, then noticed that Geo was no longer with them. He looked back and saw the stall of the Green Teachers where a vast array of oils and medicine plants were set in careful piles to be distributed with advice to anyone in need of a cure. Geo seemed deep in conversation with Tantas, and believing his brother had lost interest in Isis and horses Atlas led her on to the oval stadium whose towering stone walls lay directly ahead.

Even he was awed by the sight of it, as he always was, but even more with what lay within. "Your father is my horse-master," Atlas told her. "Geo and I ride with him every day."

Isis looked at him with a cocked head. She seemed to be grasping for words. "Then you know my father very well," she finally said. "Better than I do."

"You'll soon know him very well, too. You'll live with him."

She smiled at the thought.

"Your father and my father are friends. They're the two greatest horsemen in Atlantos. Every year in the races they ride. Some years my father wins. Sometimes it is Boah."

He led her in through the high portal and arched tunnel and emerged into the massive oval stadium with its tiered seating that rose to the top of its walls. The finest racing mounts were galloping around the track, proud horsemen crouched low on their necks. Other horses in teams of two were tethered to small sleek chariots, the drivers urging the animals on with cracks of a whip above their flanks.

"There are two kinds of races…" Atlas began, but stopped as the blurred figure of Isis rushed past him. Her forward progress was stopped only by the wooden railing at the edge of the erthan track. As he came up beside her he saw that her fingers tightly clutched the beam and her eyes were round as two full moons. She was hardly breathing.

"Oh," she sighed. "Oh…"

Isis watched in rapt silence with only an occasional gasp at a near-collision of chariots, or a sharp intake of breath as one of the magnificent beasts thundered by in front of them.

Atlas was surprised when he felt her small fingers grasping his own. She turned and he saw now that happy tears glittered in her eyes. His chattering cousin whose barrage of words in Taug and Terrerthe streaming endlessly since the moment she'd walked with her mother into the residence gathering room had, at the sight of the beloved horses of Atlantos, been rendered speechless.

Atlas turned back to face the track, happy with the day and the thought that the golden-haired girl at his side was his family. And he felt, though it hadn't been spoken aloud, that she would be his friend. For ever and ever.

Ninety-Seven

T HIS PAIN, THOUGHT Persus, *is beyond the level of endur-*
ance. Stop it now! But she could not stop. Would not stop.
Self-inflicted pain was an archaic behavior of the unstable
mind. But her mind was certainly intact. Stronger and more finely
tuned than the vast majority of Terresians on the home planet and
here on Mars. *Then why am I alone in my quarters, the trans-screen*
before my eyes glowing with anatomical diagrams and procedures,
cutting into my thigh bone with a surgical phaetron?

When the vibrus sequence ended Persus delivered a brief jolt of
local anesthesia to her leg and fell back on her bed with a relieved
groan. Such major surgery was normally accomplished with the
patient fully narcotized, always conducted by a specialized medic,
not the patient herself. But these were less than normal circumstances, she silently argued. Then she thought, *Perhaps I am more*
unbalanced than I'm admitting. Perhaps I've gone slightly mad.

Blessedly the pain was abating. She lifted onto one elbow and
gazed down at the right thigh, horribly mottled with green and
purple-black bruises and a not-yet-healed incision. The cosmetic
after-surgery to remove them would be easy and painless. But she
reckoned with grim satisfaction that the leg was a full four inches
longer than it had been just hours before. Would she have the

fortitude to proceed with the other one? Persus chuckled as she lay back down to rest. The vision of herself limping around with legs of two different lengths was ludicrous. She was ugly enough as it was.

Her mother had been beautiful – statuesque, with strong but feminine features and piercing blue-green eyes. She had self-inseminated with the sperm of a physically attractive, maximum cortex donor. It was discovered as Persus grew into a small, rather unattractive child that somewhere in the donor's genomic profile lurked a sequence of strong recessive traits that, while impacting her prodigious intellect not at all, had deeply influenced her physical appearance and stunted her growth. In fact, all that remained of her mother in Persus were those startlingly lovely eyes. Otherwise she looked like some distant ancestor of her biological father – short, with squashed features and thick wiry hair.

Her youth had been excruciating and her blandly emotionless mother had neither shown affection for her, or revulsion. It was commonly expected that Persus would enjoy the accolades awarded her from her earliest schooling through a stellar course at the Academy. She'd proven as adept in scientechnos as in administration, and had been recruited by Federation long before her final term.

She'd grown accustomed to her physical defects. And she was anything but isolated because of them, sought after as much for her kindly nature as her myriad skills. She'd been reasonably happy in her life and had believed her appointment as Colonial Governor Athens's aide a just reward for a life well-lived.

She had never anticipated falling in love with him.

The emotion itself was ancient. She'd read about the earliest quasi-civilized Terresians loving another person with this strange magnitude of passion. Athens's brother Poseidon had curiously fallen victim to it on Gaia, but it had never occurred to Persus that it could happen to her.

For his part Athens had taken to her immediately, correctly perceiving her talents and finding a true friend in her. He was even affectionate in private moments, often complimenting her pretty, bright eyes. She most treasured the times that they would work together late into the night, companionable, sipping goblets of jog, sharing a laugh. He trusted her implicitly, exposing to her his innermost thoughts, wildest dreams, even his fear. She suspected he did none of that with his other women.

His many, many women.

All of them were beautiful. All of them desirable. All of them stunningly sensual. Everything she was not.

In the beginning she had rejected any notion that she could be experiencing the obsolete sensation of jealousy that, together with violence, lust, greed and warmongering, had long ago been bred out of the Terresian genomic sequence. But each and every time Persus found herself in the company of Athens and one of his sexual partners, watching his hand unconsciously dandling a soft curl of her hair, caressing a bare shoulder, the delight on the woman's face as she accepted a gold bauble or intimate garment – perhaps something that Athens had had Persus procure – a tightness developed in her chest. Her eyes began to sting, and many times she would have to excuse herself from the couple's company.

When had it first occurred to her that she could make herself more attractive? She couldn't remember now. At first she had dismissed it out of hand. A ridiculous idea. Embarrassing really. Then the thought had materialized. *I can do it myself. Slowly, over the course of time. No humiliating visits to the cosmetic techs. She would study anatomy and physiology. She would learn the techniques of phaetronic surgery. It would be a gradual self-transformation.*

No one really looked at her anyway. She was simply there when needed. Taken largely for granted. Her physical appearance was of no importance to anyone. So she would make the changes. Perhaps she could, with the lengthening of her legs and facial bone structure, the plumping of her lips, the shaping of her cheeks and breasts become a worthy companion of the man she so adored.

This was the first of the procedures. The adding of bone tissue to her femurs was not over-complicated. If he questioned her added height she could say that she'd had a procedure done to straightened her spine. But she guessed the changes would be noticed only subliminally. The more obvious modifications might require explanation. She hoped the results would prove so pleasing to Athens that he would overlook their unnatural origins. Together with her deeper, more substantive attributes Persus would become the ideal mate for the governor.

She sat up in bed and took the phaetron in hand. She consulted the trans-screen to locate the major blood vessels and nerves and inhaled deeply, hoping to fortify herself against the coming agony.

This is worth the pain, she told herself as the targeted vibrus shattered, then began building skin, muscle and bone.

Worth every moment of it.

NINETY-EIGHT

THE GOVERNOR'S MOST recent visit with his brother had left Athens in a black mood. He'd admitted to Persus that sight of "that woman of his," or the adored sons – two more of them every year – flayed him raw. There was never anything but good news from Erthe, while everything here on Mars seemed to be crumbling. Each of Poseidon's successes on his paradisiacal world were these days experienced by Athens as wounds that would not heal. The governor's perpetual optimism had begun to sour in the years since the phibious monsters had begun their attacks on the coastal settlements, sending them inland. And growing confirmation that tears in the fabric between dimensions – caused by the Marseans themselves – had allowed the creatures to pass through them to breed and proliferate was driving Athens mad with guilt.

A briefing in his office presented by Captain Vargos of the Shore Guard to Athens, Kyron – head of the Colony's Defense Ministry – and Vice Governor Praxis had just concluded. He'd reported that the crew of yet another submersible had been lost and that in the open ocean whole schools of the beasts were attacking their defensive vessels in larger and larger groups.

Persus observed Athens as he listened. She thought his mouth looked pinched, and the shadows in half-moons under his eyes were growing more pronounced. When everyone else had filed out she moved to his side at the head of the long table.

"Are you ill, Sir?"

Athens's barked laugh was sharp, bitter. "I guess you could say I'm sick of this place. Of course this latest incident will do wonders for my already stellar popularity."

"The colonists can't possibly blame you."

"Oh, but they do. Not just for the deaths of the hunters. What rankles them most is the death of life as they knew it. What was once peace and luxury at the seaside has become…it's no different from what we endured on Terres." He pushed away from the table and moved to a large window looking over a vast forest of ferns.

"It's not as bad as all that," Persus reasoned. "The sun rises every morning. You've dug canals from the ocean to the city…"

"Persus…" He sighed with exasperation. "The city is ten miles from the sea. For a culture that reveled in seaside living artificial waterways are a miserable excuse. We all loved the sand between our toes. The ocean breezes. We loved our little solies. Now we're left with the horror that we deserted them to those *things* when we fled inland."

She wished desperately to refute his words, but he was right about everything. She came to his side.

"We've had to go to war," he said. "At first it was awful to think that we'd become a bellicose people with terrifying weapons. But it's worse to realize that we've become used to it. Some even enjoy it."

He looked at Persus then with a question on his face, one he seemed unable to form. Did some part of his brain recognize that the level of her eyes next to his was higher than it had been the last time? Perhaps. But his level of self-absorption was so extreme that comprehending it was nearly impossible. She guessed he would adjust to this new perception of her, and the next time they stood side-by-side the question would not reoccur.

"I tell you, the people are beginning to hate me," he continued. "I've let them down in the worst possible way."

"You're wrong," Persus said with a smile – one that with a simple procedure would soon be just a little prettier. "You are still the most beloved person on Mars.

And, she did not add, *the most beloved man in my heart.*

NINETY-NINE

ATHENA FELT THE merest stab of guilt as she packed her small holiday bag. It was one thing to admit to herself that she was longing to visit the new solie park more than she wished to see her father. It was another to confide it to her classmate. Not that Grantae felt any differently about holidays with her mother, or any of the children at Academy their parents. Parents – if they intruded at all in the lives of their offspring – were tolerated with various levels of interest and affection. Rarely did birth parents cohabitate, and few pairings produced more than one child. Only occasionally might a child become aware of a half-sister or brother. So visits were rarely experienced as a family gathering. Going home – to Athena and Grantae and all the children they knew – meant returning after a holiday to the Academy campus.

Still, when you had a father like Athens Ra everyone expected something a little different. Athena didn't mind that her father was famous. He was the governor, after all. He was rich and handsome and popular with the people, and all the older girls whispered about growing up fast so they could take a turn in his bed. It used to upset her, all the fuss about her father, but Athena had realized last year when she was eight that she was privileged liked no other child she knew.

Her father doted on her. Brought her presents. Frequently invited her to his lavish residence. Made public shows of affection. Some of the time they made her cringe. But other times, when they'd be walking side-by-side and he playfully pulled her close and teased her gently to hear her giggle she felt a warm rush of heat in her chest, and a rosy flush climbed up her neck to her cheeks. She had to admit she enjoyed those moments when she was the object of his attentions.

But Athena knew as well that this level of parental warmth bordered on deviant behavior. There were other whispers about her father that she tried hard to avoid hearing, or if she did hear quickly put out of her mind. She gathered, with her still-evolving intellect, that something was mildly amiss with both the governor's overly exuberant manner as well as his administration of Mars. Colonists no longer lived by the sea but in inland settlements and cities. She understood that people blamed him for this change in circumstance. But she was largely loyal to him. These days the more unpleasantness she heard merely strengthened her resolve to defend him, show pride that she was his one and only child.

But this morning when she was having breakfast with her housemates she had announced – to be honest she had bragged – that she was far more interested in visiting New Solie Shores than seeing her father. Athena didn't know why she had said it. It had escaped her lips before she knew what she was saying. Perhaps she had secretly wished to be more like the other girls, cool and detached and ordinary. Perhaps it was a way to put distance between her and her famous father. Her *infamous* father.

"He's here, Athena!" Grantae trilled, peering out their bedroom window. "Get him to stay as long as you can."

"Why should I? All you girls do is stare at him and drool."

"You just want to keep him for yourself."

"He's my father."

"And this morning you said you'd rather swim with a furry animal than spend time with him."

Huffing impatiently Athena grabbed her bag and raced out the door of Girls House Four to see the shiny shuttle disk hovering at roof level above the grassy quadrangle, just in time to see her father descend on a slender blue beam to the ground. Girls, old and young, teachers and even a few boys from across the campus were already gathering to catch a glimpse of the planet's highest dignitary. For Athena this was the most difficult part of the ritual. Watching the little girls fawn and giggle, the older ones flash seductive eyes and budding breasts at him. Sometimes she'd hear snide whispers from the older boys, but always she was torn between the thrill of Governor Athens's boisterous greeting to the largely adoring crowd and mortification that his laughter was so loud and his embraces so unabashed.

This morning was no different. Her father stepped from the elevator beam with that incandescent smile and flung open his arms at the sight of her. Athena decided to make a good show of it, sorry she had denigrated him so blithely at breakfast. Of course he was more important to her than playing in the surf with solies, no matter how adorable they were. And truly, when she felt his strong arms go around her and heard the girls calling out their star-struck greetings to him she was very, very glad he was her father. And that he was special. Even deviant.

She was, she thought to herself as he led her into the silvery disk, the single luckiest girl on Mars.

*

Everything changed the moment they were settled in the shuttle lounge. The pilot wasted no time speeding away over the campus, and before they had reached the Academy's boundaries Athens had slumped into the long seat and grown silent. Athena watched as the light behind his eyes faded. She grasped that the previous moments in the quad had been nothing more than a spectacularly successful performance. She squirmed as she took a seat across from him. Of course she had seen "moods" come over him before, but this was somehow more alarming.

The silence lengthened and became unbearable.

"Are we going to New Solie Shores tomorrow? Or the next day?" Athena blurted, grasping for something, *anything* to say.

"When would you like to go?"

She was relieved that the silence had been broken, then realized his voice was flat, lifeless.

"Tomorrow," she said, insistently. "You promised."

"I said we'd go," he agreed, then ceased conversation altogether.

She drummed her fingers on the seat and twitched her foot impatiently. "What's wrong with you?!" she finally shouted at him.

Athens looked up at her. "I'm poison," he said in so low a tone his words were hardly discernable.

"What?"

"If I stay poisonous…" Athens continued thoughtfully, "…no one will be able to devour me."

Athena felt her stomach twist into a sudden painful knot. She was not yet nine and had spent precious little time in her father's company. She didn't know him very well at all. But something of the whisperings about the governor began nagging at the edges of her mind. Something unsettling. Dangerous even. She felt a prickly wall materializing before her, *between* her and her father. *Defense,* she thought. *Don't let him hurt. Don't let him near.*

"I want to go *tomorrow,*" she demanded, knowing how spoiled she sounded. But she didn't care. "I want to go *both* days." She set her teeth together, and her jaw tightened.

"All right," he said, amiably. Absently. "Both days it is."

*

Of course he hadn't meant it. She knew after the painfully silent dinner when she'd climbed into her bed that his promises had all been empty ones. She became convinced as she dressed this morning –donning her swimming suit and sandals – that her father would not being taking her to New Solie Shores that day, or tomorrow, or maybe ever. Yet here she sat, waiting for him in the great room, watching water cascading down the gold ore waterfall, the morning ticking by. Remnants of her prickly wall were still in place. She concentrated, trying to strengthen it, multiplying the thorns, turning the thorns to razor shards of titanum. *The best defense.*

"Athena…"

She looked up, startled. There stood her father's assistant, Persus. It had been some time since they'd seen each other, but something was vaguely different about her. She was still the most unattractive female Athena had ever known. Her kindly nature did nothing to enhance the overall effect of her unfortunate physical appearance.

"What are you doing here?" Athena knew, even as she spoke, the reason Persus was standing in the governor's great room.

"Your father's not feeling well. I'm going to take you to Solie Shores."

Athena thought to say, *No you're not. If my father won't take me I'm not going at all.* But she wanted to go. Very, very badly. She was sure that nothing could soothe her more than a real living solie to snuggle in her arms, its warm whiskered snout poking into her neck, the excitement of swimming in rolling surf alongside its strong, sleek body.

It pained Athena to stand, pushing up and out through the defensive shield she'd so carefully erected. "Let's go," she finally snapped, knowing exactly how rude she sounded. "Half the morning is already gone."

ONE HUNDRED

THE PHAETRONIC HORIZON RING was surely the most frivolous use of Terresian technos ever devised. Yet, Persus thought as they approached the entrance of New Solie Shores, it delivered unmatched pleasure to pleasure-starved Marsean colonists.

The earliest solie parks had simply relocated the animals to inland lakes and salinated the fresh water to something approaching the ocean's chemical balance. But bathing at a lake lacked the sheer glory of days spent frolicking at the seaside. Having to look across a placid body of water to the opposite shore was a grim reminder of what the colonists had lost from their lives with the coming of the phibions.

Sedula Xeres, a recent Academy graduate who could remember growing up on the beach, had conceived of a device that created continuous waves approximating those that broke along the ocean's shores. More importantly – and not unlike the machine that projected blue skies onto the contour domes of Terresian population centers – the Horizon Ring, as she named it, once set in the center of any lake would project to all the beaches along its perimeter a startlingly authentic limitless horizon, complete with changing cloud patterns in a variable sky. Crisp salted air, a slight breeze, the sound of waves crashing on fine pink sand, and the calming vision of a far horizon instantly transported visitors to their beloved lost beachside world.

When the gorgeous solies came surfing along the foam and onto land inviting Marseans one and all into their playground the illusion was complete. Desultory attendance at the first of the traditional solie lakes erupted into utter mania with the advent of Horizon Ring technos.

Persus glanced at the little girl walking next to her. She hadn't spoken a word since leaving the governor's residence and never once looked her way. At nine Athena was already proficient at suppressing any angry emotions that might disturb her or ruffle her cool Marsean affect. Clearly she was furious with her father and worried by his behavior.

But as they passed beneath the park gates Persus recognized flashes of a child's pure joy. Athena was imagining herself swimming with the solies to soothe her aching heart. Seeing an empty space on the crowded beach she sprinted ahead and stood on it possessively until Persus arrived.

Together they laid out the blanket. The Enviro-Settings produced so strong a breeze this day they were forced to hunt for rocks to hold down three corners, their picnic basket securing the fourth. They stripped down to swimming suits and picked their way through the blankets towards the water. Athena's eyes were on stalks, her head swiveling left and right, watching children being sought out and lured into the waves by one solie after another.

When Athena looked up and smiled at Persus she felt a small clutch at her heart. This was after all the child of the man she adored. She hoped, but never expected, Athena to love her. But in that single moment of shared pleasure they were friends. That was enough.

All at once a young solie exploded from the breakers onto the shore at Athena's feet. Squealing with delight she bent down and nuzzled the creature's comical face. Then encircling its neck with her arms she allowed herself, laughing loudly, to be towed into the surf. The two of them disappeared.

Persus could feel her heart warming and expanding in her chest, and for a moment she forgot her worries. About Athens. About the torn fabric of the universe. About her own loveless life. So when a great silken solie came crashing gracefully down at her feet and gazed a silent invitation with its large liquid eyes Persus felt her world suddenly and quite unexpectedly complete. She inhaled the fresh salted air, then setting her eyes to the far horizon waded with her new companion into the shining sea.

ONE HUNDRED ONE

S HE HAD DRUNK too much again last night and now Talya's head was splitting. She would have opened a vein to have use of the blood-balance function of her phaetron just now. *Lighten up on the kav*, she admonished herself. She'd experienced several signs of pregnancy, though without her device she could not be sure. Her estrus cycle – held in check all the years on Gaia until her exile in Taug – had not yet regulated to the thirty-day lunar cycle of Atlan women.

Out their back window came the slapping of water against the dock and boatmen calling out to each other as they passed on the canal. She felt Boah rising from his side of the bed and pretended to sleep, though the sight of his naked body moving about their room through her slitted eyes was soothing. She hated to admit it but she never tired of the sight. He was a magnificent specimen of manhood – the hard but gracefully rounded buttocks and thighs. The strong hands that finished his beautifully muscled arms. The broad sculpted chest and belly with fine curls of black hair that formed a tantalizing triangle and seemed to point to his groin always aroused her, though this morning her head hurt too much for even the tiniest shock of pleasure between her thighs.

When he turned her way she quickly dropped her eyelids.

If she was awake he would ask her, as he did every single day, whether she wished to go with him up to the High Atlantos stables. Why could he not see how futile, how sickening it was for her to visit the place where she had once ruled as a goddess? Who with her natural magic had produced a lineage of strong, magnificent horses and even the pure white foal? The Brotherhood, who'd never learned the truth about her five-year absence, therefore had no understanding of her abandonment of them when she returned. "They believe you changed with motherhood," Boah had recently told her. "That you are now content to be my woman and bear my children."

This blatant misconception had torn at her. Driven her to drink…or drink even more than she had been doing. Wasn't it enough that she was forced to live in this humble home devoid of technos when not far under her feet lay the place of her greatest longings? The *Atlantos*. How she had taken the phaetron for granted! In no circumstance of existence that Talya could have imagined before her banishment would she be forced to live without the device that defined the life of every Terresian.

Her birthright had been stripped away from her. In the Taug village – the early days after her arrival when she had wept in the dark of her hut – she had sworn she'd have given both legs, given her beauty, rather than be abandoned in a desolate life without technos. It was then, however, that she realized the one thing she would not have sacrificed for the phaetron.

Isis.

The thought had shocked her. Perhaps it had saved her life. For if she put her child above a man-made instrument, no matter how critical that instrument was to the core of her, then life lived among savages could indeed be survived.

Out through the bedroom archway she could hear Isis moving about. She would be dressing for the day. Would she go to the high stables or the low? At first when they had returned to

Atlantos it had been offered that Isis could attend a neighborhood school. The little girl believed she wanted the fellowship of children her own age, as she had had in Taug. But she was far advanced of the city's children in every subject, and worse they knew little of Isis' beloved "natural world." What kind of playmates could they possibly be?

Within two months of their homecoming Boah had gifted her a horse, and that was the end of any talk of schooling. Talya continued with all the education she thought her daughter needed and could provide with her limited resources.

She was only seven but already consumed by horses. In this passion the little girl believed that she was her father's daughter. Boah's daughter. Ironic that the city's fabled "God of the Horse," and "bringer of the beast to the Atlan culture" – Poseidon – was Isis' father by blood.

But there was nothing to be done about any of it. When she was old enough Isis would attend the Academy like other common Atlan children and choose a course of study there. Talya sighed deeply at the thought. Calling it an academy was a cruel mockery of the word. Aside from the Green Teachers who admittedly knew much about the botany and medicinal uses of the continent's plant life, the other respected scholars – of astronomy, navigation, boat-building, agriculture, metallurgy, mechanics, mathematics and physics – had less knowledge than any eight-year-old Terresian child. Poseidon's insistence that the leaders in the disciplines instigate invention and innovation at their own pace, with only the merest hints and prodding from him, made Talya want to scream. Progress towards technos and science was glacially slow, though it had to be admitted that some of their original architecture, design and artistry was quite extraordinary. The species had the necessary intelligence for developing a great culture. It would simply take them forever to attain it.

Talya lifted her lids enough to see Boah embracing his daughter before leaving the house. He was ridiculously lenient with her, and she adored him. She had done since the first moment she'd set eyes on him outside the Taug village and claimed him for herself. The girl loved her mother, but the love between Boah and Isis left little room for much, or anyone else.

Even as Isis began pulling away from her, the child was discovering a most perfect world for herself. She had her father. She had horses. She was the darling of the stables, both in the city and High Atlantos. She had the run of an enchanting new metropolis. Took voyages on great ships and small. That the "First Family," as it had come to be known, was largely indifferent to her was of no consequence. She never once commented on her Aunt Cleatah's remoteness towards her, even though the woman's warm affection towards everyone else was her most famous attribute. Isis seemed pleased enough to be invited to the Central Isle on festival days, and got along well with the boys she called her cousins.

As every citizen of Atlantos did Isis stood in awe of Poseidon. Talya closely observed his behavior towards his daughter on the few occasions when they were in each other's company, and there was no cause for complaint. Just shy of demonstrative he was tender with the little girl. Seemed to enjoy making her laugh. And his eyes lit up sincerely as she entertained him with her spirited stories. Talya knew that nothing more would be permitted. Poseidon's undiminished love for Cleatah and his deference to her would far outweigh whatever feeling he might have for Isis.

When Talya saw the slender figure enter the room she pretended to come sleepily awake, and smiled. As her daughter bent to kiss her cheek Talya smelled the horsy scent that was always on her clothing and skin.

"Which stable today?" Talya asked, her first words little more than a hoarse croak. "High or low?" She hoped she did not reek of kav.

"Low. Then high. Then low. Then high." Isis was teasing – she loved teasing – and nuzzled her face into her mother's neck.

Talya reached out to embrace the girl but she was already disentangling herself. "There are some people outside," Isis said. "I think they want to come in."

"People? Who are they?" Talya sat up in bed.

"I don't know. From the Academy, I think. I'll let them in."

"No, don't!" Talya called, but Isis was out the bedroom archway and at the inland door. With a groan she forced herself up and out of bed. The shift she had worn the day before was crumpled on the floor. She tugged it on over her head as the door opened and a small phalanx of Atlans crowded into her small gathering room. She ran her fingers through her hair and with no other choice went out to meet them. Isis was already gone. As the girl had correctly guessed it was a delegation from the Academy. What could they want with her, and at this hour?

"Good morning," Talya said in the most pleasant voice she could manage. All in the group were women. She only recognized one. None were teachers of the sciences or mechanics or building. Nor were they Green Teachers. They were older, and though they were city people there was something vaguely tribal about them. But they all smiled pleasantly, and Talya invited them to sit amidst the cushions around the small cold hearth.

"My name is Catna," said the oldest of the women in perfect Terrerthe. She was deeply wrinkled, her fingers twisted with age, but her eyes were clear and glinted in the first morning sun that pierced the eastern window. "We are weavers at the Academy," she continued. Then with nods of encouragement from the others she added, "We are here to ask you to join us. Become a teacher of the loom. There is much we can learn from you. From your teachers in Taug." Then she smiled with unabashed eagerness, and the other women nodded their encouragement.

"You want me to teach at the Academy?" Talya said, trying to absorb the sweet sincerity of the offer and its ridiculous incongruity. The unintentional insult – the foremost genomist of Terres a teacher of weaving! She was silent for so long that the women began to squirm and exchange sideways glances.

But Talya felt a strange warmth beginning to spread inside her chest and sensed a momentousness in the humble request, an opportunity to exchange her endlessly angry existence for something comfortable, even fruitful. She would never abandon the quest to regain entry into her *Atlantos* laboratory. Of course she wouldn't.

She was surprised to hear herself saying, "I'm honored by your invitation. I'll be happy to join you." She found herself smiling.

Perhaps there was, after all, some measure of joy to be found in her days.

ONE HUNDRED TWO

ISIS COULD HEAR thunder rumbling far in the distance but overhead the sky was the same clear blue that Zanza used in the corners of her weavings. At the base of the South Ramp with morning traffic clattering past on both sides, her horse stamped and blew with the same impatience she was feeling. *Where was he? He was always late!* She would have to scold him, give him a sharp poke in the ribs, though she'd do it with a grin. *Why did her cousin Atlas always do better with a little prodding from her?* She wondered sometimes if he was pretending to be slow or stupid so that she would take a teacherly tone with him, goad him, sometimes shout with frustration at him. He would listen patiently to her badgering – the correct place on the horse's side to kick that would spur him to run faster without hurting him; where not to waste his time digging if he wanted to find the largest hoard of turtle eggs; the right way to weave a fishing net.

She also wondered why he chose to spend so many hours with her when he could be playing with Geo. They seemed sometimes to share one mind between them. But they were not the same. Not really. Everyone else claimed they could never tell who was who. True, their features were identical. Even their voices were hard to tell apart. Recently they'd cut their hair differently, Geo's

long and wild about his shoulders, Atlas's clipped above his ears –
this to avoid constantly being called by the other's name.

"I can *always* tell you apart," she'd told Atlas.

"How? How do you know?"

"Easy. Geo moves like a panther. You move like a wolf."

He'd looked at her as if she had two heads, but then had gone
away and thought about it. The next time they'd met he said,
"You're right. Geo does move more gracefully than I do. I'm more
definite with my steps."

That was what she liked about Atlas. He listened to her. Took
what she said to heart. Her mother certainly did not. And her
father, well, she did not presume to teach him anything. She was
content to be his student in all things.

"Ho, Isis!"

Finally. She saw him riding towards her on a horse that was
too small for him, and shook her head dismayed. But she wouldn't
tell him. The day would surely hold lots of other "corrections" for
her cousin, and while she enjoyed teasing him she did not want to
annoy him too badly. She loved Atlas very much.

"Come on, I want to make it past the stables before the mares
and foals are set out to pasture," she told him as he came alongside her.

"Why?" He was wearing that inquiring and mildly dubious
expression that encouraged her to explain and expound.

"Because…" she said and spurred her horse up the ramp, calling after her, "…my father is up there today and I don't want him
to know where we're going!"

*

By the time they were approaching the High Atlantos Stables
the herd was already in the field, and it seemed every man of the
Brotherhood was out among them. Isis therefore led Atlas into
a path in some tall brush on the other side of the road from the

pasture. Twigs caught in their hair and scratched their faces, but he never complained, clearly satisfied with a secret adventure with his cousin on the Great Plateau.

When they emerged from the bush some way beyond the end of the stables they could see Manya and her sister mountains looming in the distance. The sky above the range was dark with thunderheads.

"Where are we going?" Atlas finally asked.

"The far end of the Wild River." Isis didn't look at him, just kept her eyes straight ahead and her self-satisfaction concealed behind tight-clamped lips. She wondered what objection he would offer. *It was very far and they needed to be home by dark. It was dangerous, with herds of stampeding oryx. The plateau was inhabited by savage, long-fanged panthers and poisonous vipers.* But he said nothing. Just came abreast of her horse and fixed her with a curious gaze.

"What?" she demanded.

"Why do my mother and father dislike your mother?" he asked.

Isis shrugged.

"I asked my father," Atlas said.

"You did? What did he say?"

"That sometimes brothers and sisters don't get along very well. He told me there was a time that his brother – our Uncle Athens – was angry at him for no reason. But now they're great friends."

Isis knew who Athens was, but her mother went strangely quiet when she spoke of him. One day she would hear more about him, her mother promised. But truly, Isis was unconcerned.

"See the forest over there?" she said, pointing to the southeast.

"Of course I can see it," he answered, a bit more sharply than usual.

Perhaps Atlas wished to talk further about their parents. But she did not. There were too many wonders ahead to be sunk into matters that bored her.

"Let's race!" she cried, and without waiting for him to argue took off down the road at a gallop, laying low along her horse's neck, whispering the sounds of encouragement her father had taught her would make the beast run for its life. She smiled when she heard Atlas's thundering mount gaining on her.

Perhaps, she thought, his horse was not too small for him after all.

ONE HUNDRED THREE

ATLAS HAD NEVER before been so far from the city without his parents. Each year the family would take horses and a wagon to visit Manya, the mountain that had been named after his father's mother. They would climb to a slope covered by ice and packed snow and spiked with sheared-off tree trunks, to honor Poseidon's friends who had died there a long time ago. Despite the solemnity of the occasion Father would encourage them to play in the snow. There would be rough-housing and shrieks of delight as they rolled and slid down the slopes, their parents watching dreamily.

Atlas and Isis were still many miles from the foothills of the range, but they'd crossed a wide expanse of meadowland and skirted a massive herd of oryx whose bulls were engaged in the most astonishing behavior. Pairs of males ran at each other, fiercely butting their curve-horned heads together with such shattering violence that the sound echoed across the plain.

"My father says it's a mating dance," said Isis, knowingly.

"How can it be?" Atlas was perplexed. "Those are two males dancing."

"True. But see..." she pointed. "There is a female watching them."

She was right, Atlas thought, then said, "I still don't understand."

"You will one day," Isis replied. "At least that's what my mother says."

To their relief they encountered no long-fanged panthers nor poisonous vipers, but in the thick patch of forest they traversed on a path that Isis had cleverly found – a place her father had shown her just months before – the children were briefly frightened by the sight of a huge brown bear and her cubs. Their luck was that the animals were too preoccupied with their meal of honeycomb pulled from a tree trunk to give the humans a thought.

"Look, Atlas, they're twins, like you and Geo!" Isis whispered excitedly.

He had only heard tales of such creatures, and seen carvings of them in stone at the public baths. He couldn't tear his eyes away from the enormous mother, but he feasted on the sight of the two brown balls of fur tumbling and rolling around, licking honey from their paws. He thought of how excited he would be to tell his mother and father what he had seen, but then wondered if this adventure was to be a secret held strictly between him and Isis.

At the far edge of the forest they began to hear a roaring louder than anything Atlas had ever known.

"What is that?!" he called to Isis over the sound.

"The first waterfall of the Wild River. Just wait!"

They rode on, emerging onto a sandy bank with patches of trees and shrubs that overlooked the vast untamed river of the Great Plateau. The other river to the north *had* been tamed, formed into a deep ditch and lined with stone to be fed into the gridwork of canals and that irrigated the fields and orchards of High Atlantos, then to fill the aqueducts of the city with sweet water.

"Look, Atlas," Isis said, dismounting and walking to the river's edge.

He jumped down and came to her side. Just beyond a gentle

curve was a sight that left him breathless. The falls, as wide as the river itself and as tall as the walls of the stadium was the source of the mighty roar. Rainbows played in the mists thrown up by the crashing water that plunged into its base.

"Do you like it?" Isis demanded.

"Oh, yes," Atlas whispered, awed into further silence by the majesty of it all. There he stood rooted like a tree, his jaw agape, wondering if he had ever seen a thing so wonderful. He wished for a moment that Geo was at his side and wondered how he would ever describe this to him. He considered whether he would tell his parents what he had seen. *Then it will not be Isis' and my secret,* he argued with himself. This reverie was broken by a scraping sound at his side. He turned to see Isis, her tough little frame dragging a small overturned skife from the nearby bushes.

"You get the paddles," she ordered him and gestured towards the green patch from where she'd come.

There was no arguing with the girl, so he pulled the two long oars to the river's edge where she was trying to upturn the boat to no avail.

"Wait!" he cried.

Then putting his own wiry muscles behind it with hers they flipped the skife right-side-up. The children beamed with their small victory. And then there was nothing to do but push it into the shallow eddies.

"Get in," he ordered her, taking command. To his great satisfaction she did as she was told. With a great shove the skife was afloat, and he leapt in after her.

Downriver they went. Atlas's grin stretched wide across his face. Then his expression fell. "The horses!" he shouted in sudden panic.

"It's all right. Look."

Isis pointed to the shore and he saw their two mounts – led by Isis' horse – following their riders downstream.

Atlas, mightily impressed, sat back on the seat and regarded his cousin with newfound respect. "How did you find this place?"

"My father brought me here. He showed me the waterfall. He showed me the boat. That horse I rode here today has been trained to follow."

Atlas began to laugh, but the sound was swallowed up by the river rushing all around them.

"I like this better than the city," Isis told him.

"I like it, too. But it scares me a little."

"There's nothing to be afraid of. If you fall out, you swim to shore."

"Let's paddle. We'll go faster that way."

They took up the oars and one on each side began to stroke. Isis was skinny but strong, and their paddling soon had them skimming down the river, the horses having to gallop to keep up.

"I have to stop," Isis finally conceded. Her face was flushed and she was panting with exertion.

They put down their oars and allowed themselves to float lazily down the gently bending river, content to watch the forested banks and creature of every kind coming for a drink or bath. Long-beaked white birds that were not unlike those that sailed above the seawall flapped madly, higher and higher into the air. They hovered momentarily, folded their wings tightly to their sides and dove like shot arrows into the water, emerging every time victorious with a fish wriggling in their beaks.

Only gradually did the children become aware of a sound — an oddly familiar roar, but this time it was ominous. Isis' look of alarm frightened Atlas.

"Is there a waterfall up ahead?" he asked, hardly daring to breath.

"No," she answered. "Not for a long distance."

Together they turned to look behind them. There was nothing

to see save the placid river from where they had come. But the sound was there, and it was growing louder.

"What *is* that?" Atlas said.

Isis raised her arm slowly and pointed to the mountain range far behind them. It was thickly wreathed in swirling black clouds. "Oh…" she moaned, "…that is Thune, the Storm God warring with Indra, Goddess of the Rain."

"But they're far away," Atlas objected. "It must be another god, one much closer, because…" The words choked in his throat.

From around the gentle curve of the river came roaring a great wall of water, half as high as the trees. It was on them before they could scream. The flood mercifully lifted the skife on its forward edge, not tumbling the craft and crushing it beneath the weight of the water. They were flying at such a speed that the banks were a blur and all they could do was clutch tightly to the sides of the boat and pray. At the very moment Atlas suspected they might ride out the wave in safety a huge broken tree trunk slammed into the back of the boat, sharply up-tilting it.

And suddenly Atlas was in the water, submerged, tumbling and choking.

He flapped his arm seeking the surface but found himself sinking deeper. Panic rose in him. He turned, and seeing what he believed was daylight stroked toward it.

His head cleared the surface!

"Atlas!" he heard Isis screaming. "Atlas, here!"

He saw her, the boat but an arms-length from where he bobbed in the rushing water. "Give me your hand!"

He shot an arm in her direction and saw her leaning far over the skife's edge, reaching, reaching… Their hands clasped and held, the feeling like no other he had ever known. Her small fingers were hard as steel and he trusted somehow that this girl would never let go her grip on him.

Never.

Dragged as he was alongside the boat, water crashed about him, blinding him, filling his mouth and nose. Still she held. He could hear her calling his name like a chant, "Atlas, Atlas, Atlas!" a reminder that she was there. *Don't let me go,* he wanted to shout, but the words were choked by the water, and her viselike grip was all the answer he needed.

Finally he felt the rush begin to slow, and slow further. The tide flattened, the flood spending itself. Atlas took his first unspluttered breath and looked to the end of his aching arm into the face of his cousin. She was drenched, her cheeks blotched and eyes wild, the golden hair flatted against her head.

With a strength she should not have possessed after such an ordeal she pulled him close to the skife and he clutched its side with both hands. She fell back dazed, and spent with her exertions.

"Isis..." he whispered, but could say no more.

She managed a small triumphant smile before she began to cry.

ONE HUNDRED FOUR

FOR ATLAS IT had been a memorable day.

The musicians and dancers and all but a few guests that had come to the residence for Atlas's and Geo's eighth solar celebration had gone, and night had fallen. Earlier Atlas and Isis had chanced many sidewise gazes at each other – and little more – as the punishment for their recent adventure had included an enforced restriction of their playtime together. Their journey to the Great Plateau had proven a most serious offense. Atlas's horse had been badly injured in the river flood and needed to be put out of her pain. This was especially wrenching for Isis, realizing she had been the cause of a horse's death. They couldn't count how many times between them they'd heard, "You could have been injured as well. Or killed!" Blame was placed on both children, but no one seemed to care that Isis had saved Atlas's life in a most heroic effort. That, they realized, would be their private memory, a cherished and unbreakable bond.

The only moment they'd been allowed to speak to one another even briefly was at gift-giving. Isis had given Geo a colorful saddlebag cut and sewn by her own hand from one of her mother's finest weavings. But when Atlas opened the cloth wrapping of his present, an object that filled both his hands, he found a wooden, long-beaked bird. Though it was carved in great detail and polished to a rich glow its true significance was lost on everyone but the two of them. Atlas beamed with pleasure.

"Everyone will think it's a seabird," Isis whispered.

"*We* know it's a riverbird." His hand caressed the sleek wing with supreme satisfaction. "Thank you, cousin," he said.

Her eyes gleamed as brightly as his did, their hearts eased by the knowledge that they had been partners in a great adventure and that he owed her his very life.

But now Atlas became aware that the three remaining guests were Isis, her mother and father...and they seemed to be making no show of leaving. This was rare. The family was usually the first to leave a celebration. They would slip away quietly when no one was looking. But there were Boah and Talya near the arched entry speaking calmly and quietly to his mother and father. Geo played with one of the new wolf pups on the floor, seeming entirely unaware of the strangeness of the scene.

Isis sidled to Atlas's side.

"Why are you still here?" he said.

Isis kept her wary eyes on the four parents. "More punishment?"

"Not on our solar day."

The two couples' voices rose momentarily, as though something had been decided.

"Geo, Atlas, Isis, come here to us," Cleatah called.

Geo didn't hesitate when summoned. He never did. When an order was given he instantly obeyed, unlike Atlas who went his own way whenever possible. He had learned this from Isis, and they quietly reveled in breaking any rule that was breakable.

Now the three children followed their parents out of the residence into the dark. The full moon had just begun to rise.

"Everyone, please sit," Poseidon said with an inviting sweep of his hand.

This is becoming stranger and stranger every moment, Atlas thought as he sat himself in the short-clipped sweetgrass under the boughs of the yew. He and Isis didn't dare look each other in the eye.

"One day many years before you children were born," Cleatah began, "Poseidon sat me down under a tree on the Great Plateau and told me what we are about to tell you tonight."

The children were silent and dared not move a muscle. Atlas barely breathed. Though it was still and quiet it felt to him as though the air around him was thrumming.

"Atlas, you once asked me where I was born," his father said. "Do you remember what I answered?"

"Far away," Atlas replied.

"Isis," Talya began. "Where did I tell you your Uncle Athens lived?"

"Far away across a great ocean. Was that a lie?" she asked.

"No," Talya said. "It's just that the 'ocean' is made not of water. It's made of sky."

All the children gazed out at the blackness and the multitude of winking stars growing dimmer as the moon's light grew brighter.

Boah took Isis' hand in his. "Your mother, your uncles Poseidon and Athens were born out there on a planet called Terres." He raised his arm and pointed into the dome of the night sky.

Geo giggled uncomfortably and sought his brother's gaze.

But Atlas was perplexed, even fearful, and sought the comfort only his twin could offer. He took Geo's hand.

"There's no need to be afraid," Cleatah told them. "What we will show you now is a very great wonder."

"We're going to take you inside the 'ship' that brought us from our home out there," Poseidon said, pointing skyward, "to here. And then…" he smiled mysteriously, "we're going to introduce you to your Uncle Athens."

ONE HUNDRED FIVE

I T WAS A most unlikely group that approached the high circular hedge all knew as Poseidon's Grove. Atlas had never thought much about the wall of green at the center of the isle, or considered why it had no entrance. His mother's medicine garden did. Now he, Geo and Isis watched with rapt attention as their parents stepped through a brambly curtain of green *air* and into what had moments ago appeared as a solid hedge. When the children followed they found that the narrowest of spiral paths had been hidden only by a trick of the eye. One needed simply to know where the green air doorway and narrow gash were to be found.

Geo muttered exclamations as they circled deeper and deeper into the hedge, until finally they all emerged into the center of the circular grove. There was nothing here but a thick covering of shortgrass under their feet – something of a disappointment after the strange maze.

"Where is Uncle Athens?" Geo want to know.

"We have a little way to go before we find him," Poseidon said, putting an arm around each of his sons.

Their mother wore a peculiar expression that seemed to Atlas something less than a smile but more than a frown. Isis held Boah's hand tightly.

"We're going to take you aboard the ship that brought Talya and me to Erthe. It's buried beneath your feet, right here. That is why no one but a few of us know it exists. You've actually come here before," he said to the twins, "as all your brothers have, soon after they were born."

"You were much too young to remember," their mother said. "In fact your uncle has laid eyes on all six of you."

Geo was turning round and round in the grass. "But where is the ship?"

"Here," said their father, tapping his foot lightly on a raised mound under the grass.

Instantly a vertical column of transparent blue light shot up from the ground before them. Atlas and Geo fell back upon each other, and Isis squealed with terror at the sight.

"Poseidon..." their mother said with mild admonition.

"I knew no other way," he said with amusement. "Come, boys. Stand next to me and your mother. Isis..." he began, but saw she was already clutching Boah's waist.

Then with his long arms around them all Poseidon guided them closer and closer to the glimmering beam of blue light.

Once within the beam the ground seemed to evaporate from beneath their feet. As they began their descent the sensation was a *whisking downward* through a tunnel of solid rock. Atlas tried to make sense of what he was seeing but everything was moving too quickly.

Then their downward movement stopped and all at once they were standing in an alien world. Unnaturally quiet. Oddly shaped. Strangely lit.

"This is the *Atlantos*," Poseidon said.

Atlas and Geo turned slowly around in the core of a 'ship' that had brought their father and Aunt Talya through the sky to Erthe, observing five straight equidistant corridors fashioned of a muted silvery substance. Isis was still as a post, her eyes huge and staring. Atlas had never seen her show fear before. Not ever. But now she was afraid.

Their parents took off down one of the hallways and the children followed. Atlas's head swiveled side-to-side, wondering what could be found behind each of the doorways.

His mother had been right. These were the most wondrous sights that in all of his wildest flights of fancy he had never thought to imagine. Beside him he felt Geo trembling. Then he realized he himself was trembling. As they were led down each of the five corridors designed in the shape of a starfish Atlas could barely put one foot in front of the other, fixed as he was to each and every sight, sound and smell he encountered. He didn't wish to be pulled so quickly away. But then the next miracle overtook the last. Each was more thrilling than the former – curved walls of polished metal, a door that slid open with the slightest *whoosh*. Chambers his father called "laboratories" in which "devices" created light from a source other than the sun. More marvelous still were diagrams and maps of their planet and stars that danced in the air! Atlas stood slack-jawed in the "landing bay" staring at a silver "shuttle disk" – a miniature, his father told him, to the shape and appearance of The *Atlantos* if you had been able to see it outside of its Erthan burial place.

"It once flew the skies of Erthe," Poseidon told them. But never since the larger craft's entombment in rock had this shuttle seen the light of day.

Their mother smiled. "Your father took me in it on a journey to the moon."

Atlas hooted with laughter at the ridiculousness of such an idea. Geo appeared stunned at the thought.

"How?" Isis suddenly demanded to know. "How could you fly to the moon?" Her forehead was wrinkled with consternation.

Talya addressed all three children, her voice grave. "There is something called 'technos,'" she began. 'It is a *force*, like moving water, or fire or wind. It has the ability to change things, create things. Heal things. There is a machine called the 'phaetron'…"

"Talya," Poseidon interrupted her. "This will all be explained in time. Children…" he turned to them. "Are you ready to meet your Uncle Athens?"

"You said he was in the sky," Geo objected.

Poseidon pulled the boy to him. "It's difficult to understand. But trust me, you *will* understand. This is only the first day of your education. Let's go into the library."

The five of them walked to the far end of the fifth corridor and stepped through a sliding doorway into a circular chamber. The room had a single continuous wall made of a solid white material that Atlas could not identify. Its cavernous round space was empty but for a simple pedestal at the far end of the room. His father moved purposefully to a place on the right of the door and spoke the word "Mars" aloud. An instant later an entire section of the wall came alive, dozens of slender cylinders slowly emerging from it. They were as long as a grown man's hand, but otherwise unremarkable.

Poseidon studied the section of protruding cylinders and reaching out, plucked one from the wall. He walked with it to the pedestal and inserted it vertically into the top. To Atlas's amazement the pedestal sprang to life with rhythmic patterns of light and an intense – while nearly inaudible – droning hum.

That is not a stone pedestal, Atlas thought, then watched as his mother leaned towards his father's ear and heard her teasingly call this machine "The Godmaker." Atlas reminded himself to ask why the thing was called by such a strange name. But in the next moment a flickering of the air in the room's center had begun. It increased, intensified and finally transformed into an *image* – one so startlingly real that Atlas entirely forgot the Godmaker. He felt Isis' body press close to his. He heard a small whimper.

What had emerged from the flickering was the figure of a man. He looked slightly younger and slightly smaller than their father, still powerfully built with bold, even features. The thick dark hair was clipped short. Cheeks were high and square. Proud brows overhung deep-set eyes. Even considering the dark shadows beneath them, anyone would have said he was handsome. His body was clothed in gleaming blue cloth that clung tightly to limb and torso, so different from the simple tunics Atlan men wore. A pendant of shiny yellow metal hung at his breast, and thick bracelets of the same circled his wrists.

This was Uncle Athens. He was standing in a chamber, and behind him was a large window overlooking a green forest as vast as the sea beyond their own city's seawall. Athens raised a hand in graceful greeting and smiled brilliantly.

"Brother." His voice rang rich and deep. "And who do we have here? My eldest nephews. How they've grown. Haven't they become handsome boys? Come, let me see you." He was looking directly at Atlas and Geo, an unnerving vision, for the man was not really there at all.

Poseidon nodded and they moved forward, tentative and shy.

"Are you on Mars?" Geo asked in a hushed tone, his eyes wide as the silver shuttle disk.

"I am. And you are...?"

"In my father's ship under the ground of the Central Isle."

"Yes, I know that," Athens said with an indulgent grin, "but what's your name?"

"Geo."

"Aha. Then you, standing behind your brother, you are Atlas."

Atlas hesitated, feeling strangely fraught, as though a step forward towards his uncle was thick with meaning, even *destiny*, the thought of which had never crossed his mind before.

"I'm Atlas," he said, finally moving towards the all-too-real image of his uncle.

"I'm glad to see you two look like your mother, not my ape-faced brother." His laugh was a rich, rolling melody. "Are you there, Cleatah? Come into the vision field. Let me see you."

Their mother took a single step forward. Atlas saw something in her expression. He thought it was the same reserve she showed towards his Aunt Talya.

"Beautiful as ever," Athens said. "Speaking of beautiful women, where is my sister, Talya?"

When his aunt moved into the field the boys stepped back. He tried to catch Isis' eyes, but she was standing behind Boah, clinging to him.

"It's been too long," Athens said to Talya, looking suddenly serious. "I'm happy to see you."

"And I you."

Atlas thought he saw something flicker between them that was unspoken but somehow understood – the same as happened sometimes with his twin brother.

"Introduce me to your family."

"My life mate, Boah…" Talya said, looking behind her "… and father of our child."

The men nodded to one another, but Isis remained behind Boah's back. Atlas had never known his cousin to be so timid. He wondered then if he knew her as well as he believed he did.

"Isis, come here," Talya said. "Say hello to your uncle."

Atlas watched as Isis set her back straight and lifted her chin, as if finally screwing up her courage. She moved out from behind her father and walked slowly forward till she was an arm's length from the man who was there and *not* there. Uncle Athens lifted his hand and placed his palm outwards, toward her. Without a word or a moment's hesitation Isis lifted her own palm to face his. Their hands "touched" and Athens beamed with pleasure.

"Lovely. You are your mother's daughter – casting no aspersions on your father, of course," he said with a smile, then nodded towards Boah who wore what Atlas thought was a peculiar expression.

"But look at you, Isis. You have her features, her build, her hair. You are exactly like your mother when she was this age."

"Do you ride horses on Mars?" Isis finally blurted, ending her silence.

"We don't have horses on Mars."

"No horses?" She giggled to think of something so absurd.

"Geo, Atlas, come closer again."

They came to stand with Isis, one on either side of her.

"Well, what do you think?" he said to the children. "Here we are on different worlds, separated by countless miles, and I can see that little freckle on your cheek, Atlas."

Atlas's hand flew to his face as his uncle's words swirled and crashed in his head.

"And you can see this little scar on my cheek where your father took a bat to my face when I was your age. Make sure you don't bully your brother like he did me."

This sounded like a tall tale, even to Atlas. But he was utterly compelled by the conversation with a man speaking to him, if he dared believe his parents, from a tiny pink light in the night sky.

"What could *I* see?" Atlas asked. "Could I see Mars? Does it look like Erthe?

"Of *course* you can. With the phaetron you can see all the other planets in our star system. You can see Terres! If you wish you can stand in Federation Square and watch a parade."

"Can we, Father? Please, can we!" Atlas cried.

"All in good time."

"Where are *your* children?" Isis demanded.

"I only have one." He grinned and called behind him. "Athena, come meet your cousins."

A dark-haired girl who looked about twelve walked boldly into the image. Tiny breasts were budding beneath the elegant, intricately patterned dress of fabric that glimmered like metal. She bore a striking resemblance to her father, though there was a healthy bloom in her cheeks and a mischievous glint in her obsidian eyes.

Atlas was intrigued. "How old are you?" he said.

"Older than you." He suddenly felt tongue-tied, and Athena seemed unwilling to engage in conversation.

"What is that you're wearing?" Isis asked. "I never saw a weave like that."

Athena shook her head uncomprehendingly. "Why are they staring at me like that?" she demanded.

"Be kind, Athena," Athens said. "I told you they've never seen a diffracted image before."

"They don't look like savages," she observed mildly.

Atlas heard his mother gasp, and his father stepped in between the children, bristling. "All right," he said. "Say goodbye to your uncle and Athena."

"Father, wait!" Atlas cried. "We haven't…"

"Follow your parents out of the library and up to the residence," Poseidon told them.

But Isis had planted her feet defiantly. She was fixed on her cousin's image, as though she knew some insult had been delivered but could not quite comprehend it. Geo, ever obedient, was already walking towards the door.

Cleatah's firm hand moved Atlas and Isis back. "Now, she said."

ONE HUNDRED SIX

POSEIDON STOOD OUTSIDE the closed library door watching Cleatah, Boah and the children disappear into the blue elevator beam, trying to calm himself. It was not Athena's fault. He knew that. She had simply absorbed her father's most deeply felt sentiments about Erthans and spoken them sincerely with no malice intended. The only malice was his brother's. Would he never change?

As promised, Poseidon was allowing Talya to stay behind for a private moment with Athens. Poseidon had argued with himself as long and passionately as he had with Cleatah the wisdom of allowing Talya into the *Atlantos*, even for the briefest of visits with Athens.

The debate about an education for Isis along with their sons had nearly torn them apart. The compromise had been hard-won. It was finally agreed that the child could not be punished for her mother's transgressions. Neither could she be denied her Terresian legacy. But the terms and conditions of Talya's return to the city – aside from this one visit with Athens – would have to stand.

She had taken the news resignedly, even seeming grateful for the concessions made on Isis' behalf. Perhaps the years in Taug had softened her after all, he thought. It stood to reason that in the future the children would want to know why Talya made so few visits to the ship, or expect an explanation for the years in the Taug village. Talya herself had devised one. *She had "misused Terresian technos and had seen the error of her ways." Not wishing to misuse it again, she had herself decided to stay away from any use of it. Her years in Taug were an opportunity to learn weaving and have a quiet life with Isis while she was young. She always expected to return to the city.*

The library door slid open and Talya emerged looking serene. Silently they walked the length of the corridor to the hub.

"Thank you for that," she said, "and for Isis. Especially for Isis."

"There would have been no way to keep it from her. She and the boys are very close."

"You can't be looking forward to your role of Terresian teacher," Talya said with a sardonic grin. "All that time spent away from your beautiful planet, thrashing around in the jaws of technos."

Poseidon smiled, wondering if she had finally begun to know the man he had become. He missed his intellectual friendship with Talya. Missed their conversations, ones that presupposed in both of them the razored edge of science.

"May I occasionally come back down and talk to Athens?"

"We'll have to see." Poseidon hoped he'd not revealed the regret he felt to say this.

"I understand. Cleatah doesn't trust me yet. I hope she will one day."

Talya stepped into the elevator and turned back to him. "Your brother doesn't look well," she said, "I'm worried about him."

A moment later the blue light whisked her away.

*

"Thank you for your cooperation," Poseidon said to his brother. He could now see shadows under Athens's eyes and downturned creases at his mouth. Talya's assessment had been correct. Something was taking its toll on him.

"For a man who so spurns godhood you've become quite the tyrant," Athens said, his jovial demeanor dissipated. There was no mention of Athena's callous remark. "Hideous, your treatment of Talya."

"You know what she did."

Yes, thank the stars, she provided your world with a fully Terresian child. And so, tragically, you and Cleatah will only have sons. For these so-called crimes the poor woman was banished to the primitives. Now she's restored to your city but forbidden the only thing that gives her joy in life. I tell you, it's *your* woman who's behaved atrociously."

"That's enough."

"For someone with such humble beginnings she's a very harsh judge."

"I suppose you think her judgment of a man who created a race of slaves to mine his gold is harsh as well."

Poseidon saw Athens flinch visibly. "I'm doing the best I can," he said quietly. "But those phibious creatures are relentless. And I dream..." His eyes fluttered nervously. "I dream of those glowing plasma spheres that tore into the *Atlantos*. I can't get them out of my head."

"I'm sorry." Poseidon felt himself soften. This was his only brother, and he did mean well. "Is there anything I can do?"

Athens composed himself and relented with one of his famous smiles. "Listen to me complaining. We're the two luckiest men in the solar system." He moved to his window and gazed out over the forest of giant tree ferns. "I like your boys. They have spirit...and kindness. And Isis...what an amazing creature. Do you love her?"

Poseidon felt stunned, as though he'd been thrown from a horse. No one dared ask him that question. "I...I..."

"She's your *daughter*, Poseidon." Athens skewered him with his gaze. "Don't let anyone take that from you."

That "anyone" surely referred to Cleatah, Poseidon thought. What had she done to make Athens despise her so?

Athens turned away. "I'm being called to a meeting, brother."

His aide walked into the transmission field. "Say hello to my own personal slave-driver."

"Good to see you, Persus," Poseidon said, meaning it sincerely. This woman had been indispensable to Athens on the colonial mission since the moment they'd awakened from MicroMort.

"Good day, Sir. I trust you and your family are well."

"They are very well. I wish you were having a better time of it over there."

"Your brother is leading brilliantly under increasingly difficult conditions. The phibions are brutal, but they're no match for the phaetron." She looked at Athens as if to remind him. "New weapons are being developed every day....I do need you now, Sir."

"Till next time," Poseidon said.

"Till next time."

Athens held his brother's gaze for an over-long moment before his image winked into nothingness. In his eyes, thought Poseidon, had been a desperate plea for help.

ONE HUNDRED SEVEN

66 **I**'M PREGNANT WITH your child."

The moon was so bright on their dock that Talya could see countless emotions animating Boah's face – some great, as he saw a happy future flash before his eyes, some as tiny as a muscle twitching his lower lip. Rendered speechless he could only sweep her into his arms and crush her to him.

It was not difficult to imagine his joy. Now it would all be complete – a wife, a beloved adopted daughter, a natural child of their own. He was weeping silently into her neck. She held him to her, surprised at the surge of affection she was feeling for him.

"Take me out on the water," she whispered.

As he readied their skiff Talya went inside and found that Isis was sleeping soundly. She tucked the blanket around her and pulled back the hank of pale hair that had fallen over her eyes. The child didn't stir. *What was she dreaming?* Talya wondered. *What could Isis be making of the stupendous revelations of this night and the promise of a limitless future?*

To be perfectly honest, sight of the *Atlantos* had stirred Talya's own mind. Something unspoken behind Poseidon's chilly, "We'll have to see" had given her a thread of hope that things could change, a sense that if she moved slowly, carefully, she would one day return to her laboratory.

Outside she found Boah readying the skife for launch. It always surprised her to see how naturally he handled a watercraft. She had to remind herself that before his immersion in the culture of the horse, even before the skills of hunting had been acquired Boah had been a child of fishing people. It was easy to forget the existence of the Shore Village, now that it had been scoured entirely out of existence.

Boah gave Talya his hand and she stepped down into the small craft, settling in among the cushions. He shoved off and in moments they were moving along lazily with the pull of the outgoing tide, he sitting tall on the seat at the rear of the boat, steering with ease. It was quiet on the inner canals at this hour, with few family skifes and barges afloat. At the far edge of the city, on the wharves of the Outer Canal, the great triremes would be loaded, awaiting their dawn launchings.

She was glad Boah was quiet, contemplative. Her own thoughts needed space to crash around in her head. Until this evening she hadn't dared hope to return to her true vocation. But now the broad outlines of a strategy were coming clear. Her new teaching post at the Academy would afford her visibility with educated Atlans, as well as a road back to Poseidon's confidence in her. Once she gained his complete trust Cleatah could be made to follow. She knew she must be patient. It might take years.

But wouldn't it be worth the wait? To finally complete the scientechnic agenda to which she'd been assigned by Federation those many years ago? It was all there in her laboratory. Every step of the evolutionary protocol, just awaiting her return. There were only a few genomes left to introduce into the aboriginal species – cortical enhancement for heightened cognition and perception; immunity to certain virulent microbes; increased body size and bone density; evenness and refinement of facial features. She would embed that elusive genome that fostered artistic brilliance, and of course all the instructions that would nullify the violent and aggressive predilections inherent in the populace. When she had fulfilled her mission there would live on this planet a race of superior beings, beautiful and cultured and deserving of the civilization Poseidon was providing them.

He could simply never know of her master plan.

There was more to it, this need to regain her privileges on the *Atlantos*. Of course there was, and not simply the evolution of *Gaianae pithekos intermedius*. She was facing the frightening reality of her future on Erthe without that which she held most dear. The years and decades – perhaps centuries – would pass. While she might phaetronically retain her youth and health and beauty Boah would age and die. Poseidon would never be hers. Her children, when grown, would certainly go their own ways.

All I really have is technos, she thought. *The magnificent library. Genomic research.* These would keep her stimulated, evolving intellectually. Sane. They would one day be hers again. Of this she was sure.

Boah turned the skife into the Great Harbor. Ahead was the arched gateway piercing the seawall, and beyond it the ocean. She turned and saw the moonlight reflected in his eyes and knew he was making for open water.

A thrill ran through her. He was bold, this Ertheman of hers. This horseman and adventurer. This beautiful lover. His child was safe in her belly, and here in a tiny vessel soon to be navigating the dark waves they would be safe in his care. She lay back and gazed up at the night sky and wondered where in the great avalanche of stars was her home.

Perhaps home is here *after all,* she suddenly thought. *Perhaps I should think of ceasing the endless struggle and scheming. Perhaps all I need for this moment is contentment.* She allowed the word to lay warm on the walls of her mind. *Yes, contentment.*

Let it be so.

ONE HUNDRED EIGHT

"PHIBION ACTIVITY HAS increased dramatically along the shoreline. It's not about the damage to the houses along the coast. They're long deserted." Captain Vargos of the Shore Guard was once again addressing Athens, Persus, Vice Governor Praxis, the assembled heads of Defense, and today the physics men. "But the behavior of the phibions is changing. The larger group attacks – the frenzies – these are now apparently triggered by the *residual scent* of human beings in the homes. We're concerned that their behavior may be shifting in other ways as well."

"Such as…?" Athens said. He prided himself for displaying a cool reserve in these ever more frequent and unpleasant circumstances."

"We have evidence that the creatures are straying further inland."

"How is that possible?" he asked Vargos. "Why are they not taken out by our weapons the moment they come ashore?"

"That's another thing, Sir," Vargos replied, unaware of how despairing he sounded. "The sensors are failing in places. As it stands we haven't enough manpower to visually guard every mile of the coastline, and they're just…slipping through."

"Slipping through?" muttered Athens disbelievingly.

"So far none of them have crossed the inland barrier – three miles in from the coast."

"I'm *aware* of how far the barriers are from the coast," Athens said, his reserve beginning to falter.

"Could we be talking about further dimensional tears?" Persus asked the physics men.

"No new ones. But progress is slow in repairing the existing ones."

"You don't know how to fix them, do you?" Athens snapped.

What had been the physics men's proudest discovery had become the colony's nightmare.

"They're amphibious creatures, and we've always assumed they needed water to exist, "Vargos interjected, "but if they're acquiring the ability to stray further and further inland it could mean they're evolving."

"So what do you propose, Captain?" This was Praxis speaking. All heads turned to him, attentive.

To Athens's intense irritation the once-wimpish vice governor had lately taken on an air of stern, levelheaded authority. Worse, the men in the room were responding well to him.

"We think that you and Governor Athens should accompany us on a fact-finding mission into the restricted area," replied Vargos. "Decisions will to have to be made about extending barriers further inland and improving weaponry – decisions we cannot approve on our own authority."

"I see," said Praxis.

"*You* see?" Athens shouted with sudden indignation. "And who are you, Vice Governor Praxis, to be coopting authority!" Athens glared defiantly around the long table at the defense ministers. Praxis was flushed with embarrassment. This gratified Athens immensely. He turned to the captain of the Shore Guard. "When do you propose we leave, Vargos?"

"Immediately, Sir."

As Athens stood he could see Persus making ready to join them.

"I want you to stay here, Persus."

"But Sir…"

He blocked her body with his own so no one would be privy to their conversation. He spoke softly. "I've signed an Executive Act stipulating that if anything happens to me you're to assume command just under Vice Governor Praxis. I need to know you're safe."

Her jaw hung slack in surprise.

"You're speechless for once," he added, and leveled a grim smile at her.

"Thank you, Sir. Thank you for your confidence in me."

He turned back to Vargos. "We'll meet you on the coast."

*

Athens had seen to it that Praxis was forced to share a shuttle with him on the short flight to the sea. They'd sat side-by-side in cold silence for some time before Athens said, "When did you plan to make it public?"

Praxis seemed to freeze and refused to meet Athens's eye.

"The report," Athens went on, "the bone-dry two-hundred page tome you gave me back on Terres before we left. The one that you plan to embarrass me with."

"Ah, *that* report. Yes." Praxis was beginning to recover from the shock of being found out, his manner becoming defiant.

"I doubt you remember *any* of it, Sir. You were too busy with…other things." His tone was contemptuous.

"So you think you can do damage to me with the publication of an old report that specified virtually nothing except that some life *might* have existed in the coastal waters of Mars and that the creatures *might* be large? You think this will place the blame on my shoulders for my ignorance of the dimensional tears and the phibions' finding their way through them? For my not having warned the colonists about a phenomenon that didn't exist before we arrived here and began drilling? That we should have taken precautions? One inconclusive sentence in one long, tiresome report?"

Athens thought he saw Praxis squelch a smile. "Not only the 'one long, tiresome report' that proved correct," he answered evenly. "What I'm considering is how you ignored solies' deaths along the shoreline in the months preceding the first attack of the phibions. And your refusal to make those reports public so they might take precautions. I'm afraid these two lapses of judgment together will be construed as irresponsible. Reckless. Perhaps criminal."

Athens felt so black and murderous an emotion rise in him he was forced to squeeze the arms of his seat so he wouldn't reach out and strangle the life from this little worm who sat beside him. His spies had discovered Praxis's plans to make his pathetic report public, but they had not warned him about the other more damaging evidence.

"How long have you known about the solies?"

"I don't think it matters how long I've known," Praxis answered. "I will *say* I only recently found out. I will *say* that your disregard of my report about the phibions, by itself, might have been an innocent error, but that learning of your withholding the facts about the solies' deaths shocked me profoundly. Forced me to speak."

"You knew about the solies when it happened?" Athens said. It was as much a question as an accusation.

Praxis stared straight ahead. His silence was self-indicting.

"Why didn't you say something to me then? Why?! Mine was a mistake, Praxis. You knew all the facts! You might have saved lives!"

"A *mistake*?" Praxis said with feigned incredulity. "The first instance was your laziness. The second…expediency. No one will ever know that I had information about the solies, so I rather doubt that I will be blamed."

"It will ruin me," Athens whispered.

"Yes, I think it will."

"How long have you been savoring this little scheme?"

"You know, I don't remember. You've been humiliating me for such a long, long time now…"

The pilot's voice from the cockpit surprised them both. "We'll be landing in a few moments."

Praxis turned and with a sweet smile looked Athens square in the face. "Sorry to have ruined your day…Sir."

ONE HUNDRED NINE

EVEN IN ATHENS'S terrible state of agitation he could still perceive something unutterably sad in the derelict homes along the shore. Where once had been pulsing life, there now was only desolation. The brilliant sunshine gleaming off the water only made it worse. During the afternoon as the group examined evidence of the phibions' inland forays and discussed new placement of barriers and stronger weaponry Athens had moved and listened and reacted quite capably, but he felt as if he was walking through a dream.

They had visited residences on Halcyon Beach in which he had once been a guest feted in luxury and adoration. Now these places were desecrated by monsters from the sea – rooms ravaged, furniture destroyed, walls collapsed. A putrid odor remained from a yellowish slime the phibions had left in their wake, and the occasional dead jelly creature lay decomposing where it had been unintentionally sloughed off the larger creatures' bodies as they'd moved through the houses searching for human meat.

"Haven't we seen enough, Vargos?" asked Athens wearily. "We can tie up the details back in the city."

"I believe Captain Vargos wants us to see some tracks that may give us an idea of the phibions' movement patterns," interjected Praxis. He turned to Vargos. "You indicated that this was important...?"

"Critical," answered the captain with an appreciative smile to the vice governor.

"Then we'll go see the tracks," said Athens, displaying perfect control over the rage he was feeling for Praxis.

The group, numbering nine inspectors besides Clax and Callas, Praxis and himself, had come in armored land vehicles each manned by a small but well-trained team of shore guardsmen. They'd driven north up the Eastern Shore Road which paralleled the seaside residences behind them. The house they now exited sat on a flat section of beach where a row of modest homes had been built right on the sand. Athens turned his gaze south, down the beach to the significantly more luxurious neighborhood in which he had lived. All the sprawling houses there were perched on a high cliff overlooking the beach. He'd considered asking to be taken to what had been his home, but now in his already dispirited state wondered if it would be too devastating to see.

His musing were interrupted by a commotion of sound, though nothing could be immediately seen. But something was clearly happening on the shore road behind the row of houses and the forest of giant ferns that lined the road's western edge. Shore guardsmen were shouting, the tree trunks were splitting and finally the party could hear the sound of phibions squealing horribly as they died, falling against the trees. A group of them must have emerged from inland and taken the patrol by surprise.

"Report, Tarkas!" Vargos spoke into his wrist device. "How many..."

"Dozens!" came the shouted reply. Someone screamed.

"Look, there!" Athens pointed above the garden greenery to the fern forest's canopy. A huge swath of the treetops was being shaken from below.

"Move to the beachside!" Vargos called. "There's a shuttle…"

No one waited for Vargos to finish. Everyone scrambled single-file along the path at the side of the house and emerged onto the beach. The disk was hovering a hundred feet over the sand, two houses north of them. But the blue elevator beam was not shooting to the ground from its center as they expected it to be. Instead the pilot was engaged in battle with the phibions, a wild barrage of phaetron fire directed across the houses and Shore Road at the chaos in the fern forest.

"Follow me!" Vargos called to the group and made a run at the hovering shuttle, trying to activate the elevator beam with his own phaetron. "Go, go!" he cried, standing his ground.

"Look there!" Clax cried, pointing out over the sea.

A jagged gash in the blue sky above the waterline began ripping open before their eyes. Impossibly the tear grew wider, exposing behind it a starry night sky and a simmering orange ocean.

"Don't stop!" Athens bellowed at the men.

Shore Defense Minister Kyron and the rest were halfway to the shuttle when three phibions surged through the rupture. Their trajectory would intercept the men's approach to the craft. And the blue beam had *still* not blinked on, the pilot yet engaged with the beach defense.

Vargos abandoned his own efforts to activate the beam. "Drago, come in!" he shouted, trying to raise the pilot. "Drago!"

As the phibions reached the shore their jelly creatures released themselves and came skittering with bewildering speed toward the men.

Panic ensued.

Armed with their phaetrons they began firing desperately at the immediate threat. But phibions themselves – having grown in number to at least eleven – were moving inland, their tentacles waving before them as if deciding which of the humans they might like to attack.

Suddenly the shuttle's elevator beam blinked on. The ship began firing at the phibions on the beach, but more were emerging from the new tear with every passing moment.

Athens, a good shot, had picked off two dozen jelly creatures, clearing a path for himself to the shuttle. The first human scream of agony shattered the air. Athens could see Vargos twitching beneath an undulating mound of the parasites. Athens ran, side-stepping more of them, taking aim and downing one of the approaching phibions as he went.

Two more were felled by the shuttle's phaetron, but one of the huge creatures had intercepted Kyle on his way to safety, and was returning with the shrieking man into the waves to devour him in peace.

Athens made it to the craft. Standing in its shadow next to the elevator beam he fought the impulse to dive through and be lifted to safety above. But men were fighting for their lives around him. He would help from where he stood.

Clax was nearest the shuttle, but a hoard of jellies blocked his final yards to safety. Together they blasted the creatures to oblivion and the man fell into Athens's arms, crying in relief.

"Go on, into the ship!" Athens commanded him, and he obeyed. Three more men were making good progress, and several more of the phibions lay dead on the beach.

He spotted Praxis, a less than physical man who'd lagged the farthest behind the group and had made the least progress toward the shuttle. He was surrounded by jelly creatures already slain in piles around his feet. There was sheer terror in Praxis's eyes, and perhaps disbelief that he'd survived this long. He killed one that was racing straight at him. It was the last of them. He looked up and caught Athens's eye in that moment of triumph. He had survived.

Then he felt the shadow looming over his body.

Athens had seen the phibion approaching Praxis from behind.

He had given the vice governor no warning. There was the barest moment for a furious look of betrayal before the man was snatched up in a muscular tentacle. He began screaming horribly.

A reflex, Athens raised his phaetron. He had a clear shot of the beast and adequate opportunity for the kill as the phibion was hesitating, the tentacles waving almost languidly, its hideous, snouted head cocked as if deciding which part of his prey's anatomy he would like to sample first.

Praxis's screams rang out across the beach. His and Athens's eyes connected once again. He must have seen Athens glance around him, must have known the governor was making quite sure no one was closely observing his actions. Then Athens fired – wide – missing the creature entirely. Praxis would have known Athens had purposely missed. It would have been his last thought before the phibion, in a strangely delicate movement, bit the vice governor's head completely off his shoulders.

ONE HUNDRED TEN

"UNCLE!" ISIS EXCLAIMED," there are mountains inside the dome!" She was straining forward with every muscle, as though she'd like to jump through the window of the shuttle now exiting the transport bay for its entry into the airspace over a diffractor image of Atlas City.

This was the children's first journey to the surface of Poseidon's home planet, and they were utterly transfixed. He had attempted to prepare them for the strange sights they would see on Terres, and the first city other than Atlantos that they'd ever known. It was an alien world filled with unimaginable technos. They'd almost become accustomed to their phaetronic "visits" to the moon, Helios and the planets of the solar system. In the last few Terresian expeditions to Erthe the planet had been fully explored from pole to pole, the continents and the seas, above and below the waves. And all of it had been documented. What better way to be educated about their home world than to walk in perfect safety among the diverse animal life and with various aboriginal tribes with bodies of all sizes and colors of skin? They could even sit at the campfires of earlier evolutionary species from past Terresian missions. Poseidon had found to his surprise – and at odds with

Talya's expectation – that he didn't at all mind "thrashing around in the jaws of technos." He loved teaching agile young minds.

Loved teaching his own children.

They were so different from one another. Atlas's fascination with technos had been instantaneous, and was now nearly obsessive. Geo enjoyed their travels much as his mother had during her phaetronic education – solely for the natural splendor of the worlds. Isis, Poseidon quickly learned, was the adventurer of the trio. She was a thrill seeker not unlike her Uncle Athens. And while she relished her experiences in the *Atlantos* library – grateful to be sharing them with her beloved cousins – she strained against the close confines of the ship, wishing fervently to be outdoors.

More precisely on the back of her horse.

Isis was a sensualist, requiring the feel of things, the smell and taste and sound of them. She was entertained by the perfect diffractor images shown her, but she was never fooled by them. The real world, the natural world, was her true home.

"The contour dome covers the mountains as well as the city," Atlas observed, studying what appeared to be blue sky above them, but what he knew must be an illusion. Poseidon could see his son reasoning that the "shuttle" they were in had recently approached from the blackness of space to Terres's surface, then entered the airlock that transitioned all crafts from the planet's sterile non-atmosphere into the comfort and safety of the dome.

"What allows the dome to retain its shape and integrity?" Poseidon asked the children. He was not surprised when Atlas answered first.

"A specific phaetronic vibrus."

"That's correct."

"Explain the principle of phaetron technos," Poseidon asked Atlas, "and Strand Frequency Theory."

"It is the unifying principle of the micro and macro-verse. In the smallest and most indivisible micro-particles – energy strands

– " Atlas recited from memory, "vibration can be found. These resonant vibrational frequencies oscillating at different frequencies create the particles' particular signatures and properties. Everything in the universe is given form and energy by vibration."

"That we sometimes call…? Poseidon looked at Isis who was distracted by the sight of the city below them. "Isis?"

"Vibrus," she finally blurted with a wave of her hand, reminiscent of her swatting a fly from her horse's eyes.

"And by manipulating the vibrus," Atlas interjected, "the phaetron-powered by titanum produces a multiplicity of effects."

"Very good." Poseidon smiled indulgently as he maneuvered their "craft" from a great height to one lower, nearer to the tops of the edifices, some that rose to staggering sizes. Now they sped between two rows of these massive structures, over broad thoroughfares where flying vehicles hurtled towards them terrifyingly, but deftly avoiding collision as they sped past. Over city parkland they streaked and headed for the sprawling campus of the Academy.

"Athena goes to school here," said Atlas.

"Correct," his father said.

"Is that the Astrolarium?" Geo cried, excited to see the large, half-round dome on one end of a neatly manicured quadrangle. "Where you lectured?"

"The very one."

Their craft cast a shadow on the Terresians strolling singly and in pairs on the paths and through the quad. In front of the Academy's most imposing building stood an impossibly tall, pyramid-topped stone spire.

Poseidon leaned down and spoke into Isis' ear. "That is where your mother did her research."

Isis turned with a satisfied smile. "In genomics," she offered.

"That's right."

The craft began its descent next to the spire. So close were they that they could easily make out the carvings that stretched its entire length. It was the twin helix – the double-spiraled ladder that Poseidon had many times explained was the basis of all life on Erthe and Terres.

But in the moment that ground-level was achieved the stupefying image dematerialized, vanishing entirely as though it had never existed. The four of them were standing near the pedestal in the *Atantos's* library. All three children looked dismayed at the abrupt ending of their adventure, perhaps expecting to exit the shuttle and walk on Terresian soil.

"Can we do another…on Terres?" Atlas begged. "Please!"

"Yes, I want to do another," Geo agreed.

Isis squirmed. "I have to go," she said.

"You can ride any time," Atlas told her. "Don't you want to see Terres?"

"Yes. But I want to go see the new foal I helped birth yesterday."

"Can I come?" Geo asked.

Poseidon saw Atlas roll his eyes, annoyed at the fickle streak that was every day becoming more apparent in his twin brother.

"Yes, come. You too, Atlas," Isis ordered seriously, then gave him a playful poke in the ribs. "We'll come back and see Terres, won't we, Uncle?"

"You go on, all of you," Poseidon said. "We'll begin again tomorrow."

With a whoop Isis led the way out the library door, the twins racing each other, bumping and laughing as they went.

One Hundred Eleven

THE STADIUM TIERS were largely empty, but those Atlans who sat cheering the riders under the blazing sun were shouting their encouragement and glowing with pride. Most were men of the Brotherhood and their families, as many of the riders were their children and this the first racing event for horsemen of the future. It had been conceived of by Joss. His own son Rosco, fourteen, was even now thundering to a decisive victory across the finish line.

Poseidon had arrived late to the races, delayed by a meeting of the High Atlantos growers. The situation was not yet dire, but if a second year's harvest proved meager because of the long drought afflicting them Atlantos could face the first food shortage since the gathering of the tribes. He caught sight of Boah just inside the track giving last minute instructions to his finest students, Atlas and Isis. They were mounted side-by-side, flushed with elation and ready to ride.

Poseidon knew that Ammon and Evenor were somewhere in the stands. Geo had foregone the races, offering to stay home with his mother and younger brothers, the most recent set of twins born just days before.

"Don't they look wonderful?" Poseidon heard behind him. He

turned. Talya stood appraising her daughter and nephew on their horses, her two-year-old son slung easily on one hip. Giza was a beautiful boy with his father's dark curls, rich honeyed complexion and long-lashed eyes. His disposition was already legendary. He possessed a sweetness and warmth with a joyfully burbling laugh that melted even the hardest of hearts.

It had melted Talya's.

This child – more even than Isis – had softened her, opened her to those who wished to know her, touch her. Her neighbors on the Middle Isle, the weavers at the Academy, the Brotherhood who had never lost their love for her but whom she had pushed away after her return from Taug. Now Talya and Boah's home was a welcoming place, and even Cleatah could occasionally be drawn to a celebration there.

"They're competitors of the first order," Poseidon said. "Equally matched."

"Boah's placed them in a heat with older boys." And more quietly added, "They're both their father's children when it comes to horses."

Poseidon thought Tayla's tone non-adversarial, and he found himself smiling, relaxed in her company as he had been in recent months. He lifted Giza out of her arms into his. "He's heavy as a brick."

The little boy wrapped his arms around his uncle's neck and Poseidon kissed the dusky cheek. He was not immune to Giza's charm.

"You met with the growers," Talya said. "Are they worried?"

"They are. We've never gone this long without significant rain."

"Are *you* worried?"

"How could I not be?"

"I realize that you have no intention of using the phaetron to control the weather," she continued carefully.

Poseidon tensed and subtle as the movement was, it was felt

by the child. Giza began to whimper so Talya took him back into her arms.

"There are genomic protocols that would render our crops drought resistant," she said.

"Talya, you know I cannot…"

"I know very well you won't allow me into my laboratory. But I can talk you through it, step-by-step. *You* would facilitate the modifications."

He considered this. "It would still be tampering."

"I don't believe you want your people to suffer unnecessarily. Make the changes once and it will incorporate into future generations. It can all be forgotten. Wouldn't it be better than playing God with the weather?"

A bright red flag sliced down across the starting line, and the heat was on.

"Look Giza, there's your sister!" Talya told the child who squealed and threw his arms overhead as the horses raced past.

Poseidon regarded the woman who had brought so much pain down upon their heads and found himself wondering if he dared trust her again. It was evident that Taug had changed her. Her children had changed her. It wasn't as if she had asked for entry into the ship.

Giza demanded to be put down. Once both feet were on the ground and his eyes fixed intensely on the horses and their young riders, he began a song of excited shrieks and a stomping dance so comical that Talya and Poseidon began to laugh.

Are we not all connected by the children? he thought. *By friendship? By desire for the greater good?* Should he take the chance of trusting her? Make her a colleague again? She was making perfect sense. He could not let Atlantos fall, not now. He had to do this. He *wanted* to. That was the truth of it.

The horses approached, their deafening hooves shaking the erthan track. His son and daughter slung low over their mounts were leading the pack, racing neck-to-neck. His heart leapt in his chest at the sight. They were his – both of them – his blood pounding equally in their veins. He raised his voice to spur them on. Heard himself calling out wildly, joyfully.

Calling out in nameless shouts of pride.

ONE HUNDRED TWELVE

66 "I HAVE AN IDEA," Atlas whispered.

Isis wondered why he did not want his father to hear. Uncle Poseidon was a few paces ahead of them in the library corridor, making for the elevator. Their lesson today had been thrilling – a visit to the largest of the moons of Kronos, a small ice-covered world to the naked eye, but beneath a sea teeming with many strange forms of life.

She looked forward to the evening when Giza was asleep and she could regale her mother and father with stories of what she had seen that day. Sometimes she embellished them, and her mother always knew it. She had had the same lessons, visited the places and knew every exaggeration. But Patu hung on her every word. With his hands twined behind his head he would lay back on the cushions and close his eyes, seeing everything as she spoke. He'd imagine the surface of the planets he had only seen as twinkling lights in the sky, their mountains and craters, swirling gasses and colored rings, the terrifying storms on the sun.

"Not *another* idea," Isis teased Atlas.

"Shhh!" Atlas hissed.

Her uncle stepped into the elevator and made room for the children. They whooshed to the surface in moments and emerged into Poseidon's Grove. Atlas didn't speak again until his father had taken his leave of them, heading over the bridge to the Middle Isle and his afternoon courses at the Academy.

"Well?" Isis prodded when Atlas remained silent. She was eager to get to the City Stables for her daily practice. "If you don't tell me I'm leaving."

"It's a new adventure," he finally said.

"New?" She was suspicious. The two of them had explored every street and alley of Atlantos City. They'd stolen up to High Atlantos and the narrow paths of Itopia, sitting in the darkened huts with elders of the Gathered Tribes who'd refused to live in the city. They listened to their stories of ancestral villages left behind, memories that Isis could herself remember but had no grieving ache for, as the elders did. The cousins had gone farther afield and explored every meadow, swamp, forest and cavern that they could reach on horseback and return by nightfall.

"What adventure could be new?" she asked.

"You heard my father say he's leaving for his Solstice voyage. He'll be gone for half a moon."

Isis leapt across the Central Isle stream as Atlas took the footbridge. "And I'll be happy for that time to spend at the stables. My horse..."

"My horse this! My horse that! This is better!"

"Nothing is better than my horse," she said, stopping to face him, her arms folded obstinately over her chest. But Atlas's eyes were sparkling with mischief, and his lips were twitching with wanting to tell her. "All right. What adventure?"

"We steal into the ship without my father and..."

"No!"

"You haven't heard the rest."

"I don't want to hear the rest. It's forbidden."

"When has that ever stopped us?" he said, suddenly sounding older and more commanding than his twelve years.

"Stealing into the library is not much of an adventure," she said and huffed with irritation.

"It would be more than visits to the library," Atlas said, the words taking on a tone of mystery.

"Other places in the ship?"

He nodded but said no more, forcing Isis' curiosity.

"The laboratories," Atlas finally said, then amended the thought. "Your mother's laboratory."

She was sure he could see the excitement in her glittering eyes.

"No one will ever know," he barreled on. "We'll go down when my mother is at the Academy. We'll be very careful."

Now Isis fixed Atlas with a stern gaze. "Why do you want to go there? What do you want to see? Where's the adventure in it?"

He struggled for words. "We've seen everything that is *without*. Places on Erthe – the highest mountains, the deepest oceans. We've seen the planets and our sun, clusters of galaxies and clouds of stardust. They're all wonderful. But we've seen nothing *within*."

"What do you mean? You're not making any sense."

Atlas sighed and his lips pursed with impatience. "Don't you ever wonder what's inside a flower? A drop of water? What the force is that makes things live and grow and die. No, you *don't*. All you think of is horses," he finished, throwing up his hands in exasperation and walking away.

Isis followed after him. She didn't like Atlas getting cross with her. It was true what he'd said. She enjoyed their lessons in the library with her uncle but they were curiosities to her, diffracted images. And yes, they were adventures shared with Atlas, but to be perfectly honest she much preferred the ones they had in their own world. With the sun on their faces, breathing horse musk and a salty breeze, and not the stale metallic air of the *Atlantos*.

"What *is* inside a drop of water?" she finally relented, wishing to please him.

He shrugged. "Who knows? But it must be something

wonderful. Or else your mother would not have studied it. I think…" he hesitated, "our bodies are matter, so there must be frequency strands inside us, each with its particular vibrus."

They were both silent then, contemplating her mother's prohibition from her own laboratory. "A misuse of technos" was all that had ever been explained to the children. It had been Talya's own decision to keep her distance from the ship. Isis had never taken time to consider the truth of this explanation. Her mother and father were happy enough, she thought. They loved her and Giza very much. She knew her mother was different from other Atlan mothers and wives, though she could not precisely say how.

But now that she was thinking on these things she saw the secrets lurking in their family like sly little foxes in the bush. She wanted to know more about why she had been brought up not in Atlantos but in the Taug village. The true reason there was no love between Muta and her brother. Something to do with Aunt Cleatah. *Why have I never asked about these secrets?* she wondered now.

"I don't know," said Isis. "If we're caught…"

"We won't be caught," Atlas insisted. "And what if we are? We've been caught before and punished before. But if you don't want to do it," he said with a sly grin, "I'll go alone. I'll be sure to tell you *most* of what I saw…"

Isis gave him a shove, knocking him to the ground. She jumped on top of him, harmlessly pummeling him. He grabbed for her flying hands.

"Are you going without me?" she cried. "An adventure without me?"

"No!" he shouted through the happy barrage. "Never, dear cousin!" Atlas was gasping through a fit of laughter. "It would not be an adventure without you."

ONE HUNDRED THIRTEEN

I AM THE FIRSTBORN son of Poseidon and Cleatah. I adore my mother and love my father. How many times had these thought crossed his mind? *I love my father and I fear him, too.* Since he'd been small, since he'd acquired the sense to understand his place in the world Atlas had thought these thoughts, ones that weighed heavily on his still-narrow shoulders. He peered furtively through the green hedge frequency curtain of Poseidon's Grove. *Yet here I am waiting to disobey him, violate his most fervent prohibition.*

What could he be thinking? He wanted to thrill Isis. That much he knew. But was stealing into the most forbidden location in their world the only choice left to him that would satisfy her? Isis seemed to be tiring of the simpler odysseys. He knew she loved him, but more and more she craved her horses. Atlas could not be certain of what mysteries lay hidden in his aunt's laboratory, but that they were Isis' mother's mysteries had finally seduced his cousin into the adventure.

The plan had all been his. He waited until his father was several days gone on his Solstice journey. It was the first year that he and Geo had been tasked with speaking to Poseidon during his travels. They'd been given leave to enter the library and use the diffractor for transmissions. His mother was consumed with her youngest twins and had become a stranger to the *Atlantos* since their birth. She'd always loved her lessons there, but she said that even as the phaetronic journeys expanded her mind, the dead air of the ship sickened her body. She'd been content with Atlas's and Geo's reports that were made to her and their brothers every day.

It wasn't the first time Cleatah had had to stay home with newborn babies. To relinquish her beloved treks around the planet with Poseidon. But she seemed to be content with her babies. In fact, Atlas imagined that his mother was never happier than with an infant or two in her arms, her eyes closing in pleasure as a tiny hand reached up to caress her face. That was how she listened to the daily reports – incandescent descriptions of the sights and sounds and smells and tastes of Erthe – with her eyes gently shut, lids fluttering and her lips moving into smiles and "O's" of surprise.

One day his father had come upon the fossil skeleton of a creature of unimaginable proportions. Atlas and Geo had seen the bones of the long-necked, mountain-backed, long-tailed monster in the diffractor report. There was their father standing dwarfed next to the fallen beast. But it fell to the brothers to adequately describe it, to elicit wonder in their mother's eyes and cause their younger brothers to clap their hands in glee.

Father always had messages for each of them. "Tell Evemon to stay out of the stable. Give Siris a tickle under his arm. Thoth, sit in your mother's lap and kiss her hand for me." Atlas would watch his mother's eyes dampen and glitter. Then she would tell Atlas and Geo what she wanted them to say to Poseidon the next day. It might be a remembrance of one of their past Solstice adventures. A medicine that one of the Green Teachers had used to heal a difficult wound or illness. It could be a new galaxy the star gazers had discovered with their long-necked lenses. She would share the tenderest sentiments of her love for him. Sometimes these made

Atlas blush, both to hear them and repeat them to his father. They had placed the greatest trust in their two sons.

And today he would break that trust.

Atlas considered for the hundredth time since he'd recklessly proposed the scheme to Isis to abandon the plan. To sacrifice the chance to learn the forbidden and risk his cousin's displeasure.

But she'd come! He could hear her footsteps as she rounded the circular hedge. Isis seemed lit from within, excitement radiating out through her eyes. His chance for retreat was lost, but in the next moment any worry, any advance regret he had suffered was forgotten with the sight of her eager face. Yes, she was pleased with him. With his boldness. With his arrogant disregard of Poseidon's commandments. Atlas prayed silently to the God of Important Things that what they would discover in Talya's laboratory would rock his cousin, shake her to the core.

She stood defiantly, her hands planted almost comically on her hips. "Well," Isis demanded, only a small tremble in her voice to belie her confident stance. "Let's go. Show me this wonderful world."

*

He had stumbled around at first. The devices in Talya's laboratory were at once familiar – the controls for basic phaetron technos resembled those on the library's diffractor pedestal. But here in the large spare chamber hung a dozen rectangles of light, what Atlas believed were called "trans-screens." They came to life at a single touch and projected two and three-dimensional images that were easily manipulated – moved and enhanced, magnified and diminished.

To his and Isis' surprise a touch on a constellation of light pinpricks at the bottom of the screen caused the image of three-dimensional creatures swimming in water to suddenly surround them, so that the pair found themselves watching wide-eyed as amorphous one-celled animals the size of a wolf pup floated by their heads. Its hundreds of tiny hairs seemed to propel them along, and miniscule hearts beat within transparent bodies.

Atlas had an innate understanding of the phaetron's functions. Even in theory it had come naturally to him. Not so with his brother. And certainly not so with Isis. He quickly mastered magnification of an object – first one of the water creatures, then the fabulous craters and precipices of a grain of pollen. A human skin cell.

Isis grew most intrigued with the human magnification.

"Make it bigger," she said. "Again." "Again!"

And now, after enlarging a cell to a hundred times its size, they were hovering between the curving ropes of two organic spirals linked together by a crosswise ladder. It was the same twin helix that had been carved on the stone spire near her mother's laboratory on Terres.

"Where are we?" Isis whispered.

Atlas searched the controls, but his fumbling fingers only caused the ladder stairs to glow and pulse in four different colors.

"Wait, wait. Let me try this." He punched a series of light pricks and suddenly Talya's voice filled the room, startling the children and causing Isis to lurch backwards into Atlas. They gasped in nervous laughter, then calmed so they could hear what her mother was saying. It was an explanation of the image within which they now existed.

"…dual helix and the matrix of the four acid packages – the building blocks of all carbon-based life. The indivisible unit of genomics."

"Show me something else," said Isis.

Atlas couldn't say whether his cousin was suddenly bored with the simplistic dual helix, or if her mother's voice grated on her, unnerved her. With his fingers flying over the controls he transported them into unthinkable realms. Human genomes integrated in phaetron com-cons creating robotic machines with human thought capacities and emotions. Micromachines for healing living tissue, building and replacing a human heart. They observed a surgery *from within an eye* during which a damaged optic nerved was repaired and sight restored. They marveled as they stood inside the electrical web of a human brain, a microbot fusing broken neural pathways.

They were brought to their knees in shock to see furred, long-fingered creatures the size and shape of human beings laid out upon tables while Terresian technoists operated upon their bodies. They watched their Uncle Athens standing at one end of a long dining hall as thousands of identical, dead-eyed young men with the same triangular-shaped birthmarks in the center of their cheeks brought spoons mechanically to their lips and ate a thin grey gruel without apparently tasting it. This had shaken the cousins. Atlas could see Isis' lips hanging slack with confusion. But something made him press on.

With a few more flicks of his fingertips the army of drones was gone and the cousins were standing in a Terresian laboratory behind a scientechnic team who peered eagerly into a sealed glass chamber where sat a small furry creature on a pedestal, chewing on a seed. Atlas could hear snips of conversation – "…S-T Diffractor Protocol 1633…" "I'm sure this time…" Hopeful looks were exchanged. But when a subtle frequency wavelet swept across the glass chamber the animal dropped its meal and suddenly died, slumped flat with sunken eyes. Within seconds the once-plump body collapsed in upon itself. An accelerated decaying process began, reducing the body to a shapeless pile of fur. Decomposition was swift – from red-black muscle to a picked-clean skeleton. Even this lost its attachments and in moments was a pile of bones. The bones disintegrated into dust.

"I don't like this," Isis complained.

Next they were touring a dim cavernous space. Along its sides were what appeared to be long rows of enclosures. Atlas dared to enhance the sound, and the voice of a man neither of them recognized came forth clear and emotionless. It echoed in the vastness of the dark-walled space and was occasionally drowned out by a guttural moan, a high-pitched wail, a terrible animal gibbering.

Atlas dialed in one of the enclosures. It was a barred cage. There were only shadows to be seen within, but as the perspective grew closer they could peer in between the bars. Exploding with a strangled cry from the deepest corner came a winged, feathered animal that grasped at the bars with bloody, razor-tipped claws. Isis screamed as the rest of the creature crashed into view – the writhing head of a snake!

With that the trans-screen dissolved. Sitting slack-jawed on the floor Isis and Atlas were momentarily blinded by the cold light of Talya's laboratory. When their vision returned they were greeted with a sight more terrible than anything they had witnessed.

Cleatah loomed above them.

Atlas could feel the sharp edge of her fury cutting into his skin. When she'd turned her sights on Isis he saw his cousin shrink under her aunt's withering outrage.

Isis' eyes darted to him and in the very next moment she was blurting, "I made him come! It was me!"

"No!" Atlas's voice was a ragged cry. "Mother, it was *my* idea!"

"Get up." She spoke with unnerving calm. "You Isis, go home and bring your mother back here." Cleatah watched steel-eyed as Isis stood. For a moment the girl hesitated, trying to read her aunt's expression, but Cleatah's posture said, *Get out of my sight.* Isis scurried away, quick as a lizard. Atlas scrambled to his feet.

"Come with me," his mother said.

*

His misery was complete. Poseidon's entire demeanor – the sag of his shoulders, the pained tightening of his features – twisted knots in Atlas's stomach. Mother's voice was raised as she spoke to the image of his father near the library's pedestal. The two had come very close, but Cleatah's tall figure was stiff, her motions made in small jerks. Where was his slow-limbed, honey-voiced mother?

Atlas stood well back from his parents but he could hear her nevertheless. "…Talya's doing…they saw it all…please come home…" Atlas watched her body soften at the response. Atlas longed for his father's presence, yet shuddered at the thought.

"Mother, may I speak to…?"

"No," she snapped, dissolving the image. "You'll see him soon enough."

She strode towards the library door and he hurried along behind her, out into the hallway.

"I'm sorry!" he called after her.

"You love her too much." Cleatah refused to stop or to listen to him.

"Isis is my cousin. I *do* love her. Mother!" He tugged on her shift and finally she turned, her eyes liquid and shimmering. "Go to the residence stables. Groom the horses. Stay there till your father comes home."

"Yes, Mother."

"Do not leave this island." She fixed him with her sternest gaze. "You understand."

He nodded.

Then she stepped into the elevator and was gone. She was so angry at him. She wouldn't even ride the beam with him. Atlas had been wrong. *My misery is not complete,* he thought. *There is a lot more of it to come.*

*

They were all, humiliatingly, there before the residence hearth. But this was no ordinary family gathering. All the younger twins were absent. How Atlas missed their childish presence! Even Geo had been exiled from this punishment. He knew it would be worse this time. The other infractions were mere missteps. He had the feeling of the ground about to slip out from under his feet with a great sickening free-fall just ahead.

Boah seemed hardly troubled, as though nothing could possibly be so dire. "Children were being children," he'd murmured when they arrived.

Now Poseidon turned to Atlas. "I trusted you," he began.

"I'm sorry. I'm really, really sorry."

"Your blame is misplaced," Cleatah hissed at Poseidon. "Blame Isis. No," she amended. "Blame Talya."

"This was not my doing," Talya said. She fixed her pleading eyes on Poseidon. "You know it was not. Tell her!"

"It doesn't matter, Talya," he said wearily. "You may not have put the children up to this silly game," but you were scheming. You wanted to get back to your laboratory. To your 'master plan.'"

"What is this master plan?" Boah demanded.

"When the children are gone," Cleatah warned.

"It was not Muta's fault!" Isis shouted at her aunt. "I told you it was mine!"

Atlas watched as dark, angry gods darted around their parents, fear and hatred rising and engulfing them like a foul mist.

Then came his mother's voice, a series of small smart slaps, her eyes falling like a blade on Isis. "Your Terresian education is over. You and your mother will never set foot in the *Atlantos* again."

ONE HUNDRED FOURTEEN

THE MEN AND children had gone. The two women stood beneath the skylight bathed in clear morning sun.

"You've been waiting for this moment for years." Talya skewered Cleatah with her gaze. "Pretending forgiveness. You basked in the admiration of our husbands, the only two men on the planet whose admiration we require. 'Wise and Magnanimous Cleatah, Great Lady of Atlantos.' True, isn't it?"

"I was not waiting," Cleatah answered, meeting every quiver in Talya's stare. "I prayed to the Goddess every day that this moment would never come."

"This moment. The expected betrayal. But you're wrong. I haven't betrayed you. I did not send my daughter into my laboratory. It's ludicrous to think I did." Disdain hardened Talya's features. "Either you lack the science of subtlety or you're incapable of applying such subtleties to me. You're still blind with anger."

"And what is it that I do not properly understand about you?"

"That I'd already begun to regain Poseidon's trust. He was planning to convince you of that trust. To restore me to my birthright. The work I do. Technos – aside from my family – is the only thing I value in this life."

"You may have gained Poseidon's trust…until we saw your plans."

Talya fell silent. Her teeth ground together. "My abhorrent plans. To improve our species? Make us stronger? Less prone to disease? *That* is my crime? No, silly me to forget. I stole Poseidon's seed. I stole your daughters from you." Talya took a step closer. "You took my *mate* from me. Whether you two see your pairing as written in the stars means nothing to me."

"You could have gone home to Terres with the others. You chose to stay."

The accusation – true – caused Talya's unexpected and embarrassing flush. "I hated you." The words choked in her throat. "Perhaps that's more rightly my crime. Terresians are not meant to hate. Not meant to feel things so…excruciatingly. That I was so debased by emotion that I could restructure another woman's body for reasons not strictly bound by science appalls me to this day." She clutched Cleatah's arm with rigid fingers. "But I did *not* send Isis into my laboratory. Why won't you believe your son? He claims responsibility."

"He's protecting her."

Talya sighed. "You haven't heard a word I've said."

"She's just like you."

"What an easy way for you to insult my child…" Talya opened her mouth to finished her thought.

"Don't say the words," Cleatah threatened, "or I will strike you down where you stand."

"…Poseidon's child," Talya defied. She tensed, waiting for the blow to come.

"Just go," Cleatah whispered.

Talya managed a brittle smile. "You win," she said, feeling a sharp ache in the back of her throat. Her spine straightened as she turned to go. "Once again, you win.

One Hundred Fifteen

HER MOTHER'S NORMALLY milky skin burned with the colors of a summer sunset, and a thick vein at her temple throbbed alarmingly. At the doorway of their home she loomed over Isis and the words, when they finally came, were clipped. Icy.

"Do you know what you've done?"

"Mother, I…"

"Don't speak. Don't utter another word. Your words, your *lies* have cost me…" Talya's lips twitched soundlessly for a long terrible moment, "…everything."

"I only meant…"

"What? You only meant to spare your cousin a just punishment? You only meant to lay the blame of his misdeeds on my head?"

"Not yours. Mine!"

"In all the time you've known of the ship and my laboratory you've never wondered why I was kept from them? You never knew how it pained me to be kept from my work? You never knew that Cleatah hated and mistrusted me? That she was waiting for the moment to finish me? You claim ignorance of that?"

"No." The single syllable was whispered shamefully, its full impact only now becoming apparent to Isis. "But I didn't mean to harm you, Mother. You have to believe me."

"I do believe you."

Isis felt her shoulders sag and relief began to flood over her in a warm wave. Then she saw her mother's face harden, her gaze narrow into a fine, pointed lancet.

"You simply put Atlas before me."

"No!" Even as she cried out the denial Isis admitted a shameful grain of truth in the accusation.

"Yes. Yes you did!" Talya was shouting. "And now everything I care about is lost to me!"

I don't know what you mean." Isis felt her eyes stinging. Her mother's words confused her. "You have Patu and Giza…and me. You have your weaving, and the Academy…"

The slap was hard and unexpected. Isis raised her hand to her cheek, but the blow had been more numbing than painful. She fought the urge to reel backward but as understanding dawned, unwelcome as it was shocking, she stood her ground and glared in defiance at her mother. Her own fury began to well up like an eruption of boiling water from the hot pools at Ankra. Isis' own words formed and flew at her mother like an arrow shot of its own volition.

"How can you love machines in a cold ugly room in a buried ship more than you love me? More than Giza? More than Patu?" Isis watched her mother's face fracture for a moment, broken by surprise at the truth of her daughter's words.

Their happy family life was a lie.

Talya groped helplessly as though wanting to reply. To deny this appalling charge. But it was impossible. Isis could suddenly see her mother's secret life laid bare. It had always been there. Boah had known. Poseidon and Cleatah had known. Only Isis had been fooled.

"Isis, I'm sorry. I didn't mean…"

"You can't take it back. You can't take it back because it's true."

"I do love you. I love you so much!"

But the words were muffled, meaningless sounds, echoing as if from a distance. Isis had already turned away. She slammed from the house and walked quickly along the street of the Central Isle towards the nearest bridge.

The Goddess was her mother. Her real mother. Her *only* mother who smiled down with every Erthely blessing and true, infinite love. Isis was feeling the pull of the stables now. The place of solace. Her father was there. The horses were there. They would never let her down. She didn't need her mother. She didn't need Atlas either. She would go and saddle up Arabo. Ride up the South Ramp to the Great Plateau. Ride until the city was far behind her. Whatever she needed was out there – the solid ground beneath her horse's pounding hooves. The dome of the sky. The wind on her face.

She would ride. That was all. She would ride...

ONE HUNDRED SIXTEEN

"I T WAS ME. *I* did it," Atlas intoned miserably.

"I know." Standing at the door of the Central Isle stable Poseidon watched the boy grooming Arrow, his anger and frustration transfigured into long powerful strokes along the horse's flank. Terresian control was strong in him, Poseidon thought. He was a good boy.

"Isis didn't even want to go down there. Why did she take the blame?"

"She was trying to protect you."

"I don't need protecting! She thinks I'm weak. That I ride small horses to make myself look big."

"I doubt she thinks you're weak. She wouldn't have you as a friend if she did."

Atlas pierced Poseidon with his gaze. "If you knew it was my idea, why did you let her take the blame? Now you're going to keep her from the library. Her lessons."

Poseidon sighed with the weight of the world on his back. "It went beyond what you saw and heard today. It was your Aunt Talya's mistake."

"She didn't put Isis up to *anything*."

"Atlas...she had plans of her own."

"What plans?

Poseidon squirmed in his skin. These days he tried to avoid remembering Talya's unspeakable violations. "She'd been trying to get back into your mother's good graces, and mine. So she could return to her laboratory. Carry out certain protocols. She was going to modify the human strain."

"Like they do with horses? I thought it made them better. Stronger. Why is that so bad?"

"You'll understand one day."

"I will not!"

"I promise you will, Atlas. But now...now we have a lot of work to do. There's so much you need to know about our technos." Poseidon saw his son straighten at these words. He knew they were the ones Atlas most dearly wished to hear. "One day you and I will oversee all this together. And there'll come a time when I won't be here. You'll need full cognizance of the ship and the phaetron. But you must let me teach you how to use it...in a measured way."

Atlas was straining towards him. He looked to be hardly breathing, as if a single errant breath might change his father's mind. "We'll begin tomorrow," Poseidon said.

"Tomorrow?"

"Too soon?"

"No, no Father!" Atlas threw himself into Poseidon's arms and clutched him with a boy's bony fingers. Then he pushed away and looked up at his father with blazing eyes. "I saw something in Aunt Talya's laboratory. An experiment. An 'S-T Diffractor,' I think they said."

Poseidon nodded. "You know that a normal diffractor encodes light fields and produces three-dimensional images. On Terres, physics men are working with the *fourth* dimension – time. They've developed a 'Spatial-Time Diffractor.' In theory it should encode time and allow backwards and forward movement, but the correct vibrus sequence has always eluded them. The same way trans-location of living things kills the organism, so does time diffraction, so they've…"

"Backwards and forward movement in *time?*" Atlas said.

"That's right."

"I want to do that! Will you teach me about the S-T Diffractor?"

"I'll teach you anything you want to know."

"I might find the correct vibrus!"

"You might. But the experiments devour huge amounts of titanum, so the work is only theoretical, and…"

Atlas had gone silent and still. He was staring at Arrow's side but, Poseidon could tell, he was seeing something different before his eyes. A great opening. His future. This world that would one day be his to tend and defend. The limitless expanse of starry heavens. Not yet a leader, he would come to that in time. Learn what was necessary to benevolently govern. He was the marvelous product of love. A child of Erthe. Poseidon felt a warmth and fullness in his chest that could only be pride. Or love. A giddy delight that threatened him with tears.

"Let's go talk to your mother. She's in her garden. She looks unhappy."

Atlas shook his head. He resented being torn from his beautiful vision.

"She needs to know you'll forgive her."

"But I won't."

Poseidon said nothing.

"Not yet."

"Fair enough," Poseidon agreed.

"So we start tomorrow?" It was a demand as much as a question.

Suppressing a smile Poseidon nodded once in agreement. Then he turned in the doorway, leaving Atlas to his dreams. He stepped out into the soft day, allowing his feet to lead him across the meadow and the stream's red bridge. Cleatah's high garden hedge was ahead. He couldn't see her, but he was sure he would find her kneeling before one of her medicine plants, seeking solace, a healing for the anger that bedeviled her, might always bedevil her. She would look up and see him, and the tight folds of her anger would unfurl like the petals of a flower. She would stand and open to him. Take him into her embrace. He would be whole.

His ship moored. His heart home.

The Saga Continues...

Enjoy an excerpt from the upcoming sequel to ATLANTOS ~

CHILDREN OF RA

The Early Erthe Chronicles

Book II

CHAPTER 13

ATHENS STOOD IN his rear viewing deck aboard the nameless craft on which he and his colonists had arrived on Mars – now designated the "Command Ship." He stared dispassionately out at a sight he never, in his worst nightmares, believed he would ever see. Stretched out across space in two flanks on either side were four human transport vessels, hastily constructed and every bit as unlovely as the original had been. Following directly behind the Command Ship like a long metallic tail was an even uglier craft – the barge train, a powerful tow engine and its six linked cargo holds: the first four carrying titanum, the last two raw gold.

Ugly or not the barge train was the only thing that mattered anymore – all that Athens had left to show for his efforts on Mars. The titanum would assure him adulation and tribute when finally Terres came round again. The gold would be his solace and sustenance while waiting on Poseidon's blasted "Erthe" for that day to come.

In the distance, behind the escape flotilla was Mars. Moments before, a worried Captain Delos had cautioned Athens that they'd not put enough distance between themselves and the planet they were fleeing. The three massive asteroids had silently targeted the globe's southern hemisphere as though faultlessly aimed by the hand of some distant, sharp-eyed marksman. Athens might be observing the scene with his eyes, yet it was unreal to him, an evil diffractor construct designed to entertain by way of horror. It was preposterous that he should in the next moments be witness to the death of a world.

It was only when the first of the three asteroids plunged into the Southern Ocean that the scene took on an aspect of reality. A mushrooming white dome of steam and gasses billowed huge and ominous as half the ocean vaporized and the other half, in a wave large enough to be seen with the naked eye, began sweeping into oblivion all that lay before it.

In the next moment the second asteroid – a rock the size of Mars's smallest moon – struck. By then the planet had revolved more than a hundred degrees, and the missile smashed onto land not yet inundated. As Athens watched in horrible fascination the point of impact exploded into brilliant conflagration, setting the atmosphere afire. Only then did he feel the first dagger of fear in his belly. He knew there could never be so enormous a detonation without a far-reaching shock wave.

He was certain now that his delays had left too little time for unscathed escape. Confirmation came with an invisible but shattering blow to the ship. It knocked Athens across the deck, tilting the entire vessel as if a large hand had backswiped it. Lights flickered momentarily. Screams could be heard outside his door. He struggled to the window.

Mars and the barge train were no longer in sight. The shock

wave had shifted the vessel's alignment. Only the two ships that formed the left flank of his fleet – numbers Three and Four – were still visible. Both vessels were listing badly, but only Four was regaining its equilibrium. A stream of vapor bled from the propulsion deck of Three, and the angle of its tilt was growing more extreme.

The image of Captain Delos materialized before Athens. He was white-faced with rage, his normally sanguine demeanor having failed him. It was understandable. His pleas to evacuate Mars sooner had gone unheeded.

"Every one of our passenger vessels has sustained damage," Delos spluttered. "One, Two and Four can be repaired. But Three is entirely disabled. We're ready to begin the rescue operation…"

"Very good, Captain," said Athens, interrupting Delos. His voice was listless. "Keep me apprised."

"Keep you *apprised*, Sir? There's another asteroid about to impact Mars. It's twice as large as the first two and it will be striking landmass. We have no idea how large a shock wave it will produce, but if we're in mid-transfer, lives will be lost, *Sir*. I need orders!"

Athens, dull and confused, wished desperately for Persus's counsel, but she was at the end of the right flank on transport Number One…or was it Four…? Almost as soon as his thought had been projected he heard the vice governor speaking.

"I heard your report, Captain Delos," said a disembodied voice. Athens looked around for her diffracted image but only saw the beginnings of it – a flurry of pixels and static trying, but failing, to take form. "We can't risk beginning the rescue operation till the next wave of ejecta has passed," she continued.

"I agree," Delos said. He was clearly relieved to be speaking with someone other than Athens. "Have your passengers brace themselves, Vice Governor. And you, Governor, strap yourself into your chair and activate trans-screen 4."

Athens did as he was told.

He switched on the exterior monitor moments before the final asteroid made contact with the surface of Mars.

Its trajectory was straight on, and the force and velocity with which it finally slammed into the landmass seemed almost to stop the planet in its rotation. But the expected explosion failed to materialize.

The asteroid had been swallowed up in its entirety by Mars.

When it came several moments later the wave was muted and only rocked the vessel gently, as a rolling swell would tilt a large seagoing ship.

"What's happened?" Athens demanded. "Why was there no explosion?"

Delos was maddeningly silent while he retrieved the readings. Finally he spoke. "The asteroid pierced the planet's crust. We should see the counter-action on the opposite side of the planet eventually," he said, "but the worst of it was apparently absorbed by Mars's mass. It's very good luck for us. We can begin transporting passengers immediately. Are you ready to receive a quarter of the displaced, Vice Governor?"

"Any time, Captain."

"Very good. Governor…"

"Yes," answered Athens, vague and defeated.

"A delegation from the other ships has just arrived onboard. They wish to see you."

"What about?"

"Look out your window."

The command ship had regained its alignment and the window of the viewing deck again had Mars squarely in its center. But strung out – like the scattered beads of a broken necklace – were the tow engine and its six barges. The cargoes of titanium and gold were floating one by one into the deep blackness of space.

"No!" Athens shouted, moving quickly to the window, his

palms flattened against the glass. He stared miserably out to see that the rescue shuttles had already begun flying to and from the disabled passenger craft. Four more shuttles were chasing the ore barges. He looked past scenes of selfless courage and naked greed, and saw in the distance the ruined planet that had once been his glory.

Athens put his head in his hands and wept.

AUTHOR'S NOTE

THERE EXISTS ONLY one of Plato's works left unfinished – it literally breaks off mid-sentence – and this suggests it was written near the end of the great man's life. *Timaeus* is a treatise describing, in immense detail, the lost civilization of Atlantis – the continent and capitol city, its government, the character of its inhabitants, and its stunning end. It illuminates the god Poseidon and his mortal beloved Clieto, their five sets of twin sons (the first and favorite, Atlas) and the "daughters of the earth" whom they married – the progenitors of the Atlan population. It is a story that found its way, in some form, into every ancient civilization on the planet and is now deeply rooted in most cultures of the modern world.

In *Timaeus* and another of his dialogues, *Critias,* Plato explains the origins of his account. Two hundred years before he held sway as the renown philosopher of Greece, the priests of the Nile Delta related – from their written accounts – the story to Solon who was known as "the wisest of the Seven Sages." Through the oral tradition of history-keeping it was passed down from Solon to his great-grandson, then to *his* nephew Critias, and finally to Plato himself. Plato ponders the reasons why such a gloriously wrought civilization should have become debased enough to go to war with the other fabulous city of its time, Athens. Plato takes great pains insisting to the reader that what he is relating is not fiction - but an actual history of a world that existed (amazing even to himself) *nine thousand years before his own time.* It is, he claims, "a tale which, though strange, is certainly true…not a mere legend, but an actual fact." (*Timaeus*).

Despite his efforts these two works, since their writing, have caused extraordinary controversy, beginning with Plato's own student Aristotle, who claimed they were merely allegorical in nature and not to be believed as factual. More recent researchers have postulated – to fall in line with their own ideas about the location of Atlantis – that Plato actually meant nine *hundred* years as opposed to nine *thousand,* and that the continent he described in *Critias* as "greater in extent than Libya and Asia" was actually Thera, a tiny volcanic island in the middle of the Mediterranean. The topic of Atlantis has been relegated by many to the lunatic fringe, and any historian, scholar or scientist who takes it seriously risks being thought a crackpot. But Plato was an extraordinary thinker and author – revered even in his own time – hardly a deluded or gullible old man. These writings are the singular historical source that exists describing Atlantis. Without them we would have no knowledge whatsoever of that civilization.

Who, I asked myself, was I to second-guess Plato? I have simply chosen to take the man at his word.

In every one of my novels I've made an attempt, with what I call "filling-in the holes in history," to solve an historical mystery. The one that presented itself here was *why Atlantis went to war with the ancient city of Athens 11,500 years ago.* Remember that this is not the later Athens of Plato's time (5th century B.C.) but the one the Egyptian priests claim existed contemporaneously with Atlantis. There is no explanation or provocation given by the priests, Solon, Critias or Plato for the war. As an author of fiction it's my prerogative – my job – to take my best guess about such motivations. I decided that if Athens had not originally been a city but, instead, a *man* after whom the city was named, and if that man was the jealous brother of Poseidon, this could have sown the seeds and become the driving force behind later hostilities. Poseidon and Athens might be the first family members in earth's ancient history to go to war with one another, but they were certainly not the last.

There is a corresponding scientific mystery. 11,500 years ago the last Ice Age, known as the "Younger Dryas," came to an end, and massive flooding is known to have taken place all over the globe. Today, off the coastlines of numerous countries, ruins – some humble, some mighty – can be found under more than one hundred feet of water. It seems too great a coincidence to me that Plato's Atlantis sank beneath the waves in a single day and night at exactly the time of the Younger Dryas' conclusion.

For the book that truly rang my bells about ancient civilizations lost to the deluge I thank Graham Hancock for his *Fingerprints of the Gods* – a big, juicy book of great scholarship that reads like a ripping novel. His *Mars Mystery* educated me on the fate of the red planet, inspiring me to wonder what it might have been like to live on that world before its tragic demise. That Mars might have been a habitable planet with oceans, continents and an atmosphere, provided me with a logical place to send Poseidon's rival brother. Hancock's more recent geological research for the *Fingerprints* sequel, *Magicians of the Gods*, helped me place my antediluvian civilization where it now seems most likely to have existed – not in the mid-Atlantic, but the Indonesian islands south of Southeast Asia (what is left of a continent-sized land mass). It also pinpoints the dates and nature of the cataclysms that brought the last two ice ages to an abrupt end and caused the world-wide flooding that wiped out the Atlan empire.

Zecharia Sitchin's *The 12th Planet* and *There Were Giants Upon the Earth* offer translation and analysis of 6,000 year-old Sumerian texts and seals, and the poem, "The Epic of Gilgamesh." His contention that our solar system includes a planet called Niburu with an uber-long elliptical orbit, sparked the idea of my off-world protagonists' home planet, Terres. Some modern astronomers have postulated that there exists a massive dark planet at the fringes of our solar system with a similar orbit called "Nemesis" or "Planet X." Sitchin also held that the gods of our most ancient *proven* civilization, Sumeria, were simply humans beings with advanced technologies believed by the primitives to be supernatural. He points to the texts that suggest these individuals were capable of genetic manipulation, and used these techniques on the human population. When one considers the minute numerical probability of one woman birthing five sets of twins sons, as Plato said Cleito did, the theory begins to sound plausible.

The late, great Terrance McKenna's *Food of the Gods* makes a masterful case for the role that psychotropic plants played in the evolution of human consciousness, another of my favorite pre-historic mysteries. By casting Cleatah as a mushroom-eating shaman I was able to integrate his brilliant theories and research into my novels.

Erick Von Daniken's *Chariots of the Gods* stands as the first book (1968) that stimulated me, and millions of others, to begin questioning conventional wisdom and what we had been taught in our dry old history classes about Earth's deep history. He made a good argument that prehistoric humans might have been influenced by visitors from other worlds whom they believed to be gods by virtue of their advanced technology.

Over the course of fifteen years, four individuals became my tireless and faithful editors and critics. To Chris Vogler, Billie Morton, David Forrer and Max Thomas I owe the greatest debt of gratitude for their perseverance, honesty and good humor during what must have seemed like the Ground Hog Day of book projects. They never failed to steer me towards clarity and simplicity, much needed in so complex a saga. I appreciate Greg Michaels and Ginny Higgins for their tough critical analyses that kicked my butt and made me work even harder.

I am in awe of consummate actress and dear friend, Suzan Crowley, for her stunning performance of the audiobook version of ATLANTOS. She brought the characters to life in ways that even I had never imagined.

I'm so grateful to Debra Deyan of Deyan Audio, who so generously opened her studio to me, allowing me the opportunity to learn a new skill-set and direct the ATLANTOS audiobook.

Finally I thank Linda and Ron Shusett for twenty years of support for all my Atlantis-themed projects. Ron, a writer-producer considered by many as the Godfather of Hollywood science fiction, is the monster-meister who literally dreamed up the stupefying chest-burster sequence in "Alien." I'm honored that he created my Marsean creatures – the phibions, jelly parasites and solies – as well as the architecture of the planet's gargantuan titanum mines.

I have, with deep gratitude, liberally borrowed and stolen ideas from some of the best minds in the most exciting areas of historical and scientific research in our own world and beyond. But in the end it all comes back to Plato. Scholars, students and skeptics are still arguing over *Timaeus* and *Critias* 2,500 years after they were written.

The old man would no doubt be amused.

– Robin Maxwell
Pioneertown, 2015

Robin Maxwell would be delighted to hear from you.
You can contact her at:
www.RobinMaxwell.com

Follow her on Facebook...
facebook.com/AuthorRobinMaxwell

...and on Twitter
twitter.com/TheRobinMaxwell

Made in the USA
San Bernardino, CA
18 July 2015